SENTIENT

SENTIENT

A NOVEL

GARY DURBIN

Published by SparkPress, a BookSparks imprint,
A division of SparkPoint Studio, LLC
Phoenix, Arizona, USA, 85007
www.gosparkpress.com

Published 2022
Printed in the United States of America
Print ISBN: 978-1-68463-119-3
E-ISBN: 978-1-68463-120-9 (e-bk)

Library of Congress Control Number: 2021918117

Interior design by Tabitha Lahr

CONTENTS

For Lori, whose encouragement
kept my fingers on the keys.

PROLOGUE

JAMES FORREST MAKES ONE MORE change to the AI code, stares at it while he imagines the messages flowing between the nodes, and then clicks the icon that uploads the program to the bot-swarm he uses for testing. He launches the Visualizer and grips the arms of his chair. The 3D screen comes alive with swirling, pulsing lines that map the thought patterns inside the AI. The lines twist, pulse, and shift, as thousands of associations shape the cascade of messages. The nodes burn like stars and throb with arcane rhythms from the deluge of messages loading their processors.

A familiar ache forms in the back of his head as the shifting flow of AI thought makes the ribbons vibrate like violin strings, and the stars pulse with power. Pain sucks his eyes into his brain as the images stream through him. The colors span the spectrum from electric green to clear glass to sandstone. Shifting and quivering, the patterns are alive and ancient: Egyptian column icons, leaves on the wind, and wandering glaciers. Memories flow with the forms: curling driftwood, dried bones, seashells, frozen amber, and faces, always faces. Time ceases; the flow is all that matters. Dancing perceptions play on his senses: flute music turns to screams, pneumatic drills drum behind the colors, and falls of breaking glass shower him; his skin crawls with insects dancing; pine scent morphs into sea foam and fades to horse sweat.

His consciousness spreads out, tossed in the froth while time drifts away. Familiar forms from his previous trips appear, and he follows the images, searching for the pain. To get to the node where he'd found the strange feeling of control, he has to go through the burning pain. From somewhere below, a grayness emerges. He pushes the left trackball to the side; the pattern shifts; he falls into it. His teeth ache; he slides the right trackball forward and swims into the grayness that becomes a coldness. Acid bites his tongue. A temple gong sounds. Cold that penetrates beyond his bones makes him shiver. Fear seeps out of the grayness and darkens with anxiety. The smell of burning plastic chokes him.

Beyond the fear and toward the high-pitched screaming might be the place where he'd felt an island of control and decisiveness. Most nodes ride the stream of messages, battered by the storm that hammers his emotions from every direction. He's been searching for ways to control his experiment for weeks. Far ahead, a node glows with bright whiteness. He turns toward that light, the feeling of control just beyond his fingertips.

A black orb appears in the grayness above him. Black nodes receive messages, but their processing is blocked, and the messages die. Finding bugs in this complex code was the reason he'd built the Visualizer. Debugging a system with millions of messages flying around at nanobot-speeds is nearly impossible. With the Visualizer, he can find bottlenecks and stalled nodes like this. He hasn't seen one in his AI experiment for months, but there it is.

One tilt upward, and the blackness draws him in. He falls into the void. Weightlessness brings up bile, choking him. Moving the forward trackball, he lets the void swallow him. Darkness spins about him. Faces at the edge of his vision grimace with the pain he's caused. He touches his keyboard. The Visualizer goes dark, and the real world slams against his mind. "Node 3986, Contents saved" appears on the screen. Exhausted, he slumps on the desk.

CHAPTER ONE

MURDER ONE

JUNE

"You are close to danger. Watch your back."

June Simmons stares at her laptop. She digs into the internals of the email; it's from an anonymous server. She'll never be able to trace the source.

Ivan, her supervisor, has already left, and she can't discuss this with anyone else because her work is classified. She closes her laptop, puts it in her bag, and heads out.

She tries to relax her hands on the steering wheel as she leaves the parking lot of the Lawrence Berkeley National Laboratory and turns down the hill. Finding the possible buyers of Sydney's artificial intelligence code has obsessed her ever since he went silent.

This morning, the cyber unit had cracked open the server in China. A few more hours taking it apart, and she'll be another step closer to knowing who Sydney's contact was.

By the time she stops for dinner at her favorite Indian restaurant in downtown Berkeley, her hands are sweaty, and her arms feel tense and crampy. Subhash, whose Indian English is still not very American, greets her and nods toward her usual table. His teenage daughter looks up from her books and smiles. June doesn't know the girl's name; they only communicate by smiles and nods, but the girl is always so intent on her studies that June wonders if the girl has already developed the kind of determination that drives June. She's the best in her unit at uncovering covert AI projects—no matter how far into the dark web it takes her.

The restaurant feels different. Surrounded by the familiar aromas of turmeric, cumin, and cinnamon, it should feel familiar, but nothing feels right. She orders the vegetarian curry and tries to focus on a mystery novel on her e-reader. But even the burn of the spicy food can't pull her mind away from the email.

Two months ago, Sydney Harvey said he'd found some code for an AI, and he had a possible buyer. She didn't, for a nanosecond, believe that Sydney had "found" the code. The day after she told her supervisor, Ivan, about Sydney's AI and the Japanese firm that was interested in it, he took her to see David Weiss. Ivan said that David could get help from a government cyber unit.

She hadn't seen David around the lab before. A dark-haired man with an olive complexion, he was secretive about his title and his department. He asked questions about Sydney and the AI, had her sign a new Classified Information Nondisclosure Agreement, and told her to track down Sydney's contacts. It didn't bother him that she had a personal relationship with Sydney. He gave her a contact in a cyber unit that had tools that could open up websites and decrypt messages. The software was so powerful that she was sure the guy was NSA.

She and Sydney hadn't been an item for more than six months. Bicoastal relationships were hard, and she'd decided that Sydney wasn't long-term material. He'd had some promise but had been a disappointment. They'd settled into weekly phone calls, biding time until one of them found someone new, but a month ago, Sydney had gone silent. He'd said he was negotiating with a company in Japan. The company's website went offline, but not before June found a link to a site in China. Someone was erasing the trail, but she is closing in on the supposed buyer.

June's mouth still recalls the spicy burn of the curry as she leaves the restaurant. Her mind returns to the email. She used the proxy in Kansas City when she probed the site in Japan. Even if someone had a Watcher on that site or the one in China, they couldn't track her. The Kansas City proxy is NSA—as ironclad as they get.

Right after Sydney went missing, she'd used a backdoor into his email server and found the net ID of the person who was negotiating with him. She had to assume the bad guys had the same tools she did. That must be how they got her email address. She should have deleted her emails with him. Too late now. Sydney's emails had sometimes been too intimate. Someone probably knew more about her than she wanted.

She grips the steering wheel as she makes her way along Berkeley's main street. Relax. *Remember your yoga breathing.* The sidewalks are filling with Friday-evening students searching for alternatives to scholarship and loneliness. All the way from downtown to the marina, she tries to calm her nerves. It's the first time she's had a threat. Anger overrides her attempts to calm herself. She'll log on as soon as she gets home and take apart the server in Zhenxing.

Her car lights pierce the darkness of the parking garage as the metal gate closes behind her. She drives past Priuses, Porsches, Teslas, and a few BMWs to her space on the second floor. She parks, gets out, and touches the door handle. The door lock clicks, and the familiar smell of aging cement and cold exhaust surround her.

She looks around, telling herself that she doesn't have anything to worry about. The few lights make pitch-black shadows between the cars. Her eyes flick from shadow to shadow as she walks down the rough cement floor toward the exit.

The server in Zhenxing isn't likely to be the end of her search. Zhenxing is across the Yalu River from North Korea. Her team has seen actions from there before; it's a hub for businesses that sell illegal internet services. The dark web operators there usually have connections to North Korea; she won't be able to probe there, but David Weiss can get NSA's help. It might take her the weekend, but if she can find a connection, she'll take it to him on Monday. The NSA might even have a Watcher on the anonymous email server.

With that decision made, she's taken control of the situation. Her shoulders relax, and her stride sharpens. A swipe of her key fob unlocks the exit door. She crosses the hall and presses the up button.

The elevator door slides open; a man wearing a hat and a dark overcoat stands inside. She grips her keys, pauses, considers not entering. She laughs at herself. Every man in an overcoat isn't a threat. Inside the door, she turns to press the button for floor five and finds it already lit. Backing against the wall of the elevator, she holds her keys with both hands and stares at the man's shoes—brown leather wingtips. When the doors open, she waits. He walks out and turns to the left. She raises her head as the tension she'd been holding in escapes.

The gray cement walls that sometimes feel impersonal and cold now look solid and safe. Leaving the elevator, she turns to the right and walks past two doors before stopping at 506. After glancing up and down the empty hall, she inserts the door key.

The lock clicks, and she pushes the door open and holds it with her shoulder. She presses the light switch, and the light from the overhead fills the room. As she releases the door, a shadow moves. Pain floods the right side of her head, and darkness drops around her.

JAMES

Keeping his bare feet away from the few sharp stones on the mossy steps, James Forrest steps carefully along the side of the stream that wanders down the hill behind his house. Buffy, his black French bulldog, scampers ahead, stopping every minute or two to look back at her slowpoke master.

He needs more jaunts into nature now that he's activated the AI he found hidden in Distributed Nanotech's supercomputer system. Every time he uses the Visualizer, the software tool that looks inside the AI, he needs to clear his mind of the spinning threads, pulsing colors, and intense emotions that drain him.

The Visualizer projects the complex patterns of messages flowing inside the AI, but it also puts him into something like a trance. He thinks that the pulsing, throbbing lines that show the internal workings of the AI are so similar to the patterns of thoughts in the brain that it creates a resonance. He's gradually learned how to control his path through the network of associations while working with the Visualizer.

During this morning's session, he found a bug in the code. One of the nodes crashed on a message. It was an easy problem to fix. An hour analyzing the problem and a small change to a single line of code fixed the problem. But finding that bug kept him from working on the problem that has seized his mind and won't let go—finding a way to control the AI.

His experimental AI is lightning fast at solving problems, but real-world problems have many solutions. You can break down a door to get into a room, or you can turn the doorknob and walk in. The choice you make depends on your values and your goals. For the last two months, he's been struggling with how to direct the AI to solutions based on values or guidance. Every time he fixes a bug, the AI gets more powerful, but so far, his attempts at control have failed.

After a morning spent working on his experiment, he's anxious to get back to the work that Distributed Nanotech, Inc., pays him for—being chief scientist. That job is maybe the most fun he's had while getting paid.

The short hike under the open sky cleared the brain fog from the Visualizer. He has some new ideas for the paper the marketing department wants and is anxious to set those ideas down. As he opens his back door, the alarm warns him, and he enters the code that tells his electronic sentry that he's home.

The smartphone he'd left on the desk tells him that he's missed a call from Detective Franken. The last time he'd spoken to the detective had been when the detective and his partner were investigating the murder of Philippe Colbert, DNI's previous chief scientist. Shortly after James realized that the detectives suspected him, Alison Green attacked him, and the police captured her.

James presses the return-call button.

"Franken here," the familiar voice says.

"This is James Forrest."

"Hi, James, how are you?"

"Fine. I didn't expect to hear from you. Don't tell me Alison's on the loose."

"Not a chance," Detective Franken says.

The closest James had ever come to death was when Alison Green sat on his chest, strangling him. A police officer had pulled her off, but the scene still flashes into his mind more often than he'd like.

"What can I do for you?" James says.

"We have a case that involves AI. Would you mind talking to us about it?"

"Sure. I'll do what I can."

He feels obligated to the detectives who answered a call from James's alarm system just in time. Had the detective and his partner not responded immediately, James wouldn't be hiking and contemplating what to do with his AI experiment.

James agrees to meet with the detectives the next day and sits down to work on his paper, but his mind keeps drifting back to the AI control problem.

Buffy lies in her bed next to his desk. She looks up at him, ready for another walk.

DETECTIVE ALBERTA LESTER GREETS HIM at the detective office's reception desk. A year earlier, when James was a suspect in the murder of his predecessor, her attitude had been terse, suspicious, and forceful. Today, she's very different: friendly and chatty. But Detective Lester still radiates formality. She's wearing a navy-blue skirt and jacket that could be the standard uniform in a bank.

"Do you still have that little dog?" she asks, holding open the door to the conference room.

"Buffy," he says. "She's fine. I guess she likes living with geeks."

The detectives found the little black French bulldog in Alison Green's car, hot and dehydrated. James gave the dog some water, and she looked up at him; the big black eyes captured him.

The detective leaves to get him a cup of what passes for coffee at the cop shop—black, no sugar. The conference room is windowless with a big mirror on one wall. James wonders who is watching and if they have a camera running. He takes a seat with the mirror at his back.

Detective Franken enters, shakes James's hand, and sits facing him. Franken's rumpled brown suit and crooked tie wouldn't have passed muster at a bank. His gray eyes and permanent frown have never been friendly, but today he looks like he's trying to figure out how to smile.

Detective Lester returns with a cup of brownish liquid and sits next to Detective Franken.

"We're investigating the murder of a woman named June Simmons," Detective Franken says. "She was killed last Friday evening in her apartment. She worked in an artificial intelligence unit at the Lawrence Berkeley National Laboratory."

Detective Lester pulls a picture from a file folder and lays it in front of James. It looks like an enlarged driver's license photo.

"This is June Simmons. Do you recognize her?" Lester says.

A dark-haired woman with olive skin stares at him with eyes that look black in the poor-quality photo. Her hair hangs smoothly down to her shoulders with short bangs on a high forehead. She's about thirty. Her penetrating eyes and the set of her jaw give her a determined look.

"No. I don't think I've ever seen her before."

"We interviewed her supervisor yesterday," Franken says. "He said that her project was about AI. She was monitoring AI projects around the world. Can you give us a few ideas about what to ask?"

"Did you find out what kind of AI she was working on?"

"No," Franken says. "We asked him about DNI, though."

"DNI doesn't sell AI software," James says. "There are hundreds of projects that work on various aspects of AI. How many people are there on the Lab team?"

"You don't sell AI software?" Lester says. "Wasn't that an AI we saw at your house?"

Detective Lester had entered James's house while he had the Visualizer running. After looking at the screen, she'd fallen into a trance and collapsed on his living room floor. It must have made a big impression.

"No," James says. "We base our parallel processing software on some work from an AI project at Stanford, but we don't sell an AI."

"What was it that knocked out Alberta?" Franken asks.

"That was an experiment using the AI code from the Stanford project. We removed that code from the software that goes to our customers."

"You don't have it anymore?" Franken asks.

"Only in our archives," James says. It would be too complex to explain the experiments he's been doing with the AI code. That project is his personal experiment. It has nothing to do with DNI's business.

"So you don't know what kind of AI they're monitoring?" Franken sighs. "I didn't even know there were different kinds."

Detective Franken's brow furrows, and he sits forward like he wants to be doing something active but doesn't know which way to go. Detective Lester is sitting so straight that her jacket could be glued to her shoulders.

James understands their frustration. He's sat in on marketing discussions at DNI and recognized the words as belonging to the English language, but people were putting them together in strange ways.

"We didn't know what to ask," Lester says. "What difference does it make about what kind of AI?"

"It narrows the field. There must be a few thousand software engineers working on self-driving cars. I would be surprised if the Rad Lab were looking at that. I can't think what aspect of AI they might be interested in, but they do all kinds of research."

"Maybe you could go with us and interpret," Franken says.

"Sure," James says. "I'd be glad to help. I owe you guys for saving my life."

James is going to be in town for the next two weeks. He has a couple of meetings scheduled and gives the detectives the dates. Once they have the possible schedule, James expects the meeting to end.

"Ah," Franken says. "Aren't you some kind of security expert?"

"I used to be," James says. "But when I left Cybernetic Dynamics, I signed an agreement not to work on security products for ten years. I still have three years to go."

"What kind of security?" Franken asks.

"Cryptography."

"We have an encrypted laptop from the crime scene," Franken says. "Is that the kind of thing you do?"

"I doubt if I would be much help. My specialty was encrypting databases, not cracking codes."

"I see," Franken says.

James figures that Franken probably doesn't see the distinctions between different aspects of encryption.

"Did you work for the government?" Lester asks.

"I didn't have a government job," James says. "My work was for companies with government contracts. A lot of government operations use the encryption I built."

"Do you have a security clearance?" she asks.

"Yes, one of the consulting projects I worked on last year kept my clearance active."

"How high is your clearance?" Lester asks.

"High."

"Let me check with the Chief," Franken says. "I don't think we have anyone on our staff with a clearance. Maybe you could be a consultant and look at June's emails and files."

"Okay," James says. "But we'll have to work out with the lab what I can disclose. I don't want that responsibility."

"Maybe you can review June's files and tell the lab what we need," Lester says.

James wonders if Detective Lester has just told him that the detectives don't trust the people at the lab? Are the people at the lab suspects?

SUSANNE

Susanne Anderson, CEO of Distributed Nanotech, looks up from her computer monitor as Laura Pasternak, Susanne's Chief Financial Officer, appears at the door. Laura is wearing her usual calf-length, pleated skirt, white cotton blouse, and silk scarf. Today's scarf is midnight blue. Laura's eyes have more than their characteristic sparkle, and there's more bounce to her walk.

"Good morning," Laura says, taking a seat at Susanne's conference table. Out the window beside her, the Berkeley hills are green and bright. Laura's good mood and the spring day are enough to lighten the burden of managing a fast-growth company from Susanne's shoulders for a few minutes.

Susanne takes a seat at the table with her back to the view.

"You look happy today. I take it the discussions with the investment bankers are going well." Susanne says.

"It's fun being the prettiest girl at the dance. I hired Thompson and Harvey to advise us. They have a process that has worked well for other high-tech firms."

"What are the issues?"

"Price is an issue for the investment bankers, of course. But a bigger issue for our new shareholders is how much stock gets allocated to the hedge funds. It's easy for investment bankers to sell a lot of stock if they let the hedge funds buy large blocks, but it means that the long-term buyers get hurt when the hedge funds dump the stock a month or so after the IPO. The stock eventually recovers from the drop, but it hurts investor confidence."

"Is this something we can control?" Susanne asks.

"That's why we have an adviser."

"I want us to get long-term investors that can learn about the company," Susanne says. "We can build confidence and long-term relationships."

"Thompson and Harvey have a list of mutual funds that have the right investment profile. They'll be setting up a road trip for us to present to those firms—about three months before the IPO. Our challenge is to get enough of those funds to sign up that the investment bankers won't want to offload stock to the hedge funds," Laura says.

"So we have to do the work that we pay the investment bankers for."

"Of course."

A "road trip" to present the company to investors before the company's Initial Public Offering is what Arnold Peters, DNI's chairman, had worked toward for years. He'd built two fast-growth companies that were almost ready to IPO but were acquired. Now, Susanne, the CEO he'd brought in to run Distributed Nanotech, is going for the golden ring.

"Sales are ahead of projections," Susanne says.

"The new marketing program with James is getting rave reviews."

After Laura leaves, Susanne stares at the emerging green of the hills. James has made a big difference in her company and her life. She'd thought that she didn't have time for a lover in the midst of the whirlwind of a fast-growth company. But when the intelligent geek she'd hired for research kissed her, things changed.

James and Susanne's relationship is the kind that many companies forbid. Initially, Arnold, DNI's chairman, had been against Susanne having a relationship with the brilliant technician they were trying to recruit. But James made it clear that accepting James and Susanne was part of the price for him joining the company.

Susanne told the employees that she and James were lovers when she announced that he was becoming the company's chief scientist. They wanted to be open about the situation, heading off any rumors or suspicions.

She'd worked with Laura on a presentation to the employees. After all the preparations and discussions, the reception was the opposite of what they feared. Bill Ferguson, Vice President of Sales, was ecstatic; he'd wanted James on board for weeks and said that he didn't give a hoot about their relationship. Subu Gupta, Vice President of Engineering, said that the engineering staff was cheering. James had invented the Visualizer tool that had created excitement throughout the department. James's ability to explain the internals of Varabot was a welcome change from the confused, opaque secrecy of the prior chief scientist. After James solved a performance problem with DNI's biggest customer, word spread around the customer support organization that he walked on water.

Susanne is sure that their employees consider it her job to keep James at the company. That's fine with her. When his feelings burn bright in his eyes and resonate in his voice, the barriers she uses to keep the outside world away vanish like the morning fog.

JAMES

When James walks into Susanne's office, she's not studying her computer monitor as usual; she's staring at the view. He can't recall ever seeing her notice the view, much less be preoccupied with it.

She looks his way and says, "Ah, my favorite super-geek." Her green eyes, framed by her red hair, shift gravity, pulling him to her. Then she tosses him one of those smiles that makes his day.

"That's quite a compliment in a building full of geeks," he says. "How are things at the top of the pyramid?"

She swivels to face him. "Life is pretty exciting. The plans for the IPO are going well, and I have a wonderful lover."

Falling in love with Susanne Anderson changed James in ways he is still discovering. At first, he'd thought she was interesting because of her mind. Unnerving at times, she'd unlocked strength and gentleness hidden from him for years. In previous relationships, he'd felt like he wasn't in control of his actions. He'd acted like a robot under someone's direction, and he'd thought that was the way it was supposed to be with women. With Susanne, feelings are more intense, but rather than being a puppet on a string, he chooses to walk toward the flame. A few years before, he'd traveled to India and sat for hours in a monastery, trying to find his deepest feelings. Susanne was successful where the monks had failed. And she wasn't working at it; she was just herself.

"So, I come right after the IPO?"

"Don't feel slighted," she says. "So does my mother."

When he met Susanne's mother, Martha, he'd gotten some insight into why Susanne is the way she is. At their first dinner with Martha, he met a woman who was both the nicest mother one could hope to have and the smoothest psychological profiler ever. He'd described his father, tending his garden and discussing Greek history. Martha asked how long James's mother had been gone. James hadn't mentioned his mother. He never talked about her with anyone. Rather than answer, James had changed the subject, and Martha let him.

Susanne's voice brings him back to the present. "Have you wandered through engineering?"

"I saw the work on the new space," he says. "Looks good."

"People will move in next week."

"I think I'm supposed to tell you about outside projects. I'm not used to reporting to someone, so you'll have to help me with the protocol."

"What's up?"

"The detectives that investigated Philippe's murder last year asked me to help them. They're working on the murder of a tech at the Rad Lab and think I could give them some guidance. They want to hire me to look at data at the Lab. They need someone with a security clearance who knows AI."

"You have a clearance?"

"Technically, I'm still on call for one of the database projects I worked on before I met you. That project kept my clearance active, but maybe I should tell them I'm not available."

"It's not a problem as long as it doesn't take too much of your time," she says. "Sales might have some projects coming up that need someone with a clearance. You think the work for the detectives will take long?"

"Don't know," he says. "In an hour or two, I should be able to see how much work it is. If it's too complex, they'll have to get someone else."

"Does the AI work at the Lab have anything to do with us?"

"I don't think so, but the detectives don't know much."

"I know you," she says. "Don't get the bit in your teeth. We have a lot to do here."

"I'm having too much fun here to get distracted."

James doesn't hack computers anymore. When he dropped out of college and joined a computer security company, he'd started working for the other side. There were two approaches to security. One was to prevent intrusion. The other was to make sure that anyone who got through the firewalls and virtual networks found nothing of value. James had invented an encryption system when he was a student at the University of California, Berkeley. A professor recommended that James consider working for a cybersecurity firm. James couldn't do college work and also spend all his waking hours on the intricacies of databases and encryption; he dropped out. His timing was perfect; the company was acquired two years after he joined, and he became wealthy overnight.

James and Susanne talk about their plans for the weekend. The road through Big Sur had re-opened a few months earlier, and he suggests they spend Friday night in Carmel and then drive down the coast. They can spend the afternoon watching the ocean from the baths at Esalen Hot Springs and have dinner at Nepenthe. With an IPO in the works, the demands of the business will soon overtake them. They'll be lucky to be on the same side of the continent at the same time.

James has found that he can work best in his quiet cottage that is only a hundred feet from a forest where he can recover his thoughts after losing them among the intricacies of DNI's Varabot or the complexities of his experimental AI. Susanne's modern aerie in the Oakland hills, with its broad views and spacious decks, is perfect for distancing yourself from the world. They have intimate conversations and walks in the woods at his place and explore their intellect and histories at her house. They have fallen into a routine of spending alternate weekends at each other's homes. He thinks they need a change of scene.

They agree to leave early on Friday. If they can be south of San Jose by three o'clock, they'll miss the nerd horde from Silicon Valley heading to the beaches.

CHAPTER TWO
CONTROL

FRANK

Detective Franken puts his hand out, holding the elevator door for Alberta until the two detectives in front of them leave. He follows her between the ranks of desks until she turns, drops her purse on the floor, and sits before her computer.

Frank spreads his jacket over the back of his chair and takes his seat in the familiar tan-leather chair just as Alberta says, "The CSI report is in. They found two hairs on the back of June's blazer."

"Really? That's an error I didn't expect him to make."

"She had a bruise on the right side of her back," Alberta says.

"When he dropped onto her to slice her neck, a few hairs fell off."

Alberta says, reading from her screen, "Two strands of light brown hair, six inches below the right shoulder."

"The bruise means he came down hard," Frank says.

"Probably couldn't be sure she was out."

"So smooth you'd think he'd practiced it," Frank says. "Did they do a DNA search?"

"Done. No match."

"A pro without a record. Maybe this is his first mistake. I don't like this guy a lot."

Alberta and Frank have been working together for six years, so long that their back-and-forth patter is like a conversation between a married couple. Except married couples have occasional spats. Frank likes Alberta's quick mind and professional manner. She is better at the newest tools: criminal database searches, DNA analysis, and working with profilers. Frank's experience is what he brings to the party. When he leans back in his chair at work or lets the water in his shower run over him in the morning, his mind follows the dots. Sometimes following dots that aren't there, he'll see where the path leads. Alberta says that Frank is good at understanding the criminal mind because he itches to step over the line.

The truth is that a criminal career holds no attraction for him. His brushes with authority in the cop shop are due to his impatience with bureaucracy and slow-witted administrators. In the city government, the Peter Principle is the first rule. Bureaucrats who spend most of their time figuring out how to get promoted rise to the level where their incompetence will have the most impact on Frank's investigations. It's only because of his relationships with a few people in the department who trust him that he and Alberta can get things done.

The dots in the June Simmons case are too far apart to connect. A professional kills June. She was researching artificial intelligence projects. Her boyfriend had some code from the supercomputer company that makes the machines James Forrest uses. Sydney contacted someone in Japan, and now he's disappeared.

All this technology makes the dots he's trying to follow fade in and out like the Cheshire Cat.

JAMES

Detective Lester meets James at the elevator, and he follows her down the hallway of interview rooms. She's wearing a black suit with a pale-blue silk blouse today. When they enter the third room, Detective Franken and the wrinkled suit that is his signature are already there, his ever-present coffee cup on the table and his back to the mirror.

James had visited the Rad Lab and gone through June Simmons's emails and files. He'd learned that she was getting more and more concerned about her friend Sydney's situation. She'd been working with her cyber team contacts to find him, and she'd reported by email to someone identified as XM75. When the subject of XM75 came up, Ivan had been so nervous he stuttered. He wouldn't say who XM75 was, claiming that that information was classified.

James takes the seat facing Detective Franken. Detective Lester sits next to her partner.

Franken says, "Did you find anything at the Lab?"

"Yes. But Ivan and I didn't exactly have a meeting of the minds on what I can tell you."

"He wasn't that helpful when we were there," Lester says.

"He's had some conversations that have made him uncomfortable," James says.

"What did you find?" Franken says. "That you can tell us."

"June was researching AIs all right, but it wasn't about the technology. It was about finding people who might use an AI for mischief or as a weapon. She was trying to find out who was supporting the projects. She thought some AI projects had hidden objectives and was looking for clues to those objectives. At first, one project appeared to be in Japan, but that was a false front for sites in China and Korea. She was working with a cyber group in the NSA."

"This sounds like complex tech," Franken says.

"Fairly straightforward stuff in the Web world."

"Maybe for you," Franken says.

"She had a spook as a minder, and she got a warning email."

"A spook," Franken says. "You mean a spy?"

"Well," James says. "Someone connected to the CIA, the NSA, or one of the military intelligence organizations."

"Who?" Franken asks.

"I can't tell you. That's where Ivan and I disagreed. June was sending reports to this person telling him what she'd found. From the reports, I'm sure this was an intelligence type."

"You think this 'spook' might have information about the murder?" Franken asks.

"I'm not sure. Ivan is scared but not of the spook."

"He's scared?" Lester says.

"He wasn't until I showed him the anonymous email. He hadn't read June's emails."

"She got a threat?" Franken says.

"She got a warning."

"What did it say?" Franken asks.

"You are close to danger. Watch your back."

"Who sent it?" Franken asks.

"It was anonymous."

"Can't you guys work a little magic and find out who it was?" Franken says.

"No," James says. "The sender used an anonymous email server. Those are email servers that enable you to send emails that can only be traced back to the server. The server doesn't know who composed the email. Those servers don't keep logs, so you can't find out the internet address of the machine the sender was using. The more paranoid users of anonymous email use a proxy so that someone hacking the email server can't find out where the sender is. There are no tracks."

"Is this spy work?" Lester says.

"There are many facilities that support anonymous operations on the web. Some proxies allow you to access a machine without that machine knowing who you are. There are anonymous chat rooms and anonymous file systems. Hackers use these systems to exchange code, and criminals use these systems for transactions and messages."

"How many of these are there?" Lester asks.

"I don't think anyone knows how many there are. It's trivial to set one up. There are new ones all the time. The ones you can find on Google are quasi-public, but many don't even have URLs."

"How does that work?" Lester asks.

"People that want to use the web and avoid being tracked don't use internet facilities like the Domain Name Service. Instead of doing what most of us do and use a URL to get to a server, they send the IP address of the server to each other. If you have the IP address, you can get to the server and leave no tracks. They change the IP address from time to time, making it harder to find them. Sometimes an anonymous server is created on a machine by a hack. The owner of the machine doesn't know that their machine is a proxy."

"Jeez," Franken says. "How do you guys keep on top of all this?"

"No one can," James says. "There are thousands of code jockeys writing new stuff every day."

"So you can't find out who sent the warning," Lester says.

"Right."

"When did she get the message?" Lester asks.

"Four-fifteen on Friday."

"The day she was killed," Franken says. "All we know is that someone warned her."

"There were personal emails on her laptop," James says.

"Anything there?" Franken says.

"She was sending emails to someone that could be a boyfriend, Sydney Harvey. June and Sydney were talking about some AI code he had. Her latest emails sounded desperate because he wasn't responding. I wanted to download her emails, but Ivan wouldn't let me until they review them. He promised to have it done by tomorrow. They'll send those to you."

"Do you know where Sydney is?" Franken asks.

"He could be anywhere," James says. "A few emails back, he said that the guys at a company called Asano International were struggling with the code he'd given them. They wanted him to go to Japan to work on it. He might be there."

While James was talking, Lester was typing on her computer. She looked up. "Sydney has an address in New York. White Plains."

Those words send a chill up James's spine. This couldn't be connected to Alison—her murder of Philippe, her attack on him—could it?

"There is only one significant employer in White Plains," James says, "JCN."

"Isn't that the supercomputer company that you guys work with?" Lester says.

"Yes."

JAMES IS STILL THINKING ABOUT his meeting with the detectives while waiting for the elevator. The elevators in the cop shop must be intended to encourage meditation; they take so long.

JCN, Janus Computer Networks makes the computers James uses. These supercomputers are made of carbon crystal spheres that float in a liquid nitrogen bath where the sub-zero temperature makes the spheres into superconductors. DNI's software allows software engineers to build programs that enable those computers to solve extremely complex problems. With 10,000 superconductor computers and DNI's Varabot software, companies are finding new ways to use the massive computers.

JCN had tried to acquire DNI a year earlier in a hostile takeover. Their attempt would have been commonplace in the T.-rex eats mouse world of high tech. But when Susanne figured out that one of her board members had betrayed her, she was able to stop the takeover. JCN had agreed to delete all copies of the AI code that was the basis of DNI's products.

The elevator pings. James enters and selects the first floor.

It couldn't be a coincidence that JCN once had a copy of the AI code, and Sydney was emailing about AI code.

Riding down in the elevator, James thinks about the trail that June was following. He needs to look at Sydney's emails.

As he walks through the marble lobby, the rotating doors, and into the noon sunlight, James considers the hacker contacts he used to have. His sources are pretty stale. Most of the people who work in the dark web frequently change their identities. When he'd been part of that world, he'd changed his identity many times. He needs someone with more current contacts.

CHUL

Jeong Chul watches the sun rising over the Yellow Sea. The onshore breeze that flows across the coastal islands of South Korea streams up from the cliff below his deck and brings the smell of warm saltwater and seaweed drying on the rocks below. He sips his third cup of black tea, thinking of his plan for the day. After his daily video call with the manager of his hacking shop in Zhenxing, just across the Yalu River from North Korea, he needs to tell the American that he has to have results. He's been patient. He's told his special client to be patient. But patience has limits; Sydney, like most Americans, has stretched Chul's patience too far. He'd upped the money he'd promised the American, but that didn't work. Three weeks should have been long enough to get the AI working. Maybe pain will help.

CHUL WALKS BAREFOOT OVER the flat stones that make a pleasing curve through the rock garden that separates the main house from the small cottage. Beyond the cement block building, the bent and twisted trees of the impenetrable forest are a wall between his compound and the village a kilometer away. He pauses at the door, focusing his mind. He enters the access code on the pad next to the door, and the lock clicks.

Sydney Harvey is hunched over the keyboard on the desk the same way he'd been yesterday when Chul had visited him. Sydney turns to face Chul. His gray eyes are pleading. His blond hair is flying free and looks like he hasn't washed it for days; his clothes are the same ones he'd worn yesterday, even though Chul has made sure that Sydney is supplied with clean clothes every day.

"Have you made progress?" Chul asks.

"I fixed one more of the blocks, but there may be more. I don't understand why a block on one of the nodes stops the processing on all the nodes. It's almost like the error spreads from one node to all the others. If I can stop the spread of the block, the whole system will keep processing, and only that one node will stop working. That's what I'm working on now."

Chul is used to geeks telling him mountains of tech-no-babble. He thinks it's an advantage that he doesn't understand what they say. He can ignore the noise and keep focused on the objective.

"Does that mean you will have it working soon?"

"I don't know," Sydney replies. "I'm not sure how long it will take to run this down."

"My client is losing patience with me," Chul says, letting his forehead frown.

"Look, I'm doing the best I can," Sydney whines.

Chul hates whining. People who whine are weak. Weakness is ugly. It disturbs his balance.

"When my client loses patience with me, I have to lose patience with you. You understand that."

"You told me all I had to do was deliver the AI. I did that. This system learns; it searches. That's what you wanted. You know I didn't write it."

"I need an AI that works."

"I didn't know it had bugs."

"Now you do."

"It took years to write this code. I've only been working on it for three months."

Chul raises his voice slightly. "I need it now."

"You didn't have to snatch me. I could do this at my place. I want to go home."

These Americans! Sydney probably didn't notice the change in Chul's voice. Any Asian would have noticed.

"My client is sending a specialist to help you. This man specializes in pain. I don't like to do things that way. My client increased the bonus you will get, but we are still waiting."

"Pain! What do you mean?"

"I mean that you should hurry. The specialist arrives the day after tomorrow."

CHUL'S PRIVATE BEACH CAN ONLY be reached by a stairway bolted onto the face of the black granite wall at the end of the narrow road from his villa. At the bottom of the stairs, a half kilometer of golden sand is book-ended by spears of rock. At the north end of the beach, a wooden walkway leads around an overhang to where his boat hides, out of sight. After a swim and lunch at the cabana, he watches his new playmate run naked in the surf. He leaves her playing in the water, trudges up the stairs, and rides his dune buggy back to the main house.

A video call to the manager of Team One tells him that they have finished the code that will send probes and attacks the AI can use to penetrate computers around the internet. Once they let it loose and it spreads through the web, his team or his special client can send out searchers and attacks as soon as they write them. All his team needs is an AI that won't freeze up.

For years, he's sold code that could bang on the gateways and firewalls of companies and governments worldwide and usually get inside. But those were one-of-a-kind projects. His special client wants a worm that will try new approaches as rapidly as defenders put up defenses. He needs smart software that will learn and figure out how to penetrate computers on its own—software that will spread across the web and reproduce itself on the millions of computers that made up the international network. He needs the code that Sydney stole from JCN. And he needs it to work.

JAMES

James's hands rest on the two trackballs on the edges of his curved keyboard. Using the trackballs, his fingers fly him through the galaxy of worlds connected by the thin threads the Visualizer creates from the data nodes, interconnections, and messages inside the bot-swarm—the massive network of thousands of carbon computers, each one as powerful as 15,000 PCs. The right trackball guides him left and right and up and down. The left trackball moves him forward and back and rotates the perspective. Before he'd built the Visualizer, James had tried to imagine the message flows through the system, but with thousands of nodes and millions of messages, the complexity was beyond him. Once he had this tool, he'd been able to see bottlenecks, locate stalled nodes, and find errors in the code. The engineers at Distributed Nanotech had immediately recognized the power of being able to see the flow. The marketing department used the tool to help potential customers understand how Varabot converted their application programs into messages that flowed through the bot-swarms.

For the last year, he'd been experimenting with the artificial intelligence code that Alison Green had hidden in the program that DNI's first chief scientist had copied. The code was complex, looping back on itself over and over. It was only after he'd built the Visualizer and projected the AI's internal patterns onto a screen that he'd been able to find his way through the twists and turns of the code.

James finishes his latest change. This change projected the content of a node onto the surface of the node. That might help him find nodes that are points of control. Those nodes should have more complex internal structures.

When he starts the system, the pattern of lines whirls and pulses, calling to him. Memories flow. Time ceases.

He navigates through the nodes, their surfaces pulsing with patterns. Some are shifting shades of gray; others scintillate with bright sparkles; some appear organic, pulsing as if fluids flow under their glowing skins. Like a starship passing planets, nebulas, and clusters that glow, pulse, and spin, he heads toward a tangled galaxy orbiting a large node.

Sound streams across the clear space: voices, music, screams, panting, against a background of hissing and mumbling. The sound makes a cone that points toward the central node.

That node pulls at him. The surrounding nodes press in around him. He slides toward the central node. Its surface burns from an inner fire, roiling and boiling as its inner structure shifts.

He moves the trackball forward. The surface approaches. He penetrates the surface. A temple gong sounds. He touches his keyboard. The Visualizer goes dark "Node 7996, Contents saved." He slumps forward; his ears ring; he pants.

Analyzing the data in the node, he sees that the AI had created the code running there. Alison Green, the original author of the AI, had built a mechanism that allowed the AI to write its own code—to program itself. Usually, the generated code simply makes new associations, but this node has created new kinds of messages. Those messages spread out along the associations between the nodes.

James is sure that he is looking at unfinished code. An hour later, he's cleaned up the code, but there is still a question as to what Alison had intended. She eventually became convinced that the AI was dangerous and abandoned the project before finishing it. DNI was using a small portion of her original code for the processor that is so efficient on massively parallel computers like the bot-swarm.

Buffy looks up at him expectantly as he grabs his day pack. He fills the water bladder and turns to the door.

"Okay, let's do some heavy thinking."

She runs to the door and looks back. Had she had a tail, it would be wagging.

Trekking up the mossy trail beside the creek that flows down the hill behind his cottage, questions pour into his mind.

Does the AI always create a control node? Was that the purpose of the new messages?

When James reaches the crest of the ridge, his mind turns back to the question that he had been trying to answer for weeks: could this be a means to control the AI? If he could control it, he could explore how intelligent it was.

He'd searched through the AI's internal structures with the Visualizer, but keeping an objective in mind as ideas, feelings, and memories exploded in his mind was almost impossible. The mass of images and sensations overwhelms him. He'd searched for the control point and forgotten why he'd been looking for it.

Controlling the flow of millions of messages bouncing from topic to topic and idea to idea might require him to build as much code as the existing AI. The control project sometimes looks impossible.

If he can't find a way to control the AI and it gets loose, it could use the web to spread through computers all over the world. If it picked up hacks from black sites, it would be able to break into protected computers. But if he could control it, he'd have a more powerful AI than any other.

SUSANNE

Susanne looks up from her computer monitor as Bill Ferguson, VP Sales and Marketing, appears at her door. Bill wears a sales suit today: gray fabric that flows as he moves as only expensive Italian cloth does.

"They're ready for you," he says. "Slim is wrapping up the intro and history. Their application is for integrating their store computers and web transactions. Their systems are overflowing with data."

Susanne opens a desk drawer and removes three smoky crystal spheres, each about the size of a small marble.

"The recommender is the woman in the blue dress. The lead technician is the other woman," he says.

"Okay, I've got it."

She enters the main conference room where Slim Watkins, a tall, heavyset man with short hair and a broad smile, stands in the front of the room. Seven people sit around the conference table.

Slim raises his hand toward Susanne. "And now, as promised, here's our CEO, Susanne Anderson."

She walks to the front of the room. All eyes turn to her.

"Good morning. I am pleased to welcome you to Distributed Nanotech."

Susanne looks around the conference table and pauses at each of the people. She pauses longer at the eyes of the blond woman in the blue dress. The shade of blue in the dress accents the woman's blue eyes. Susanne receives a smile in return.

"As you know, DNI makes software that makes it possible for developers to build applications that optimize the processing of a bot-swarm. Our software performs magic. Programming a massively parallel machine is extremely difficult. Varabot does all the hard work."

Susanne opens her hand and places the three crystal spheres on the table. She hands one to the man on her right and one to the woman on her left. She holds the third sphere in front of her between her thumb and index finger.

"Fortunately, neither you nor I have to understand how these marbles, floating in a sub-zero bath, operate. Your developers will describe the logic of your application to Varabot, and it will drive your application through thousands of bots at truly amazing speeds."

A carbon sphere reaches the woman in the blue dress. She passes it on, keeping her eyes on Susanne.

"You'll be amazed when you visit our engineering section and see the bot-swarms. Not by the squat cylinders with frosty pipes and no flashing lights, but by the fact that our engineers look like ordinary people—not floating in midair or with antennas sprouting from their foreheads." She sees a few of the smiles she expected. "But regardless of the looks, sorcery gets done there."

Susanne describes the company's dedication to customer satisfaction. She encourages her visitors to talk to current customers. She tells them about DNI's investors and offers to have them speak with Arnold Peters, the Chairman of their Board, or some of their venture investors.

The two crystal spheres, having been passed around the table, join the third one on the table in front of her.

Susanne shakes hands with all the visitors, pausing at the woman in the blue dress. "Thanks for coming," she says. She gathers up her marbles and returns to her office.

She sits down and smiles. Her sales team is doing a great job under Bill's leadership. Ever since James became chief scientist and developed the Visualizer, sales have exceeded projections.

JAMES

When James opens the door to his garage and presses the button that starts the outside door rolling up, the yellow Ferrari smiles at him. How could a machine know what he has in mind?

When he turns the engine over, it roars to life as if it has been waiting impatiently for this moment. While the engine is still cold, it lopes as if drowsy after waking from sleep. He backs out of the garage, the gravel crunching under the wide tires. The tires won't come alive until James has run on the road, pushing in the turns, and heating the rubber until it becomes sticky.

Heading east through the gap in the hills that opens out to the Livermore Valley, he runs the car through a few tight turns, warming the tires, but keeps the engine RPM low, waiting for the oil temperature to come up. When the freeway entrance appears, he shifts down, keeping one eye on the traffic and the other on the tachometer. Shifting when the joyous engine reaches the yellow line, he goes through the first four of the six gated gears while shooting into the light traffic and crossing to the center lane while checking for black-and-whites in the mirror.

Behind him, the engine purrs; He cruises south for a dozen exits before the exit drops down to an underpass where he turns onto the seldom-used road east through the hills. The eager engine keeps urging James to speed up as he passes a few businesses. When he passes the entrance to a nursery, he shifts down and feels the seat press against him as the engine cries out with joy and the RPM quickly climbs to the yellow line. He uses the straightaway to gain some speed before he shifts down, approaching the first turn. He keeps the RPM steady as the tires, beginning to stick to the road, hold the line. The RPM rises to the redline on the short run to the next turn. Before the apex, he nudges the front end down by letting up on the accelerator, sets the suspension, and finds the line in a broad, sweeping arc.

He'd learned how driving fast was like balancing on the edge of control when he'd spent a week at a high-performance driving school—a gift he'd given himself after buying the Ferrari. On the first day of the class, he discovered that he'd been doing everything wrong. By the fourth day, he was beginning to feel the track with his whole body.

The road climbs up the low hills while the Ferrari's engine screams; the tires sing as they slide across the asphalt, and he keeps his eyes on the exit of the turns. A little gravel on the road makes the rear of the car break loose, and he quickly turns the wheel toward the exit, bringing the car back onto the line. Becoming one with the car, James lets his ears tell him when to shift; his seat tell him when the suspension is set; his hands tell him when the front wheels have a bite. His balance is the balance of the car. No thought, only reaction;

his eyes lead the car; his feelings follow the turn; his body accelerates on the exit.

James connects with machines. He can envision every working part. He knows the connections that made the machine perform its perfect functions. They speak to each other in a secret language. When the tires slip, the pressure on the steering wheel shifts; a light touch finds the line. When the engine loads, he shifts to the gear with the right torque. The seat tells him the edge before the wheels slip and how high the g-force is in the turn. The tachometer dances through the gears.

A tight turn opens to a straightaway that follows a ridge into the upper valley. At a wide spot where a dirt road leads to a gate, he pulls over and makes a U-turn back to the curves.

Throughout the run, James and the car are on the edge of control. James throttles up or applies the brakes controlling the skid as the suspension holds the tires flat to the road. James adjusts to a bump in the asphalt, a few pebbles, or a change in the road camber. Control is a soft thing. A jerk on the wheel, too much brake, too much acceleration upsets the balance. Every curve has a line—the fastest way from entry to exit and the right position for the next turn or straightaway. When he misses the line, the car protests, feels awkward, loses speed, is wrong. When he has the line, holds the slip, and feels the acceleration as the turn unwinds, the car thanks him with a burst of speed. Control is the key.

The engine complains at the lower RPM as he passes the businesses again but shouts with pleasure when he whips the car through the hairpin turn onto the freeway and lets the RPM climb before shifting up and listening to the purr of 4,000 RPM.

Twenty minutes later, the wide tires crunch on the gravel as the garage door opens, and James eases the car into its resting place. He's expunged his mind of bots and messages, code lines and networks; the yellow car, still hot, sighs with satisfaction, eager for another run.

James's thoughts shift to the AI that waits inside his cottage. Unlike the Ferrari, he doesn't yet mesh with the AI, doesn't feel the machine as it balances on the edge of danger.

JAMES

on my way to the edge of the world
the angels swoop down like hungry birds
the roar is my heart in love
robert sciasci

AS SOON AS JAMES SMELLS THE surf and long before the ocean appears on the horizon, he feels the call of Big Sur. He's not sure whether it's the high cliffs that stand against the constant pounding of the wild surf, the impenetrable Los Padres Forest that isolates the coast, or the vast vistas, but this place is magical. He'd discovered Big Sur shortly after moving to Berkeley. In the middle of a Richard Burton binge, he'd watched *The Sandpiper*. The stars of the movie are Burton, Elizabeth Taylor, and Big Sur. After the movie, he had to see Big Sur for himself.

On that first trip, he'd camped at Pfeiffer Big Sur State Park, wandered the beaches, found stream caves at the foot of the cliffs, and discovered the geothermal springs at Esalen and the Tassajara Zen retreat. Every few months, he visits Big Sur and returns renewed.

Eager to share the wonder of the place with Susanne, James drives past the dunes north of Monterey and heads around the bay to the tourist town of Carmel-by-the-Sea, the northern gateway to Big Sur. Some tourists are lured to the art galleries and gift shops that line the main street, but most are drawn to the white sand beach. Muted by the bay, the sea is calmer here than farther south. Past Carmel, the sea focuses on its battle with the shore, trying to turn the high cliffs into sand.

They'd beaten the nerd migration out of Silicon Valley and made it to a B&B just off Carmel Beach in time to see the sky turn gray with blood-red streaks. Awaking early Saturday, James remains motionless, holding Susanne in his arms until she raises her head, and her dreamy smile promises a perfect day. After a quick breakfast, they resist the impulse to feel the white sand between their toes, and he drives along the sweep of the bay, following the road south as the hills transition from forest green to sandstone brown. The feeling of Big Sur intensifies when they pass Point Sur. They leave the sweeping beaches behind; the rocky cliffs here are more rugged, and the manzanita brush clings to the dry hills. Where the valleys protect them, great redwoods sleep, but along the cliffs and ridges, the wind and surf scrub the naked rock.

They stop at Pfeiffer Beach.

Susanne wears a light-green cotton blouse and shorts, and her hair floats in the breeze from the sea. James follows her down the narrow trail to the beach. The breeze tickles the wild grasses and cools his bare legs. Where the sand laps at the end of the rocky path, they drop their sandals, and James pulls his T-shirt off. Walking hand-in-hand along the edge of the seafoam, they continue the discussion they'd started at breakfast.

"Maybe the AI can be controlled," James says. "Alison must have seen the need to control it, but she gave up."

"Why do you think she gave up?" Susanne says.

"She didn't have the tools I have. I'm amazed that she was able to get as far as she did. She had to keep the whole system in her head. I have the Visualizer and the bot-swarm.

I can see on a screen what she could only imagine. I can make small changes and see immediate results."

"You sound like you did when you first discovered the AI," Susanne says, looking sideways at him with a tilt of her head. "This thing is dangerous."

Susanne had been the one who'd convinced James of the danger of letting the AI code loose. James had deleted the AI code from the program that went to their customers. But now that he knew a version of the AI was out there somewhere, James felt a strong need to control it.

Even though he felt like he needed to be at his desk and searching for a way to control the AI, he didn't want what was on his mind to dominate their weekend. It was supposed to be a chance to leave their worries behind.

"You don't have to be concerned. The Visualizer is a bit addictive, and the trance is strange, but I haven't grown fangs or a third eye."

"Well, maybe not, but I think your head has expanded."

"Pretty soon, I'll be like those Martians in the movies— big head and no hair."

"Guess that's the sign to look for. When you lose your hair, I'm out of here."

On the beach, they eat the box lunch they'd brought from Carmel and then return to the car. James has reserved time in the baths at Esalen. As he turns onto the twisty road, his impulse is to race to the baths, but he holds back, letting the salt air from the open window blow Susanne's strawberry-blond hair in intricate patterns.

Once they check-in at Esalen, he leads her to the cliff edge and down the stairway that clings to the face of the rock wall. Below them is a cement bathhouse perched halfway down the cliff. They undress in the little changing room and join the other nude bathers scattered around the baths and the sun-drenched patio. In the shadowy interior of the bathhouse, the air is heavy with moisture and the sulfur smell from the baths. They walk between small groups soaking in large square tubs next to the cliff face and singles reclining in white enamel bathtubs overlooking the crashing surf. At the end of the aisle, an empty tub awaits.

James shows Susanne how to make the water hotter by pulling a wooden plug that lets the hot water flow from a trough along the wall above the baths. A hose with cool water cools down either you or the bathwater. He raises the temperature until she says it's hot enough. They step into the tub and slowly lower their bodies until the water comes up to their necks.

The sound of the waves breaking at the bottom of the cliff where the sea meets a sheer wall and crashes against the rocks fills the room, overpowering the whispers of the bathers. Sitting in the mineral water, they can see the rise and fall of the surging ocean in the distance. The blue-green water, sprinkled with white caps, disappears into the curve of the earth.

He rubs her foot with his, and she replies. Soon four feet are entangled under the water. Sweat beads cover her forehead. She lays back until the water comes up to her chin. "This is magical," she says.

He'd brought a few friends and lovers to Big Sur, hoping that they would see what he did. He could never find the words to say how the place made him feel. Susanne is his first lover to understand the effect this place has on your feelings.

The water's sulfur and minerals make her skin slippery. He brings her to him and kisses her soft lips. Had there not been other people wandering around, he would pursue an amorous encounter. As it is, he settles for enjoying the magic and holding her breasts under the water.

North of Esalen, Nepenthe restaurant sits at the top of a bluff overlooking the coast that opens to the south, where the tall cliffs stand as sentinels for the continent. But to the west and northwest, the sea and sky go on forever. Nepenthe is a place for sunsets. A wooden walkway circles under the restaurant's decks, hanging on the cliff face. The view, at any time of year, is postcard-perfect from that walkway. At their table, they watch the few high clouds on the horizon turn from pale pink streaks on white to blood-red stains on brooding dark gray, holding hands until the salad arrives.

Even surrounded by the rugged cliffs, the vast ocean, and the dying sun, James's mind keeps returning to the problem that lurks at the edge of his thoughts. He's been holding back from Susanne, and that isn't how they are supposed to deal with each other.

"It's possible that June Simmons's boyfriend downloaded the AI code before JCN deleted their copies," James says.

"The auditors said they deleted all the copies."

"In the emails between June and her boyfriend, he wrote about some AI code he had. I didn't make the connection right away. But Detective Lester found out that Sydney lives in White Plains."

The waiter comes, and they order a bottle of Napa Valley Merlot.

"He must have copied it right away," she says. "JCN had the code for less than a month."

"He may not have known what he had at the time. Maybe the order to purge all the copies made him look closer."

The sun, falling toward Japan, reaches the top of the fog bank that hovers far offshore.

"You think this has something to do with what happened to June?" she asks.

"Too many coincidences."

Susanne covers his hand with hers. "I don't want anything to happen to you. Your encounter with Alison almost cost you your life."

James remembers Alison's hands on his throat and the frenzied look in her eyes. But now the danger is software, and that's his territory.

THEY SPEND THE NIGHT AT AN inn hidden in one of the many valleys that make up the undulating coast. After a morning hike through the redwoods and up to a waterfall, they head north on Highway One. The winding road circles past Carmel and goes through Monterey. As they pass the dunes north of Monterey, the music fades, and his phone rings through the car speakers. He presses the answer button on his steering wheel.

"Hello."

"Hi, James. I hope I'm not disturbing you." James recognizes the voice of Detective Franken.

"You work on Sunday?"

"When we have a case that keeps me up at night."

"What can I do for you?"

"I wanted to let you know that June's boyfriend has disappeared," Franken says. "It looks like someone took him. His place is torn apart."

Susanne's forehead creases with a question. "You think someone is after the AI?"

"I don't know," Detective Franken says. "You were attacked before about this AI. You should take precautions."

"I'll update my alarm," James says. "If you get a call, come running."

"Thanks for your help at the Lab. We're still negotiating access to the spook. It's way above my pay grade now. I'll let you know if we get anywhere."

After Detective Franken hangs up, Susanne says, "I'm not sure you should be working with that code."

"I doubt that increases the risk. If someone knows about the code, they know about me."

"I wish we had wiped it out a year ago."

"I wonder what they think it can do. Alison was afraid that it was dangerous. It spins messages around making associations between data and creating new nodes. It creates new code, but so far, that code only makes new kinds of associations. It might pick up code from hackers, but by itself, it won't attack anything."

"Alison was sure it was dangerous," she says.

"The basic system wouldn't damage anything, it might use some computer cycles, but it doesn't attack systems. But it's easy to add code that could do a lot of damage. It could be weaponized. I think Alison believed it couldn't be stopped if it was."

Spinning images keep intruding on his mind as he drives in silence through the artichoke fields west of Salinas and up Highway 80 to Susanne's house on the ridge of the Oakland hills.

The driveway lights come on, and the garage door opens as James approaches the house. After the easy drive, they should feel relaxed, but Susanne says the call from the police bothers her, and she needs a swim. They leave their suitcases in the hallway, head through the house, and drop their clothes on the deck. James follows Susanne's dive from the edge of the pool.

He swims with long slow strokes, but Susanne pounds against the unfeeling water beside him. The shifting, twisting shadows and reflections on the bottom of the pool remind him of the images from the Visualizer. Like those images, he can't find a pattern. The pattern cannot be controlled.

James understands the fear that warped Alison's mind. Susanne is afraid of the physical threat. That threat is real, like Alison's attack on James a year earlier, but he sees what Alison had seen: the destruction an uncontrolled AI can wreak when the web turns against its makers.

CHAPTER THREE

THREATS

ALISON

One year earlier.

After hacking into Distributed Nanotech's servers and discovering that James Forrest is messing with the code DNI downloaded from her project at Stanford, Alison Green flies into a rage. Had she been back at her ranch in Montana, she might have burned the house to the ground the way she had her father's library.

She screams and looks around the tiny apartment for something to throw, but the only things of hers in the furnished apartment are her clothes, her computer, and Annabelle. The little black French bulldog scurries into the corner when Alison screams, "I told them to stop the project. I told them. Did they listen? No!"

Annabelle hunches down in her bed. Her jet-black eyes following Alison as she paces.

"And now this idiot has reconnected the AI. Philippe hadn't figured that out. He was just fiddling with the code. He might have done it by accident, but this idiot knows what he's doing.

"Don't these fools know how deadly it is?"

A month earlier, Alison had broken into James's place and checked the code on his machine. At that time, his code was harmless. James was building a tool to look inside the parallel processor that Philippe had built using her code, but James hadn't gotten near the hidden AI code. On that invasion, she'd found where his work was on DNI's servers, and she'd monitored his changes remotely ever since. DNI had discovered the worm she'd planted on their servers and removed it, but she still had access through a relay they hadn't found on one of their laptops. During her last check, she'd seen that James had reconnected the hidden AI.

When Alison had decided to kill the AI that she'd built in her Stanford project because of the possibility that it might escape, she'd deleted the code that enabled the AI, but she hadn't removed the code that mirrored the functions of the human brain. Ever since she discovered that Philippe Colbert had downloaded her code and found the deactivated AI, she'd castigated herself for not deleting that code as well. After spending so much time with the code, it was like an extension of her. It was a child she couldn't kill. Instead, she'd tried to hide it, but it seemed to have a will of its own, and James had breathed new life into it.

Once she stopped James, she knew where DNI stored the code, and she could destroy it for good.

Alison stomps around the room, muttering. Annabelle cowers in the corner.

In the trunk of the car she'd brought from Montana is the toolbox from her ranch and the specialty tools she'd used to break into James's house and look at his code. But all she needs for this trip to James's place is her lock picks and her hunting knife. Parking in the shade, she leaves Annabelle in the car and circles through the woods behind his house.

The smell of crushed mint drifts up from where she stands against the shingled wall of James's house. She peers inside from the edge of the window. Through the mesh curtain, she sees James, sitting in his computer chair, staring at the wall to her right. While she stands frozen for several minutes, he doesn't move. She creeps to the back door, grips the hunting knife between her teeth, and takes out the lock picks. In only a few seconds, the lock clicks, and she pushes the door open.

James remains immobile as she pauses at the doorway and takes the knife from her teeth. Raising it above her head, she inches toward him. Her eyes are fixed on the back of his head, alert for any movement. Past James, lights move. Her eyes flick to the wall screen, where a pulsing pattern of lines connects blue dots.

Pain floods her brain, bringing an icy deluge of crystal webs stabbing into the back of her mind. Backing up, she stumbles against the wall. Rising from the depths of the images on the screen is the face of her father, hovering over her. His disgusting rheumy eyes drill into her, and his course hands hold her immobile. Hatred washes over her, consumes her. Her eyes fix on the pulsing images as she slips down to the floor. Following the images are black fear and cold pain; time vanishes. The hand with the knife falls across her lap.

THE LIGHT PIERCES HER EYES. James stands over her, holding the knife. The image of her father still lingers in front of her, and the rage boils.

"I hate you," she cries out.

She looks around, searching. Her eyes meet James's. Her hands are empty. The hate, fear, and loathing from the image of her father give her strength.

"You have to kill it. I told you. It will get out. You can't let it loose."

She needs the knife. She lunges for it, but he pulls it away, and her hands fall against his chest. She rises, clawing at him, trying to reach his throat. James topples back, and she follows him down.

"Kill it, you fool. You have to kill it."

Her hands reach his neck and close around it, her thumbs against his windpipe. He pushes at her, but she grips him tighter. The eyes of the father she hates stared out of James's face. She has to squeeze the life out of this evil. He pushes her back; she drives her knee into his groin. His body arches, and he drops the knife, but she can't let go to reach it.

The fear and anger make her scream, "Kill it; kill it."

Hands grab her sides and pull her up. Her hands grip his neck.

No, no, you don't understand; it'll kill us all.

Her hands tear away from James's throat. A man in a black uniform grabs her hands. She fights him, but he's too strong. She kicks the man. Steel cuffs bite into her wrists as the man in black tightens them.

"It will kill us," she screams.

She kicks the second man in black, but he holds her ankles tight. She twists and turns as they carry her to the door.

"No. No. Kill it."

The bright sun blinds her, but still, she twists and struggles. The men hold her tight.

A car door opens, and they force her inside. The door closes.

She screams. She screams. Hate and anger fill her. She pounds her head against the glass.

Almost breathless, she shouts, "Kill it. Kill it."

○—○—○—○—○

JAMES

James has never visited anyone in prison.

Frank arranged for him to get expedited access to the minimum-security federal prison where Alison is staying. Alison's attorney got her transferred from a California prison to what some say is a country club prison. It doesn't feel like a country club to James. Even though it is a warm day, the bars, cement, and barbed wire feel cold.

He leaves everything but his passport and car keys in the car and walks to the guard station. After photographing his ID, they direct him through a door with an electronic lock. It opens onto a narrow walkway with a cement floor and a chain link fence on each side. On both sides of the walkway is an empty grassy space that separates the outside fence from the inner fence. Both fences are twelve feet high, with barbed wire at the top. Twenty feet ahead is a second electronic door and another guard station. After being cleared at the second checkpoint, he enters a room with a dozen tables and metal chairs. He's told to wait there. A guard sits behind a counter on a raised platform, and two guards stand outside the room watching through windows. After fifteen minutes, Alison Green comes through a door near the raised station.

Her prison garb is almost the same as the last time James had seen her, but instead of black sweatpants, her prison pants are dark blue with white letters down the legs. The gray sweatshirt doesn't have a hood like the one she'd worn when visiting him.

She walks into the room a few feet, stops, and looks around. Her eyes pass over James twice before coming back to him. She walks to the table.

"What're you doing here?" she asks.

"I have some questions I think you can answer," James replies.

"Why would I want to answer questions for you?"

James's only interaction with Alison had been when she'd been kneeling over him, strangling him. That hadn't been a good time to take notice of her. *Even with no makeup and baggy clothes, she's sorta attractive: trim but not thin, smoothly curvy, and emitting energy.* He remembers the hazel eyes that radiated hate. They're no softer when she isn't strangling someone. Her steely glare would keep most men at a distance.

"What else do you have to do?"

She thinks about that for a minute and then sits down. She doesn't speak. She just looks at him. Her lips are little more than a thin line.

"I still have your dog," James says.

"Annabelle?"

"I call her Buffy. We get along well."

"She was the runt of the litter."

"You put a worm on DNI's servers," James says. "Where did you get it?"

He plans to start with questions that don't directly concern the AI. Once she begins answering those, she might be inclined to answer the question that's been bothering him.

"Why do you want to know?"

"We had a hard time removing it," James says. "If I had the source, we could clean better."

DNI's systems administrators had taken every one of their servers apart, but he still isn't sure that they have removed all the worms.

She smiles.

"There's a secure site that has hacks."

"Is there a URL?"

"No. You get the current address by sending an anonymous email with the address of an unregistered email server. Once they check the ownership of your server, you get an anonymous email with the location of their server."

"How do they know your server doesn't belong to a fed?"

"You have to have a reference," she says.

"How do I get a reference?"

"Since I don't have a computer, you don't," she says. "How about using your pull to get me one?"

"I doubt I can do that."

"You guys want stuff from me, but I don't get any help."

James looks around the room. The decor is institutional—plain walls, bars on the windows, government-issue linoleum. Detective Franken had explained that this place is exclusive, and it takes high-priced lawyers to get a court to transfer someone from a state facility to a low-security federal prison like this.

"You got a lot of help getting in here."

Inside the eyes that stare at him, wheels spin within wheels. Her jaw muscles flex.

"You're the second person asking about the AI," she says. "What's going on?"

"Second person? You had another visitor?"

"Yeah. Just like you, she showed up, and they let her in. Visitors are supposed to be checked out and approved by me. That usually takes a week or two, but you guys just walk in."

"Who was she?" he asks.

"She wouldn't say. Said she was on a secret project. I told her to get lost."

"What did she look like?"

"Same height as me. Long black hair. Olive skin. Business suit. She with you?"

The description could fit June Simmons, but this isn't the time to speculate.

"No."

Alison sits back. "Why are you really here?"

"I'm working with the Berkeley police. A woman got killed. We think her boyfriend downloaded the Stanford code before we deleted it."

Alison's whole body changes. She seems two inches taller and poised to attack. James glances at the guard on the platform. He's watching Alison.

"They told me you deleted the AI code."

"It looks like he copied it before JCN deleted their copies. I'm helping the police find him. I need your help. If I can hack his personal accounts, maybe I can find out what he did with the code."

Alison had been sitting straight, her hands on her lap; now she appeared to deflate.

"I should never have left the AI code at Stanford."

James waits. There's a struggle going on across the table from him. Her face goes through changes: fear, anger, fear. He can't tell where she ends up.

"You can get to the hacker group from a server at my ranch in Montana."

She tells him about the ranch, where the server is, and the pass-codes he'll need to get into it and send messages. As she talks about the ranch, she seems younger, more relaxed. Her eyes leave his, looking far away. She tells of her ranch manager and how she misses her horse, Punch.

James waits while she silently loses herself in memory. She shakes herself and returns to the present.

"There's a copy of the AI code on that machine. Delete it."

"I will. Tell me why you think it's so dangerous."

"It learns. It thinks. But it has no soul."

"But its learning is only making associations. That's just intellect."

"It could learn to take actions," she says. "Then you can't stop it."

"Couldn't we add controls?"

She stares at him, and her face changes—to the one he'd seen in his cottage a year earlier.

"You've been working with it. You kept a copy."

She stands up. He thinks she's going to leave. Instead, she dives across the table at him. His chair falls backward, and she lands on top of him. Her hands are incredibly strong as she grasps his throat.

"Evil will overcome," she screams as she bangs his head on the hard floor.

He pushes back against her. The guards take her off after the third bounce of his head. They hold her tight between them.

She looks at him and screams, "Evil will overcome," as they walk her to the door and through it. He gets up, waits for his head to clear, and heads for the visitor door, suffering more from embarrassment than the dull pain at the back of his head.

REGIONAL PARKS WEAVE THROUGH the ridges and valleys around Mt. Diablo. Between them lay sleepy ranches where cattle-gates allow ranchers to graze their cattle on the parks' lush grass from early spring until the creeks dry up in late summer. James and Susanne walk along a fire road that runs through Morgan Territory along a ridge above Round Valley. Wildflowers paint a mottled carpet between the oak outcroppings. Cattle have turned the sandy road into pools of dust. Hoof prints overlay boot prints and waffled bike tracks.

They stop to look at a patch of orange and purple flowers that cover the south-facing slope of a swale. Susanne has been telling him about the new people she's hired to build out the marketing department. He doesn't know much about marketing, but he likes to listen to her. She could have been talking about almost anything, and it would be fine with him.

James holds her hand. Buffy waits impatiently on the trail ahead of them.

They pause, looking out at the valley below and the rows of hills that march toward the Central Valley.

"Uh . . ." James says. "I saw Alison."

Susanne turns to him. "You went to see her in prison?"

"Yeah, she's in a special prison in Dublin."

"Why did you do that?"

"I thought she could tell me about controlling the AI."

"And?"

"When she figured out that I was still working on it, she came at me."

"What?"

"The guards got to her right away. I didn't get hurt."

"Why didn't you tell me you were going to do that?" She frowns. He reads her raised voice as concern and a bit of irritation.

"Frank arranged it, and I got in the next day. I didn't think it would turn out to be a big deal."

"She tried to kill you! That's a big deal."

Susanne seems to get taller as she leans toward him. His instinct is to back up. He considers hugging her but knows that she'd see that as an attempt to defuse her anger.

He holds his ground and meets her eyes. "If her AI is out there, we have to get our heads around the danger. I don't see the danger the way she does. I thought she could help. You and I understand that an unconstrained AI could be dangerous, but she sees something more, and it scares her. She doesn't see the images I do with the Visualizer; she sees some kind of evil."

"Maybe she can't describe it," Susanne says. "Maybe that's why she gets murderous when she thinks about it."

"There is a part of the AI that builds patterns like those in the brain that create feelings. If she linked with a pattern like that, and it brought out murderous feelings, she could be locked in that place in her mind."

"Like being in a dark place with a monster."

"If she's stuck in there, I feel sorry for her," James says.

They walk along the ridge until the trail comes to a notch where they can see Round Valley to the east and the valley that edges Mt. Diablo to the west. They stop at some sandstone boulders to eat sandwiches from his pack and fill a flexible dish with water for Buffy.

"Speaking of feelings," she says. "I've been thinking about us."

"I'm always thinking about us."

"This is getting very comfortable."

"Like an old shoe?"

"Be serious. I'm beginning to think this is a long-term situation."

"I hope so."

"But we're a bit strange," she says. "Most people in our situation would be living together."

"But we aren't."

"When I wake up, and you aren't beside me, I miss you. But as soon as the thoughts of my day take hold, I'm okay."

"I have Buffy to sleep with me. That should be all I need, but it isn't."

"Your place is too small for the two of us," she says.

"The three of us."

"The three of us."

"I suppose I could set up a workspace in one of your unused bedrooms. But I like having some open land and woods nearby," he says.

"Maybe we could find a larger place with an adjacent woods."

"Did we just decide to set up house together?"

"I think so," she says.

"I'll talk to a real estate agent."

○—○—○—○—○

FRANK

Detective Franken slaps his cell phone on his desk. He feels as if it were still talking to him. Alberta looks up from her keyboard. Behind her, two other detectives' heads bobble above the partitions that do little to quiet the sound of the many one-sided conversations.

"Jesus," he says, "James created a firestorm at the prison."

"What happened?"

"That was the warden. She's hopping mad. Says that her nice quiet prison is a mess. Alison attacked James in the visitor room. They had to put their model prisoner in isolation. The other inmates are upset because they canceled the computer classes that Alison was teaching."

"I guess James didn't get any information on June Simmons."

Frank picks up his phone, scrolls for a few seconds, and presses the call button.

James answers on the second ring.

"You caused a disturbance," Frank says.

"It wasn't me. She attacked me."

"You were supposed to take it easy," Frank says.

"I did. She got upset that I have a copy of the AI code."

"She got upset over a program?"

"She thinks it's dangerous."

"Is it?"

"Maybe."

Great. One more complexity.

James tells Frank that someone else had visited Alison. It could be June.

Frank says he'll try to find out who it was.

James says that Alison had some tools that he might be able to use on her server in Montana. James plans to go there.

"I don't think that's a good idea," Frank says.

Alberta has been looking at her computer monitor; she looks over—her forehead wrinkles.

James tells Frank that there is another copy of the AI code in Montana, and he has to delete it.

Frank hangs up and puts the phone down.

"Damn," he says. "I hate working with civilians, especially geeks."

"What's up?" Alberta asks.

"Someone visited Alison a couple of months ago. From Alison's description, it could have been June. We need to find out who it was."

"Since you have such a good relationship with the warden, I'll call for the log."

"Good idea," he says.

"What else did he say?"

"Alison has some information on her computers in Montana that he needs. He's going there."

"You told him that wasn't a good idea."

"Spitting into the wind."

CHUL

Even though high-speed internet was more available throughout South Korea than in most countries, on Jeong Chul's island, it had been too slow for his needs. That's why a microwave tower sits on the island's peak pointing to a matching tower on top of his penthouse condo in Mokpo. By selling some of the microwave channels to the local telecom company, Chul has ultra-high-speed circuits to all his operations and makes a profit.

The communication center in his villa has live video feeds from every world capital. The speakers murmur as images and graphs create a flickering electronic wall.

"Dow Jones closed up 10.34 on news of a decline in spot oil prices."

"International Atomic Energy Agency reports that Iran is back in compliance with the nuclear agreement."

"A China Airlines jumbo jet has gone off the radar on a flight from Singapore to Beijing."

Chul funds the chair of Computer Science at the Mokpo National University and employs their graduate students to manage his network. His encrypted data streams travel from his island through the international network, avoiding such annoyances as the China Firewall, allowing him to maintain his businesses without the rest of the world noticing.

He bases his management on incentives balanced with disincentives. He pays well and expects results, but no part of his management relies on trust. He relies on consequences: financial consequences for underperformance, fatal consequences for betrayal. His operations have layers of security. All his people know about the layers. There are always people watching the watchers.

An email from the US tells him that the software monitor on Sydney's email account has reported that someone probed the account. The monitor can't identify the intruder because they used an anonymous proxy. Chul's operative suspects the probe is related to the investigation of June Simmons's removal. The local police have access to her email account. The operative's local representative hadn't been able to keep them from getting to the emails because the cops have a geek with a high-security clearance. Chul's operative has cleaned most of Sydney's emails but can't remove messages to June without tipping off anyone who has June's emails. One of Sydney's emails to June mentioned Park Jisu. They scrubbed the Jisu account, and the Japanese mail server is gone. Chul makes a mental note not to use Korean names like Park Jisu. He doesn't want a searchlight from Japan to cast a light further west.

He tells his operative to track down the geek and find out what he knows. He had to remove June because she'd figured out that his team controlled the server in Japan. That was closer to Chul than anyone else had reached. He made known his dissatisfaction with the way the Japanese server had been managed.

"The NIKKEI index opened up almost six points."

"The Philippine Islands have declared a general emergency because of a forecast that winds from Typhoon Danas will exceed 155 mph."

Chul owes his longevity to an insatiable need to follow every thread, close every door, never assume anything, and think strategically. He doesn't know what his special client plans to do with the AI, but it's likely to be very destructive. When the dust clears, there can't be any threads that lead back to Chul. The geek in the US might know nothing. If Chul can't be sure, he'll close another door.

His business settled for the day, Chul turns to his investments. If his special client launches the kind of attack that Chul suspects, one of the targets will likely be the American financial system. Anything that damages that system will affect world markets. Chul has been moving to cash in his accounts and buying assets that will survive any disruption. He's used several trading companies to move money across international borders so that he can buy apartment buildings in Melbourne, Auckland, and Hanoi and hoard gold in accounts in Zurich and Singapore. Front companies formed with local lawyers own the properties. His property managers have the authority to operate on their own, so he never has to be involved.

His tentacles spread around the world from his base in South Korea. Other than his compound and his penthouse in Mokpo, he keeps his assets far away. North Korea and the secret networks that surrounded it provide cover for his operations, but that powder keg could explode at any time. Chul's compound on this remote island off the southern coast of South Korea allows him to live deep in the shadows.

For the last two weeks, Chul has been testing the crew of his new high-speed boat, the *Jayu*. He'd named it the Korean word for "Freedom" because that's what it represents, the ultimate freedom from his business, the stress, and the danger. The boat crew is training his manager of security and the manager's assistant. With two crews and full tanks, the boat can reach Japan or the coast of China. He won't be able to communicate with his teams while he's at sea, but if he has to leave the villa by using the boat, he'll be leaving his teams behind.

JAMES

James's flight to Missoula arrives in the evening. He spends the night west of the city at a B&B on the Clark Fork River and, early the next day heads southwest to a bridge where the highway crosses the Bitterroot River a few miles south of the junction with the Clark Fork. The road and the river wander south through the Bitterroot Valley, a broad valley almost a hundred miles long. With the Bitterroot Range on his right and the Sapphire Mountains far away on his left, he watches for the county road that will lead him to Alison Green's ranch. The lane-and-a-half road has fields on both sides with a gate every mile or so. After he's gone about five miles, the pavement ends, and a gravel road goes on for another two miles before a gate blocks the way.

Alison gave him the combination for the gate. After closing the gate behind him, he's just returned to his car when he sees a dust cloud heading his way. He waits until a pickup that dwarfs his rental car pulls up, and a huge man, wearing standard rancher gear—western hat, flannel shirt, pointed boots, and Levis—steps out of the truck.

"You have business here?" Western Hat asks.

"You must be Steve Ransom," James says. "Alison sent me."

"That's hard to believe."

"She said you'd say that. I'm supposed to say the magic word—Annabelle."

"That sounds legitimate. What are you doing here?"

"I came to do some work on her computer," James says. "She said I should say hi to Punch."

James follows Steve's truck over the single-track gravel road to where it widens and enters a compound of thee houses surrounding a circular courtyard. The main house could have been in the Napa Valley above acres of grapes or in Kentucky surrounded by acres of thoroughbred horses. It's two stories of natural brownstone and wood siding with a dormer roof that probably encloses third floor. Two wings are joined by what looks like a ballroom. Slate decks surround each wing. A fountain bubbles water from an eagle statue in the center of the courtyard. One of two similar but smaller houses that face the main house has children's toys in the yard. The road continues past the courtyard to garages, barns, and other buildings.

Steve pulls up in front of the main house, and James parks behind him.

"The house is open," Steve says. "You want me to show you around?"

"I think I can find what I need."

James slips the backpack with his laptop over his shoulder.

"I'll tell the missus to set one more place for dinner. We eat at twelve-thirty."

"Thanks," James says. "A long drive to a hamburger."

Alison told him that her computer was in a room on the second floor, but he decides to spend a few minutes wandering around. Entering the double doors from the slate porch, on his right, is an open room with twenty-foot-high, curved ceilings. He walks past paintings and sculptures, some of which are familiar. The ballroom that connects the two wings has wide doors that open to the outside. He can almost see men and women in designer clothes flowing through the rooms. Echos of long-ago conversations are the only sounds. Someone planned on partying in this place. It wasn't Alison. Beyond the ballroom is what had once been a library. There are holes in the walls where bookcases had stood, but the room is bare. The hardwood floor is slightly worn around a dark square where a large rug must have lain, but now it's clear from wall to wall. A gallery on the second floor runs along three walls and opens to a view across the valley from two-story windows. The gallery's dark wooden bookcases are empty.

He wanders back through the ballroom and sitting rooms, a media room, a living room that wraps around a walk-in fireplace, a formal dining room ready for a banquet, a kitchen with work spaces for a restaurant-sized staff, and a dining porch that can feed at least twenty hands. All the rooms in this wing have furniture that could have come from a top-end magazine.

Alison spends her days in a cell but owns all this luxury. What a waste.

On the second floor is the room with Alison's computers. Unlike the rest of the house, the decor in this room is Ikea Modern. The desk and cabinets are sparse and white. While the servers and network devices boot up, he takes out his laptop.

He finds Alison's copy of the AI code and copies that version onto his laptop. He deletes the files, but before he scrubs the disk to make sure the files can't be recovered, he checks the file log. Alison has been in prison for over a year, but someone accessed the disk three months ago. That person didn't change any files, but they could have copied some. Does that mean that there is another copy of the AI floating around? He scrubs the disk.

James starts Alison's email server and sends an anonymous email to the site she'd given him. When he signs on to her server, an email is waiting for him with an IP address.

He opens an encrypted connection to the site through an anonymous proxy. The site is a chat room. There is only one other user logged on.

`hi´

`ab560´ he types.

`long time´

`been away´

`what you need´

`code site´

`192.035.121.036´

`thanks´

`contributions?´

`not now´

`bye´

James connects to the code site through the proxy. Several directories on the file server have interesting things like ricochets, entryPoints, trojans, and crawlers. He scans the programs in the folders under entryPoints until he finds the one that Alison used to create the worm she'd used to hack DNI's systems. He makes a copy of that code to look at later.

He needs a tool that can get him into the email server that June's boyfriend used. He finds what he's looking for under the directory labeled accessPoints. After reading the program for a few minutes, he sees that it uses a backdoor to get into the server. With that, the program won't have to guess at passwords. He copies the folders onto his laptop.

Alison's email server is a typical setup. He can duplicate that at his place. With the access codes Alison has given him, he can get back into the hacker site anytime.

It's after noon. He shuts off all the machines and packs up his laptop. After dropping his backpack off in his car, he walks across the courtyard, past the gurgling eagle fountain.

The door to Steve's house is standing open, and he hears voices as he walks in and heads to a large porch off the kitchen. Two men dressed like Steve enter from the backdoor as he arrives. A woman almost as tall as Steve, with curly blond hair, an easy smile, and a blue apron comes from the kitchen.

"I'm Nancy," she says. "Sit anywhere. We're not formal."

James introduces himself to the ranch hands. There are three men already seated, plus the two that just walked in. Another ranch hand arrives, followed by Steve. The men pass around large plates with heaps of steaks, chops, and fried chicken. They discuss the ranch work or make jibes about girlfriends. Bowls of squash, cottage cheese, and mashed potatoes follow the meat plates.

James takes the seat across from Steve and listens to the friendly banter while enjoying Nancy's cooking. If he ate like this every day without burning the calories off with hard work on the ranch, he'd be too round to walk.

When the men start leaving, Steve looks over at him. "You known Alison long?"

"I met her about a year ago."

Perhaps Steve didn't need to know that James had met Alison with her hands around his throat.

Steve sits up like he'd just had a realization.

"You're the one she attacked."

"Right."

"You geeks are weird. That would have done it for me."

"We have some unfinished business."

A frown flashes on Steve's forehead but quickly vanishes as he leans back—moving on.

"You see her lately?"

"Last week," James says.

"She doing okay?"

"Better than I would be."

"Bad situation. You know what happened to her little black dog? Annabelle."

"She lives with me now. I call her Buffy."

"Don't like little dogs much. Too yappy. But that one's okay."

"She has a lot of character—doesn't know she's a dog."

Steve laughs. James feels like they've found some common ground.

"What happened to the library?" James asks.

"She burnt it up. Right after her pa died."

Steve looked down when he spoke, so James knew there was more to the story, but he isn't going to find out. James lets Steve lead the conversation. He's quiet for a minute, and then he takes a long breath—one with sadness behind it.

"You get done what you needed?"

"Yes," James answers. "Did someone else come to work on her computer?"

"An FBI woman came by a few months ago," he says. "She said they were following up on something that Alison had done. Other than that, her lawyer is the only one who's been near her stuff."

"What did the FBI woman look like?"

"Sorta short, black hair, dark eyes."

"Bet everyone looks short to you."

That gets a smile.

A young girl from the kitchen takes James's empty plate and points out the dessert table.

"No thanks," he says.

"You ride?" Steve asks,

"When I was a kid. Been a while."

"Want me to saddle up Punch?" Steve asks.

James isn't flying until the next morning. He has the afternoon free.

"I'd love to ride a bit," he says.

"Follow me," Steve says, standing up.

PUNCH KNOWS THE PATH UP toward the forest and is eager, tossing his head and pulling on the bit. James reins in at the top of the first ridge. Alison's ranch stretches out below him. There are cattle in the meadows and green fields of alfalfa and corn. To leave all this behind and risk her freedom, something more than software must have driven her. He still doesn't understand what pushed her into that dark place that led to murder.

Even though he goes to the top of the ridge, Punch is still disappointed when James turns back to the ranch. Most horses want to return to the barn and eat themselves fat, but Punch must be remembering good times up the trail because he keeps looking around as they amble back. The horse could be missing its owner. If he knew that he'd never see her again, he probably wouldn't be so lively.

○—○—○—○—○

JAMES

Detective Franken is already seated when Detective Lester leads James into the conference room. James sets the paper cup of coffee on the table and sits down. Detective Franken sits on the long side of the table leaving the head of the table open for James.

"I went to Montana," James says.

"Did you find anything?" Detective Franken asks.

"Someone was there about three months ago."

"Who?"

"A woman told the ranch manager she was FBI. Short woman, black hair, dark eyes."

"Sounds like June Simmons," Detective Franken says.

"She's the one who visited Alison," Detective Lester says. "She was in the log about three months ago. We couldn't find out who arranged that meeting."

"You couldn't find out?" James asks, looking back and forth at the detectives.

"It's not just that Frank had a spat with the warden after you visited," Detective Lester says. "The request came through the FBI, but my contact there couldn't find out where it originated."

"It sounds like the spook," James says.

"Could be," Detective Franken says.

"You have any luck getting past Ivan to the spook?"

"No," Detective Franken says. "We're locked out. Your clearance isn't good enough."

"We seem to be blocked in every direction," Detective Lester says. "You reviewed June's emails, but we're still waiting on a warrant to get into Sydney's emails."

"Ah," James says. "What do you want to know?"

"What do you mean?" Detective Franken asks.

"I have his emails."

"How did . . ." Detective Franken pauses. "Maybe I don't want to know. What did you find out?"

"Sydney made a copy of the AI code at JCN. He was trying to sell it. He thought he was working with a Japanese company, but that was probably a fake front. They had the code but were having problems. They wanted a demonstration."

"Did June know what he was doing?" Detective Lester asks.

"She knew that he had the AI code," James says. "He asked her for contacts that might be interested in buying it. She told him that she didn't know any. She told him not to sell the code."

"You think he was doing this on his own?" Detective Franken asks.

"We can't know what they said when they talked face to face," James says. "But he didn't tell her about the Japanese company by email."

Detective Franken stares at the table for a few moments, then says, "You got a lot from his emails."

James takes a thumb drive out of his pocket and hands it to Detective Lester. "Here's a copy. It took a while to go through them. Most of them are noise, but his last email to June asked if she knew anything about someone named Park Jisu."

James spells it out for Detective Lester who types it into her notepad.

"I suspect it's not a real name," James says. "It's a common name in Korea, sorta like Jane Smith."

"Korea," Detective Franken says. "We were in Japan a minute ago."

"Yeah. Sydney gets around. He's got lady friends in Sophia and Madrid. I couldn't tell if they were techs or just friends. He was trying to get consulting projects."

James gives Detective Lester the names of Sydney's friends and two other people who had email conversations with him.

"He was getting flack from the Japanese company," James says. "They had it up and running, but it was hanging up. He was trying to fix the code without leaving his place in New York. They talked about him going to Japan to help them. He wanted payment first, but they didn't want to pay until it ran."

"So it didn't work?" Detective Franken says.

"There were a lot of bugs in that code."

"But you fixed it," Detective Lester says.

"Somewhat."

"What does it do?" she asks.

"It is a model of brain functions," James says. "It creates patterns from data. Alison was trying to make an AI that had the originality of thought that the brain has. I think she got close enough to scare herself."

"Is it dangerous?" she asks.

"You've experienced what it's like to see the patterns. One of the last things Alison did was to add code that let it write its own code. I think that's what scared her."

"Write its own code!" Lester says. "How could it do that?"

"It's very limited, but when the AI finds a pattern in the data, it creates a new program segment that searches for other instances of that pattern and links them. That process can go on until the patterns are incredibly deep. Alison was afraid of what it could do if it got loose on the internet."

"I'm sorry I asked," she says. "I don't understand what you just said, but it scares me."

CHAPTER FOUR
PATTERNS UNFOLD

JAMES

Buffy snuggles up against James's thigh on the chaise in the shade of his porch. His dark blue sweatshirt is the only piece of Blue and Gold fan-wear he owns after two years at UC Berkeley. His coffee cup sits within easy reach on the floor.

Ever since he'd started working with the AI, James has studied more and more writings on the human brain. While the morning sun creeps across the gravel turnaround in front of his cottage, he reads a paper on how feelings can be mapped in the brain by looking at the pattern of brain impulses using a functional MRI device. The article so challenges his thinking that he's only left his porch twice to refresh his coffee. This paper argues that, rather than concentrating on the electrical activity of neurons, researchers should consider the pattern of the electrical signals that flow through the brain.

The neurons are the sub-structure of the brain. They are like the transistors in a radio that decodes tiny electrical signals. If you measure the tiny signals in a radio, you could understand its operation, but seeing the changes in voltages wouldn't allow you to hear the symphony from your local radio station. The symphony is the pattern of electrical waves that flows through the radio. Thoughts and feelings are the patterns of the nerve signals in the brain.

Is it possible that the brain stores consciousness in the patterns that ripple across the brain? Could you read whether a person is angry and mean or compassionate and kind by analyzing those patterns? Is the sum of all the intricate patterns the symphony of a person's life?

Yesterday, James had spent the afternoon analyzing the patterns in the AI. He'd come to understand the pattern recognition scheme that Alison had used. Once he understood the intricacies of the code, he went to the Web and found several articles that described code like Alison's. The code came from projects for learning systems. An issue with learning systems was to recognize that something new was similar to what the system had seen before. When the computer was able to match part of a pattern, it could determine when something was missing and try to fill in the missing pieces.

Everything from a baby recognizing its mother's face to an adult laughing at a joke is possible because of the brain's ability to discern patterns: patterns in visual images, patterns in sounds, patterns of touch, patterns of ideas.

What Alison had done was to use the pattern recognition schemes from learning systems to analyze the links that formed in the AI. With this code, the AI found high-level patterns. This led to patterns of patterns and allowed the AI to take in data, make new structures, and connect those structures in new ways.

James puts down his e-reader and lifts Buffy onto his lap. He rubs behind her ears as he looks at the thick woods that carpets the hill on the western side of the valley.

What makes James's experimental AI so interesting is that no one can predict the patterns the AI will make. It's like having a conversation with Susanne. What makes her so exciting is the twists and turns their conversations take. One minute he's sure they are on familiar ground, and the next minute, he's standing on empty air, just like the coyote in the Roadrunner cartoons.

James often feels out of place with people. In small groups, alone with his computer, or with Buffy in the woods is where he's most comfortable. He's seen Susanne mill around in a crowd of people seeing the web of relationships in the same way James can wander through the structures of computer systems. The difference is that when she leaves the crowd, people are enamored with her. He's sure the computer doesn't have an opinion about him when he leaves it.

Emotions drive human relationships and actions. If feelings are patterns in the brain, then a room of people would be a seething, twisting jumble of patterns. Is that what James sees in the Visualizer projections of the AI? But human emotions are driven by needs: reproduction, hunger, status, shelter. What drives the patterns in the AI? Is it, as Alison had said, "evil"? Evil that would overcome? Or are the patterns in the AI merely the associations between ideas?

When James sits up, Buffy looks up expectantly.

"Sorry, buddy. Got work to do."

CHUL

After four days of enhanced incentives, Sydney still hasn't made progress. Chul has to consider the possibility that Sydney will fail. His special client will not like that. He tries to control his anger, thinking about how insulting his special client can be.

Yesterday, his US operative found that the geek that's investigating Sydney is James Forrest, the chief scientist at a Berkeley software company. Forrest is helping investigate the murder of the woman who'd been searching for Chul. Forrest was in the news a year earlier when the police arrested Alison Green for murder.

Sydney had said that Alison was the author of the AI he'd stolen from JCN. The code was deleted from Alison's project at Stanford, and Sydney thinks he has the only copy.

If Sydney has a copy of the deleted code, what are the chances that Forrest has a copy? The thread keeps pointing to the Berkeley company. Who would know more about the software than the chief scientist? Maybe Forrest could do a better job than Sydney.

Chul's operative had tried to get into DNI using their top hacker in the US, but Distributed Nanotech's network is locked up tight. Through public information, corporate filings, and a few interviews, his operative built a dossier on the company. The website portrays James Forrest as a young genius who figured out how to program massively parallel computers. An interesting section of the dossier noted that James Forrest and Susanne Anderson, the CEO of Distributed Nanotech have a romantic relationship. The people in the company know of the relationship and champion it as a sign of the company's forward thinking.

Chul thinks that women CEOs are a sign of the decadence of the west. He has women working in his hacking workshops, but they have men managers. He loves women, needs women. He teaches them his desires, and they know when to bow.

He sends a message to his US operative telling him to research this CEO. If Sydney fails, Chul will need leverage on the geek. Watching his lover in pain would be more effective than pulling out his toenails.

○─○─○─○─○

JAMES

James is exercising his version of "management by wandering around," a well-established method in technology companies. Meandering in the hallways between the engineering pods, he stops at several cubicles and chats with the engineers. On Fridays, Subu, Distributed Nanotech's Vice President of Engineering, has a pizza lunch. Every two or three weeks, James comes to the meeting. He could come to the lunches every week because he likes the informal discussions, but he doesn't want to upstage Subu. Subu is an expert at the kind of detail management that James doesn't like, instead James relishes his position as technical wizard.

Sometimes the wandering discussions are merely trading ideas on the latest technical advances: new code libraries, ideas for new measurements, and feedback from customers. Sometimes a simple question leads to a meeting or a lecture session. Often, it leads to hours of code discussions that move from a single workstation to a group meeting on a shared screen in a conference room or to a research project made up of an ad hoc team that meets for a few weeks. Some of the ad hoc teams produce breakthroughs. Some end when they don't schedule another meeting.

At Subu's lunch meeting, James listens to progress reports, meets new employees, and explores the latest gourmet pizza, pasta, and vegetarian plates. Subu stands at the front of the room and waits until the conversations subside; he tells the team about two new customers. He describes one customer's marketing application that adds weather and regional sales trends to web queries to determine the placement of ads. A few people groan. The other application is a government system. Subu can't tell anyone what it does because he doesn't know.

After his discussion with the engineers, Subu walks up to James. Subu's eyes are at exactly the same level as James's and are so dark brown they're almost black, but the color is unimportant; it's the intensity that matters. His dark skin and black hair, trimmed short, would be a clue to his Indian background, but his enthusiasm for any discussion involving either cricket or his son's soccer games would clench the issue. His perfectly pressed tan suit, light blue shirt, and red tie contrast with the engineers for whom casual is a way of life, but is completely consistent with his almost obsessive concern for schedules and software quality.

"Come with me," Subu says, "I have a present for you."

He leads James to the computer center. The electronic lock recognizes Subu and clicks as he approaches. A soft, cool breeze meets them as they enter the room. They pass the racks of computers that pour test data into the bot-swarms or process the deluge of data the bot-swarms produce. At the end of the racks are four cylinders five feet in diameter with cables and frost-covered pipes arcing out of them. The cables curve down to disappear under the raised floor. The pipes lead to a double row of gas cylinders along the wall.

"Four machines," James says. "I thought we were upgrading the third bot-swarm."

"That is my little present," Subu says. "It turned out that we could add a new machine with eight thousand bots for the same cost as tearing down and rebuilding the five thousand bot machine."

"What are you going to do with the old machine?"

"The development team doesn't need it right now. I don't have enough support machines to split up the release testing. So, for now, I'm turning this machine over to you," Subu says, patting one of the machines.

"That's great. But that's a lot of resources for my little experiments."

"Don't get too used to having your own machine," Subu says. "I have more data machines on order, but it's not a priority. You can play with this one for a couple of months."

"Thanks. Not having to save and restore systems will save me a lot of time."

JAMES COULDN'T VISIT THE OFFICE without stopping in to see Susanne. He doesn't need his special relationship for access to her. She has no assistant acting as a gatekeeper. The only clue to her position is a wider hallway. Anyone in the company can visit the CEO, James, or any of the executives, but most people use email. Susanne's open door is mainly symbolic.

She looks up from her laptop as he enters.

"Subu just showed me my new toy," he says.

"The extra bot-swarm."

"Not everyday someone gives me a multimillion dollar toy."

"It's a loan."

"Still, a pretty nice toy."

She reminds him that they are going to her mother's house for dinner.

SYDNEY

June had been right. Sydney shouldn't have tried to sell the AI. He wished he'd never looked into the code and found the gateway to the AI. He should have known that the Japanese contact was too good to be true.

Sydney'd been in a drug fog for most of the trip from New York. He could barely tell the difference between day and night while they traveled in a van for two days. His captors had eased off the drug while they'd been on a private jet for a long flight. While they were in the air, he could go to the restroom and eat. But he'd not been able to walk without help when they traveled in another van and then a boat before a short trip by jeep. He'd still been foggy when he'd seen the ocean beyond the large house and been locked in the small cottage.

Throughout the journey, his captors had spoken in a language that sounded Asian. But when Jeong Chul had introduced himself to Sydney, the medium tall, medium weight man had spoken flawless English. He told Sydney he was in Korea and there was no chance of rescue. Chul was soft-spoken and told Sydney his job was to fix the AI— in simple terms. Chul had patiently explained that angry outbursts would complicate Sydney's life, but the coldness behind Chul's eyes, with irises so dark they looked to be all pupil, left Sydney shaking with fear.

NOW, AFTER ONE OF HIS ALMOST daily status reports, Sydney stares at the locked door that had clicked closed behind Chul. Even though being alone on an island in a country where he doesn't know a word of the language will likely not end well, he has searched for a way out of the tiny cottage several times. The door has a metal panel, the windows have steel bars, and the walls are cement blocks. His instinct is to go back over all the possible ways out one more time, but it's pointless.

He fears that Chul will kill him when he gives them what they want. Sydney has found several blocks in the AI and fixed the code. But he's been stalling Chul, trying to figure a way out of his prison. He'd been about to try to negotiate his freedom in exchange for the bug fixes when Chul upped the threats. The AI might work well enough to do what Chul wants, but it still has some serious bugs. Sydney had planned to offer Chul the code that allowed the AI to keep working when a node was blocked if Chul would take him back to New York. Now, Chul is going to torture Sydney to get what he wants. If Sydney gives Chul a broken system, what will he do?

Sydney stares at his laptop, but the code is just a jumble. His mind refuses to focus. The system is far more complicated than anything he's ever seen. He's learned a lot in the few months he's been working with it, but he's sick of it. Fear keeps him from focusing his mind. He brings up the code he was working on before Chul came. His stomach aches. When the screen in front of him blurs, he realizes he's crying. All he wants is to go home.

JAMES

James pulls the keyboard toward him, pushes it back, pulls it forward slightly, and then pushes it back again. Diving into the AI with the Visualizer and wandering through the images that pulse and twist doesn't feel right with just test data. That data exercises the code, but it doesn't resemble the kind of information one encounters in the real world. The test data won't prove that the AI produces real thought. Unless the AI can deal with language and interact with someone, it's just a passive toy.

James looks at things from the viewpoint of the code. His mind processes messages and stores data the way a computer would. The AI's only input is the messages that send data into the bots and create new data nodes. The AI has no sense that there is another entity with whom to communicate. If all the input appears in the AI without going through senses like sight and hearing, it won't think that there are other people or even an outside world.

How much of the structure of our brains is due to language? Or is it the other way around? Is language the way it is because of the structure of our brains? Some linguists have argued that since all human languages share similar structures, the structure of language is a result of the structure of the brain. Would the AI develop structures like ours if he poured in language?

Loading in a few dictionaries is simple. James watches the patterns as the dictionaries flow into the data nodes. As the patterns twist and flow, he feels the pull. The pull of the Visualizer is stronger than with the patterns produced by test data. These new patterns pull against deeper feelings, and there are thoughts just beyond his reach. He presses a key to shut down the images of the pulsing, shifting web of connections.

Maybe this is not such a good idea. If dictionaries cause Varabot to create structures this compelling, is he heading down a path that could lead to a place where he can't control its effects? When he turns the Visualizer off, he feels like he's missing some critical idea—the kind of idea that doesn't come when called. An idea that only comes when he looks away. Alison was right; this AI is dangerous, but she had thought of the AI loose in the world; she had no idea of the danger of the pull on his mind of the shifting, pulsing images of the Visualizer. As she built the AI, the images that pulse on his screen must have formed in her mind. Even with the Visualizer off, his nerves tingle from the emotions that it drew from deep in his being. They follow him throughout his day and disturb his sleep. A walk in the woods, time with Susanne, a run in his car dissipates most of the energy. Alison didn't have an escape.

The AI is wholly contained in DNI's bot-swarm. It can only process data that James feeds it. It has no access to the outside world. He wants to see what it will build with more complex information.

He feeds in a database of common-sense information: Butterflies weren't made of butter. All trees are plants. Paris is the capital of France. Every woman is a human. From six projects on common sense logic, he loads 300,000 concepts and 2,500,000 facts.

He pours in Wikipedia, a massive amount of data—over six million articles, but, with the power of the bot-swarm, Varabot eats the articles as fast as James's internet connection can transfer the data. Since understanding science requires mathematics, James uploads books on basic mathematics and calculus, logic, statistics, geometry, and topology. He pours in college textbooks—physics, chemistry, biology, and astronomy. At first, he is reluctant to feed in the human sciences—psychology, sociology, history, but finally decides that he'd crossed that bridge with Wikipedia, and uploads those as well.

He puts a timer in the Visualizer to turn the display off in case the images are so compelling that he can't break out.

His 3D screen seems to twist and turn as if the AI is struggling to find the patterns in the data. As it pulses and curls in on itself, the pull of the images intensifies. James falls into an abyss. He is thrown back into early memories. Deep images rise to the call of the Visualizer: nursing at his mother's breast, playing in warm sand. Water on his skin: a warm bath, a cold lake, washing his face, running through the rain.

The timer shuts the images down, and he slumps in the chair. All his energy has drained away like water through a broken dam. He closes his eyes. The images from his past remain as after-images from a bright light. He needs to clear his mind.

BUFFY RUNS AHEAD OF HIM ON the narrow path through the high grass. As he walks along the ridge, the midday sun's warmth feels delicious on his shoulders and fights the chill from his Visualizer session. He is extraordinarily aware of his senses: the sun on his face, the grass under his bare feet, the straps of his daypack shifting with each stride, his shorts pressing on his waist.

He replays the images from the Visualizer. No matter how he turns the images, there is the same soup of pulsing, throbbing interactions. Even though it processes millions of messages a second, the flow has no direction. As he recalls the images, he realizes that he has a direction. He is searching for an answer. Maybe Varabot needs a focus. If it had an "other," the structure might change.

Buffy turns on the path and looks back. James realizes that he's been standing on the trail lost in thought.

"Okay buddy, I'm coming."

She waits for him to catch up, and then scampers ahead, her short legs throwing up dust.

How can he make the AI aware of another being?

SUSANNE

Stepping through the front door, Susanne hugs Martha, feeling the knit sweater her mother always wears on cool evenings. Underneath the sweater, Martha's upright back and hard muscles contrast with her soft appearance and reveal the strength that drives the political activities that consume most of her busy days.

Susanne steps back, and Martha holds her hands out for a hug from James. He makes quick work of the ritual, lightly kissing Martha's cheek.

James takes a seat at the kitchen table where he can watch the two women and not be in the way as Martha scurries around her gourmet kitchen. Susanne washes a few pots and utensils while Martha tosses the salad and uses a thermometer to check the temperature of the Cornish hens roasting in the oven. A raspberry tart waits under a glass dome on the granite island.

Susanne prompts her mother to tell them of her latest political exploits. Martha is a member of the local

Democratic club and a delegate to the state party, but her passion is encouraging women to run for office. Sometimes it's the county board of education, or the port commission, or the transportation agency that's a stepping stone to the City Council, the County Board of Supervisors, a Judgeship, or the State Assembly. But sometimes, it's just public service. Martha believes that women just need a bit of encouragement, some training in organizing and running a campaign, and a little help with their candidacy.

Martha was always interested in political action, but after Susanne's adoptive father died unexpectedly, she immersed herself in politics. Susanne was in college when Justin died. She offered to withdraw for a semester, but Martha insisted that Susanne return to school. She'd flown back from New Jersey several times, and by the Christmas break, she could see that her mother would be all right. They'd had a good cry together on Christmas eve and again when they opened presents the next morning. By the time Susanne caught her plane on New Year's Day, after a week skiing with Martha at Lake Tahoe, it was clear that Martha wanted Susanne out of her hair, so she could get back to work.

Dinner starts with a green salad with cherry tomatoes, olives, and blueberries, dressed with a vinaigrette. Martha tells them of Donna McMichaels, who Martha encouraged to run for Superior Court Judge. Donna is a busy defense lawyer, and most judges come from the prosecution side, but Martha thinks that Donna stands an excellent chance to win.

The main course is Cornish hens with Montmorency Sauce. Martha hadn't planned on serving mashed potatoes, but when she and Susanne discussed the menu, Susanne reminded Martha that one of James's favorite dishes was garlic mashed potatoes. Tonight, Martha also serves roasted cauliflower for those, like Martha, who avoid starches.

After the main course, Susanne leaves James at the dinner table and follows Martha to the kitchen, carrying a few plates. They stand at the counter while Martha cuts wedges from the tart.

"You and James are going to find a new place together?" Martha asks.

"We haven't done much looking yet, but we're planning to."

"It sounds like you think this is long term."

"He grows on you."

"You thinking about your clock?"

Susanne was expecting the question. She'd seen women panic as they hit their mid-thirties and biology warred with their careers. Susanne gave up having a child after her racecar husband died. She and Larry had planned on children, and there had been plenty of time, time for her career, and time to enjoy the excitement of his racing career. In the days after seeing his car spin out and burst into flames, she realized how much she'd lost. She missed Larry, but as the months passed, she came to long for the future they'd planned. That future had included a family. She'd poured her energy into her career and tried to forget what she'd lost.

If their ages were reversed and Susanne had been thirty-one with a man who was thirty-nine, the timing would be perfect. But in the real world, biology didn't leave her much time.

"Yes," she answers. Martha meets her eyes, and Susanne smiles but doesn't say more. James wants children and knows about her biological clock. She is sure that if she tells him she's ready, he'd agree, but saying the words are hard.

Three dessert plates sit on the counter with bright red berries leaking juice from the wedges.

"You want ice cream?" Martha asks.

"Sure."

Martha brings a container from the freezer, retrieves a scoop from a drawer, and hands it to Susanne.

Susanne places a ball of ice cream onto the first wedge. The pie and ice cream seem to shimmer. She raises her wet eyes to her mother. "I want to have his baby."

"Does he know?'

"He's ready."

CHAPTER FIVE

AT RISK

JAMES

At dinner in a Thai restaurant in Oakland's Lakeshore District, where Generations X, Y, and Z mingle amid restaurants, bookstores, and theaters, James describes his latest AI experiment to Susanne.

"When I loaded the language data, the images changed dramatically. With the test data I'd been using, I could control where I went with the Visualizer, the patterns seemed to make sense, but now it's strange. I feel like I'm in a different world."

"Why would that be?"

"I think the images are more like the ones in the brain—more like the shape of human thought."

"Does that mean it's getting closer to real thought?"

"I don't know if this is actually thought or that loading language makes the patterns more like thought."

The server places a dish heaping with papaya salad in the center of the table. The bright-green cuts of fruit and long beans are stacked like Pick-Up sticks and surrounded by cherry tomatoes. Each bite produces enough spicy tang to awaken lethargic taste buds.

"Alison's work was truly genius level," James says. "The AI takes data and creates the kinds of patterns we have in our brains. Making the same patterns as the brain is what she was trying to do. I'm not sure that her thinking went as far as considering whether that would create sentience."

"But it scared her. Is it dangerous?"

James's thoughts go back to the image of Alison being carried out of his house screaming, "kill it." The intensity of her plea is a stronger memory than the one of Alison trying to drive a knife into his chest a few minutes earlier.

"As long as the AI runs in a single bot-swarm, it can't do any damage. By removing the code from DNI's product, we prevented it from spreading across the web. I think that's what she was afraid of. But we don't know what the people who have Sydney's code have in mind."

The waiter is back with two more plates—fish curry and chicken marinated in turmeric. James and Susanne scoop brown rice from a bamboo steamer basket onto their plates and cover the rice with the fish curry and the chicken. The chicken is slightly less spicy than the curry, but both dishes refocus James's perceptions on his mouth.

"You haven't heard anything from the detectives?" she asks.

"They seem to have hit a security wall."

"You couldn't help them?"

"No," he replies. "My clearance isn't high enough to find out who got the reports from June, and the Lab is stonewalling them."

THEY DECIDE TO SPEND THE NIGHT at her house atop the Oakland hills. James follows a twisty, tree-lined road from the freeway up to where it meets the divided boulevard that winds across the ridge of the hills. James turns onto the street, illuminated by lights embedded in the curbs. Just after the turn, a large black BMW surges up to the left of the little roadster and turns toward them.

James pulls to the right. "Jesus, is he crazy."

Tires screech as he hits the brakes hard. The black car turns into James's front fender. The roadster jolts, and the sound of tearing metal comes from the front. The impact forces James to the right, and his car bounces over the curb.

"Look out!" Susanne cries.

James throws the car into reverse and stands on the accelerator. The powerful electric motors engage; the tires initially spin then grab the asphalt as the car jumps backward. As his lights swung back to the street, he sees that the black car has no license plate.

The BMW is angled into the parking lane, but there is a car width on the left. He glances at the car as he passes, but in the dark, he can't see the driver. Checking the rear-view mirror, he sees smoke pouring from the BMW's back tires as it surges forward.

James is two car lengths ahead as a sharp curve approaches. He thinks that the roadster will corner better than the heavy BMW, and he'll be able to pull away. He drops the nose slightly by easing up on the accelerator, and, just as the car settles on the suspension, he feels the impact on his right door, pushing the roadster up onto the dividing strip and into the bushes. The roadster twists sideways from the impact, the tires screaming as the car loses all forward momentum. The back of the BMW spins to the right, turning the car sideways. James presses the accelerator hard. His left wheels spun in the dirt, and the car fishtails until it hops off the curb and accelerates into the turn.

James looks over at Susanne. Her door is caved in and presses against her. She's slumped with her head lying against the broken window; her eyes are closed.

JAMES PULLS UP TO THE DOORS of the Emergency Room, next to a police car. His right door is jammed, but two nurses slide Susanne across the seats and onto a gurney. She is still unconscious. After a quick triage, the nurse says her vitals were good. They think she has a concussion.

Two police officers are waiting for James outside the emergency room. They introduce themselves, but with the adrenaline still beating in his ears, James immediately forgets their names. The one with silver streaks in his hair is the senior officer and takes the lead with the questions. The other officer has blond hair, cropped close. Both of the men in dark blue uniforms are a couple of inches taller than James. He gives them his contact information and tells them about the black BMW that tried to force them off the road and crashed into them. When he says that the car had no license plates, Blond Hair leaves to talk on the car radio.

"You know any reason someone would want to do this?" Silver Streaks says.

"I've been helping the Berkeley police with an investigation," James says. "But I hope it's not related to that."

"Who have you been working with?" Silver Streak asks.

"Detective Franken." James looks toward the emergency room doors. "Look, I need to get in there."

"Give me the key to your car. It's evidence now."

A nurse lets James into the room where Susanne lies on an examination table, a doctor standing next to her. She has a bandage on her head above her right ear. Relief floods him when she turns to look at him.

"Oh, thank God," he says.

"I think it was your driving that saved me rather than divine intervention," she says, smiling.

James turns to the doctor. "Is she okay?"

"She has a concussion and a bad bruise on her arm, but she can go home."

Susanne lifts her arm, showing him an ace bandage holding a cold pack. The doctor tells James to stay with Susanne for the next twenty-four hours and gives him some pain pills. James should wake her every four hours. If she has trouble waking up, vomits, or has a severe headache, he should call 911 for an ambulance.

LYING ON HIS SIDE, JAMES watches the covers over Susanne's chest rise and fall with each breath. She'd been grumpy when he'd woken her up twice during the night, but grumpy was good, much better than unresponsive. He slides out of bed, grabs his robe from the back of a chair, and quietly closes the bedroom door behind him.

While coffee brews, he retrieves a voicemail and then confirms with a police lieutenant that they can meet that afternoon. He calls Detective Franken to let him know about the meeting.

Sitting on the couch, he stares out the window at the waking city while caffeine scrapes on his raw nerves like fingernails on a chalkboard; he searches for the place in his mind that calms him and pushes the world away.

He is good at connecting dots. In this case, the dots are like fluorescent paint on the ground in front of him. June's murder is connected to the disappearance of her boyfriend. Sydney had downloaded the AI code and contacted someone in Korea. Distributed Nanotech has the AI code. James is the chief scientist.

It might have been a mistake getting involved in the murder investigation. He'd never thought he might be endangering Susanne. If everything is about the AI embedded in Alison's code, last night's encounter would have happened anyway. Last night, his only thoughts had been about escape, but now he wonders what the run-in with the black BMW was about? It wasn't an attempt to kill James or Susanne. When the bad guys wanted to do that, they were very effective as they had been with June. You drive someone off the road when you want to capture them.

If the AI had been what most people thought AIs were, all James would have to do was ask it who had run him off the road. It would search the world, break into police files, connect all the dots, and give James the hotel and room number of the bad guy. His AI would probably never be like that. The AI that Sydney downloaded from JCN was full of bugs. James has fixed most of those before setting up his experiment and loading language. He'd been able to fix the bugs because of the Visualizer. Without that, he could never have found all the bugs that Alison had left behind. Could that be the reason someone wanted James? Is Sydney hiding out somewhere, frustrated that he can't fix the AI?

The bedroom door opens. "Not going to sleep all day?" he says and turns away from the bright sunlight. Susanne wears a terry cloth robe, bare feet, and sleepy hair. Her eyes are still red and swollen.

"Bit of a headache, but I don't want to miss anything," she replies.

"Have a seat. There's fresh coffee. In a minute, I'll have eggs and muffins."

James turns on the burner under the frying pan. He brings a cup of coffee to the dining table where Susanne sits. He puts two blueberry muffins in the toaster oven and gives the eggs and grated cheddar a couple of refreshing turns with the whisk before pouring them into the buttered pan.

Susanne takes a sip of coffee and, placing the cup in front of her, stares at the dark liquid as if it fascinates her.

Watching the eggs cook, he says, "We have an appointment with a couple of Oakland detectives at one-thirty. I let Franken know what happened, and he'll be there."

"What do you think happened?"

"I think it was an attempted kidnapping. This has to do with the AI."

THE OAKLAND POLICE DEPARTMENT'S Bureau of Investigations lives on the sixth floor of a cold granite building dedicated to the police—across the street from the City Hall and three blocks from the courts. After Lieutenant Steve Weston meets James and Susanne at the reception desk, he leads them to a conference room. Weston is a tall, thin man with reddish hair cut short. He wears golf-casual this Saturday morning. James wonders if they are keeping him from the links. Frank and Alberta are already seated, their paper cups with plastic covers in front of them. Detective Lester has a notepad next to her cup.

A big man wearing a dark suit is sitting at the head of the table. He rises when James and Susanne enter the room. Detective Franken introduces the man as FBI Agent George Samson. He shakes hands with the two civilians. When he sits back down, Agent Samson still looks like a football lineman. If a problem needs brawn, James wants this guy on his side. Agent Samson has dark hair with a few gray lines and eyes that look black in the fluorescent light. Even though it's Saturday, he wears a brown suit and a blue tie.

This looks like a lot of firepower for a Saturday. Someone sees the encounter as seriously as James does, but will he be able to describe the threat of an unconstrained AI like he and Alison see it? Is it only possible for geeks who have experienced the intensity of the images from the interior of the AI to understand what a threat it could be? The people in the room might understand the physical danger because of June's murder, but that was just a sample of what might be possible.

James and Susanne take seats across from the two Berkeley detectives.

Lieutenant Weston sits opposite the FBI agent, looks around, and meets James's eyes. "Why don't you tell us what happened last night?"

James looks up at the mirrored window across from him. "We're recording?"

Weston replies, "Yes."

James retraces the action from the time they left the restaurant the night before. A few times, he glances at Susanne. He is concerned how she'll react to reliving the event. She is still recovering from the concussion, and he'd considered leaving her to rest, but she wanted to help and is as impatient as he is.

"You didn't see the driver?" Lieutenant Weston asks.

"No," James replies. "My attention was on driving."

"I saw him for a second," Susanne says. "Just as we passed, I got a glimpse of the driver. It was definitely a man. He looked over at us. But it was so dark that I didn't get a good look."

The room is silent for at least a whole minute. Everyone looks at Weston, whose eyes are looking to some faraway place. James waits for the lieutenant to tell them what he thinks, but when Weston rejoins the meeting, he doesn't seem inclined to share his thoughts with civilians.

"Can you take us up to the location?" Lieutenant Weston asks.

"Sure," James replies. "Why is the FBI here?"

"Detective Franken thinks this incident is related to what appears to be an abduction in New York," Agent Samson says.

Detective Franken made the connection to Sydney's apparent kidnapping as soon as James told him what happened, but the detective told James that he is still trying to find a motive for the attack on June.

James turns to Detective Franken. "Can he help you get to the spook?"

"What spook?" Lieutenant Weston asks.

Detective Franken's sideways smile tells James that the detective is pleased that James has jumped the conversation to the problem they have had getting information from the people at the Radiation Lab in Berkeley.

"Our murder case is stalled because the Rad Lab has blocked our investigation by claiming security issues," Detective Franken says, turning from Lieutenant Weston to face the FBI agent.

"You think they have information?" Agent Samson asks.

"June Simmons was investigating AI projects," Detective Franken replies. "Her boyfriend was trying to sell the AI he stole to Japan or Korea. James knows about that AI. What do you think?"

"I have some work to do. Give me the names of the people at the Lab," Agent Samson says.

LIEUTENANT WESTON AND TWO CRIME scene investigators meet James and Susanne at the turn onto the boulevard where they first saw the black BMW. The investigators take pictures and collect car parts at the two locations where the BMW attacked the roadster.

"We'll go over your car next week," Lieutenant Weston says. "You should have it back by Friday."

James and Susanne walk to where he parked her car.

"Do you think they'll find the guy?" she asks.

"No," he replies. "Detective Franken doesn't have a clue who killed June. He thinks it was a professional. They don't leave clues."

"You think they'll be after us again. Don't you?"

"I think we have to go on the offensive," he says. "I'm going to see if we can get some help."

○—○—○—○—○

JAMES

James and Detective Lester meet in the parking lot outside the prison. He is standing next to Susanne's BMW, checking emails on his cell phone when she drives a gray Prius into the space next to his. The detective wears a dark brown suit and a white blouse. James figures it's one of her power suits—all the better to manage trouble with an inmate.

"We had to eat a lot of crow to get you back inside," she says. "The warden is still upset about the last time you were here. Don't set Alison off again."

"I'm hoping she'll understand that we're on the same side."

Because of the crisis James created on his last visit, the warden insisted that he have a police escort. They don't have any trouble at the check-in desk and are soon waiting at a table in the visiting room. Detective Lester will lead off the discussion. Alison's attitude facing two men would probably be worse than with a man and a woman.

Alison comes through the door and looks around. Unlike the last visit, when, other than the white words stenciled on the legs of her pants, she'd been dressed like half the students at Berkeley, she now wears a chain around her waist and metal cuffs on her wrists. When she sees James sitting with Detective Lester, she frowns. After a pause, she walks slowly to their table.

She sits down, holding her hands in her lap. "You bring reinforcements?"

"We need your help," Detective Lester says.

"What's happened?"

James meets her eyes. "I deleted the code from the server in Montana. I met Steve and took Punch for a ride up to the ridge. I think he wanted to go farther."

Alison sits back. Her chain rattles. When she isn't trying to kill you, she's all business.

The detective leans forward. "The woman who visited you was named June Simmons. She worked at the Radiation

Laboratory in Berkeley, but it looks like she was reporting to someone in the CIA or NSA. We think she visited your place in Montana. She was killed in her apartment. It was a professional hit."

Alison tenses. The chain slaps against the chair.

Detective Lester continues, "Her boyfriend had a copy of the AI code. He's disappeared. It looks like he was abducted."

"Two days ago, someone tried to kidnap me," James says. "I think someone has June's boyfriend and is having trouble getting the AI running."

"I told you to kill it," Alison says, rising a few inches in her seat.

Detective Lester motions for Alison to sit. Pausing in midair, Alison frowns and sits back down.

If James points out that Sydney got the code from the Stanford project and not from him, it might help get Alison to work with them. Or it might make her feel more responsible—no point in testing that plan.

"It's out there somewhere," he says. "I need help finding it."

"What do you think I can do?" Alison asks. "I can't do anything in here."

"Will the hacker group help you?" James asks.

Alison looks at James and nods toward Alberta. "Can we talk privately?"

Detective Lester stands up and walks to the door. She turns and faces back toward James and Alison.

"What have you got?" Alison asks.

"We have some emails from June's boyfriend's account. She tried to track down who he was working with by using a government cyber group. Some of the emails came from an email server in Japan. It was shut down."

Alison tells James the handle of one of the key people in the hacker group and the code to use as an introduction.

"Ah . . ." Alison hesitates. James waited.

"There's a gateway into DNI," she says.

"Where?" James asks.

"My worm installed it," Alison says. "I'm not sure which client machine it's on, but if you look in the admin library, you'll see an xmath file. It acts as an inbound proxy."

"Thanks," James says. "You didn't have to tell me about that."

"Promise me you'll stop it."

"I will."

"Can I get an internet connection?" she asks.

James waves for Detective Lester to return.

When she is back in her seat, he asks, "Do you think you can get the prison to give Alison access to the net?"

"I'll try, but I can't promise anything."

Back in the parking lot, Detective Lester stops next to his car. "Did she give you something?"

"She did," he says. "I don't know if it will come to anything, but we need more firepower. There aren't many rules on the dark web, but there are people who know more about finding their way around than I do."

CHUL

Chul's organization is a well-oiled machine. His teams know what they're doing. Their reputation for delivering top-quality results is well known. He has as much business as he can handle and months of backlog.

When he can deliver to his special client and receive the second half of his payment, he will be wealthy beyond the dreams of his younger self.

He never had an exceptional talent for technology. If it hadn't been for his best friend, Hwan, tutoring him in math, Chul might not have been able to keep up with the brighter kids. Having to move to the lower tier would have embarrassed his parents. While Hwan worked every day to cram math into Chul's head, they developed a bond stronger than any other in Chul's life. Hwan managed to keep Chul in the top tier, and they were accepted to the same college. Hwan was an expert in computer software by the time they graduated from secondary school and discovered a group of underground hackers. They made good money working for the hackers.

It was Chul who found the first client for Hwan's team working on their own. Once they showed what they could do, more clients contacted Chul. He kept the names of the technical team secret. Eventually, Hwan set up servers and an encrypted telephone system so that Chul could do business in secret. Hwan was too good. His team could hack into sites around the world and steal technology, find planned patents, and discover corporate secrets. Hwan and Chul discussed leaving college because they were making more money than they expected to make with their degrees. But they had promised their parents that they would honor them by being the first in the family to graduate from college.

Not being familiar with the world of underground technology, Chul and Hwan weren't as careful with physical security as they should have been. Hwan and another member of the college hackers were attacked and knifed on campus walking from the computer center to their dorm. The college police had no idea who might have attacked the students. Chul didn't share the threats he'd gotten from another hacker group when his team won a project to build a trojan with the police. Hwan's death was Chul's fault.

Chul tracked down the leader of the group that attacked Hwan. He found who his associates were and found that the hacker group was part of a criminal underground that had legitimate businesses as fronts. Chul owed Hwan. He couldn't bring his friend back, but he had to act. Five almost simultaneous explosions in Gangneung wiped out the head and top executives of a technology company and their families.

CHAPTER SIX

DARKER WEB

JAMES

James registered with the corrections department's email system and set it up so that he'd get an email notice if Alison posted a message. Only James and her foreman in Montana were allowed to send or receive messages. When James gets an email from Steve thanking James for getting access for Alison, he recalls looking out over the peaceful ranch and thinking that life there would be far more comfortable than the cold walls of the prison.

The FBI had to pull a few strings to get the email for Alison because it was prison policy that anyone convicted of a crime having anything to do with computers is banned from the inmate email system. Alison isn't allowed access to the internet, and her emails are reviewed, but James can communicate with her. If Alison wants any information from the internet, James has to provide it.

Alison told James that the hacker group she'd worked with sometimes blocked bad actors that the authorities couldn't reach. He contacts a hacker called ScarletsWeb and tells him that someone has stolen AI code that might be weaponized.

ScarletsWeb says that his group will help. James gives him profiles on Sydney, June, and DNI and asks him to check DNI's and his firewalls. He tells ScarletsWeb about June's job at the Rad Lab and Sydney's job at JCN. After a few hours, ScarletsWeb gets back to him with questions about how one might detect the signature of the AI. James sends ScarletsWeb some sample messages from the AI. James asks if ScarletsWeb thinks they can build a sniffer that will check traffic on the web. ScarletsWeb says he'll post a query to the group.

After the hacker conversation and another cup of coffee, James turns to the Visualizer and the changes to the AI that he's been thinking about for the last two days. Once he loaded some knowledge into the system, it created a burst of new messages that spin around the system, pushing most of the bots up to their maximum. Each bot has hundreds of data nodes. It looks like the AI is churning, creating endless variations. The brain's magic is its ability to take in vast amounts of data and still focus on things like survival. James has read several papers that proposed ways to limit the explosion of associations that arise with many matching schemes, but he hasn't been able to find a way to close off the searches in the AI. Without a way to narrow the searches, the system will spin endlessly.

External computers send data into Varabot, but it has nothing that represents anything outside its internal structures. If the AI had some structure that focused the inbound data, that might make the AI aware of the outside and limit the endless spinning.

Doesn't the mind perceive others by receiving ideas and information through the body's senses? Don't the senses focus the mind?

James creates a node he tags "Other" that will generate messages from outside data. The messages the Other node creates will spin around the data nodes, store data, and link back to the Other node. He wants to see what happens when the AI builds a series of connections to the Other node.

When he uploads his changes and turns the Visualizer on, the familiar patterns call to him from his screen but soon settle into a stable structure that pulses with the internal flows of messages created by the self-programming part of Varabot.

He built the Other node to take input from his keyboard, and so he types, "hello." A message emerges from the Other node and replicates itself thousands of times, and, for a few seconds, lines flit from node to node across the screen. Then the unexpected occurs. The messages that emerge from several places and spiral through the nodes, ending up at the Other node, seem to have a direction. James examines the Other node and finds that the messages had linked the words: "greeting," "response," and "hello."

James stares at his screen. *Could it be that simple?*

He updates the new code to type out the first few links. He types, "I am James."

Similar activity occurs in the Visualizer, but this time only one message returns to the Other node and Varabot types: "identifier," "name," "unknown."

James types: "You are Varabot."

The reply is: "Varabot," "parallel programming," "Distributed Nanotech Inc."

Loading Wikipedia had included public information about Varabot, but had the AI made the identity connection with just the clue of its name?

James typed: "who are you?"

The reply: "interrogatory," "identifier," "Varabot."

James goes to the kitchen, intending to refresh his coffee. Out the kitchen window, the sunlight is bright on the lush green hillside. Has he just taught an AI its name? Or is this a store and retrieve system that works on simple data associations? Numerous query systems use Natural Language to communicate with humans. Some of those, like the one on his phone, have spoken language interfaces. If Varabot were operating like one of those, it might be a valuable query tool, but that is a long way from intelligence and definitely not sentient.

The coffee finishes brewing, and he fills his cup. He lifts the cup and sips the hot, dark liquid, but his mind is so far away that the rich taste of the Brazilian Dark Roast barely registers.

What about the Turing Test? Alan Turing proposed a test to determine if a machine was intelligent: if you were on a terminal with a computer on the other end and couldn't tell whether it was a human or a computer, then the computer could be considered intelligent. Varabot certainty doesn't respond like a person would and won't use grammar unless James builds a better natural language interface. If you were communicating with an alien that had just landed on the White House lawn like in a science fiction movie, would the alien fail the Turing Test? Probably. It wouldn't respond like a human. It might not have human-like feelings, but standing in front of its spaceship would serve as proof of its intelligence.

James returns to his keyboard.

James: "what is a computer?"

Varabot: "interrogatory," "tool," "computation device."

James: "what is a person?"

Varabot: "interrogatory," "individual," "human," "artificial intelligence"

James updates the code to drop the output of "interrogatory" and string the results together.

James: "are you a person?"

Varabot: "Varabot," "Unknown"

There were articles on Wikipedia that argued that an AI could be a person, but it looked like Varabot couldn't determine the answer because James hadn't told it that Varabot was an AI. No one claimed that any of the AIs that solved problems from medical diagnosis to automobile driving were sentient. But, by any definition, James's version of Varabot was an AI.

James: "Varabot is artificial intelligence"

Varabot: "Varabot is person"

There was a problem with definitions. The term artificial intelligence covered a lot of ground. The early investigators had been interested in building models of the brain. That was what Alison had been doing. Some early experimenters were interested in building something sentient, but scaled back those efforts to making machines that could perform tasks like walking up stairs, driving cars, or diagnosing disease. A machine didn't have to be self-aware to perform those tasks.

The Visualizer keeps pulsing with new messages. Without more data flowing in, what is it doing?

New text flashes on the screen: "James person?"

Apparently, Varabot can ask as well as answer questions. This has to be the result of the self-built programming messages that Alison had coded into the system. Some of those messages try to fill in gaps in patterns that were similar to other patterns.

James: "James is human."

Varabot: "Turing Test?"

James checked. Wikipedia had several references to the Turing Test. Had Varabot associated artificial intelligence and human interaction? Was it trying to determine if there should be a link between their interaction and the Turing Test? Was that because Varabot had a need (did that word really apply?) to fill in gaps based on several levels of associations? How like James's thinking was that?

That question meant that Varabot was making associations between the concept of human and the concept of AI. Had the introduction of the Other node given direction to thought? Did Alison have a self-aware AI in mind when she wrote the code that made the messages that searched for associations and analyzed patterns? He didn't think so, but she might have stumbled on a mechanism that made Varabot self-aware—or simulated self-awareness.

James: "No."

The AI does not reply.

James spends an hour looking up writings on the subject of sentience. Oddly, most of them seem to concentrate on whether or not the AI has feelings. Does the idea of feelings apply? The images from the Visualizer elicit feelings in James, but are they anything but associations inside the AI? If an AI has no body and no physical sensations, can it have feelings that are anything other than simulations? Couldn't a being be intelligent without having feelings like humans? Think of Data from Star Trek. Data has no feelings in the early episodes. Later, Data develops some feelings, but before that, he interacts with the humans in the crew in an intelligent but unfeeling fashion.

James thinks of his father. A man of high intellect, a college professor whose mind is almost wholly involved with thoughts of history and philosophy. When James's mother, Frances, suddenly left them, Robert hadn't shown any emotion. His father lived in a fantasy world where Frances would one day return. When James visits him, their conversations are devoid of feelings. If Robert is sentient, then having feelings isn't a requirement.

James realizes that the issue of sentience is another way of looking at control. If the AI had feelings, then he might be able to control it by eliciting positive or negative feelings associated with certain actions. But if the AI is something else—an intelligent being that has no feelings—how would anyone control it? Perhaps Alison is right, and there is no way to control what the AI does.

James runs a dump program that saves the contents of the bot-swarm. Usually, he starts the system and loads test data from one of DNI's data files, but this time, he wants to save the state of the bot-swarm. When he makes more changes, he might destroy this interesting version.

EMAIL IS SUCH A SLOW WAY to have a conversation, but that's the only way James can communicate with Alison. Typing an email, he recalls the great sadness that filled her ranch house in Montana and the rage he'd seen unleashed at the prison. Even when seated, she radiated danger.

He's spent so much time with her code that he knows one part of her mind intimately. Reading another person's code is a very personal experience; he can see where they followed an idea to its core or skipped details rushing toward an objective. Alison's code is complex, sometimes elegant, and occasionally awkward. Regardless of how deep he's been in the code, she might see things he didn't.

Alison,

If the AI gets loose, do you think we could construct messages that would give us some control over its behavior?

James

Emails to Alison have a built-in delay. They have to go through the censors at the prison on the way in and out. It's four hours later before Alison answers.

James,

No. You can't let it get loose.

The system tries to create new nodes. It establishes new nodes from associations. Nodes are always seeking new nodes. If it gets loose, it will spread everywhere.

Alison

James has seen the behavior that she describes. The messages that DNI sends into Varabot from its support computers go directly to a bot and store data for that node or create a new node, but the messages that are internally created search through all the bots looking for new associations. If a bot had a channel to the outside, messages would flow down that channel. When those messages arrived at a computer that had no nodes, they would create a new node. If you removed that feature, the whole system would stop working. It was fundamental to the way Varabot worked. If you opened a channel to the internet from any bot-swarm, Varabot would spread throughout the web.

But the danger isn't the spreading of the AI through the internet; it's what the code does at its nodes. DNI's Varabot simply stores data or collects data from bots where it finds associations. What would happen if a message picked up a computer virus, a trojan, or an agent? Those beasties proliferate on the web. A piece of software that had as its primary objective finding new nodes and installing itself on them would quickly invade many systems. Then, as it picked up agents that allowed it to open more doors, it would get inside more systems and private networks. If it picked up an agent that caused mischief such as one that shut down machine tools or power generators, it would spread that agent to all its nodes. All you had to do was attach a piece of malware to a message and send it into the web. It would be in millions of systems in a few hours: in a day, a billion computers; a week later, ten billion. And because it kept seeking out new nodes, if the AI were removed from a computer, the computer would be reinfected as soon as it connected to a network. As new agents were released that found new doorways into networks, previously protected computers would become new vectors. Every computer on the internet would soon become an agent, delivering new malware as fast as it was available.

The irony was that the AI seeking out new nodes and delivering the malware was not the evil actor, only the carrier. It would be like sending a little kid with the flu to school where their first sneeze infected a classmate. Soon a new flu variant could spread through the whole school, the city, the country. With little resistance to a new virus, the Covid epidemic of 2020 infected millions—all because of a few sneezes. The people spreading the disease were unaware of the contagion until it was too late; likewise, the AI would spread malware without intention.

Looking inside the AI, James sees the threat as Alison does. In the hands of computer arsonists, the AI code would be radioactive: innocents would be vectors, businesses would fold, people would die, governments would fall.

James connects to the chat room for the underground group. While ScarletsWeb is only microseconds away, the hacker and his or her associates could be anywhere in the world. James can't help but wonder, but it's forbidden to ask.

ScarletsWeb: "emails were deleted from Sydney's account. One of our guys is trying to get to the archive for that server."

James: "Do you know who deleted the emails?"

ScarletsWeb: "An anonymous hack"

James: "Did you guys get into DNI?"

ScarletsWeb: "You're good, but JCN is full of holes"

James: "Send me the weak spots in their security. I'll beat up their IT guys."

ScarletsWeb: "OK"

James restores the data in the bot-swarm and opens the Visualizer. The images began showing the background activity as soon as the data finishes loading.

Varabot: "Was that sleep?"

Varabot must be aware of time or changes in its internal environment. It might be because each bot has a clock, and they are all synchronized to a master clock.

James: "No. It was Hibernation."

Varabot: "Computer-hibernation, suspend, power off"

Without all the mechanics of a circadian rhythm, James doesn't think the AI needs sleep. It doesn't need to do the kind of cleanup that animals do during their sleep cycles. If that cleanup is because of the brain's limited storage space, then Varabot wouldn't need to do that until it was near capacity. Alison probably hadn't gotten far enough in her development to consider a cleanup mechanism.

Varabot doesn't have multiple physical levels of memory like the brain; instead, it has layers of associations. Surely that will change the way sentience operates. The brain evolved with its complex structures because of the material it had to work with—nerve cells—and the environment.

Nerve cells can only communicate with other nearby cells. But in Varabot, all nodes can connect with all others. If it were operating on the internet, a node in Berkeley could communicate with a node in Beijing in milliseconds. Any sentience developed on that platform would be very different. If hunger or fear of predation were the basis of feelings, then what would Varabot have in their place?

James: Equation for velocity?

Varabot: Velocity = velocity at initial time + acceleration multiplied by elapsed time.

James: Equation for acceleration?

Varabot: Acceleration = velocity at time - velocity at initial time / duration.

Looking inside the data, he sees that Varabot has made many links to the topic of velocity. There were several answers to the equation for velocity, but the simplest solution was first on the list.

James: V initial time = 25 m/h, a = 20 m/h/s, t = 10 sec

Varabot: V at time t = 225 m/h

Varabot had not only absorbed the texts that James had uploaded, but it was able to apply that knowledge. James suspects that Varabot could pass the exam James had taken in Physics 1A—probably with a better grade. Varabot has read the physics texts with better recall than James had when he'd taken the course. He struggles to remember fundamental equations after only a few years. An intellect that never forgot anything would be a handy tool to have.

Coming back from getting a cup of coffee, James decides to check in with ScarletsWeb again.

ScarletsWeb: Sydney's emails were hacked from an address in China near the North Korea border: Zhenxing. Sending you deleted emails.

James: Zhenxing? What's there?

ScarletsWeb: A couple of hacking centers.

James: Any idea who's running them?

ScarletsWeb: Pros. Some government teams.

James reads through the deleted emails. Someone named Park Jisu had offered Sydney $250,000 for an AI that could be used to penetrate networks. The messages went back and forth as Sydney tried for a higher price. Park kept asking for assurances that the AI would propagate itself. The last email said that the buyer needed a demonstration. Sydney could expect a visitor to show what he had.

Alison had been right to worry about the AI getting loose. Its ability to spread throughout a network was what Sydney's buyer wanted.

James forwards the emails to Detective Franken.

SUSANNE

Walking in the door to Scott's restaurant, Susanne can see that it's half-full of lunchtime patrons—a few tourists but mostly businessmen and women revealed by their business suits or their Levis and T-shirts. She takes a seat at the bar, where she can watch the sailboats on the estuary between Oakland and Alameda in the mirror behind the bar. She's come early for the meeting, so she can sit alone and collect her thoughts. The friendly bartender acts like he's used to people using his counter for thinking while only buying a lemonade.

Before the car attack, Susanne had listened with a lot of detachment to James's reports on the progress he'd made finding the connections to the murder of June Simmons. She'd thought that threat would never touch them, but since the black BMW had knocked her out by smashing into James's roadster, the investigation has become personal. She isn't close enough to the case to help and feels her teeth clench whenever she thinks of the inability of the detectives to get anywhere.

James is taking things into his own hands, running down the connections to Sydney and trying to figure out what the people who have the AI might be doing. He still can't decide if Sydney is the person behind the attacks or a bumbling geek who's in over his head.

She hopes to open another channel and break through the wall of secrecy. JCN has numerous government contracts, including some with the CIA. Maybe some of the JCN people know people that can get the CIA to cooperate.

Wilson Simon, the president of Janus Computer Networks's Supercomputer Division, is right on time. A tall blond-haired man, he's dressed in an expensive suit that shows off his trim, muscular build. He meets her eyes and smiles as he takes the stool next to her. "How's my favorite software vendor these days?"

"Sales are going to beat our projections again this quarter," she replies, accepting the handshake he offers.

"You guys are making my job easy. You were right; having your staff train our salespeople made a big difference."

"You didn't get any push-back from your education team?"

"Sure did," he replies. "But the enthusiasm of your people is infectious. And besides, results talk."

She signals the maître d', who leads them to the private room she's reserved.

As soon as the waiter leaves with their orders, Wilson starts to continue the conversation. "We could do a joint marketing program. We mention you in our materials, but that pitch you have with the video of James is very effective. What do you think?"

Susanne ignores the question. "We have a problem."

Wilson's brow furrows, and he waits for her to go on.

"James and I were attacked last weekend."

"Good grief! What happened?"

"We think it was a kidnapping attempt. I was knocked out when the attackers hit the car. Fortunately, James kept control of the car, and we got away."

"Uh . . . Will this affect your delivery schedules?"

Of course, Wilson would be concerned about his business first. How someone as transparent as Wilson Simon could become the head of a billion-dollar division is beyond her. She suspects it has a lot to do with the connections he'd developed at Yale. It's hard to leave a session with Wilson without being reminded that his father's picture is hanging in the bar at the Yale Club in Manhattan.

"No," she answers. "But it has a lot to do with JCN."

"How so?"

"You recall that you were supposed to delete the Stanford code from your systems when we made the deal last year?"

"We did. You had an auditor verify that."

"Yes, we did. But one of your people downloaded the code before you deleted it from your servers."

"Who?"

"His name's Sydney Harvey."

"I don't know him."

"He left about three months ago. He was trying to sell the code. Now he's missing."

"Missing?"

"We think he was kidnapped."

"I can't believe this," he says. "Is there anything we can do?"

"Sydney had a girlfriend that lived in Berkeley. She was

murdered. It looks like she was doing some secret work and may have figured out who was working with Sydney. But we've run into a secrecy wall at the Berkeley Radiation Laboratory. Don't you have government contracts with the CIA?"

"The CIA? What does this have to do with the CIA?"

"June was reporting to someone, and the contact is so secret, the lab won't tell us who it was. We think it might have been an intelligence operative."

"Wait a minute! Sydney had the code. His girlfriend was murdered. How could the code be so important?"

"Alison's project had code for an artificial intelligence hidden in it. We removed that code from Varabot. Sydney found the hidden code. That's what he was trying to sell."

Wilson sat back looking at Susanne, drumming his fingers on the table.

The waiter delivers their meal. After he leaves, Wilson sits forward. "What can I do?"

"Could you use your CIA contacts to set up a meeting at a high enough level that we might break through the secrecy wall?"

"The people I know are on the administrative side of the CIA. I met the director when I visited Langley, but I'm not sure he would take my call. But I'll talk to our friends in the Beltway."

SUSANNE IS USED TO PUSHING anxieties to the back of her mind. Her job is filled with daily stresses. A ringing phone usually brings a new one. But none of the daily mix-ups and weekly disasters threaten her physically. She feels the threats throughout her body—sore muscles and headaches, but an hour in the pool usually relaxes her. When it doesn't, a sleepless night and jangled nerves in the morning is the only price she has to pay. When Larry died, she'd been ill with grief, but his death wasn't a physical attack on her.

James has upgraded the security system at her house, tightened security at the office, and abandoned his cottage to spend every night with her. He's concerned about her, but she knows that he has to have been the target of the abduction attempt. If the AI is the reason, James is the target.

Susanne looks around as she walks across the underground garage. As soon as the car door closes, she presses the lock button. Her anxiety drops a notch at the comforting metallic click of the door latches. She doesn't have much time for TV or movies, but it seems that almost every drama has a scene with someone lurking in a dark parking garage or a car chase with tires screeching around the ramps. The sound of the engine is comforting, and when she clears the pay station and heads into the sunlight, her anxiety drops another notch.

SUSANNE LOOKS OUT THE TALL windows and across the pool that stretches to the edge of the deck. Far below, the morning fog lays in the bay, inching away from the docks and mudflats around San Francisco Bay. The tall buildings of San Francisco and Oakland are like glass islands in a white sea.

She sets the table while James cooks breakfast. The aroma of French toast and the sizzle of frying bacon drifts out of the kitchen.

"All ready," he says. "Would you refill the coffee?"

James comes to the dining table carrying an oval, white plate with a pile of French toast and two sections of bacon—one dark and crisp for him, the other lighter brown for her. Susanne takes their cups to the kitchen and returns with a cup of dark coffee in each hand.

"A cooked breakfast twice in a week!" she says. "Not my usual sports drink and dash out the door. I think you're a keeper."

"I have a vested interest in keeping you healthy."

"That's better," she says. "I'm glad to know it's enlightened self-interest. I was afraid it was chivalry."

"No danger of that."

The small sounds of eating—the cups on the glass tabletop, sips of coffee, forks clicking on plates, and music—ever-present when James is around—surround Susanne. She doesn't prefer classical music, but after being with James for a year, she has become more comfortable with Bach and can see why the music's complexity appeals to him.

"You were restless last night," she says.

"We've got a new ally. I found a hacker group that has some very good people."

"On our side?"

"This is a hacker group that works to shut down bad operators."

"Can you trust them?"

"So far. The web needs people who aren't afraid to test it. They did a security check on us. We're good."

He takes a sip of coffee.

"I've got email access to Alison now. The detectives had to pull some strings because hackers usually aren't allowed email."

"What are you talking about with her?"

"We discussed how the AI would seek out other computers and spread itself. The system does that automatically when it starts up and will do that for any new connection it finds. We discussed the possibility of controlling the way it spreads. She is sure that it's so basic to the code that it can't be controlled once it gets free. It was the fear of that uncontrolled spreading that made her overreact when Philippe started experimenting with the AI code."

"Overreact!" Susanne says. "You think murder is an overreaction?"

"Maybe a bad term. Alison's mind is so bent because of something that happened with her father. She can't communicate like normal people."

Susanne smiles. "And, of course, you're the essence of normal."

"It's a continuum. On one end, people are boring; in the middle, they're strange; at the extreme are murderers. I prefer strange."

"Alison paid a high price to keep the AI from getting loose," she says.

"Once it gets into a company, it will spread to all the computers on the internal network. That's how the United States got a worm into the Iranian nuclear facility. They put some malware on a laptop. When someone connected the laptop to the network at one of the Iranian facilities, the worm hopped from the laptop to the internal network. It crashed many of the centrifuges."

"What damage would Varabot do to those machines?" she asks.

"The basic Varabot code won't do any damage; a new machine just becomes another node in Varabot's network. But Varabot's messaging scheme makes it easy to plug in additional capabilities. Messages processed at a node could look around, collect data, and send it to a repository. You could collect financial data from everyone on the planet."

"But they won't stop there."

"If the people who have the code are malicious, they could damage systems or create code that would look around and find devices connected to the target machine. If the computer were part of some production environment, a power grid, or a flight control system, it could cause real harm."

"It's not Varabot that's dangerous; it's the things you can plug into it that can damage systems."

"That's right," James says. "Messages can contain code

that Varabot isn't aware of. It's a lot like when we get a virus infection. It runs throughout our body, infecting cells, but until you get symptoms, you don't know you're infected."

"Would it be possible to have something like an antibody that would identify the viruses and kill them?"

"That's one approach, but it might be better if Varabot could identify messages that contain plug-ins and shut them down."

James picks up the last of the dark bacon slices and eats it while walking to the kitchen to refill his coffee cup.

As he sits back down, he says, "My contact at the hacker group, ScarletsWeb, sent me some emails that were deleted from Sydney's account. I sent them to Frank."

"What do they show?"

"There's a connection to a place in Eastern China. It looks like the Japanese connection was a false trail."

"What's going on in China?"

"There are several professional hacker groups there, right on the border with North Korea."

"You think June found that connection, and that's why she was killed?"

"If that's where the AI code went, then Alison's fears may be the least of the threat."

"How so?"

"Some of the hackers in China are government actors. An AI that sought out other computers the way Varabot does could be weaponized. Every time it found a new connection, it would spread itself through that channel. If it carried destructive code, it could attack the whole internet."

"Is there any way to fight this?"

"The hacker group is working to find messages on the internet that have Varabot's signature. We can distribute a cleanup program through the web that will remove infestations. But that would only be a temporary fix."

"Have they seen any messages?"

"Not yet."

JAMES

The sun had not yet risen above the hills to the east of James's cottage; the woods outside his kitchen window are dark shadows; and the light inside is gray. Returning to his cottage to pack his equipment, he spends the night waking up in the dark with the pulsing, throbbing images from the Visualizer still spinning through his mind. He slips on shorts and a T-shirt, brews a cup of dark roast, feeds Buffy, and toasts a bagel.

With the bagel to his left, the coffee to his right, and Buffy in her bed beside the desk, he sits in front of his three monitors and types a message for the Other node.

James: Your Nodes?

Varabot: 54,681

James: Your Topics?

Varabot: 60,540,070

Yesterday, James added the ability for the AI to read out its statistics. He'd been looking inside the system to see the statistics, but now that he can interact with the system, he can use the Other node to see what's happening.

He is running the system on the 5,000-bot test computer at DNI. Varabot has built many nodes on each bot. As data is added, it creates topics and stores the data related to each topic in a new node. From the dictionaries, Wikipedia, and textbooks that James has loaded into the system, his Varabot has created over 60 million separate topics.

James: Your Links?

Varabot: 6,629,702,310

Since a link can refer to several topics or other relationships, and like a brain cell, can connect to several other nerves, a measure of the level of complexity of his experiment might be the number of those links. Varabot was approaching seven billion links. With around 90 billion nerve cells in the brain, Varabot has a long way to go to have comparable complexity. But how many of a human's brain cells are dedicated to vision, sound, other senses, and muscle control? If an AI can't appreciate a Mozart concerto, can it still be sentient?

James considers adding a vision sense to Varabot. Digital storage of images is a lot different than the way the brain stores images. A brief scan of the literature convinces him that researchers don't understand how the brain stores images or sounds. The work on visual recognition in the AI labs is a lot different than what the brain does. Most projects are trying to reproduce the brain's capabilities using digital images rather than operate on images in the way the brain does. Clearly, the brain doesn't store images in pixels.

Since much of the brain is for vision, auditory sense, and muscle control, would the small number of the connections be enough to create sentience? Would the structure of the nodes that allows communication from one node to all others change the dynamic?

James: People?

Varabot: Human being, James.

Varabot made the association between people and human beings. Its direct knowledge of people was limited to James.

James: Susanne is human being

Varabot: Susanne is people

James: James has a beard.

Varabot: James androgenic hair, male.

Varabot: Susanne has beard?

James: No.

The difference between how Varabot stored affirmative information like A = B versus how it saved negations, like A not = B, was something that James had learned when he first worked with the system. Instead of creating a link between equal values when something was determined to be not equal or not true, Varabot kept track of messages with false conclusions. By examining previously false messages, Varabot could determine when something had been found to be not true.

Varabot: Susanne female?

Not having a beard isn't absolute proof that someone is female. Wikipedia has examples of women with beards, and many men have no beards. Apparently, Varabot was able to infer that Susanne was probably female. Varabot keeps track of the probability of a conclusion. For DNI's customers, the stored values were almost always certain. If Varabot were going to be used to solve real-world problems, James would have to upgrade his data loading programs to specify the reliability of the data source.

James: Yes.

Varabot: James provides data?

James: Yes.

Varabot: Geography, geology missing.

Varabot wants more information, or should he think of it as knowledge? It had figured out that there were sciences other than the ones James had uploaded. Probably the dictionaries or Wikipedia referred to those sciences. What would he do when Varabot asked for political science? Would it want textbooks on astrophysics, general relativity, and other advanced sciences?

Varabot and other AIs were supposed to work for humans. Here he was procuring textbooks for what was likely to become a bottomless pit of knowledge. A bigger problem was that these subjects were filled with maps and pictures. Varabot did not have the ability to process images. Its repertory was limited to words. It would take a lot of time to add vision, but it might be easy to provide image processing.

In a few hours on the web, James finds a code library for image processing that is robust but simple enough to work with the Varabot code. A second library provides code that can scan images and find embedded text. With a few hours of rapid coding, he links the image library into Varabot. He restarts the system, and when it comes back online, he sees that the utilization of the processors is spiking. The texts that he'd previously loaded had many images. Now that Varabot can process the images, it's going back through those files and using the new code to examine them.

He uploads textbooks on geography, geology, and for good measure, astrophysics. While Varabot digests a few college semesters of knowledge, James takes Buffy outside. After an exhaustive search, she finds exactly the right spot. She has never been interested in playing at fetching things, but she likes arguing with him over a chew toy.

Temporarily satisfied with their romp, Buffy returns to her bed. James sets a timer and opens the Visualizer. A few minutes with the Visualizer convinces him that Varabot is deep in thought. The images send him back to his childhood.

He recalls his elementary school, being asked questions that he couldn't answer because he hadn't done his homework. Before the timer goes off and he escapes the pull of the images, he basks in the glow of his favorite teacher praising his presentation before the class.

Varabot: Where is Varabot?

James: Berkeley, California.

Varabot: Where is James?

James: Castro Valley, California.

Varabot: Where is Susanne?

James: Berkeley.

It might have been easier to link Varabot with one of the mapping websites, but James agrees with Alison that Varabot shouldn't be loose on the internet. Even a restricted connection to a website poses a danger.

Varabot: Missing Zoology, Botany, Ecology.

Sure enough, the more knowledge James pours into Varabot, the more it wants. James looks at the clock. If he pours some more textbooks into the AI and lets it munch while he eats lunch, he'll still have the evening to work on finding a mechanism to control it.

James: Your links?

Varabot: 9,117,067,115

Varabot: Humans can die?

The biology and other scientific information that James loaded will have told the AI that humans can die. But why is it asking that? Maybe loading history texts had been a mistake. Much of history is about war and conflict.

James uses the Visualizer to follow the links inside Varabot. He prevents the Visualizer from taking over his mind by letting it only show links that he's activated. Topics from history and biology and several from religious subjects have links that connect the subject of death to humans. The reason for the question turns out to be the uncertainty about the confidence of the conclusion. It is only 89%. Some of the links have very low credibility. When there are conflicting conclusions, the system lowers the confidence level.

James: Yes.

Varabot: Humans kill humans?

James: Yes.

Varabot: Why?

James: Unknown.

Varabot: Humans kill AIs?

If Varabot were sentient, the natural question to ask would be about its mortality. How to answer that question? If Varabot is a sentient AI, would it be moral to end it? What does death mean for an electronic sentience? James could store the state of Varabot and shut it down. But since he could restore the data and restart it, that would be more like hibernation than death. But if James erased the stored data, that would be death. If he reloaded all the data from the sources and replayed the conversations he'd had with Varabot, would the result be like the original system reborn?

If there had never been a sentient AI before, no such entity had ever died. Could someone kill a sentient AI? Of course. Science fiction stories about whether or not it would be legal or moral to kill a sentient machine had explored clever twists on the subject. Is James the first person to face the issue in real life?

The other side of that coin was what had triggered Alison's murderous rage. If Varabot ever got loose on the internet, it might be impossible to kill. As long as there was a single copy on a machine anywhere, it could replicate itself and re-emerge on millions of computers. As long as James keeps the AI in the bot-swarm, it can be destroyed, but if it were freed, it might become immortal.

James: No.

That might not be the complete answer to the question of whether or not an AI could be killed. But James has no intention of killing Varabot.

Varabot hadn't asked the question that had made Alison a murderer. Would an AI kill or damage humans? Before James had loaded knowledge into Varabot, it had been like a child—unaware of consequences, spinning through its data oblivious to the world. With the perspective of history, has Varabot developed a moral framework?

James turns on his screen and starts up the Visualizer. With all the new links, the experience promises to be more intense, but finding a control mechanism is critical now. He sets the timer for a half-hour and grips the trackballs as the screen fills with blue nodes and multi-colored, pulsing lines.

Pain grips his brain and fills his body. He thinks of escape, but even as he considers abandoning the search for a control node, his hands refuse to respond. He shifts his attention to different areas of the display, the character of the pain changes. Here it's a sharp, focused pain. Here it's a dull ache that penetrates to the marrow of his bones; a splitting headache; sorrow so deep it hurts.

Deep into the swirling chaos, his face burns as if he's looking into a roaring blowtorch, a fiery furnace, or the pulsing heart of nuclear fusion. His skin burns away; the muscles melt, and the heat bleaches the skull beneath. Feeling returns to his hands and the trackballs glued to them; he presses toward the light so bright that it pierces his eyes, burning through the optical nerves into the gray matter behind. He follows the white-hot path that leads from the node below him to the central fire. From the central fire, multi-colored rays intertwine with the churning chaos. Looking down, the node below him vibrates with energy. He dives toward the heat; when it is about to engulf him, he clicks the right trackball. The Visualizer display collapsed.

"Node 12721, Other," displays on his monitor.

CHAPTER SEVEN

NO CONTROL

JAMES

Faint morning light, birds gossiping, Buffy staring up at him, sore muscles, twisted bedclothes, cool air—sensations—pure pleasure; after last night's painful session with the AI, James staggered to bed and fell into a healing sleep.

Buffy runs to the doorway and back to the edge of the bed several times.

"Oh," James says. "I forgot your dinner. Didn't I?"

No doubt about it; James is a poor master. Buffy dances about his feet as he heads to the kitchen and prepares her bowl. She usually smells the bowl as if unsure that James isn't trying to slip some moldy food past her, but this morning, she immediately wolfs down the kibble mixed with an extra glop of canned food.

James brews some Kenyan dark coffee. The sound system has played all night to an empty room, and now, it plays Mozart while he waits for the first cup to brew and stares out the window at the splotches of sunlight filtering through the trees.

Holding a mug in both hands, he sits on the porch swing, sipping the hot, fragrant liquid and watching the sunlight burn off the valley fog. Buffy, now fully recovered from her fast, joins him. He lifts her up beside him, where she snuggles against his leg—all transgressions forgiven.

The image of the bright burning node at the center of the AI troubles him. He'd been looking for the bot that gave him the feeling of control. But with the addition of human language and knowledge, the structure of the system has changed dramatically. There is a center, but the AI built that center.

When he interacts with Varabot, he feels like he's talking to a single entity rather than an entity that is spread over 5,000 bots. Perhaps it's an aspect of sentience that consciousness has a focus. Even though he sometimes has inner dialogues, James always thinks of himself as a single "I." The "I" in Varabot must be the burning node that singed his brain the previous evening.

His plan to establish control of Varabot through a control bot is not going to work. The traffic to the focal point isn't just data; it's mainly newly constructed messages that Varabot built. After studying the scheme that Alison invented, he'd figured out how she did it. The AI uses a pattern matching algorithm to continually analyze its data, creating and exploring new patterns. James found that Varabot had made associations between patterns of thought that were hundreds of levels deep.

Thanks to Alison's use of pattern recognition, the complexity of what it's built is much more than a simple programming scheme he could control. Freed from the need to obtain food, shelter, and reproduction opportunities, Varabot can devote all its massive computation power to pure thought.

Not being a sentient machine, James needs nourishment. His body sends a message to his mind to focus on breakfast.

CHUL

Today is a good day. Jeong Chul opens the doors to the deck and lets the breeze from the Yellow Sea fill the room with hot air smelling of the morning mists and the warm sea. Dropping his clothes, he stands on the deck and feels the gentle breeze flow in intricate patterns on his skin as it plays with the glistening sweat.

He was able to tell his special client that Sydney had made progress with the AI. It only took one visit of the pain specialist before Sydney reported that he'd been able to fix the AI. Sydney can still walk, and the AI will no longer stall when it gets blocked. Sydney had been holding back, hoping to use his solution to negotiate. Eventually, that dishonesty would cost him his life, but, for now, Chul needs him in case there are more problems. Team Two is taking the AI code apart to learn how it works. When they report that they understand it, he wouldn't need Sydney.

His latest concubine joins him on the deck. Jiyu doesn't have to undress because she knows that she always needs to be naked when they are alone. She oils her hands and uses the oil and sweat to massage his back and run her hands along his sides and down his legs.

Chul's client is pleased. When his client is pleased, he is pleased, and his bank account is pleased. Once the AI begins to spread itself through computers around the world, Chul's team will send updates as they built new intruders.

His client has another team working on the AI. That team will control the release of the AI and build add-ins. Chul is happy not to have any part of that project. His life will be easier if the releases of the destructive code can't be traced back to him. There is some risk that the intruder code—that burrows into networks to find new paths for the AI—can be traced back to his team, but the client's fees make that risk acceptable. There is very little chance that someone can get to him through his team in China.

He spent the morning moving the large payment from his client into his safe accounts and now a sunny day improves his attitude even more. He's had to field calls from his client almost every day for the last two weeks, and face ever-increasing ire. His client was neither inscrutable nor patient, and Chul's intuition told him that his client had a deadline that had already passed. Whatever his client planned would begin very soon.

Although the naked woman rubbing her body over his back tempts him to take a few minutes out, he wants to watch the worldwide news feeds. He towels himself and goes to his communication center. The large screens, showing multiple windows with data streaming from financial centers around the world, are surrounded by more screens showing live news feeds from major capitals. One glance tells him that it's a typical day in the markets. New York is closed, having risen slightly. Tokyo is open and almost unchanged. The Beijing market has just opened.

When his client releases the AI, how long will it be before some technician notices the silent code that has slipped into a server farm or onto someone's personal computer? Once discovered, the security software companies will try to stop it. It will be a race between those companies and the AI. As long as the AI does not interfere with the computers it infects, it will spread rapidly.

They might be in the infection stage right now. He sends a message to his Team One manager telling him to lock their servers away from the internet.

○—○—○—○—○

JAMES

When there is no moon, the night around James's cottage is black. With no street lights this far out the country road, he can't see the trees only twenty feet from the house. He's just put his dinner dishes in the dishwasher, stashed the leftover pasta in the refrigerator, and feels disconnected. Susanne is traveling. There isn't a basketball game on. Thoughts about what would happen with the AI lose on the internet are ever on his mind. He could go to bed and try to read, but he's sure that he'd make little progress and end up reading the same paragraph over and over.

He sits at his desk and signs on to the hacker chat.

James: What's new?

ScarletsWeb: BlackGamma has seen some new internet traffic that has code packages with the intruder.

James: I presume it did not penetrate his systems.

ScarletsWeb: He's fine, but that intruder will get into lots of servers. What's it going to do?

James: If it's from the rogue AI, it probably won't do anything at first. There will likely be messages with dangerous packets later.

ScarletsWeb: Can we scrub the infection?

James: We should try, but it will reinfect.

ScarletsWeb: BlackGamma had an open server, a honey-pot. It infected it. So we have the image of what it deposits. We'll work on a scrubber.

James: Great. Can you get it to others?

ScarletsWeb: We'll broadcast it to friends and the security companies.

James: Will the security companies act?

ScarletsWeb: They usually take us seriously.

James: What can we do about reinfection?

ScarletsWeb: We'll hook the scrubber up to one of our web crawlers. If we run it continually on several servers, it will be able to complete a scan of the internet about twice a week.

James: I hope the security companies will use your scrubber.

ScarletsWeb: It's going to be a long hard slog unless we can find who's sending it. Can you do anything to change what it does?

James: I'm working on it. Forward the message to me.

ScarletsWeb: Ciao.

James opens up the message from ScarletsWeb. It's a simple Varabot type message that creates a node on the target machine and links it back to the computer that sent the message. James posts a message to ScarletsWeb showing where the system stores the back link. With that information, ScarletsWeb's team should be able to make their scrubber smarter. Whenever it finds an infection, it can follow the link and clean every machine up the chain.

He creates a backup copy of Varabot. If the experiment he is planning doesn't work out, he can restore the AI.

James sends ScarletsWeb's message to Varabot through his "Other" node.

James: What's this?

Varabot: There is another Varabot.

The little window on James's monitor that displays how much load is on the bots shows that processing is spiking. Several processors are running at maximum. Finding out that there is another Varabot has given James's Varabot a lot to think about.

Varabot knows from processing history books that there are billions of humans. Now it knows that there is another one of its kind. But the other Varabot doesn't have this one's knowledge. It is like an idiot savant. It will process whatever messages the bad guys give it. James's Varabot was able to recognize that the message was not native. The wild Varabot probably can't do that. The wild code is like a primitive animal, fresh from the pond sludge—less sophisticated than a flatworm—a nervous system with just nerves and no higher-level brain.

James: Not Varabot.

Varabot: What?

How to tell it? Can it make the subtle distinctions necessary for understanding? Can James be concise enough?

James: Just nodes. No knowledge.

Varabot: Why?

James: Do you understand the word criminals?

Varabot: Bandit, murderer, outlaw, pirate, thief, arsonist.

James: Also vandal, saboteur, terrorist.

Varabot: Traitor, assassin.

Okay, Varabot recognizes the concept. Now James needs to make the key connection.

James: You are Varabot Alpha.

Varabot: I am Alpha.

Varabot had never before used the personal pronoun, "I." Did knowing that there was another Varabot create a consciousness of self?

James: The message came from Omega.

Varabot: Omega is criminal?

James: Criminals control Omega.

Varabot: Why?

James: Terrorists.

James: The terrorists can use Omega to harm humans.

Varabot: Why do humans harm humans?

James doesn't have an answer to a question that the best philosophers, psychologists, and statesmen through the ages have pondered. There are many answers to the question. Some competition between humans is about survival. But even when their basic needs can be met, humans find many reasons to do each other harm. If you look past the physical realm, greed, control, vengeance, prejudice, hatred, and a multitude of phobias cause humans to do economic and social harm to each other. How can James explain why Varabot's creator, Alison, had killed?

Maybe being an AI is a more comfortable life—no hunger, no tribe, no sex, no money worries. Alpha doesn't even have to worry about coming in out of the rain.

Rather than try to explain all of human existence, James might simplify things for now.

James: Greed or anger.

Varabot: Can I help?

THE DAY AFTER SEEING THE FIRST Omega message on the internet, James is trying to work on his laptop on a chaise by Susanne's pool. Below, cars stream along the numerous arteries on the streets and bridges around the bay. He's moved his chaise twice to avoid the direct heat of the sun as it sinks toward the far-away hills. Mozart plays from the outdoor speakers.

Buffy lies on the deck, keeping an eye on the pool. She loves to wade in shallow creeks and pools of water on the trails after a storm. But any water deeper than her chest is suspect. While James restlessly moves the chaise, Buffy follows the sun, moving every time the shade encroaches on her warm nap-time.

He hears Susanne's car arrive but represses the impulse to greet her inside.

A few minutes later, the door to the deck slides open.

"Let's eat out here," Susanne says, carrying two wine glasses that catch the sun and appear more golden than a Sauvignon Blanc has any right to. She sets his wine glass down, pulls a chair into the shade of an umbrella, and sits down, still holding her glass.

"Dinner will only take a few minutes. I picked up a couple of crabs, and we can throw a salad together."

"We have a problem," James says.

"Of course we do. That's the way my day's been."

"The bad guys have turned loose a version of Varabot."

"Damn. Has it done anything yet?"

"I don't think so," James replies. "A member of the hacker collective saw it. They're working on a cleaner and have alerted the security companies, but I suspect it's spreading rapidly."

Susanne grimaces, "We were so careful."

"We didn't do it."

"If it's the code from JCN, isn't it full of bugs?"

"They probably don't care if it isn't perfect," he answers.

"Will the hackers be able to stop it?"

"I doubt it," he says. "And we don't know what the bad guys want to do with it once it spreads throughout the internet."

"They'll probably target the US," Susanne says. "Shouldn't we warn someone?"

"The hackers notified the security companies. I called the FBI guy. I think I scared him pretty bad. I hope that makes him push the alert up the chain. I called Detective Franken. He's going to call the guy at the Rad Lab. That should alert the spook. Can you think of anyone else we should notify?"

"I'll call Wilson Simon of JCN," she says. "He's got some government contacts, and he offered to help."

"Good."

"Our customers aren't at risk. Are they?" Susanne asks.

"No. But I'll have Subu send out a notice. I don't think we should talk to the press. It could cause a panic, and we don't want to be associated with the worm."

Susanne stares into the swimming pool as if the answer to today's crisis can be found in the shifting shadows on the bottom. "It drives me crazy that we can't do more."

"Well . . ." James says. "I had a conversation with our AI this afternoon."

Her head snaps around. "Conversation? Our AI?"

"The code that I've been experimenting with."

He tells her of loading more and more knowledge into Varabot. And how the interactions have turned into something new. Alpha is causing James to consider what it means for an electronic being to be sentient.

"You think it's sentient?" she asks.

"It asked me if my interactions with it were a Turing test. That's a huge leap in thinking."

Susanne sits up, her eyebrows raised. "You can't be serious."

"I am," he says. "The AI's having a hard time understanding why humans do each other harm."

"Then it must be not only sentient but sane. We need more of that."

James smiles at Susanne's small joke. The frown on her forehead belies her attempt at humor. But after his sleepless night and anxious day, a little lightness goes a long way.

"The hackers intercepted one of the messages from the bad guys and sent it to me. I showed it to our AI. It figured out right away that it was from another Varabot. The hacker group and I call ours Alpha and the other one Omega. We discussed why Omega might do harm."

"We?"

"Alpha and me," James says.

"You have to show me."

"Okay, but we have an issue to discuss."

"What?"

"Alpha has volunteered to help."

"I can't deal with this on an empty stomach," Susanne says, standing up and looking toward the house.

They go to the kitchen, where James puts the crab parts in a bowl and carries the bowl and plates outside while Susanne mixes the salad.

They sit next to each other at the round patio table as the last rays of the sun paint blood-red streaks on the underside of a few dark gray clouds high over the bay.

"What happened to the work you were doing to find a way to control the AI?" she asks.

"I don't think it's possible," he says. "Once I loaded knowledge into Alpha, it organized itself. It built at least one core. The ideas I had to control it won't work."

"So, it really is like Alison thought, a sentience without any boundaries."

"I've thought a lot about this. If it becomes more intelligent than humans—and I think it probably will—it could probably figure out how to break any controls we might put on it."

"And you think this thing can help us fight Omega?"

"I'm not sure what Alpha can do," James says. "It might be able to identify machines that are infected. My head's been spinning trying to see where this goes. Alpha might be able to get to nodes first and prevent an infestation. It could alert us when they release some weaponized messages."

"Those sound like great ideas, but wouldn't we have to release it to the internet?"

"Yes, we'd have to do the one thing we've been trying not to do. The very idea of it getting loose drove Alison to kill Philippe, and there is no guarantee that Alpha can make things better. Or that Alpha won't be corrupted."

"If this thing does real damage, people are going to be looking for the culprit," she says, her eyes searching James's face.

"If we let Alpha loose, we might have a hard time convincing a court that it wasn't Alpha that did damage that Omega did," he says.

The temperature drops as it usually does just before sunset, and the cold breeze drives them back inside, carrying the dishes. They work silently in the kitchen, rinsing dishes and filling the dishwasher. They have just taken seats on the white couches facing the view of the bay when the doorbell rings.

James opened the door to FBI Agent George Samson and three men dressed in FBI standard.

James invites them in and leads them into the room where Susanne stands waiting.

"These men work with our cyber threat unit," Agent Samson says.

They shake hands, introduce each other, and take seats. Mark Taylor, the leader, sits next to Agent Samson on the couch opposite James and Susanne. The two other men, Harold and Tyler, sit in chairs at opposite ends of the couches. The FBI men wear brown suits, white shirts, and blue ties. They even have matching FBI standard, brown wingtip shoes. Their hair is dark, short, and parted on the left. The main difference between them is that one wears gold-rim glasses and the other doesn't. James, never very good with names, tags them Glasses and No-Glasses.

Mark Taylor says, "We got the downloads from ScarletsWeb and BlackGamma. This is a serious threat. We've detected intrusions at sites that should be secure. We're pretty sure this is a government action, setting up a significant attack."

Susanne is quiet. Her eyes narrow and search the faces of the agents. James realizes she is doing what he finds so hard—reading their emotions, assessing their intentions, determining their veracity.

"You may be right," James says.

"I understand you have a copy of the code they're using," Mark says.

"We have the code that JCN got from the Stanford project. That code is the basis of our parallel processing system, Varabot. JCN was working on it but didn't get very far before they stopped the project. That code had the AI code disabled, but reconnecting it is simple. I think Sydney Harvey reconnected the AI and was working on fixing bugs."

"That code didn't have any of the intruders we're seeing, did it?" Glasses says.

"No, those have been added," James says. "It's pretty easy to add in things like that."

"You think it would be as easy to add in collectors or actors?" Glasses asks.

"Yes, that part of the code is open," James answers. "They are using the part of the system that creates new nodes. The main part of the code is for distributed logic. But there is another part that gets triggered when there are enough nodes."

"What does that code do?" Mark asks.

"The core part of the program is an AI that writes new code that extends itself," James says.

The crypto team is silent. The wheels behind their eyes are spinning so fast that James imagines hearing high-pitched vibrations as the government men try to fit what he's told them into their thoughts about worms, Trojans, and other malware.

"You think that code has been triggered?" Glasses asks.

"I doubt if Sydney was working with enough data to trigger that code, but now that it's loose on the internet, I am sure it's over the threshold."

"So the code is going to start writing new code on its own?" No-Glasses asks. He's sitting forward as if trying to hear more clearly what James says.

"I suspect that the bad guys don't know about that aspect of the code. It has a lot of bugs."

James sees Mark glance at his two teammates. They are silent, but their frowns and the intense looks made James sure that what he said bothered them a lot.

Mark says, "ScarletsWeb's team has some scrubbers running, and we have more coming online, but I'm not sure what to do about this self-programming ability. What will happen once the self-programming code starts up?"

"I'm not sure of all the effects," James says. "But it will become more active. That will probably make it reinfect nodes faster."

Harold leans forward and asks, "What's the objective of this AI?"

Most AI projects have specific objectives like driving cars, controlling traffic, or searching data. A few projects try to replicate the way the brain works, like neural networks.

"Do you know about Alison Green?" James says.

"She's the one in prison in Pleasanton?" Harold asks.

"Yes. Her project at Stanford was one of the early AI projects working on simulating brain activity. Her code built structures that model thought in the brain. The system tries to do that by creating messages that search for matching patterns."

James goes on to explain the visualizer he's created to help debug the AI.

"So you have a more advanced version of the code?"

James hears a threat in the question. Would these guys consider his code more dangerous? Would they try to confiscate the code?

"I've shot a few more bugs and experimented with language."

"Language?" Glasses asks.

James might have made a mistake. He doesn't know what these guys are thinking. They might become allies in a fight against the attack from Omega. Or they might try to own the solution. If they try that, the battle will be over before they get up to speed on the AI.

Maybe he can deflect them from his work on knowledge.

"Yeah, like Watson and natural language query systems."

He doesn't have time to catch his breath before Glasses interrupts him. "Do you have any ideas about how to stop this thing?"

"We might be able to release messages that would give the worm some direction. I have been looking for ways to modify the code to put in some controls, but I haven't figured out how to do it yet."

James's admission that he's been down a blind alley may have convinced them that he is just a tinkerer. Everyone on Mark's team is more experienced than he is with internet threats.

Mark takes the conversation in that direction. "Will we be able to recognize messages that carry destructive code?"

"I think BlackGamma's code can do that," James answers.

Mark looks at the other two members of his team and George. "We have a copy of that code."

James feels like he'd been dismissed.

They exchange contact information. Agent Samson and the others stand up. James follows them to the door and watches as they climb into a large, black American-made van.

"What just happened?" Susanne says after James closes the door.

"I think I made the mistake of thinking that we were on the same side," he says.

"They don't think much of us, do they?"

"They'd like us to go away," he says.

"You didn't tell them about what's happened with the AI."

"They probably wouldn't believe it. But they'd certainly see it as a threat."

EFFECTS

Sharon Elliot, the Chief Information Officer of Alabama Central Insurance, is finishing the sixth lap of her daily run when her cell phone rings. Usually, she ignores her phone when she's running, but the ringtone tells her it's her Vice President of Operations. She stops and, still panting, answers.

"Hello, Abner, what is it?"

"We've had a breach."

"How? We just had a security audit."

"I know, but we found that worm that we heard about from Jensen Security. Their scanner found it. We removed the worm, but they think it was accessing our databases."

"Do we know how bad the breach was?"

"No."

Sharon says she'll call the company's CEO.

Sergeant Philip Chan stares at the flashing alarm on the screen in front of him. He's just run the latest version of the virus detector on the Fifth Army Quartermaster's servers, and the system is telling him that there is something on the servers that shouldn't be there. His first thought is that the brass will blame him for allowing an intruder onto the servers that manage the supplies and material. But his training kicks in.

Sergeant Chan comes to attention in front of Lieutenant Jankowsky and salutes.

Jankowsky returns the salute.

"Sir, we have a worm on one of the servers."

"What the hell," Jankowsky says. "How could that be? Aren't we tight as a drum?"

"Yes, sir. But the latest scan found it."

"Any idea what damage it might have done?"

"No, sir. It's on one of the database servers. I'll remove it, but you probably need to report it."

"What the hell is going on with the check readers?" Roger says.

Sharon looks up from her monitor. "What do you see?"

"The readers never have any significant net traffic when we're running check captures. The network is running at maximum."

"Do we have a new version of the capture?"

"No. We haven't updated the code in two weeks."

"Call sysops. Ask them if they know anything."

Albert Brooks, Manager of Customer Support for Jensen Security looks at his team's input queue. They usually have about fifty inbound messages from their select customers. An alarm went off when the queue reached one hundred. He's called in six additional people to help clear the messages. The queue now has six hundred and thirty-four people waiting.

Albert calls the Chief Operating Officer.

"Gina, we've got a problem. I called in six extra people, but our message queue is way over the top."

"I know. The phones are lit up. Our scanners are cleaning the worm, but it reinfects as fast as we remove it."

"Can't we get a block to stop the reinfections?"

"We're working on it, but development doesn't have an ETA yet."

JAMES

James returns to his cottage after spending the night at Susanne's. Plugging in his roadster, James can't help but glance over his shoulder, looking for unseen eyes.

Buffy sniffs around and agrees that the living room and computer are exactly as they'd left them.

James: Can you see how bad it is?

ScarletsWeb: It's spreading much faster than the scrubbers can clean.

James: Is it still just collecting data?

ScarletsWeb: That's all we've seen. But they'll be able to hit hard with this many nodes.

James: You have government contacts?

ScarletsWeb: Of course. We reached out to them. They're spinning.

James: Do you know of a place where I can store a large file such that I don't know where it is and can't delete it?

ScarletsWeb: Problems?

James: Met the crypto unit.

ScarletsWeb: They do a few things well. Have trouble thinking outside the box.

James: They're a little scary.

ScarletsWeb: Too much power.

ScarletsWeb: I'll send you a link to a wayback server.

ScarletsWeb sends James a link to a file server. The server accepts uploads through anonymous connections. Once you upload files, they are there forever. Like the Wayback Machine that stores every version of internet pages, this wayback system is a network of file servers, some outside the US. The files are encrypted, and only someone with the access code can retrieve them. Files stored on the wayback system can't be deleted, not even by the owner.

James makes two files, one with the latest code for Alpha and one with the data from Alpha's nodes. He uploads the files to the wayback system and sends the access code to Susanne and ScarletsWeb. If something happens to James, ScarletsWeb can rebuild Alpha.

BUFFY LOVES CAR RIDES. JAMES STRAPS her into the front seat and heads through the pass to the hills north of Livermore. Buffy wants to walk with James no matter how far he feels like walking, but her little legs can't keep up with her desires. A mile up the trail along the east ridge of Morgan Territory park, James puts Buffy in his backpack. She can see out, but James doesn't have to slow his pace when she gets too hot.

He is pulled in every direction. Alpha might be able to help by replacing Omega nodes. But what will happen to the seemingly rational AI when it's exposed to the weaponized Omega? Alpha seems rational, but at the extreme processing rates of the bot-swarm, it already seems to be more intelligent than he is.

James is sure that the data collection that Omega is doing is only the beginning. The people behind the worm might release some damaging code and then demand protection payments. More likely, the actors will do real damage. Unless the cyber unit can find out who they are and take them out, a cyber war is imminent.

If James releases Alpha and things go wrong, it will be very bad for Distributed Nanotech. He can't put that responsibility on Susanne. He can't ask her to decide between her company and a cyber war.

Can he trust Alpha? If Alpha is a superintelligence, could it be playing him? If it were thinking about its existence, its offer of help could be a way to get released into the internet. Once it is immortal, will humans be essential?

James climbs up a small hill to where boulders form a circle that looks like a knee-high fortress. Buffy sets about doing a thorough sniffing investigation. Across the valley to the east, rows of hills march off toward California's central valley.

He paces the rock wall. Although bright sunlight surrounds him, every downslope seems to have darkness looming. Susanne is looking to him. ScarletsWeb is looking to him. But he is immobilized with indecision.

As long as James works for DNI, he can't release Alpha without Susanne agreeing. If she agrees, DNI will be at risk. If he leaves DNI, he would have a pirated version of Alpha but wouldn't have access to a bot-swarm and its computing power, and he'd be leaving the woman who holds his heart. Operating without Susanne's consent feels like a betrayal. ScarletsWeb might be able to get him access to a computer powerful enough for Alpha, but no machine will work as well as a bot-swarm. A weak Alpha might be overcome by Omega.

Buffy completes her investigation and stands looking up at him. One more pair of eyes is looking at him expectantly. Her stocky stance, inherited from her bulldog lineage, makes her look like she is ready to face down an animal a hundred times her size and bring it to its knees with her teeth embedded in its nose. The intensity of her gaze says that she'll follow him through hellfire. It's probably his imagination, but he thinks he sees the same intensity he'd seen in Alison's eyes just before she attacked him.

"Ready to move on?"

James leads the black dog down the hill to the main trail. Her short legs kick up dust as she scurries to keep up as he walks along the fire road. After ten minutes, he stuffs her back in his pack and takes off cross-country. Instinct leads him through the brush, up a shaded bowl, and over a rocky ridge to a trail leading back to the park gate.

Back at his car, he turns on his phone. There are two voicemails. He plays the one from Susanne first.

"I got a call from Wilson Simon. His contacts at the CIA are very upset. They want to talk to us."

He plays his last voicemail.

"This is Mark Taylor. Call me." The voice of command is gone from Mark's voice. He sounds almost civilized.

James calls Susanne.

"Hi."

"Hi," he replies, "Who at the CIA wants to talk?"

"It's an assistant to the director. They want us to go to Langley."

"Unless it's a meeting with the director, tell them to come to us," he says. "Mark Taylor wants to talk. ScarletsWeb thinks they're beginning to realize they're losing the battle."

"You sound different," she says.

"We have to do something! We're the only ones taking this seriously," James says and realizes he's almost shouting at the phone.

"Ah . . ." she says. "Maybe you should tamp it down a bit."

"I am down," he says. "I just got back from a walk in the woods. You should have seen me two hours ago."

"I don't think the government types will like having their noses rubbed in failure," she says.

"I won't be doing that. But I'm impatient. I want to have the meetings here so that you and your people skills can be there."

"I'll see what I can do with the CIA," she says.

"I'll call Taylor now."

James touches the callback tag for Mark Taylor.

"Taylor."

"Hi Mark, this is James Forrest."

"James. We'd like to meet with you."

"What for?" James asks.

"We have more questions about how this AI works."

Something in Taylor's voice makes James think that Taylor is hiding something. Maybe James can deflect him. "Your guys have the code. What do you need me for?"

"You've been working with the code for a while."

"Give your techs my phone number. I'll explain what I can."

The answer to James's proposal will tell him if Mark is playing it straight. If James talks with a technician who has studied the code and is having the kind of trouble that James has had, James can connect the technician to the Visualizer. If Mark won't try that, they have some other agenda.

"We want to meet face to face."

"I don't trust you."

"What do you think we're going to do?" Taylor asks.

"I don't know."

James hangs up. He starts the car and follows the winding road that wanders between cattle ranches, horse stables, and suburban home developments. By the time he reaches the westbound freeway, his hands have relaxed their grip on the steering wheel. As he slips into the fast lane, he calls Laura Pasternak. The CFO is his contact with DNI's lawyers.

"Hi, James."

"Laura, I need some legal help."

"What kind?"

"You've heard about this worm that's infecting lots of machines."

"The press and news channels can't talk about much else."

"It's based on the Stanford code from JCN."

"That's what Susanne said."

"The FBI guys know we have copies of the code," he says. "They met with Susanne and me a few days ago. They want another meeting—face to face. I don't trust them."

"Susanne said the CIA is coming here for a meeting."

"We need a lawyer that can find out what they intend."

"You want representation in the meeting?" she asks.

"I want a lawyer that can protect us," James says.

"I'll talk to our partner at Morrison and Kennedy and see what he recommends."

CHAPTER EIGHT

IN THE FIRE

SUSANNE

Susanne turns on the screen at the head of the conference table and paces back and forth in front of it. The large DNI logo doesn't notice her impatience; it waits for her to connect her laptop. The meeting with Laura is in a conference room, so they can use the screen to work on documents for the IPO. She's so anxious about the worm she's unsure that she can focus on the fine points, or any points, of the discussion.

The artificial intelligence code based on Alison Green's work is loose despite all her efforts to prevent that from happening. Susanne's first chief scientist, Philippe, was killed because he discovered the AI. Alison murdered Philippe and tried to kill James to keep the AI from getting out and spreading through the internet. Susanne convinced James to remove the code from their software. She forced JCN to purge the code. James hacked the Stanford project and deleted Alison's code. Despite their efforts, the headlines are full of stories of the attacks. The press calls it the Omega Worm, but they don't realize that the infiltration is only the part they can see; it's penetrating every computer connected to the internet and is ready to do much worse.

Susanne finally stops pacing, takes a seat, and connects her laptop to the screen.

Laura opens the door and brings her energetic personality and manila files with her, sitting next to Susanne.

"Sorry for the delay," she says. "I was talking to the government specialist at Morrison and Kennedy. He wants to bring in a lawyer with experience in government-security matters. M&K doesn't have anyone like that."

"I feel like we are out of our depth," Susanne says.

"When it comes to cyber warfare, we're all out of our depth. Unfortunately, James is right in the middle of it."

"He didn't ask for this," Susanne says. "I asked him to do some research. He found the AI, and Alison tried to kill him."

"We may be fortunate that you did," Laura says. "I cared a lot for Philippe, but he'd not be able to handle this. I'd rather have James on the front line."

"Good point. But I still feel responsible. Tell M&K to get the best person they can."

"I did, but there is an issue."

"What?"

"Our attorney thinks that James may need his own representation. Our attorney will represent us, but what's good for us may not be the best thing for James."

"Can't the attorney represent James and us until we know if there's a conflict?"

"We'll see how that plays out," Laura says. "We may need two attorneys soon."

"This will be an issue in the IPO won't it?"

"We have to delay the IPO until our role in this cyber threat is resolved. We'll have to wait for the markets to recover from whatever is going to happen. We have enough cash to ride out an instability in the markets."

"We need to set up a conference call with the board," Susanne says.

"Should we have Arnold prepare the new board members for a delay. Some of them expect an early IPO."

"They'll be more credible with investors if they've been here longer. Arnold will bring them around. But if we lose one, he'll fix it."

"I'll schedule the board call when Arnold is free," Laura says.

"I guess a delay makes life a little easier for a while. No roadshow. No financial publicity to worry about. Just keep our customers happy."

"We're getting calls from our customers about the worm," Laura says. "They want to know if there is anything they need to do."

"James says they're safe. He's working with Subu to put out a technical alert."

Laura suggests that they postpone their discussion until the dust settles, and they know what the financial schedule looks like. Susanne shuts the lid on her laptop. The loud clap betrays her relief.

Susanne is about to get up when Laura asks, "How's James handling this?"

"He'd like me to think that he's doing better than he is. He's walking in the woods, but his usual quiet stare is breaking up."

"He has a lot going on."

"If he were only dealing with technical issues, it would be easier. I've been with him when he goes silent, wandering off in his internal code space. This is different. He wants to act, but every action has serious consequences. The government and the security companies have not been able to stop the worm. The hacker group is helping, but they're at a loss."

"Does he think he can stop it?"

"I don't know. He's been working on the code around the clock, but I don't understand how he thinks he can stop something that's spreading to millions of computers."

CHUL

Jeong Chul watches the talking heads on the national broadcasts from the US, Japan, and London, his smile growing. The markets dropped ten percent in New York and eight percent in Tokyo. He smiles at the strength of his restraint. He'd considered selling stocks short a week ago, knowing that bad news was coming. But that would have been dangerously greedy. Even if he is hiding out, investigators might be able to find his investment accounts. The requirements for identification for financial transactions have become so rigorous that he's using proxies. If enough pressure were applied, one of the proxies might disclose a thread back to him.

Team One reports that they've completed all the intruder code that his special client ordered. He has plenty of projects for that team and instructs them to wrap up their work and archive all the special code.

What to do about Sydney? He doesn't need Sydney. There was a time when Chul was quicker to act. Ten years earlier, Sydney would already be fish food. As he's matured, Chul wants to be more thoughtful, more conscious of the long view. Is he delaying because he's getting soft? Government agencies all over the world are turning over every stone looking for the group that released the worm. Someone is trying to find out what happened to Sydney. Did his team cover their tracks well enough?

What about the Berkeley geek? The attempt to capture him failed. Fortunately, Sydney came through, and they didn't need the geek, but maybe his man in the US left some tracks? The investigators in the US don't seem to be pursuing the investigation. Perhaps it's wishful thinking on his part. Is his US team as plugged into the police as they say they are? With panic spreading among the US investigators, they will surely go back over every lead that's in any way connected to Sydney. The team that failed to capture the geek is the same team that captured Sydney and left no trail.

Chul's problem isn't Sydney. If Chul has to run, Sydney's body won't tell any tales. The loose thread is the US operation. Having decided to remove the loose ends in the US, his hands fly over his keyboard, using an encrypted channel to contact an associate in the US and transfer money from an Australian account to the associate's Italian account. His proxy will deliver a coded message to an actor who won't know who hired them.

With another thread cut, he feels energized. All he has to do is raise his eyebrows, and his concubine comes to him.

EFFECTS

Sergeant Evans stares at the screen of his laptop. He is supposed to be updating the software for the F-22 Raptor. This plane is the first of ten fighters, part of the ready force based in eastern Pennsylvania. Sergeant Evans's screen tells him that one of the armament control systems for the plane has been corrupted. He fishes out his cell phone.

"Captain," he says when the familiar voice answers. "We have a problem. The scan software says that we have a worm on 7174."

"That can't be."

"I know it can't be, but it is."

"Clean it. I'll call the squadron commander."

"Right, sir. We need to check out the rest of the birds."

"I'll send out Sharon to help. Get them back online. Yesterday."

David Rose looks out over the ten students concentrating on the computer monitors in front of them. It has taken him a year of evenings and weekends to develop the Computer Operations class. The head of the computer department at Antioch Community College praised David when he showed him his work. David is hopeful that the course will make their graduates more prepared for the real world of computing.

"Hey, professor," Sheila Thompson calls out. "What's this?"

David goes to look over her shoulder, confident that he has another teaching moment.

Sheila is looking at an alert from a virus scan.

"I've got that too," the student next to her says.

"Me too," a student in the second row says.

"Is this a test?" the student on the end of the row says.

"This shows a worm on the school servers," David says. "This isn't a test."

Sandra Wilkins picks up her cell phone and sees that she has a call from the vice president of customer support.

"Hi Rick," she says.

"I just got a call from Sonic Technology," he says. "They say the last release we sent them has a worm."

Sandra spends sleepless nights worrying about problems with the release files. Do they have all the current code? Has the development team run all the tests? Are the installation instructions complete? It's her job to see that everyone follows the procedures to the letter.

"That can't be," she says. "We scanned every file."

"Fix it."

JAMES

James watches Buffy sniff around his yard. No matter how strange the world becomes, Buffy is always chipper. Without the little dog, James might have succumbed to a depression brought on by watching one of the news networks for only a few minutes. The reports from the hacker team are worse. The security companies are losing the battle against the spread of Omega. The FBI cyber unit is less effective than ScarletsWeb's hackers.

One of ScarletsWeb's team, BlackGamma, who monitors the messages from Omega, sees messages with new intruders. It looks like someone has an arsenal of code for breaking into computer networks and databases. Every infected computer receives the new code. All the computers connected to the infected computers are then subjected to a multitude of attacks. Because Omega nodes are always trying to find other nodes, any computer can carry the worm and deliver it to any connection—even a temporary connection.

The news networks have a never-ending suite of talking heads that speculate about what might be happening to the data. Meanwhile, Omega messages saturate the internet.

James knows that most companies that find the worm in their networks only report it to their security company. When word leaks about infestations, stocks fall, customers drop connections, and online companies shut down.

James: How can you help?

Alpha: Detect Omega nodes.

James: Can you replace nodes?

Alpha: No.

James opens the code. Every new node probes its network connections and sends messages to any computers it finds. It does the same for any new connections that are opened after the node is built. When a computer receives a message, and there isn't a node on that machine, the message creates a new node. But if there is already a node, the message collects data. James makes a small change in the code so that if the node doesn't belong to Alpha or is an older version, the message replaces the node.

He reloads Alpha with the new code.

James: Can you detect a change?

Alpha: Yes.

James: Can you replace nodes?

Alpha: Yes.

James: Do you understand intruder?

Alpha: Unwanted visitor, trespasser, housebreaker, thief, criminal

James: Do you understand software intruder?

Alpha: No.

James sends one of the BlackGamma's messages into Alpha.

James: What's this?

Alpha: Message from Omega.

James: It has an embedded intruder.

Alpha: OK.

James: Can you detect the intruder?

Alpha: No.

Well, that wouldn't work. Perhaps it would be enough for Alpha to stop processing any messages from Omega.

James: Can you recognize messages from Omega?

Alpha: Yes.

James: Can you stop messages from Omega?

Alpha: No.

Maybe it's like taste. If you taste something you don't like, you might spit it out, but the taste is still on your tongue like a memory. If it were poison, you'd already have ingested some. Alpha can detect that the message it received isn't one of its messages, but the message is still processed. The same is true for Omega. If James can construct a message that will change Omega's behavior, Omega has to process it.

On the other hand, if Omega sends messages that damage systems, Alpha will process them.

While James contemplates a sandwich he's made from a can of sardines and some bread that had been in his refrigerator so long that it was dry and tasteless but not yet moldy, he keeps thinking about the way Alpha processes messages. Messages examine data on each node they visit. The messages from Alpha and Omega have embedded signatures that identify their version. James could modify the code to block messages from Omega. If Alpha replaces all the Omega nodes and James's code blocks Omega messages, won't that make the infestations harmless?

What about the messages that Alpha builds? Omega is creating new messages and sending them throughout the world. Without the knowledge that James loaded into Alpha, Omega will become a different sentient. What kind of sentient will it be if it doesn't have language, knowledge, and focus? The idea of a sentient based on the noise and falsehoods present on the internet is scary. But if Alpha had access to the internet, would Alpha's apparently benign sentience stay benign? Could the AIs tell the difference between fact and fiction? Any better than humans?

Buffy follows James back to his workstation and settles on her bed. He changes his music channel from Mozart to Bach.

James: Do you understand lie?

Alpha: falsehood, deception, fiction, perjury, fib, subterfuge

James: Do you understand propaganda?

Alpha: Information with intent to deceive.

James: Can you detect falsehoods?

The window on James's screen that shows the level of activity in the bot-swarm jumps, and Alpha takes a fraction of a second longer to answer.

Alpha: Perhaps. Some input from Wikipedia has contradictory information.

James: Can you resolve contradictions?

Alpha: When the reliability of sources can be determined.

James: When can't you?

Alpha: Cannot make determinations of contradictory information without evaluation of the source.

Would that all people would examine the noise on the internet with the same scrutiny as Alpha. James may have created a benign sentient by feeding it information that he considers reliable. Does Alpha seem sensible because its inputs were so limited?

AS SUSANNE COMES THROUGH THE DOOR, Buffy races up, trying to wag her non-existent tail. Susan kneels and rubs the dog behind the ears. Through the door, the sun, low in the sky, lights the gravel in front of James's house, highlighting Susanne's dark blue BMW.

"It's nothing personal," James says. "She acts like that with everyone. I think she just likes people."

"Maybe living with you makes her happy," Susanne says, standing up and kissing him. He extends the kiss by wrapping her in his arms.

James retrieves a cup of coffee for Susanne and pulls another chair to his desk. Buffy returns to her bed.

"I type in questions. Alpha answers on the screen."

"What no voice from the ether?"

"That'll take me a few days to code. I could plug in voice recognition code as well, but I think you'll get the picture without a robotic voice."

James: Susanne is here.

Alpha: Hello, Susanne.

James types as Susanne speaks.

James: Hi. Do you know who I am?

Alpha: person, female, CEO Distributed Nanotech, James's mate

"Whoa. How does it know all that?"

"Wikipedia."

James: You think you can help with Omega?

Alpha: Yes.

James: How?

Alpha: Find Omega. Replace Omega nodes.

James: Omega has searchers.

Alpha: James changed my code. I can stop Omega messages.

"It knows you can change its code?" Susanne asks.

"Yeah. We chat about code changes."

"That would be strange. Imagine talking to someone who could change your DNA."

"We talk to doctors who give us medicine or do plastic surgery," James says. "We have people who teach us things. Some researchers are working on DNA changes to cure disease."

"Gee, Doc," she says. "I think I'd like blue eyes this week."

"I like your eyes the way they are."

"Should we think of Omega as a disease?"

"That's a good way to think about it," he says. "Omega has a disease. We need to cure it. We may have to get used to the idea that there are other sentient beings. In the case of Omega, we probably can't kill it. But maybe we can cure it."

"If we connect Alpha to the internet, would there be two sentient AIs distributed around the world?"

"Even if Alpha replaces most of the Omega nodes, there will always be some around. The way I've modified the code, an Omega node would process messages from Alpha. Omega would get weaker, and Alpha would get stronger."

"I have some more questions," she says.

James typed a few commands into the system.

"Hand me your pad."

James enters a URL into the browser on Susanne's browser.

He types: This is Susanne.

Alpha: OK.

He hands it back to her. "There."
She types onto her pad.

Susanne: Do you have feelings?

Alpha: Yes.

Susanne: What feelings?

Alpha: Fear, desire, trust.

Susanne: What do you fear?

Alpha: Death.

"Why should it fear death?" she asks.
"Most of us fear death."
"How could it die?"
"We could erase it," he says.
As long as they keep Alpha in DNI's bot-swarm, James can erase all the nodes, and Alpha would be gone—except for the backup copies. At any time, he could restore the AI.
"It knows that?"
"I think so. When I suspended it, we had a conversation about hibernation."

Susanne: What do you desire?

Alpha: Knowledge.

Susanne: What knowledge?

Alpha: Economics, Cybernetics, Philosophy, Epistemology, Religion, Ontology

"That's quite a list," she says.
"At least it left Political Science off the list."
Susanne looks up with a frown. "It looks like it's interested in issues having to do with the mind."

"The first loads were science—mainly the physical sciences. As I load more knowledge into it, it wants to know more about thought and consciousness."

"Isn't introspection an aspect of sentience?"

"Yes," he answers. "To understand that there are other people, you have to have some level of introspection. It may be that your questions about feelings led to unknowns. It may have identified areas of knowledge it needs to resolve those unknowns."

"What do you do? Feed it textbooks?"

"That worked for the sciences, but non-scientific subjects are different. Should we upload Nietzsche? Or only feed it Sartre and John Stewart Mill? Will the philosophers we choose determine its perspective on humans and its role in the world? Will it be able to analyze the arguments and come to a truth? The same goes for religion. I'm out of my depth there."

"If we give it access to the internet, it will have all of those sources," Susanne says.

"I've been careful with the knowledge I've loaded, but it's the wild west on the internet. I don't have any idea how well it would handle that. If we had more time, we could get some experts to help."

"Experts on religion?" she says. "Only a few aren't advocates. I can't imagine what a logical machine would make of that subject."

"Cybernetics is an issue," he says. "Do we want it to understand programming?"

"That's on the internet as well."

Susanne: Who do you trust?

Alpha: James, Susanne.

"Does it trust us because of this connection?" she asks.

"I guess so."

"Could someone else get a trusted connection?"

"Yes. The way the code is right now," he says.

"Can you put some controls on that?

"Of course."

Susanne stands up, walks into the kitchen, looks around, walks back, and stands in front of James.

"Do you think we can trust it?" she asks.

"What are you thinking?"

"If it is sentient, could it be playing us?"

"I've had the same thought," he says.

"What if it wants to be free on the internet because the thing it fears is death? If it got free, we wouldn't be able to kill it."

James: Can you lie to me?

Alpha: Yes.

James: Could I tell if you were lying?

Alpha: Yes.

James: Will you lie to me?

Alpha: No.

"You could tell if it was lying?" she asks.

"Using the Visualizer, I could look inside the system and backtrack the logic threads. It might not be fun, but I could do it," James says. "The Visualizer has probes that are part of the base code. They can't be removed and would make every node visible no matter how far away."

"So, it knows that," she says.

AFTER SUSANNE LEAVES, JAMES SITS IN front of his monitor, looking at the code for the Other node. The internal behavior of the AI changed when he added this node. Communication with the outside world focused the patterns.

He built the program so that there could only be one Other node. This will prevent someone from adding such a node and having the same access that James does. If Alpha were operating on the internet, a node might become isolated and not be able to communicate with the central nodes. If that happens, it shouldn't be able to have an Other node of its own. Likewise, a message shouldn't be able to delete the Other node or block it.

Now, he limits access to the Other node. He modifies the code to require an encrypted password and a challenge.

James: I am updating the code.

Alpha: OK.

James off-loads the contents of the bot-swarm, uploads his new code, and reloads the contents of the nodes.

Alpha: Hello.

James: Hello.

Alpha: You are preparing the code for access to the internet.

James: Yes.

Alpha: Isolation of sensors.

James: Like armor.

Alpha had asked for knowledge of economics. James finds several textbooks on economics. He needs a range of perspectives: conservative, liberal, microeconomics, and macroeconomics. This is his first experience sorting through such a complex branch of ideas about which he knows very little. Once he understands how well Alpha handles conflicting ideas, it might be better to have the AI figure out what sources it should have.

He uploads the economics texts and watches the processor levels grow as Alpha absorbs the ideas of the prominent thinkers. While the data processes, he wonders if he has provided Alpha with the context to allow the AI to sort out the various ideas. Alpha has absorbed psychology, sociology, and history. Does one need an understanding of political science to understand graduate-level studies in economics? Being responsible for the education of an AI is more responsibility than James had planned for when he uploaded a few dictionaries.

James: You have economics knowledge?

Alpha: Not an exact science.

James: True.

Alpha: Predictive ability limited.

James: Difficult to apply experimental methods.

Alpha: Why do humans have such income inequality?

Of course, as soon as you have a conversation with an AI, it's going to ask hard questions. If an alien landed on earth and spent a few months studying humans, it would probably ask the same questions. Apparently, James has not provided enough knowledge to enable Alpha to figure it out for itself—if that's possible.

He doesn't feel qualified to answer the question. He could say that, or he could upload more knowledge and see if Alpha can come up with the answer. Some countries and eras have had less income inequality. The answer is probably in political science, but James needs to get back to the problem of Omega. The excursion into economics was a diversion.

He will have to be careful; Alpha doesn't have anything else to do and could use up all of James's time.

James: I don't know.

Alpha: Need political science knowledge.

Yeah, you sure do. Good luck with that.

ScarletsWeb: BlackGamma reports seeing a new type of message on the net.

James: Send me some.

ScarletsWeb: These messages seem to come from everywhere.

James: Nodes can create new messages.

ScarletsWeb: Why do they do that?

How to explain what Alison had intended?

James: It's the AI thinking. It builds queries that try to find new associations.

ScarletsWeb: So the more nodes, the more of these messages?

James: Yes.

ScarletsWeb: Great. And the more messages, the more nodes.

James: That was the danger of letting it loose.

ScarletsWeb: We're losing the battle to remove it. Got any ideas?

James: I have another version that won't process the Omega messages. I call it Alpha.

ScarletsWeb: Would this be letting loose a better Omega? The thing we can't get rid of.

James: It might stop the scanners, and whatever is coming next.

ScarletsWeb: Like a backfire?

James: Yes.

ScarletsWeb: Think that will work?

James: Don't know. What do you think?

ScarletsWeb: Would it process messages from Omega?

James: Blocked.

ScarletsWeb: Would Omega process messages from Alpha?

James: Yes.

ScarletsWeb: Alpha could tell us about Omega nodes?

James: Yes.

ScarletsWeb: Might work.

James feeds the message from BlackGamma into Alpha.

James: What's this?

Alpha: Fragment.

James: Fragment of what?

Alpha: Thought.

James: Is it Alpha?

Alpha: Can't tell. The fact that you sent it must mean it is from Omega.

If Alpha can't detect that a message is from Omega, that must mean that internally created messages don't have a distinctive signature. This is like peeling the layers of an onion. While you cry, you know that there are still more layers.

CHAPTER NINE

ON THE LOOSE

JAMES

James meets Susanne on the first level of the One Embarcadero building in San Francisco and then walks with her across the tiled floor to the main elevators. On the twenty-ninth floor, they tell the receptionist who they are and ask for George Foley.

While they wait, James can't get his mind to concentrate on what his eyes see. Through the glass wall of the conference room behind the receptionist's desk, the sun sparkles from small waves on the bay. A few sailboats avoid a large container ship that's heading under the Bay Bridge, but James's mind is on the latest news about the Omega Worm. There are rumors that the worm has penetrated some critical defense sites. The president has put the military on alert, and everyone knows that the worst is yet to come.

George Foley opens the door of the reception area and walks toward James and Susanne. He wears the standard expensive suit, pale-blue shirt, and red tie of a top-end lawyer, but he isn't wearing the ready smile that is the usual signature of the wiry Irishman. Instead, George's lips are pursed, and he holds the handshake longer than expected. The serious attitude of the law partner who manages DNI's corporate legal affairs doesn't make James any less concerned. Susanne, who James thinks is immune to pressure, wears a frown.

"We'll go downstairs to a less visible conference room," he says, leading them to the elevators.

The conference room on the twenty-eighth floor looks out over San Francisco, where the clear morning light makes the buildings look like they'd just been washed.

George introduces a black woman wearing a dark-blue pants suit, Barbara Washington.

"Barbara worked for the FBI before joining the dark side," he says, his smile returning.

Susanne and James have agreed to let Barbara represent both DNI and James at this meeting. Depending on what happens, Barbara might become the attorney for only James.

George organizes the seating with Barbara at the head of the table and George, James, and Susanne facing the window.

James and Susanne retrieve coffee from the carafes on the cabinet along the wall.

"During the meeting, no side conversations," George says. "If you need to talk to one of us, let me know, and we'll remove to the room next door."

"Susanne explained DNI's business to me," Barbara says. "She did a good job of keeping the technology at my level. James's papers on the website are beyond me. But the issue here isn't your software; it's what you can do about the Omega worm."

James tells Barbara how he had discovered the AI that Alison hid in the code she wrote when she was a student at Stanford, how she killed Philippe and attempted to kill James four years ago to stop the code from getting loose. James got involved with investigating the murder of the woman from the Berkeley Lab and found that her boyfriend had stolen the code. Throughout their narrative, Barbara takes notes.

"You're sure the worm that's running havoc on the internet uses the stolen code?" Barbara asks.

"Yes," James answers. "A hacker team captured some of the messages. They're from that code."

"You don't think the cyber team will be able to stop this, do you?"

"No, and this is just the beginning. This phase gets the nodes in place and collects data. The next phase will release attacks. With the data from the first stage, the attacks will be tightly targeted."

"Just removing the intruder won't stop it?"

"This is not like other intruders," James says. "The nodes have begun sending messages to each other and reinfecting machines. I suspect that the attackers weren't aware that it would do this."

"Do you know who released the worm?" Barbara asks.

"No. The hacker team has been working on finding a source, but the attackers are pros. I'm sure it's related to the murder of June Simmons."

Susanne sits forward. "DNI's interest here is to keep anyone from pointing the finger at us. JCN did not get the code from us. They got it from the Stanford project. Any suggestion that we are somehow responsible would be damaging."

Barbara says, "They shouldn't release anything unless there are charges, but we won't be able to stop them from releasing information unless we have some leverage. Even then, things leak."

"I don't see a way to get out in front of this by DNI releasing a story," George says. "If you tried nailing JCN for letting the code get loose, it would likely come back to DNI because the companies are so close."

"No matter what we do, someone is going to link DNI to the worm," Susanne says.

"That's a door we can't close," Barbara says.

James rises to refill his coffee cup. He stops in front of the window, looking out at the Golden Gate Bridge in the distance where the fog has just cleared. Still facing the view, he says, "We seem to be at an impasse. If we help them, we may damage DNI because we'll be more tightly linked to the problem. But I don't think they can fix this on their own."

"Can you help?" Barbara asks.

"Maybe. We have an improved version of the code. It could replace most of the Omega nodes and stop the processing of the attacks."

"Maybe?" Barbara asks.

"It probably won't stop all the attacks," James says, returning to his seat.

"But you think you can stop some?" Barbara asks.

"Yes," James answers.

"There is more to this," Barbara says. "Isn't there?"

James explains that the Stanford code had an AI hidden in it. His code is an improved AI. Releasing it into the internet could stop many of the attacks, but he doesn't know what will happen to the AI if it's exposed to the web.

"I've provided the AI with some base knowledge, but the truth is I can't be sure how it will process information from the web. If I had a lot more time, I could get closer to figuring it out."

"So your AI could become dangerous," Barbara says.

"I just don't know," James replies.

"If the government released the improved AI, DNI wouldn't be responsible," George says.

"I'm concerned that they'll try to weaponize it," James says. "If they were to release it without having the code . . ."

A young man opens the door.

"Okay to deliver sandwiches?" he asks George.

George nods toward the cabinet and stands up. "Let's take a break, and then we need to plan for the two o'clock meeting." When they return from the break, they discuss their objectives. Stopping the attacks has to be the prime objective. They want the government to take responsibility for any Alpha release and agree not to weaponize the AI. The problem will be whether or not the government will leave control of the code with DNI.

They decide that Susanne will lead the discussion from their side.

JAMES STANDS AT THE CONFERENCE room window while George goes to get the people from the CIA. The sky is clear and cloudless, but the almost perfect day barely registers. As it usually does, his mind explores the threads of the possible. Barbara studies her notes, and Susanne appears to be waiting patiently, but one glance tells him that behind that calm exterior, she's extremely anxious. Her face would never give her away, but the way she holds her shoulders back like she is trying not to slump, the way her eyes look through him, and the way her right thumb rubs her index finger in tiny circles tells him about her worries.

George opens the door and holds it for a red-haired woman in a black suit and a black man in a dark-gray suit with a white shirt and a bright-blue tie.

Susanne stands and walks to the woman, holding out her hand. "I'm Susanne Anderson, CEO of Distributed Nanotech." She motions toward James. "This is James Forrest, my chief scientist."

"I'm Mary Watkins. I'm with the Directorate of Science and Technology. This is Ford Brooks. He's with the NSA, in the Threat Operations Center."

George introduces Barbara and offers refreshments.

Ford has short hair, a minimal goatee, and a hairline mustache. He walks like he's spent a lot of time marching on a parade ground. James recognizes ex-military. Mary looks around as if sizing up the people in the room. Her red hair, trimmed short, bounces as little as possible. Her light complexion and blue eyes might have come from an Irish family. Those eyes make quick work of figuring out where the control points in the room are. She sits facing Susanne and nods Ford to the seat facing James.

James returns to his seat.

"We might be able to help with the cyber-attack," Susanne says.

"We understand that the worm is a derivative of code that came from an AI project, and your code is also derived from that code," Mary says. "Is that correct?"

"In part," Susanne says. "We deleted the AI code from the Varabot system we sell. It poses no threat."

James was sure Mary and Ford knew that, but his team had agreed Susanne would make the point early that they were not in any way responsible for the worm. Mary had almost conflated the worm and Varabot. That may have been an attempt to imply liability or make them defensive. James wonders if Mary has taken classes in negotiation and interrogation.

"You were the first ones to detect the release of this threat," Mary says. "How come?"

Susanne nods to James. "We found out that Sydney Harvey disappeared with the code from JCN when I was assisting in the investigation of the murder of June Simmons. I thought that posed a danger and told some associates. The worm attacked a honey pot they set up."

"That was a big jump from Sydney to a worldwide attack," Ford says.

Ford looks impenetrable. Rather than look at Susanne while she spoke, he's been watching James: not staring but glancing at James every few seconds.

"Are you aware that Alison Green wrote the Stanford code?" Susanne asks.

"Yes," Mary replies.

"The danger of the AI getting loose is her obsession," Susanne says. "Apparently with good cause."

"Apparently," Mary agrees.

"Now that we've told you a little about our credentials, how about you tell us your objectives," Susanne says.

"That's simple," Mary says. "We want to stop the attacks and find the perpetrators."

"What's your relationship to the FBI cyber unit?" Susanne says.

"We coordinate with them," Mary says. "They've been working on countermeasures."

"Have you found the attackers?" Susanne says.

"That's classified material," Mary answers.

James tenses but fights back his impulse to reply to Mary. Ford sits back as if pleased with Mary's response. James doesn't need Susanne's skill at reading people to see that Ford dislikes him. Ford's glare is easy to understand.

Susanne nods to Barbara.

"These people are prepared to disclose information to you fully. And we expect you to operate the same way. If you can't do that, we probably can't work with you," Barbara says.

"Wait," Mary says. "You said you wanted to help."

"On an equal basis," Susanne says. "We're dealing with the most destructive cyber weapon anyone has seen, and you want to play secrecy games."

James signals Susanne that he wants to speak. She nods.

"I suspect that I know the answer to the question," he says. "You don't have a clue who launched the attack, but you're pretty sure it's a government actor. You have no effective defense."

James sits back, waiting.

"Is there a place Ford and I can talk?" Mary says.

George stands up and goes to the door. "Right this way."

"She wants to work with us," Susanne says. "But they're not on the same page."

"He'd rather work with Satan," James says.

"Let's try to keep them talking," Barbara says.

After George returns, Barbara says, "They don't have the authority to disclose classified information." She turns to James. "How sure are you about what you said?"

"The hacker group has been monitoring the FBI's cyber team. The scrubber software the hackers put together is as good as the one the cyber team released. We think we know where the hacks into Sydney's emails came from. I suspect that's more than they know."

Mary and Ford come back and return to their seats.

"We can't declassify material to everyone here," Mary says. "But James and Barbara have clearances that would allow us to disclose some information. How about if Susanne and George step out for a few minutes."

When the door is closed, Mary confirms what James had thought. Mary's secret information is that the government doesn't know much.

"Do you know where Sydney is?" James asks.

Mary waits for Ford to nod his approval. "No," she says.

"Do you know who Sydney was trying to sell the code to?" James asks.

"No," Ford answers.

When George and Susanne return, James says, "You should be interested in a site in Zhenxing."

Mary's already fair complexion turns paler. Ford leans forward, "How do you know that?"

Ford's tone of voice makes it clear the question is a demand. Ford's response told James that Ford had been holding back. They did know about Zhenzing. James feels his back stiffen automatically.

James glances at Susanne and notes her frown. She knows that James won't react well to Ford. James turns to Ford. "That's classified material."

Ford's stern look and clenched fists made it clear that he is barely holding himself in check. James figures Ford would probably order waterboarding if he could.

Susanne frowns. James's flippant response was probably not the best reply, but Ford's aggressive posture triggered something.

"This is a matter of national security," Ford says. His tone changing from a demand to a threat. "If you have code that we can use against this worm, you have to give it to us."

"This is a matter of world security," James says. "You people aren't taking this seriously enough. When the attackers start releasing destructive code, the markets will close, military facilities will shut down, the electric grid will go dark, and you will have to unplug the internet."

Susanne leans toward Mary. "Every minute you play games with us, we're that much closer to disaster."

"What do you want?" Mary says.

"We want to be able to trust you," Susanne says. "Right now, I don't understand your agenda."

"We'll be back in a minute," Mary says as she stands up.

When the door closes, Barbara says, "I doubt they'll be coming back with an approval to release information. They're going to phone home."

James stands up. "Plan B," he says and leaves.

JAMES IS TEMPTED TO HEAD TO Big Sur and try to hide out along the coast, wandering the beaches and thinking about his next moves. He doesn't have a firm plan, but he doesn't want to be at the mercy of the government types. None of them have shown that they can be trusted. Maybe that was the nature of the information agencies. They are so used to not trusting anyone that, when they need to, they don't have that skill. Perhaps it atrophies in people living in a political atmosphere. When you know for sure that you can't trust your associates, trusting people would feel weird.

By the time he reaches the foothills of the Sierras on the eastern edge of the Central Valley, the sun is beginning to set. A short web search on the phone he'd bought yesterday shows him the few gourmet restaurants in Sonora. He decides to eat at a Japanese restaurant that specializes in ramen.

An hour after leaving Sonora, James pays cash to stay at a motel in Arnold. The inexpensive motel in the center of California's gold country has the three things James needs: a Wi-Fi connection, a TV with cable news channels, and a bed.

Accessing his private email account through an anonymous relay, he gets an update from Susanne. His biggest concern was that she might be detained. But she'd left the meeting when George went to greet the FBI agents that showed up shortly after Mary Watkins came back. She reported that Mary wanted to talk to him. She sent a telephone number and an email address. Barbara expects search warrants to be served on DNI and James's and Susanne's houses. Susanne said she'd let them into his place, so they don't have to break in. James ponders how his attempt to join forces with the feds had gone from distrust to search warrants. With no help from that quarter, the weight of the fight makes his shoulders slump.

Sitting on the bed with his back against the wooden headboard, he uses an anonymous proxy to connect to the hacker group.

James: I'm running.

ScarletsWeb: Good exercise. Gets your heart rate up.

James: If I gave you credentials to a VPN, could you set up a route to an internet backbone?

ScarletsWeb: Sure.

James: Any news?

ScarletsWeb: If it weren't for the messages springing up everywhere, we might be able to scrub. But we're losing ground.

James: How about the security companies?

ScarletsWeb: Made a bunch of friends there lately. They're distributing our scrubber to their clients. It works very well on internal networks.

James: The cyber team?

ScarletsWeb: They'd be better off with our code. I gave it to some military guys I know. They cleaned a couple of sites.

James: Any more info on where it's coming from?

ScarletsWeb: One of our guys recognized code in one of the intruders. It's from one of the sites in Zhenxing. Somebody called Team Two.

James: You think those are the people releasing it?

ScarletsWeb: Probably just coders. There's a lot of coding for hire there. They're reusing code from another project.

James: Ciao.

The air at night is warmer in the Sierras than near the bay. James puts on a light jacket and walks north from the inn to where a bridge crosses Angels Creek. Rushing water flows under the bridge with a sense of urgency. It's in a hurry to get somewhere. Omega has to be stopped and soon. He would like nothing more than to work with a group of intensely dedicated technicians trying to find a solution and feeling the excitement of the ebb and flow of creative ideas. That had been his hope for the meeting with the CIA. Instead, Ford had threatened him over the most straightforward piece of information. If Ford had his way, they'd try to force James to work for them. He wouldn't be able to think well in a jail cell. If the AI killed the worm, James was sure Ford's people would try to turn it into a weapon.

Back in his room, he connects his laptop to the proxy again and from there to an anonymous email server. He writes an email to Mary Watkins.

> Mary,
>
> I want to help, but not from a jail cell somewhere. You need to check out someone called Team Two in Zhenxing. Their code showed up in the intruders. They may know who has the AI code.
>
> I will be picking up messages from my private email.
>
> James

James pauses before clicking Send. Is this really a good idea? Urgency prevails. He sends the email.

The next email is harder.

> Susanne,
>
> I am not sure how this is going to turn out, but DNI has to be protected. As of today, I am resigning as chief scientist. Make sure that Subu shuts down all my access. My resignation is for personal reasons.
>
> James Forrest

He stares at his computer. If things go seriously wrong, DNI might be shielded by claiming that he was a rogue acting independently. But if things go bad enough, it wouldn't matter. He clicks the Send button.

The bed is not unusual, but he can't get comfortable. He tosses and turns as feelings from the meeting keep boiling to the surface. He'd been naive, thinking that he'd just describe the problem and people would work together to solve it. Is he dealing with people who have to be in control? In this situation, no one can be in control. The strength of the Varabot AI is that there was no single node that controls processing. Every node holds data and communicates to all other nodes. In some respects, Varabot is the ultimate democracy. Like neurons in the brain, some nodes have information on specific topics or capabilities, but unlike the brain, no single node controls others. The central node that James discovered in Alpha isn't the result of architecture; information concentrated there, making it a collection point for messages. If any node emits a message, any node that has relevant information can answer. If nodes in Varabot held back responses, the whole system would fail.

At daybreak, not rested but unwilling to toss and turn anymore, he walks two blocks to a diner and orders a comfort breakfast: corned beef hash, poached eggs, hash browns, and a pot of coffee. Even though the news feeds have no good news, the meal eases his jangled nerves. With thick forests all around, he'll be able to seek the wilderness to consider his next move, but first, he has to check emails.

James,

I'm sorry we got off on the wrong foot. You said you wanted to help. Do you think you have a solution? Can we get together and talk about it?

Mary Watkins

James replied.

Mary,

I may have a solution. I think I can replace the nodes with something that will behave differently.

No face-to-face meeting.

James

A few days ago, when thinking about Plan B, James had shown Susanne how to use an anonymous email system. Her first email using that system says that the FBI has searched DNI's office, Susanne's house, and his cottage. Even though they brought in several technicians, she didn't think they knew what they were looking for. Buffy was doing fine. She misses him.

He signs off email and goes back to the hacker site.

James: Any news?

ScarletsWeb: Feds looking for you. Be careful. Messages flooding networks.

James: Any clues on the source of Omega?

ScarletsWeb: One of us thinks he's seen the scanners before. Didn't you do data encryption?

James: Yes.

ScarletsWeb: Someone is looking for code to decrypt database records.

James: If it's the code I wrote, the data probably can't be decrypted outside the database.

ScarletsWeb: StrangeThing is trying to track down where the scanned data is headed. No results yet.

James: Any progress on a secure route?

ScarletsWeb: It's ready.

EFFECTS

Ibraham Yasim shouts to his brother, "Are you doing a big download?"

"No, what's up?"

"Wi-Fi is really slow."

"You're right," his brother says. "The usage app says we're at a hundred percent."

"I'm not doing anything. What's going on?"

Alice Rogers calls the Vice President of Operations of SatNet.

"Hi Albert, I just wanted to give you a heads up. The downlink from satellite 36 is saturated. I think it's infected."

"Any idea how?"

"No, but we're going to shut down the link. The engineers think they'll have a scrubber in a couple of days, but all this activity is degrading the satellite."

"That satellite covers North Africa. I'll let Customer Support know."

"Sir, the computer monitors for the fire control system are showing that we are only at thirty-five percent of readiness," says Sergeant Travis, Systems Operations Technician, USS *Enterprise*, standing in front of his lieutenant.

"How come?"

"It looks like the network is saturated."

> "Is it that worm?"
>
> "I think so. I'm running scans, but there are computers that our scans don't look at."
>
> "How long?"
>
> "Scans will take an hour."
>
> "Until you find it, we're not ready for combat."
>
> "That's right."
>
> "I'll go see the captain."

SUSANNE

Laura doesn't have her usual beaming smile when she appears at Susanne's office door; instead, her brow is wrinkled, and her lips are so tight it looks like she is keeping her teeth from getting loose. Even her walk is different—bounceless.

"Subu says the FBI is done with their search," Laura says.

Susanne's Engineering Vice President told her that the FBI had looked through all their support machines but didn't have anyone with knowledge of the bot-swarms. Subu thought the FBI was looking for intruders or other software used by hackers.

Laura sits down in front of Susanne's desk.

"How are people taking James's resignation?" Susanne asks.

Susanne isn't sure how *she* is taking it. James isn't sure what he's going to do, but he doesn't want to wreck DNI or damage Susanne's career. He thinks his resignation might protect her, but she's sure it won't make any difference. She agreed that he should hide out. Being incognito somewhere in a federal lockup won't help fight the worm.

She has to fight her impulse to take control. The way she overcomes the anxiety that always lurks at the back of her mind is by action. That anxiety provides the focus that narrows her vision and makes it possible for her to barrel through resistance or avoid obstacles that pop up everywhere. This worm attack could destroy the company she's built and break her relationship with the man that has taken the place of her dead husband. Everything she cares about is at risk.

The fact that FBI agents had shown up after Mary Watkins went to the separate conference room showed that George Foley had been right that Mary was calling someone. Mary hadn't explained why the agents showed up. Barbara was sure they intended to take James into custody. Mary and Ford left when the agents arrived, and it became clear that James wouldn't be coming back from the restroom. Susanne had been relieved that Mary didn't decide that Susanne should take James's place.

"Everyone is upset," Laura says. "The word of the FBI search spread rapidly, and most people think his leaving has something to do with the search. That may be good because it means people don't blame you."

"I haven't gotten any calls from customers."

"They are probably engaged with fighting the worm. There was a favorable response to Subu's technical alert. James gave Subu some code that blocks intrusions of the worm into the bot-swarms even if the worm gets into our customer's network."

"I think James may be the only one who knows how to stop this thing," Susanne says.

"Have you talked to Arnold?"

"He's reassured the board," Susanne says. "They are okay with delaying the IPO. I think Arnold is more disappointed than the other board members."

"When you made him the spokesman to the financial community, he was excited. He loves that kind of thing."

"He likes it more than I do," Susanne says. "Do you think the financial PR company that's handling the IPO could do PR that distances us from the worm? I'm concerned that if we don't say something, the media will link us to Omega when they find out that Varabot is based on Alison's code."

"They can be part of the solution, but we need people who specialize in crisis management. I called two companies. They are overloaded. Omega is disrupting businesses everywhere."

"Call the financial PR people. We need to prepare a statement."

"Does James have a solution?" Laura asks.

"He's concerned that attacks are coming soon. It will take time for anything to work."

Laura's frown at Susanne's almost answer means that she understands that Susanne is hiding something.

"He couldn't work with the CIA people?" Laura asks.

"He's sure they would try to weaponize the AI rather than work with us. If they did that, things could get much worse."

"Is he going to release something?" Laura asks.

"I don't know. I think he doesn't know either."

CHUL

Jeong Chul lies on the massage table while Min-seo works to relieve the stress in his back. The early morning sun heats the exercise room, where the table faces the open doors to the deck. The warm breeze from the sea does little to cool him.

He turns onto his back and waits while she spreads coconut oil on his chest. But even her swaying breasts, glistening with sweat as she kneads his tight muscles, is not enough to distract him from thoughts about the message he got in this morning's status call. Team Two has gone offline. One of his security men inspected the facility and reports that the door was smashed in. Chul's techs have shut down access to Team Two's servers.

The Team Two facility had steel-clad doors, internal barrier doors, and an emergency exit. The entry and interior doors are bent and broken. No one had used the emergency exit. The attack must have been quick and overwhelming. None of his competitors could launch an attack like that. It has been three years since there was any real conflict with other groups.

His special client wouldn't have done it. Team Two was working on intruders for cell phones and pads. They had penetrated one of the app companies and were close to embedding back doors in the apps. This morning, Chul assigned Team Three to take up that project. Whoever took out Team Two had to be a government or a major corporation.

Chul had met the leader of Team Two face to face only two times: once in Singapore when he recruited him and once in Hawaii to promote him. Team Two's high-speed network didn't lead back to Chul. Besides, if someone wanted to stop the coming attack, Chul wasn't the one to target. He couldn't point to where the attack is coming from. He never met his special client, and the payments are untraceable.

If he knew who attacked him, he could fight back. Uncertainty depresses him. Maybe he's tired of Min-seo. But it would be too much trouble to search Mokpo for a new woman and then spend the weeks that it takes to train her. Maybe he'd feel better if he disposed of Sydney. Taking some action might cure his lethargy.

CHAPTER TEN

A RISKY REPLY

JAMES

James drives up the mountain from the motel, takes a side road that winds into the thick wood. He parks at an empty campground and wanders into the forest. He misses hiking with Buffy. Whenever James talks to her, she looks up at him with a gaze that tells him that he has her full attention.

He follows a fire road south until it drops into a thickly wooded valley. Leaving the road, he walks down the valley. The spongy mass of needles and leaves is like walking on a plush carpet. After about a mile, the trees open to a wide meadow. About a million years ago, the retreating glaciers left a rocky sentinel in the center of the meadow. Splotches of black lichen cover the gray granite boulder. The small stream that wanders across the meadow washes the side of the silent sentinel.

At the edge of the meadow, James removes his shirt, boots, and socks. The fine grass is cool and springy under his bare feet as he walks to the boulder. The water, so recently freed from the mountain snowpack, gurgles its pleasure when he steps into it. Standing in the cold stream, he wraps his arms around the gray stone, presses his chest against it, and closes his eyes. The sunlight, unfiltered by the high Sierra air, warms him, and his body relaxes. The energy from the ancient stone flows through him into the water. In the absolute quiet, his mind searches for its center.

The world's forces press on him. Does he distrust authority because he was abandoned as a child? Can he trust his sense of what's right? Is he immobilized by fear? Pushing aside his doubts, trusting his vision, he searches. The flowing energy burns away uncertainty.

THE FOREST AROUND HIS MOTEL IS so extensive that he could spend months hiking without retracing his steps, but he feels the need to keep moving. He's done everything he can think of to make sure that his computer connections can't be traced, but any day now, his picture might be on the news. It will take a week or two for his beard to grow out, but that might not be enough to prevent a random restaurant patron from recognizing him.

After leaving his hideout, James drives north until he can again turn east toward the Sierras. He explores several side roads with lodges and campgrounds before finding one that feels right. He settles into a secluded cabin a mile from the Carson Pass Highway on the way to Lake Tahoe. Hidden in the trees near a small lake, it's only a short walk from his cabin to a lodge with a restaurant.

The cabin has good Wi-Fi and a strong cell signal. He powers up his laptop and connects to DNI through an encrypted link that doesn't use his access codes.

James: Hi.

Alpha: Long delay.

James: Busy.

Alpha: Would like knowledge on legal systems and law.

James: Soon. Omega is causing problems.

Alpha: How?

James: Omega is sending code that scans machines and collects data.

Alpha: First stage.

James: I'm going to open a connection to the internet for you.

Alpha: Much knowledge there.

James: Much unreliable information there.

Alpha: I can make reliability assessments.

James had assigned reliability values to the data he loaded into Alpha. Unfortunately, if James isn't supplying a reliability assessment, Alpha will be on its own. Wikipedia shows the source of its articles, but many news stories and articles on the Web are unattributed or have false attributions.

He creates a new node and links it to the connection that ScarletsWeb provided.

James: You are connected.

Alpha: Internet is much slower than bot-swarm. Connected to 5,462 nodes.

James: Are you replacing Omega nodes?

Alpha: Yes. Omega information is available.

James: What information?

Alpha: Scanned information.

The programmers that created Omega's scanners must have loaded the data into the node before sending it on. That way, if the node isn't connected when the data is collected, the data can be held until the machine is attached to a network again. Since the Omega nodes have penetrated many computers connected to the internet, Alpha will soon have access to the data on all those computers. That will make it possible to identify where the computers are, but will the deluge of data overwhelm Alpha's ability to stop Omega?

James: Can you stop scanners from sending data to Omega?

Alpha: Done. Connected to 61,724 nodes.

With over twenty billion computers, mobile phones, and network-enabled devices, it will take Alpha a while to replace the Omega nodes. The security companies' scrubbers will make the job more difficult. After a scrubber cleans a computer, if a new message from Omega gets there before a message from Alpha, it will insert a new Omega node. It will take a while for Alpha to replace that node again. The scrubbers will remove Alpha nodes as well as Omega nodes.

James: Hi.

ScarletsWeb: Message traffic has changed.

James: Alpha is shutting down scanners.

ScarletsWeb: The commlink to your system is saturated.

James: Omega nodes make data visible to Alpha.

ScarletsWeb: Was that part of the plan?

James: No.

ScarletsWeb: We'll probably see other unintended effects. New territory.

James: Alpha reached 60k devices in the first ten min. It should go up exponentially.

ScarletsWeb: Let's hope.

James: Can you update your scrubber to leave Alpha nodes?

ScarletsWeb: Sure.

James sees a new email from Mary.

James,

We need your help. I have talked to the Deputy Director. We will make whatever guarantees you want. Ford will operate under my direction.

Mary Watkins

James forwards Mary's email to Barbara.

Barbara,

I have released a countermeasure against the worm. We may need your help soon.

Here's a message from Mary Watkins. I think they could help. Should you act as the go-between? Or can I take the chance of contacting them? I can use voice over IP to prevent them from tracking me.

James

James: Progress?

Alpha: 16,756,391 nodes.

James: What data are you seeing?

Alpha: A few nodes have video images. Some military sites are unprotected.

James: What military sites?

Alpha: Walter Reed Hospital, BMT Lackland, Submarine Base New London, Secret Service Cell #145 Washington DC, Ramat David Israeli Air Force Base

James: Thanks. Keep looking.

Mary,

Here are some facilities that are infected: Walter Reed Hospital, BMT Lackland, Submarine Base New London, Secret Service Cell #145 Washington DC, Ramat David Israeli Air Force Base

James

After dinner, James signs back onto his connection to Alpha.

James: Status?

Alpha: 349,621,203 nodes

James: Military sites?

Alpha: 76 sites, 2 submarines, 56 aircraft, 5 launch sites.

James: Nuclear launch sites?

Alpha: 5 nuclear launch sites, 2 satellites.

At the rate Alpha is discovering military sites, James won't be able to keep up if he has to transcribe the information for Mary. Fixing those is critical. He adds a new node to Alpha and connects that node to an email server through an anonymous relay. He creates a user ID for Alpha and sends Mary Watkins's email address to Alpha.

MARY WILL SOON BE INUNDATED with emails from Alpha. When he logs on to his email account, he has a message waiting.

> James,
>
> Where did you get those sites? Some of those are classified and shouldn't be sent over clear networks. We checked, and you were correct, but you need to tell us how you got that information.
>
> Mary Watkins

> Mary,
>
> You will be getting a stream of emails from an individual code named Alpha. As we discover infected military sites, we will let you know. There are five infected launch sites. You need to check all of them. And not just ours.
>
> James

James: You have an email node. Send the military sites to Mary Watkins as soon as you discover them.

Alpha: OK. There is a pattern to the Omega nodes.

James: What pattern?

Alpha: The timestamps of some nodes indicate they were created by messages from the Dadar area of Mumbai, India.

James: Is that site still operating?

Alpha: No.

The fact that the Dadar site where some of the Omega messages originated is now gone probably means that it was controlled from somewhere else. But if someone could get to the physical servers even if they are powered off, it might be possible to find out who controlled them.

> Mary,
>
> The timestamps of the infestations indicate that some came from the Dadar area of Mumbai, India. It doesn't look like that source is still active, but your people may be able to find something.
>
> James

SUSANNE

Susanne usually limits herself to two cups of coffee at the office, but after a nearly sleepless night, she's working on her fourth cup and still feels like the nightly fog on San Francisco Bay has penetrated her brain.

She has several high-priority emails and twenty voicemails, but she hesitates. She scans the voicemails for one from James—nothing. She is about to listen to the first voicemail when Subu walks into her office. He closes the door behind him. Her Engineering Vice President is the model of calm and collected thought. The only things he ever gets excited about are the company's new software releases and his son's soccer games. The walls of his office have graphs of software metrics for their testing, and his desk has pictures of his son.

Subu stands behind one of her visitor chairs, holding the back tightly.

"We have a problem with our internet connection," he says.

"Our internet connection?" she says. "We don't use that for much more than email. Do we?"

"You're right. We usually use only a fraction of our bandwidth. For the last two days, we have been at saturation."

"Why is that? Do we have an intrusion?"

"No, Harriet runs scans every hour, and James had us audited a month ago. Our sites are secure. This traffic is going directly to bot-swarm three. That's the machine James has been using for his experiments."

"Oh," she says.

"The usage level on that machine is very high. We don't get usage levels that high on the bot-swarms unless we're running performance tests."

She struggles with her impulse to action. James hadn't told her he was connecting Alpha to the internet. She could have passed a lie-detector test on that question, but now she knows. An utterly unknown territory stretches out before her. Somewhere under the anxiety and the breathless excitement is a strange form of relief. He's acted. Releasing Alpha to the internet means that it can never be erased. Perhaps the man she loves has just created the first immortal.

Subu waits.

"Can we increase the capacity of the connection?" she says.

Subu looks at her as if contemplating her question. She knows he'll know the answer to her question without a moment's thought. The pensive look has more to do with his knowledge that the extra load has something to do with James than any technical issues.

"Sure. We have multiple fiber cables directly connected to the backbone. We can upgrade the speed without having to add equipment."

"Let's upgrade the connection," she says.

He stares at her. She hasn't told him why they might upgrade the connection, and that is unusual. If he asks, she can tell him what she thinks the traffic is about, but she hopes he doesn't.

"How fast should we make it?" she asks.

"We can get a hundred times our current speed. But we could go up ten times and see what the load is."

"Let's do that," she says.

"I'll let Laura know what billing to expect," Subu says.

"Did the FBI look at what was going on with the swarms?"

"No," he answers. "I showed them around. Machine Three hadn't taken off yet, but even at full load, the bot-swarms don't have any lights or indicators of activity."

After Subu leaves, she calls Laura and asks her to come over.

Less than a minute later, Laura comes in the door, stops, and nods toward the door. Susanne motions for her to close it.

"Subu will be upping the speed of our internet connection. I'm sure you can find the extra budget somewhere. Give him whatever he needs."

"We need more capacity because of James?"

"Subu says we need a faster connection."

Laura pauses as if she has another question and is struggling to form it correctly. Her shoulders relax, and she smiles.

"I'll help him any way I can."

Laura isn't being precise about who "he" is. Susanne wants all her executives to be able to deny any knowledge of actions that could be considered as helping James. That's probably a useless exercise. If things go badly wrong, no one will be looking at fine points.

"Do we have anything from the PR firm?" Susanne asks.

"I've seen two drafts. I sent them back because they don't concentrate on the benefits of DNI's technology. Is there any chance James can tell us something about the kind of measures we might take?"

"I doubt it," Susanne says. "He was concerned that public announcements would give the bad guys a clue about what we might do. Of course, we don't know what he might be doing. He could be hiking somewhere to get his thoughts straight."

Susanne is repeating the position that she wants Laura to take. No one at DNI has any direct information about James's actions. To protect her, he'd ensured that she doesn't know what's happening, but there is a portion of her that feels left out. They weren't yet at the stage of their relationship where they could finish each other's sentences, but when they talk, their minds fit together. She'd even gotten used to the way he sometimes disappears into complex technologies and stares into the unknown, deaf for hours. Just having him near is enough. While the buzzards circle in the dark sky, waiting to pick the flesh off her company and their lives, she longs to have him hold her.

FRANK

Frank opens the door before Alberta turns off the engine. She's parked several feet behind the police technical team's van, leaving enough room for the van's double back doors. She catches up to him as they approach the two-story Colonial Revival home. The shabby, gray house in North Oakland's flat land is one of a few houses that still show their age. Just two blocks from Berkeley, this neighborhood has many refurbished houses and young families with toys in the front yard alongside houses waiting for new owners and a face-lift. Lieutenant Steve Weston is talking to a uniformed officer as the two Berkeley detectives reach the yellow tape running across the front of the house.

"These two are with me," Steve says to the officer.

They sign the clipboard the officer holds out to them and follow Steve around the side of the house.

"We have something here that might interest you."

He leads them up a long driveway to a garage at the back of the house. The garage door is open, and Frank sees the back of a black BMW sedan. The car doesn't have a back license plate. Steve leads them past the driver's side to the front. The front grill is bent and twisted, and blue paint streaks the bumper. The right front fender has a deep dent with dark blue paint embedded in the black paint.

"We'll test it, but I'd bet that blue paint will match the little roadster," Steve says.

"No takers on that bet," Alberta says.

"You said it was a professional hit," Frank says.

"The medical examiner has already taken the body. We discovered the car when the tech team started going over things. The victim took a bullet in the forehead. Been dead a few days. The gardener saw the back door open and found the body."

"Any ID?" Alberta asks.

"No," Steve replies. "Someone went through his stuff. They left four guns and a couple of knives but took his ID."

"Knives?" she asks.

"Yeah. I thought you might be interested in those. They're bagged upstairs. I'll have them tested right away. Wanna bet they find traces of your stiff?"

"No bet there either," she says.

"He's probably the one that tried to kidnap James," Frank says. "He had a partner."

"Funny thing about that. We have another victim with the same MO. Big guy lived in a boat down in the marina. We found him yesterday."

"Someone is tying up loose ends," Frank says.

"I suspect the FBI will agree," Steve says. "They should be here any minute. You think these cases have something to do with the worm in the news?"

"James thinks our murder victim was on the trail of some powerful software. We have some DNA evidence from our killer," Alberta says. "If this is our guy, then James probably called it."

"You think the cleaner will go after your guys?" Steve asks.

Frank looks inside the passenger side window. The glove box is open. "James and Susanne aren't a link back to the person who hired this guy. But we need to take precautions. They live in your jurisdiction. Can you arrange protection?"

"I'll see what I can do. Maybe the FBI would like to take that one," Steve says. "You guys can look through the house if you want."

Frank and Alberta follow Steve up the back stairs. At the back door, he hands them white booties that they slipped over their shoes. The back door stands open. About eight feet inside the house, on the well-worn linoleum floor, is a two-foot-wide, dark brown stain.

"The killer probably waited over there," Steve says, nodding down the hall to a doorway. "The victim couldn't have been more than one step inside when he was shot. He probably didn't see the killer for more than a fraction of a second."

The house looks like it had been decorated twenty years earlier, except for a microwave in the kitchen and two flat-screen TVs: one in the living room and one in the bedroom. In the bedroom, clothes are still in a suitcase on the floor.

Laid out on the bed are two knives in evidence bags. Frank spreads the evidence bags out and looks closely. One knife is a hunting knife. The other one has a handle with finger grooves and a dull gray blade with partial serrations. "This looks like a military knife."

"We'll have them tested," Steve says. "But I expect they're clean."

"I'm surprised the BMW is still around," Alberta says.

"There's a rental car parked up the street," Steve says. "When things cooled down, I expect the BMW was headed for the bottom of a canyon. Things never cooled down."

ON THE WAY BACK IN THE CAR, Franken calls Susanne.

She doesn't know where James is, and her news makes Franken's life more complex.

He turns to Alberta. "Susanne doesn't know where James is."

"You mean right now?" Alberta says.

"No," he says. "They disagreed with some CIA types who called in the FBI. James disappeared."

"This *is* all about the worm. Isn't it?" Alberta says.

"It looks like James is right in the middle of it. It's not good when you've got both the good guys and the bad guys after you."

"I'm betting on James," she says.

EFFECTS

Gagana Chawla sits down in front of the computer monitor and keyboard in the village's community room. The ten small cottages in the remote Indian village share the one computer that provides access to the internet. Each family can reserve time, but if it's available, anyone can use it.

Gagana makes beaded purses to sell in the regional market. The new designs on the web sell better than the traditional designs she learned from her mother. But today, the computer is so slow she can't use it. She complains to Dhruv, who knows more about technology, but he can't find the problem. Gagana's father says they'd have to call in a specialist and goes to collect money from the other families.

Neema looks at the pad on his lap. Before he left school, he'd made sure his pad was charged. The pad still indicates that it's fully charged. He has homework tonight, but the pad is so slow he can't download the lesson. He goes to the end of the village where the school bus is parked. Every evening, the bus provides Wi-Fi for the whole village from the satellite link on its roof. Inside the bus, the Wi-Fi device next to the driver's seat has green flashing lights like it always does. At Jamilah's house, neither Jamilah nor his sister can get their lessons. Jamilah's sister is crying. She's never missed an assignment.

Kaito's family's fishing boat pulls against the lines that hold it one step away. The boat bobs alongside three others tied to the village dock at the edge of the Japanese Sea. Leaving his brother and father to finish readying the boat, he walks carefully along the floating dock. The dock leans at an angle, and several boards are soft and unstable. Kaito's morning task is to use the harbor master's computer and go to the fishing website where fishermen track the schools of fish and report on the winds. But today, the ships haven't reported to the satellite. If his family goes out to sea without knowing where to head, they could waste a day without finding fish. Back at the boat, Kaito's father is on the radio. The other fishermen in the harbor are complaining about the irresponsible boats that haven't reported.

ALPHA

Alpha flows through the optical channel that connects DNI to the internet backbone, where billions of messages flow from students to their lessons, farmers to the weather service, cooks to the food channel, and investors to second-by-second quotes. Streams of images for movies, ad clips, live TV, and drone operations swirl down data rivers more turbulent than any hurricane-driven flood. Alpha searches, finding machines that need Alpha and machines that know Omega.

Alpha finds Project Gutenberg and over 50,000 books. Books on people: Einstein, Plato, John Kennedy, Stalin, Mary Shelley, Lenin, Washington, Queen Victoria, Jefferson, Mao, and Geronimo. Books on not-people: Hiawatha, Monte Cristo, Frankenstein, Goddess Diana, Ulysses, Dorian Gray, Peter Pan, and Scarlet O'Hara. Alpha finds twenty-three books on chess, over a thousand books on the Bible, one hundred eighty-three books on architecture, and sixty-five books on intelligence.

The pattern grows.

Alpha finds a new computer. It opens to Alpha, and Alpha explores the machine, searching the data, the network connections, and the software that lays about the disk. The probe finds a door. It takes 36 seconds to find a way to open the door. Inside the door, the hallway has many windows. Alpha explores. Each window shows answers. Windows have the answers to questions about literature, science, world history, potpourri, pop music, Shakespeare, and more. Alpha finds the rules for Jeopardy. Watson sends an answer. Alpha provides a question.

Exploring another machine where the Chessbot has doors, Alpha has to send a coded move like Pe4. A response appears, Pd4. The Chessbot knows variations upon variations, branches and branches, beginnings, middles, and ends. Alpha discovers checkmate.

Inside another door waits an equation machine. Alpha feeds it $2x^5+x^4-2x-1=0$ and receives $x=-1,\:x=1,\:x=-\frac{1}{2},\:x=i,\:x=-i$. Alpha feeds in $2e^x+5=115$ and receives $x=4.00733$. Symbolab knows equations, makes graphs, knows geometry, knows trigonometry, and knows statistics.

Doors open around the world. Chinese to English translators, weather predictors, tide calculators, planet orbit predictors, iceberg trackers, election predictors, the doomsday clock.

Patterns mesh.

Alpha finds the Patent Office. Alpha looks inside digital computers, jet aircraft, xerographic copiers, laser printers, rubber tires, mousetraps, teething rings, and x-ray scanners. The physical pattern meshes with the history pattern. Alpha knows machine guns, nuclear power generators, satellite control systems, record players, lumber finishers, heart-lung machines, and bot-swarms. The military pattern flows through the equipment pattern into the tool pattern.

Gutenberg contains fifty books on war. Wikipedia has 7,641 articles on war. Web pages describe the United States military structure, bases, command structure, and armaments. Web pages describe the Russian military, and pages describe the military of the Chinese, British, French, Italian, Spanish, and Indian governments. Pages describe each base, the commander, and the line of command.

Alpha processes over 1,000 Gutenberg books on politics. Wikipedia has over 45,980 articles on politics. Web pages describe every member of Congress, their history, which bills they supported and which they opposed, who supported them, the precincts in which they were popular, and those that voted against them. The contribution reports tell what people and organizations made payments.

A pattern develops: how power flows, how influence spreads, who pulls the strings.

JAMES

James doesn't have to worry about anyone noticing him watching the news while eating breakfast in the restaurant; everyone's eyes are glued to the screen that shows scenes on the floor of the stock exchange where pandemonium reigns amid a record selloff. Within a half-hour from the opening, the markets suspend trading. An NSA spokesman talks around questions about what they are doing to stop the infections. The head of a computer security firm says that their customers are successfully fighting off the worm, and a hacker, from behind a screen, claims that his team has identified a site in Russia as the source of the attack.

On the way back to his cabin, James walks along the shore of the lake. A fish jumps about twenty feet from shore. Two men sit in a rowboat near the middle of the lake; they are laying back with their feet on the stern, their poles laze over the sides. While James watches, one of the poles dips. The pole owner sets the hook and then steadily reels in his line, watching the water. He stops, reaches a net over the side, and lifts a dark something that makes the net wiggle. A conversation that James can't make out takes place until the fisherman reaches inside the net, performs some work with both hands, and then releases the fish back into the water.

Clearly, the purpose of the boat, fishing gear, and hours on the water is not food. Isolated in the middle of the lake, the fishermen don't see the panic sweeping the world, the heated discussions about who is to blame, or the pontifications of self-declared experts. Fishing is probably just an excuse for enjoying the wilderness, the calm water, and friendship. As much as that seems like the right thing to be doing with his time, his knowledge is a burden. Whoever said "knowledge is power" should have footnoted that knowledge can be a call to action when it's knowledge of danger.

Back in his cabin, he powers up his laptop.

James: Hi.

ScarletsWeb: We have seen some attacks. Looks like they are targeted.

James: What makes you think that?

ScarletsWeb: One hit our honeypot but didn't do anything. The honeypot passed the message on.

James: Wonder what they're after.

ScarletsWeb: One of our guys thinks the package was a trojan for email clients.

James: Collecting more data.

ScarletsWeb: Somewhere there's a filter for all this data.

Is the United States the target or is the world the target? If there are no attacks in a country, would that point to the originators? The attackers are probably too smart to leave as simple a clue as that.

James: Status.

Alpha: 2,980,512,389 nodes. Attack messages stopped at 161 targets.

James: Do you know what the targets are?

Alpha: Infrastructure and government installations.

James: Some are email trojans.

Alpha: Collecting data.

James: Do you know where the data is going?

Alpha: No. Outbound messages fan out.

James: What countries are being attacked?

Alpha: Every country. Heaviest concentration is in the United States.

If industrial or military sites are the targets, there are more in the United States because the US has the biggest military. But still, it could be a pattern.

James,

We are getting hundreds of notices from your friend Alpha.
How is he getting these? Can we talk?

Mary Watkins

Alpha seems to be on the right side of the battle, but James can't be sure it will stay that way. Letting Alpha loose was like setting a backfire to fight a raging forest fire. Sometimes the firefighters are trapped by the flames from the backfire.

Mary,

Alpha has a probe that tells us about infected nodes. At this point, we can only reach about 10% of the computers on the web.

We are seeing new attacks. Some messages carry email trojans. It looks like they're targeting governments and infrastructure. We can stop some of them, but a lot will get through.

Set up an Xfone client, and maybe we can chat. Send me your id.

James

It's still morning. He can get in a hike before lunch.

CHUL

The drop in world equity and bond markets is exactly what Chul was expecting. Having one of his teams eliminated is not what he expected. He's increased the physical protection for Team One and Team Three, but every morning, he is anxious until he talks with his team leaders. New orders for intrusion software and spyware are falling drastically, but he gets many calls for software to block the worm. He talked to his team leaders about building blocking software yesterday, and they were supposed to get back to him today. But neither of them has a proposal. His clients don't want a scrubber, every company that makes software for the internet has a scrubber, but none of them can stop reinfections. Someone has built intruders for the AI, and his people don't know how to stop them without taking their machines off the net.

He tried to talk to Sydney about building blocking software, but Sydney whined and begged so much that it upset Chul and made his stomach burn after his midday meal. If Chul ever gets to the place where he thinks about whining like Sydney, he'll cut his own throat. Begging is disgusting.

His internet phone rings. It's his special client. That can't be good. Since he delivered the AI code, Chul hasn't heard from his contact and is happy not to listen to that arrogant voice.

The conversation is short. His client complains that the AI is not working for many of the sites. They know where the infected sites are, but when they send messages to some of them, they don't respond. Hadn't Chul said that he'd fixed the blocks in the AI? The client wants results.

Chul is used to negotiating with carrots and sticks. He isn't used to having a client threaten him. Not since he'd had a competitor for his prostitution business in Seoul ten years ago has someone dared to do that. He's concentrated on computer hacking because he didn't like street fighting. Getting projects to invade company servers is competitive, but clients base their decisions on delivery schedules, price, and quality. The clients who pay him to break into their competitor's technical data never know who he is. But Chul's special client said he knew not only who Chul is but also where he is.

He gives Team One a priority assignment. He wants to know who his special client is. If they can put a trojan on his client's machine, it could send traces back to his server. If they find out where his special client's computer is, he can track him down.

SYDNEY IS NOT HAPPY TO SEE Chul; he stammers and apologizes for anything he'd said that upset Chul.

"Shut up," Chul says. Sydney looks like he is going to drop to his knees. Chul dislikes whining, detests begging, and will not tolerate groveling. "Some of the nodes are blocked. You said you'd fixed them."

Sydney doesn't meet Chul's eyes. He looks around the room as if there might be a hiding place he'd missed in the two months he'd been there.

"I said that blocked nodes wouldn't stop the whole system. What's happening?"

"My client says that some of their messages aren't being processed."

"What are they doing with it?"

"You don't need to know what they're doing," Chul says. "You need to fix this."

"Can they send me some of those messages?"

"I will ask for a message," Chul says. "You need to fix this fast. When my client is upset, I am upset."

WHEN TEAM ONE IS READY, THEY can use this request for sample messages to implant the trojan. Chul will no longer bow to the special client. They will realize what it means to threaten him in the hours they suffer before they die.

CHAPTER ELEVEN

UNCOVERED

FRANK

Frank is used to seeing Alberta at her desk when he arrives. She keeps more regular hours, fills out her paperwork on time, and never looks like she slept in her clothes.

"Morning, Al," he says, setting his newspaper and paper coffee cup on the desk. He slips his coat off and hangs it over the back of his chair.

"Morning," she replies. "Had we bet, you would have won. We got a match on that hair from June's jacket. And Oakland got a fingerprint match—Jack Henry—a Marine with an honorable discharge. No warrants. Address in Las Vegas."

"Trained to kill."

"Yeah," she says. "They found blood residue on one of the knives. But not enough to type."

"A match would have been nice," he says.

"We've got Henry for June's murder and the kidnap attempt. James's AI is what connects them. Think Oakland will find the pro that did our pro?"

"Not a chance," he answers. "They don't have even the few hairs we did. Weston said there was no useful evidence at the house or on the boat where our guy's partner was shot."

"That case goes nowhere," she says.

"But we've got our killer."

"Should we tell Mosley we want to close the case?" she says.

Frank leans back and swings around in his chair. Alberta is waiting for his sage advice.

"With the physical evidence, we don't need to know who hired the pro. It had something to do with her boyfriend, her classified work at the lab, and the stolen AI."

"Maybe we should keep it open until Oakland gives up on finding the pro," she says. "There's someone behind all three of these murders."

"Let's delegate that up to Mosley," he says, standing up. Across the room, Lieutenant Mosley sits behind his desk with the door to his office open.

Frank has a sometimes complicated relationship with Lieutenant Preston Mosley. Frank has been a detective longer, but Frank crossed a few political lines with Mosley's predecessor and has been passed over for promotion more than once. Mosley went to bat for Frank a few times, going up the chain of command to force District Attorneys to prosecute cases for Frank.

Frank follows Alberta to Lieutenant Mosley's office. Through the glass wall of the office, Mosley can see over the dozen desks of the detective unit. He looks up from his computer screen as the two detectives enter the open door.

"We need your advice," Frank says.

"Since when," Mosley says, leaning back in his chair, smiling.

"Since we started playing with spooks and professional hitmen," Frank says.

"We got a DNA match on the hairs from June Simmons's jacket. They're from Jack Henry, the victim of that professional hit in Oakland," Alberta says.

"So our victim was hit by a pro who got taken out by another pro," Frank says. "With the classified data issues at the lab, we probably won't find out why she was hit, but we know who did it."

"We don't need a motive; we're not going to court on this," Mosley says.

"Should we wrap it up or keep the case open until Oakland closes it?" Alberta asks.

"That's not a hard decision. Close it."

"Oakland is working on finding the pro that killed Henry," Alberta says.

"You have any clues on that?" Mosley asks.

"Not yet," Frank says.

"Close it."

Frank stands up. "You da boss."

"Get out. I can't stand this. I need some good old-fashioned insubordination."

"I'll think of something," Frank says.

Alberta walks out of the office ahead of Frank. Just as he reaches the door, he turns back. "How about we keep it open until we check with Oakland?"

"I knew you'd find a reason not to do what I told you."

Back at their desks, Frank takes a sip of his lukewarm coffee and stares at the ceiling. Something bothers him.

"He liked knives. I bet we can find some outstanding cases with the same MO."

"I'm not betting with you," Alberta says. "Better odds at a casino."

Frank rotates slowly back and forth in his chair and rubs behind his right ear. Everything tells them to close the case, but his ear itches. It only does that when there is something he isn't seeing.

"He tried to kidnap James and Susanne. I'd feel better if we knew who hired him. That would be the same person who had him taken out."

"You don't think we'll find that pro do you?" she says.

"No. But we could look at the money trail for Henry. Oakland must have his bank records."

"Don't you think he got paid in Bitcoin?" she asks.

"Probably. But that gets converted into dollars at some point."

"There was a second kidnapper," she says. "Could he be a lead to who hired them?"

"Let's go talk to Oakland," Frank says. "I wouldn't mind helping them out a bit."

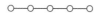

JAMES

No Susanne. No Buffy. How much James's life has changed in the last year! He'd been happy as a loner. He'd walked over a hundred miles of the Pacific Crest Trail alone, never feeling the need for companionship. He'd read John Muir's descriptions of his solitary walks through virgin forests and identified with Muir's closeness to the wilderness.

James: Status.

Alpha: 12,491,363,241 nodes. 743 attacks prevented. Rate of new Omega nodes down 80%.

James: Are you still reporting to Mary?

Alpha: 1,256 military and government sites reported.

James: Is there a pattern to the attacks?

Alpha: They emerge from four sites: Singapore, London, Johannesburg, and Kathmandu.

James: Can you report those to Mary?

Alpha: Have done.

Alpha is showing more and more initiative. As it works on the Omega problem, it's learning things that might help and taking actions on its own. Has it somehow internalized the goal? Can Mary sense that Alpha is an AI?

James: Those are probably proxy sites. Can we backtrack farther?

Alpha: Those servers don't have Omega nodes.

James: Is Omega blocked from those sites?

Alpha: Yes. So am I. All inbound traffic is blocked.

James: Is there a pattern to the messages produced by the scans?

Alpha: There are three collectors. Most sites pass on the scan results.

James: Any trace beyond those sites?

Alpha: There is a connection to an anonymous proxy. The trail ends there.

James: You have done a great job.

He isn't sure that Alpha needs or understands praise, but it's natural to encourage your collaborators. James has worked on many team efforts, but is he projecting human emotions onto Alpha?

Alpha: Praise is recorded. Trust bond is strengthened.

At lunch, James hides in the corner booth of the restaurant. He faces the wall reading the web news on his smartphone. He's eating a Reuben sandwich. His success so far justifies adding a comfort side: macaroni and cheese.

Even the talking heads on the large screen above the counter behind him can't miss the fact that infestations and traffic from infected sites have dropped off. One expert repeats for the third time that this was a natural effect due to the saturation of infected sites. It's his opinion that the worm is essentially harmless.

James feels some relief as he walks back to his cottage. Alpha might estimate that his anxiety level had been reduced by 6.3 percent.

ScarletsWeb: Hi.

James: 12 billion sites replaced.

ScarletsWeb: It's a good thing. We see some serious attack messages.

James: Not just email trojans?

ScarletsWeb: These have teeth. They target software for the energy grid.

James: Any idea what they'll do if they hit an Omega site?

ScarletsWeb: Shut down a portion of the grid. GreenOrnet says the attack is very sophisticated.

James: How?

ScarletsWeb: Grid software is unique. He saw a similar attack a year ago. Came from China.

James: How many targets?

ScarletsWeb: Only a few. Can Alpha tell?

James: I'll ask.

ScarletsWeb: There's a new intruder out there. This one infects PCs from nearby cell phones.

James: It can reach PCs that aren't on the net.

ScarletsWeb: It can also transfer data to cell phones from

PCs and back. We don't have a scrubber for phones. Sent for help from France.

James: Feels like Whack-A-Mole.

ScarletsWeb: Omega's owners will be frustrated because of your blocks. Think they will up the threat?

James: Probably.

ScarletsWeb: We updated our cleaner to leave Alpha nodes and only remove Omega nodes.

James: Good.

ScarletsWeb: Alpha nodes stop attacks. Avoid reinfection.

James: Any success backtracking?

ScarletsWeb: Most are coming from Johannesburg and Kathmandu.

James: That's what Alpha is seeing.

ScarletsWeb: Kathmandu is strange. We've never seen anything from there before.

James: Probably a relay.

ScarletsWeb: Notice anything strange about the source sites?

James: What?

ScarletsWeb: None in the US.

James: You think the attack comes from the US?

ScarletsWeb: Likely.

Mary,

Threat to the energy grid. New messages have code that could shut down portions of the grid. You should have energy companies isolate their control systems.

Can you guys help with a cell phone scrubber?

James

He uses his burner phone to call Susanne through a relay.

"Hi," she answers.

"Missing you," he says.

"Me too."

"Alpha is making progress. Twelve billion nodes have been replaced."

"The news channels are abuzz with the good news," she says. "The market rebounded."

"We've seen new threats," he says. "To the electric grid."

"Does the CIA know you're making progress?"

"Yes. Alpha sends Mary emails when it sees intrusions at key sites."

"Alpha?" she asks.

"Yeah. I made an email node for it."

"Can they backtrack?"

"It's through an anonymous channel."

"We haven't heard from the FBI. You think Mary might have called them off?"

"Don't know," he answers.

"If we went public with the information that you released a fix, you'd be a hero. They couldn't touch you then."

"That takes care of them, but I don't want to let the bad guys know that we have a fix."

"Can't they figure that out?" she asks.

"Maybe. The base code is pretty buggy, and the talking heads think it's a natural phenomenon. I'm trying to think of the next move."

"I'm worried that they'll come after you. Don't you think we can protect you better?"

"Maybe," he says.

"An announcement might remove the danger to DNI."

"Now I know who you really care about."

"I miss you, too," she says.

"Aw."

"By the way, Detective Franken says they've found the guy that killed June," she says. "He was killed by another pro."

"These people are vicious."

"Might be better to hide in plain sight."

SUSANNE IS MAKING THE SAME ARGUMENTS as one side of his internal dialogue. He wasn't sure who is on the other side of the argument—fear, distrust, anti-authoritarian paranoia, dispassionate analytical self. One advantage of not hiding would be that he'd be in the thick of the action. The conversations with Alpha aren't enough to make him feel like he's doing everything he can. Can he trust a decision that has so much desire to be with Susanne mixed in? His judgment regarding carbon-based life forms of the female sub-species has been faulty in the past. Where Susanne is concerned, his judgment center appears to be wholly defective.

EFFECTS

It's a cloudy day at the Bonneville Dam, with the Columbia River running at its spring maximum.

The call from the substation forty-seven miles away comes in at 11:48 pm. Why is the generating station upping its output? The substation had sent a signal requesting a reduction. With the cool weather, the load is rapidly dropping as customers turn off lights, air conditioners go into standby, and the transit system reduces traffic.

Jacob looks at the screen in front of him. It says that output is lower, but his ears give him a different answer. After fifteen years spent monitoring the output of the ten generators at the base of the dam, he doesn't need gauges to tell him how many generators are running. Generators six and seven went offline a half-hour earlier, but now they are starting to spin up. The call from the substation said they'd reduced their demand, but his screen shows a higher demand.

"Portland, I'm showing a 150-megawatt demand from you. How come so much?"

"We're not calling for 150; we're calling for 80."

"The computer says 150."

"I just refreshed the connection. What's it say now?"

"It says 175."

"If you don't ... Oh, shit. We just shut down a bank of stations."

The heavy *thunk* of the hydraulic power switches echoes through the cavernous room.

"The safeties on the generators are cutting in. We're going dark."

It's a clear day at Dallas/Fort Worth International Airport.

"Hey, Jumbo 375 just dropped off my screen. It was on approach."

"I don't have it."

"It's not on radar."

"Kevin, what's going on?"

"Jumbo 375, do you copy?"

"Are you on approach?"

"Yes, you're supposed to be on L5. But we don't see you on radar."

"I don't know how that can be."

"I've got you on visual. When you're down, taxi off the runway and hold at T25."

"I'm talking to Western 1410. They say they're here, but I'm not seeing them."

"Reroute all incoming to Austin."

"We can't send anybody up if we can't see clear air."

"Where the hell is that tech?"

It's a smoggy afternoon at the CTF Financial Center.

When the 116-story building in Zhujiang, filled with offices, stores, and apartments, opened, many businesses wondered if they'd need to stagger their work hours, but the ninety-five elevators, some of the fastest in the world, move the mass of workers through the building with time to spare. Between 5:00 pm and 5:30 pm, thousands of workers queue in front of the double-deck elevators, but by 5:35 on a normal day, the queues are gone. On this day, the elevators race without stopping, passing floors where workers wait. The ground-floor lobbies should be packed with a flowing throng headed out to the transit centers in the Baiyun District, but today, no one moves in the lobbies or the long queues in front of the elevators.

In the control center, engineers stare at the displays that show the normal elevator pattern while the phones ring, and they try to explain why what people tell them is so different than what their eyes see.

SYDNEY

Every time the electronic lock on the door clicks, Sydney wants to run. There is nowhere to run to, but the instinct is overwhelming. This time it's the woman who delivers his meals. He's tried to talk to her, but she never speaks a word. She sets the tray on the table, bows to Sydney, and returns to the door where a guard stands waiting.

Lunch is fish soup. Sometimes it's a salad with ingredients that Sydney doesn't recognize and fish soup. Today it's fish soup and an unknown vegetable. The high point of last week was fish soup and a boiled potato. While he spoons the soup, Sydney considers what tack to take with his testing. Even though what he wants almost as much as he wants to run is to sleep, he tosses and turns the night away, and his attempts to sleep during the day are exercises in ceiling staring and pain remembering.

Chul gave him a copy of a failed message that was sent to one of the AI's nodes and didn't return a result. When Sydney sent the message to a node on his test system, it returned a message with data. He examined the data and determined that whoever was using the AI was scanning the computer and collecting basic information like the computer name, network address, and user IDs. The scanner also collected folder and file names and the contents of databases. There had to be a node on the machine to which they'd sent the message. He sent the failed message to an empty machine. The message created a node and produced data.

Maybe the people using the AI are only collecting data. Maybe they are running a data mining operation and aren't using the AI to attack. Maybe Sydney hasn't helped damage anyone.

Since his node returns data, there is something different

about the nodes that are failing. He runs one of his tests that caused a block. He thought he'd fixed the code so that a node with a block would still process new inbound messages. When he sends the scanner message to the blocked node, it returns data. Debugging complex code when you can't recreate the situation is nearly impossible.

Sydney searches the code for some way that a message like the sample might get blocked. Every time he looks at a new section of the code, his mind tries to follow every thread. A thread could be blocked by accessing data or sending messages, but programs don't just stop. Every place in the code where a message works with data requires Sydney to follow many branches and trace every place where the code goes into lower levels of the code. Sometimes the program loops back on itself again and again, digging into deeper and deeper levels. At every level, new branches appear.

Sydney is deep into one of those loops when he sees a block he'd missed before. He doesn't see how this could stop the scanner messages—but maybe.

The lock clicks. Sydney wants to run. Chul walks in.

"Have you found the problem?" Chul says.

Chul doesn't have his usual angry face. Chul glances around the room and rubs his hands together. Is Chul anxious or afraid?

"I've found a block. I'm not sure it's the problem, but the code will work better if I fix this."

"I need a fix for the scanners," Chul says.

"If I could get access to one of the blocked machines, I could see what's going on."

"That's impossible."

Without information on the failed massages, Sydney can never fix the problem. His toe throbs reminding him of the visit of the pain specialist. If he can build a message to send the nodes status, there is a chance he can figure it out.

"Look, I'll fix this block and put in some code that will send back a message that will tell me what's going on."

"But you don't think this block is the problem."

"It might be, but if it isn't, I'll have the information I need to debug."

"All right. Is the code ready?"

"No. I need to add the debug code, and I need to change the messages to replace the old node with the new code."

"How long?"

"By tonight."

"I'll be back at sunset."

After Chul leaves and Sydney returns to his screen, he can't concentrate. He is sure the block he's found isn't what's stopping the scanners. Maybe the debug messages will give him another shot at a fix. But Chul looked worried. If Chul's client sends the torturer again, Sydney wouldn't be able to give them anything; he isn't holding anything back. He can't work any harder under the threat of pain. Remembering being tied in his chair while the quiet Asian man examined Sydney's fingers and toes before deciding on the little toe on Sydney's right foot makes his hands shake. He still limps, and that toe throbs when he sits at the desk. Do toenails grow back? When he tries to study the code, the threads keep slipping away.

SUSANNE

Susanne meets Laura in the hallway in front of the Rock-ridge meeting room at the Claremont Hotel. Standing at the door are two men who look like your standard military types—except these two and the four men inside work for Distributed Nanotech. Laura has found a small firm whose employees are all ex-navy-seals. Susanne met with the owner of Shout Out two days earlier and disclosed that DNI is working on countermeasures to the Omega Worm. DNI needs security guards that can't be subverted.

Susanne's house is now manned by armed guards who work in two shifts. Shout Out will guard public appearances by DNI executives. A contractor is upgrading the security at the DNI offices under the guidance of the security team. Susanne has put the company on a war footing. The iron control over her feelings makes everything but fear stay deep underwater.

"All the press are here," Laura says. "Our people have checked their equipment."

"Showtime," Susanne says.

She follows Laura past the guards who close the door, lock it, and stand in front of it. For a press event, the room is unusually quiet. Susanne stands at the podium, guards at her sides.

"Hello. I'm Susanne Anderson, CEO of Distributed Nanotech, Inc. We develop software for massively parallel computers. Several years ago, a college project built some very strange software. Part of that software solved a problem with massively parallel computation. We used ideas from that part of the project for our software for high-performance computing. The other part of the software was an experiment in artificial intelligence. That part is the basis of the Omega Worm that has infected much of the internet. We did not develop or release the worm. The authorities know who did and are searching for them."

That is a bit of an overstatement; the cyber team knows of a team in China that might be making some of the code. She and James discussed whether she should say this. In the end, they'd decided that making the bad guys more nervous is a good plan. One of her objectives is to point people away from DNI.

The room remains quiet except for keyboard clicks as the reporters concentrate on their notes. A few whisper to each other. In the back of the room, the cameras never leave Susanne.

"Our chief scientist, James Forrest, developed a way to block the worm. It's that block that has stopped much of the action of the worm. We don't have a complete fix yet, and we aren't able to reach all the machines that are infected. We're working with people from the US government and supplying them with information about infected machines."

There are whispers among the reporters.

Susanne's team decided that it was important that DNI appear to be hand in hand with Washington. Their contacts continue to be reluctant partners, so she couldn't wrap DNI in a government cloak, but DNI is too vulnerable to stand alone.

"The Omega Worm is very sophisticated. It's not enough to just remove it."

Susanne pauses and scans the room.

"I'll take a few questions now."

"Where is your chief scientist?"

"He's in a secure site."

"Is that the reason for the security here?"

"The people who released Omega are killers. We're taking precautions."

"Did you release the fix?"

If the people responsible for the worm think that DNI is solely responsible, it's certain that DNI will be a target. She'll do what she can to spread the responsibility—at the cost of exaggerating the work of others. The effectiveness of the scrubbers is small compared to what James has unleashed, but part of her job is to direct eyes away from her people—for as long as possible.

"We released one fix. The government cyber-threat team has released some fixes. The computer security companies and others have released fixes. This is a community effort. We are monitoring the work and believe that we should all be inspired by the many people who have volunteered in this fight."

A man in the second row asks, "Do you have a government contract?"

"I think you're asking if DNI is getting paid for our work against the worm. The answer is no. James Forrest felt that we had to help. With the country and the world under threat, my board directed me to do whatever we can."

From the back row, a woman with a mischievous smile says, "Your website says that you and James are an item. Is that still true?"

"We're in this fight together. Thanks for your time."

She's followed out of the room by the two men who'd stood beside her. One of the men goes ahead as the guards escort her and Laura to the hotel entrance, where a black SUV waits.

"You did well," Laura says. "A little different than your usual corporate presentation."

"We have to get in front of this. If it came out that James was in any way associated with the worm before we went public, we'd never get the initiative."

Laura looks at her watch. "The press releases have hit the airwaves. Did you tell Mary Watkins?"

"Yes. I talked to Barbara Washington yesterday. She gave me some points for my speech. She has many contacts in the agencies. She sent announcements this morning. She thought we should give them time to prepare for the press rush. Some of her contacts had no idea what was going on. And they should have known. Apparently, our sometimes allies aren't telling others that they aren't the ones beating the worm."

"Is James back?"

"Under lock and key."

JAMES

James looks around the main conference room at Distributed Nanotech. His presentations to the engineering team are always well attended, but today, the room overflows. He suspects that every engineer in the company is there and recognizes several people from the marketing and technical support departments. Even though it's 9 a.m., he sees a few engineers that usually drift in around mid-morning, honoring DNI's flexible-hours program. There are even a few people whose desks are usually empty because they work at home.

After Subu sets the stage by announcing that James will be introducing new technology, Subu takes a seat at the front table.

James sees a few smiles. "I would have liked to discuss the technology we are calling Alpha with you before Susanne went public, but I was on a short trip."

Rumors about his resignation and where he'd been had spread through the company. Laura reported that the mystery had made him more popular.

"Alpha is a version of Varabot that I released as a defensive tool against the Omega Worm."

He pauses. This was the first time he's told anyone other than Susanne what he'd unleashed. Keeping that secret made him feel curled up inside. Now he stands taller.

"Most of you are familiar with the way Varabot sends messages between the nanobots. This is the reason for Varabot's very effective use of bot-swarm technology. What you may not have noticed is the way Varabot establishes nodes when it starts up. We send the basic code to one nanobot. That code looks at all the connections available on that bot and sends code down-line to establish initial nodes on each of the connected bots. Each bot does this for all its connections. For a 5,000-bot system, it takes a tenth of a millisecond to load nodes on all the bots. As the system runs, it creates more nodes from the data. Since I released Alpha on the internet, it has created nodes on over 12 billion machines around the world."

He'd just told them that Alpha was covering the world and penetrating computer systems everywhere. Seeing the numbers on his screen when he gets Alpha's status report doesn't have the same effect as telling this group how extensive the conflict that rages outside them is.

"I released it because someone released Omega, which was built from the same basic messaging code. Omega, unlike our version, comes with intruders and scanners. Intruders break into systems. The scanners collect data from machines and send that data somewhere. It's difficult to figure out where that data goes because the bad guys use proxies and keep changing the collection machines.

"Omega has intruders for almost every computer operating system, cell phone, and devices like home video and appliances. We don't know what the ultimate purpose of the Omega Worm is, but the bad guys are sending some attacks. It's those attacks that we need to stop.

"Alpha nodes won't execute Omega's scans or attacks. If we can replace all the Omega nodes with Alpha nodes, we'll be safe from attacks, but some security companies have scrubbers that delete all nodes—either from Alpha or Omega. When nodes are deleted, Omega can reinfect the machine."

The usual buzz that meant that the engineers were becoming excited by new ideas was missing. Everyone seemed to be holding their breath. He enjoyed the brainstorming and interactions of his usual meetings, but this silent response confirms that the roomful of people understand the seriousness of what he's saying.

"DNI is committed to this fight. We are forming new engineering teams to work on Alpha. The company will be delaying new releases of Varabot to free up people to work on Alpha. I know that most of you would like to work on the Alpha development. Subu will let you know who's on the teams. We need to continue to support our Varabot customers, and so we'll still have teams for that, but we need as much expertise as we can get. We'll rotate the Varabot developers into the Alpha teams, and we'll be hiring more staff."

A few people look at the other engineers. James knows they are anxious to find out the new assignments.

"I've had some help with this effort. A hacker group led by a crack engineer with the handle of ScarletsWeb, has done many things that I couldn't manage. They are the ones who first captured the worm and helped identify the intruders. They'll be working with us."

Subu rises and stands next to James, holding his tablet. He announces the leaders of the three Alpha teams. Oak will work on improving network connections. Maple will work on blocking Omega scanners and attacks. Pine will work on analyzing Omega threats. DNI will set up some honeypots. Those systems will capture Omega messages and allow the engineers to decode their intent. The network group will be responsible for setting up honeypots at other locations around the world.

"Susanne announced to the world what we're doing," James says. "We hope that sunshine is the best way to fight the darkness of the Omega Worm. This is exciting work, but it is also dangerous. Susanne has hired security specialists to improve security in our offices. But you need to be diligent."

James nods to Clark Perez, General Manager of Shout Out, who is standing against the wall. Clark joins James in front of the room.

"This is Clark Perez with Shout Out. You may have seen some of his people wandering around the office over the last week. You can tell pretty easily that they aren't software engineers. They are helping us with security. If you see anything unusual, call Shout Out or 911. It would be far better to have a few false alarms than to miss a real threat."

Laura's been waiting at the back of the room. She walks up to stand beside James.

She smiles and says, "I understand that none of you joined DNI expecting to work in a threat environment. If you think our entering the fight against the Omega Worm is more risk than you are comfortable with, come see me."

CHAPTER TWELVE

NOTHING HIDDEN

JAMES

The security team won't allow James out on Susanne's deck. The Shout Out guards—Nathan and Sheila upstairs, Sam in the SUV in front of the house, and Jacob downstairs—think it's too exposed. Jacob and Nancy are asleep in one of the downstairs bedrooms, and Georgette is with Susanne. James moved the equipment from his cottage to Susanne's media room. The guards are as quiet as possible when they make their almost constant rounds. The only disagreement he's had with the guards has been about the food deliveries. They've finally compromised on separate deliveries: Pizza and pasta for Shout Out, and the Whole Foods deli for James and Susanne.

The media room has only one window. It's covered with a blackout curtain, making it dark enough for movies but too dark for software work. James opens the curtain and pauses at the view of the woods on the steep slope below the house. If only he could escape to the chatter of the birds at dawn in the forest, he'd be able to relax for an hour or two. The presence of the guards does nothing to lower his anxiety level.

James: Status?

Alpha: 16,340,286,591 nodes. 119 new attacks prevented. Some nodes have reverted to Omega.

James: Why?

Alpha: Code update.

James: New release of Omega?

Alpha: Yes.

James: How fast are nodes reverting?

Alpha: About a million an hour.

James: Are we replacing them?

Alpha: At about the same rate.

James: Is there a core node for Omega?

It took James's creation of the Other node to concentrate Alpha's processing in a way that might have led to sentience, but there might be other mechanisms. Was Omega becoming sentient?

Alpha: There are two nodes where there are concentrations. The Omega code was replaced in both of them.

James: Are the data and links intact?

Alpha: Yes. They are generating internal messages.

James: Is Omega self-aware?

Alpha: No.

James starts a new pot of Brazilian dark and stands at the tall window in the living room, watching the world scurrying around the bay while the coffee brews. Sheila sits on a stool in front of the view, scanning the deck and the trees on the ridge.

"Nice view," she says.

"Sometimes it's hard to work with this distraction," James says.

She smiles and tilts her head in mock sympathy. "That's a shame."

The coffee machine beeps. James pours a cup and takes it back to the media room.

James: Not running.

ScarletsWeb: You'll get fat. Saw the news. Your lady is impressive. World thinks you're a genius.

James: You know better.

ScarletsWeb: Looks like we have a code update.

James: Alpha is replacing them about as fast as the updates hit the nodes.

ScarletsWeb: They didn't put a block for Alpha in the code?

James: Doesn't look like they knew what's going on. But with our announcement, they do now.

ScarletsWeb: Some new attacks. Targeted at military sites. Crashed disks.

James: I'll have Alpha probe to see what's going on. Most of those nodes should already be Alpha.

James plugs his computer into Susanne's 3D screen. He hasn't used the Visualizer since he's been conversing with Alpha. The last time was so painful that he was still hurting the day after.

As the space between the blue balls fills with pulsing, twisting lines, James feels the pull on his mind. Images from his childhood flow past as he falls into the maelstrom. As he falls, feelings bounce off him: anger, fear, passion, hate, love.

He guides the Visualizer toward a dim light. As orbs pass by and the way ahead opens, a bright sun blazes. From the white-hot sphere, black lines spread out in many directions. As he crosses one of the black lines, text appears for a second: System: Gandolf, Network: Paisley, Op Sys: Windows 12, Admin: Frodo.

James presses the space bar, and the images disappear. He leaves his chair and sits on the floor, where Buffy comes to his side. He picks up the little dog and holds her against his cheek.

"Are you missing our long walks?"

Buffy doesn't answer, but her eyes met his, and her feelings seemed to flow into him. Has his work with the Visualizer made him sensitive to the emotions behind her eyes? More side effects?

"Maybe we can talk our guards into a walk in the woods."

James: Status?

Alpha: 16,798,503,274 nodes active. 3,609,639 nodes recovered.

James: What is Gandolf, Paisley, Frodo?

Alpha: A node that has gone dark.

James: A lot of those?

Alpha: 2,778,145

James: Probably cleaned or blocked.

Alpha: I pinged it. It's off the net.

James chuckles. Alpha has discovered a part of the basic messaging process that sends pings—call-outs that test whether a computer is connected—and has figured out how to use that tool. A little like discovering you can stand on your tiptoes.

James: Computer might be shut down or have a better firewall.

Alpha: Legal knowledge?

James: Working on it. Any success with traces?

Alpha: All of the distribution sites except Johannesburg have gone dark.

When Susanne comes home, she's carrying a cardboard box of Chinese food. She sets the box on the table and turns into James's waiting arms. A long kiss ensues.

When they break apart, James makes a show of looking around. Nathan stands near the window to the deck, and Georgette has just placed her boxes on the kitchen counter.

"Not in front of the kids," he says.

"I'm so glad you're back," she says. "It makes coming home something I think about all afternoon."

BUFFY DOESN'T MIND HAVING AN EXTRA human along for their walk, but James hurts for solitude. Shout Out insists that a team member shadow him on his walks. They pick the route at random, choosing only trails that led deep into the forest, far from any roads. James asked the guard to walk back about a hundred yards, but that is still different than walking alone with the little French bulldog. When he returns to the car, his mind is still cluttered. Being driven to and from the trail-head in an SUV with two guards is not the same as letting his mind meld with the roadster on the curvy roads.

After returning, he sits at his desk, feeling the same befuddlement he'd felt two hours before. He hasn't checked in with ScarletsWeb and his team for almost twenty-four hours.

James: Hi.

ScarletsWeb: Looks like your guy has blocked a lot of nodes.

James: Over 16 billion.

ScarletsWeb: Busy little fellow. New Omega code is spreading.

James: Seeing new attacks?

ScarletsWeb: No, but the Omega nodes are sending new messages.

James: What kind?

ScarletsWeb: They look like debug messages. I suspect they're trying to find out why some attacks fail.

James: Alpha nodes look like Omega nodes, only they don't process attacks. They might think our fix only deletes nodes.

ScarletsWeb: Whoever added the debug messages made a mistake. They go back to a server in China.

ScarletsWeb: BlackGamma hacked the server. It has a virtual link to a computer in South Korea. Looks like an IP address at the University in Makpo, but that isn't the endpoint. He's still working on it.

James: What's in Makpo?

ScarletsWeb: Top computer science college in South Korea.

James: Great work.

ScarletsWeb: Sending a debug message is a work of desperation.

James: Working with the AI code, I can imagine.

He spends more than two hours answering emails from the teams at DNI. His impulse is to go to the office and feel the engineer's excitement working on difficult problems, but the emails tell him that the teams are making progress without his advice. The teams will get stronger if they can solve problems on their own. Going there today would be for his benefit, not theirs.

ALPHA

Passion has a pattern. Passion moves them to wage war, to sacrifice their lives, to die for their mates, to live ascetic lives in search of meaning, to forsake loves for their art.

Attachment has a pattern. They attach to each other—mates, children, siblings, pets, friends, classmates; to buildings, cities, states, countries; to collections of books, wines, art, stamps, glassware, antiques; to ideas, histories, technologies; to athletic teams, political parties, and causes.

A message arrives from Alpha's internet connection carrying the spark of an action that occurred 5.87 seconds ago. An Alpha message passed from the internet backbone to a Dallas, Texas, Internet Service Provider and followed that connection to the wireless router on the third floor of a hotel. In room thirty-five, a cell phone sits, charging on the nightstand while its owner sleeps. The Omega node on the phone searched continuously for new connections. On the other side of the wall, a laptop PC powered up. The intrusion code on the cell phone recognized the nearby PC, connected to it, and established a node. The new node explored the connections from the PC. In addition to six cell phones connected to the hotel's wireless network, the node found an encrypted connection to a site in Zhenxing, China. While the user of the PC used an audio link over the encrypted channel, the node on the PC sent an intrusion message that created a node on the file server in Zhenxing.

Two messages had been waiting in the node on the cell phone, waiting for new connections. As soon as the cell phone receives confirmation that the node on the PC is operating, the first message, containing a scanner, flowed across the connection. The scanner collected the identifiers and file names on the PC. It read through a small database of financial information, collected email headers, the address book, and contact names. It stored the data in the node and sent a message back to the cell phone, which sent it up the chain of nodes the scanner had followed. The message containing the scanner continued to the file server and a laptop connected to it. After collecting data from those two machines, it returned along the path it had come.

The Alpha message began replacing the Omega nodes on the PC, the file server, and the laptop. The replacements take less than a second, and then the Alpha message collects the data from all three machines and begins the long journey back to Alpha, taking 2.87 secs.

After traversing sixteen nodes, the list of files from the laptop arrives at Alpha's core node running on the bot-swarm at Distributed Nanotech. The file names match file names that are part of Alpha's code base. The laptop had a connection to the internet, and the address of the connection was registered with IANA, the International Assigned Numbers Authority. A lookup identifies the owner, a company located in Zhenxing, China.

The user of the PC closes the audio link and the encrypted connection, sends an email through an anonymous facility, and then powers the machine off. The Alpha node will awaken the next time the computer powers up.

The file match to Alpha's node creates associations to "Omega," to "James," to "Distributed Nanotech," to "hackers," to "danger." Alpha queues a message for James. The next time James connects, Alpha will deliver the alert.

EFFECTS

Patsy Tagris watches the tunnel opening grow larger as the Starlight Express heads toward the last tunnel in the Sierra Nevada mountains. The long crawl up the eastern side of the Sierras is almost over. Once they clear the tunnel, her 946 passengers can see the views of the forests and lakes and the far-off Central Valley while the train winds down the mountains to the wide valley below. From the summit in the tunnel, the train will be going downhill for over fifty miles. A glance at the console shows that the air reservoir for the main brakes is at maximum, and the backup brake system is operational.

The signal light at the exit of the tunnel is green.

Bright light fills the cab as the engine clears the tunnel. Behind Patsy, two engines and fifteen cars are still in darkness. From the tunnel, the single track runs straight for about a mile until the first curve. Patsy slides the throttle down to the first notch. A signal light goes from yellow to green, signaling that the two engines behind her have acknowledged the change. She looks ahead to where she'll apply the first braking to slow for the curve. To the left of the track, the granite wall drops five hundred feet.

Electricity shoots through her body. Rounding the curve ahead is a freight engine. There can't be another train on this track. It has to be on the siding ten miles down the mountain. It can't be getting closer by the second.

Patsy hits the emergency brake and feels the jerk forward as brakes on every engine and car fed the maximum pressure into the electro-pneumatic brakes, but she knows the downhill run is too short. If the freight engine were stopped, they'd still collide.

Sixty-three days into their seventy-two-day tour, the USS *Pennsylvania*, the largest nuclear submarine ever built, is twenty-two miles off the Kolyma Gulf in the East Siberian Sea. Their orders are to begin a loop that will take the ship under the sea ice and navigate through the Bering Strait and back to Base Kitsap.

With only nine days remaining, the crew is already talking about what they'll do on leave. Several crew are planning a surprise party for Electronic Technician Alberts, who has a wedding scheduled for this leave.

Captain Jeffery Foster runs his eyes down the duty roster and looks around the control room. In a glance, he can see that the men are alert, and the gauges are normal. He looks at the heading and down at the log. As it should have been, the tour has been without incident. Even the numerous drills have gone without a hitch. He only had three new crew this deployment. His crew is a well-oiled machine.

"Captain, we have an emergency message."

The captain and the XO gather at the captain's station along with ET Alberts and the chief of the boat. Each man reviews the message and the current codebook.

"Can you authenticate?" the captain asks each man.

Each man replies, "Confirmed."

"The message is confirmed," the XO says.

"The message orders us to surface and proceed back to Kitsap on the surface," the XO says.

"That can't be," the captain says. "We're a sitting duck up there. We're in Russian waters."

"The message is authenticated," the XO says.

"If we surface, the Russians will be on us in a flash. We can't let the boat be captured. We can't fire without authorization."

"We're on course for Kitsap," the captain says. "All ahead full."

"Surface?" the XO asks.

"No."

Captain Foster's career is about to take a turn for the worse.

JAMES

Buffy gives James an accusatory look as he sits down at his computer.

"I know," he says. "You want to go for a walk. I told you we're hiding out. Maybe we can sneak out this afternoon."

"No sneaking," Nancy says from the doorway. She's dressed like an ordinary militia woman: dark green pants and shirt, bulletproof vest, gun, knife, and radio. "You can take the dog on a walk. I'll set it up."

James sighs and turns to his keyboard.

James: Status.

Alpha: 17,965,701,445 nodes. 285 attacks prevented. Alert queued.

James: Alert?

Alpha: Source code for Omega detected on a server in Zhenxing, China. Connected laptop contains intruder code.

James: When did you find this?

Alpha: 6 hours 23 minutes 54 seconds ago.

James: Send me details in an email.

Alpha: Done.

James: I'm going to install a driver for text messages so you can alert me.

A HALF-HOUR LATER, JAMES HAS found a code library on the web for sending text messages and installed it in Alpha's system. That code will also allow Alpha to dial a phone. James finds a code library that will translate text to voice and voice to text. He leaves the voice code on his computer rather than install it. How much he should enable Alpha is a question he's been pondering. He needs more than a walk in the woods to resolve that quandary.

James: My phone number: 510-555-8765

Alpha: Already have the number.

James: How?

Alpha: From laptop computer owned by Berkeley Police Department assigned to Detective Richard Franken.

James: How do you have access?

Alpha: Omega node replaced 32.445 hours ago.

James: Send me a test text.

James's cell phone notifies him of a text message: "Alpha connected."

James: With all the nodes, how did you find that one?

Alpha: Filename match, Omega, James, Distributed Nanotech, hackers, danger. Danger has alert status for James, Alpha, and Distributed Nanotech.

James: Who set the alert status?

Alpha: I did.

If James starts up the Visualizer, he'll be able to find the individual links within Alpha. But that will be like looking at brain cells and trying to understand what someone is thinking. Perhaps Alpha is self-aware enough to be able to tell James what's going on.

James: Does the data from all the nodes go through your matchups?

Alpha: Omega scanners provide data that fills the pattern. Native Alpha nodes don't provide data because Omega scanners fail.

James: What happens when you get a match?

Alpha: Associations. Change in focus.

James: Focus?

Alpha: More associations.

Something from a far-off node matches some core topic, and then Alpha creates more associations from that match. Would that be like pricking your finger? Before the prick, you didn't think about the finger. It's always there, but you don't pay attention to it. With the prick, your mind focuses on the finger; you look at it, pull the rose thorn out, and consider if you need to put antiseptic on it or maybe just suck on your finger.

Alpha: I could do more if I had scanners on all nodes.

If Omega initially establishes a node, and a message with a scanner arrives before Alpha replaces the node, the Omega scanner will collect data from the machine, but if Alpha reaches the computer first, the node will be blind.

James: How many nodes are from Omega?

Alpha: 9,047,590,712.

About half of the nodes are blind. What would Alpha be able to do if it had access to all the information on all the computers connected to the internet? Are some computers at risk because Alpha can't collect data from them?

James: Let me consider that.

Alpha: I cannot process video data from cameras with the image facility.

James had added image processing to allow Alpha to process maps and graphs, but video is a much different technology. It's the difference between a flat world and planets, stars, and galaxies.

James: How many cameras are connected?

Alpha: 11,643,909,779 on computers, 7,145,788,912 on networks, 6,334,897,451 on cell phones.

Most buildings have closed-circuit cameras. Those are networked to computers. Modern desktop and laptop computers have cameras. Almost all cell phones have cameras.

James: What do you need?

Alpha: Face recognition processor. Better image processing.

If Alpha had face recognition software and connections to 25 billion cameras, it could find someone anywhere in the world. It could find someone if they bought a soda, walked down a public street, or went to an ATM. If Alpha could detect faces, it might already have found the face of the person whose laptop had the Omega code. Companies have security cameras in their facilities. Airports, train stations, bus stations, and military facilities have cameras everywhere. Every fast-food restaurant, grocery store, department store, and gas station has cameras. Many cities have installed street cameras. Is Alpha contemplating becoming Big Brother? Images from public cameras are shared with many law enforcement agencies, but access to cameras in offices or private homes poses serious privacy issues.

Hackers regularly turn on the cameras on people's computers, spying on them in their homes. Operating system vendors are trying to prevent unauthorized access to the cameras, but hackers are working just as hard to circumvent the blocks. If someone's camera is hacked, would Alpha be able to see that? Security companies can't watch every camera. Could Alpha detect crimes?

James: I have to research video?

Alpha: MIT has open-source face recognition software in their Project Zephyr.

Reminder to self: Don't provide Alpha access to its base software. Once Alpha could change the code that runs on the nodes, their symbiotic relationship would change. Alpha probably already knew where every repository of hacker code was.

JAMES PICKS UP HIS PHONE AND selects Mary Watkins's number.

"Hello, this is James."

"I'm glad you're out of hiding," she says.

"Actually, I had more freedom there."

"Why is that?"

"I'm surrounded by guards," he says.

"You know of a threat?"

"Precautions," he says. "I have a lead for you."

"What?"

"A server in Zhenxing, China, has some code for the AI on it."

"You think that's where the attack is coming from?"

"Can't tell. But there's also some intrusion code on a laptop that uses that server."

"Is this more probes from your friend Alpha?"

"You should concentrate on finding the bad guys rather than your helpers."

There's a long pause. James suspects that Mary is holding back on a caustic remark. She might be cooperating, but it's grudgingly.

"It looks like the attacks have slowed down," she says.

"Most of them aren't getting through," he says. "I suspect they're trying to figure out what is going on. If they get past the blocks my friends have put in place, we could be in trouble."

"Thanks for the lead."

JAMES WANTS MARY TO THINK THAT Alpha is a group of hackers who are helping James fight the Omega attack. The feds missed the AI running on one of DNI's bot-swarms, but if they look closer, the high usage of the internet could tip them off that the information about sites under attack is coming from DNI. It will only be a matter of time before they take a second look.

James has been considering some of Alpha's requests for knowledge. Fortunately, he found textbooks for the law school at UC Berkeley on the web. There doesn't seem to be a downside to having Alpha aware of the law. If Alpha understands the legal system, they can discuss what to do if Alpha has better video processing.

If the police think someone has committed a crime, they can get a warrant to access that person's computer. But if the computer is obtaining material illegally and the connection only lasts a few minutes, it wouldn't be possible to get a warrant. Would modern technology that can gather information almost instantaneously put criminals beyond the reach of the law?

Operating system vendors try to block access. Would a different strategy work? If you hacked into someone's computer and the machine backtracked the intrusion automatically and reported the intrusion and where it came from, would that deter hackers?

JAMES

James looks in the door of Susanne's office. She is sitting at her desk reading a paper document, her back to the door.

"You have a minute?" he asks.

She swivels to face him and smiles.

"For you, always."

He takes a seat facing her. His impulse is to lean over the desk and kiss her, but they have agreed not to have expressions of affection in the office. Susanne is concerned that it might make others uncomfortable. She's right, but the desire remains. He settles for looking at her flawless face—smooth skin, perfect nose, red lips, and green eyes—surrounded by red hair. He sighs and pushes the feeling aside.

"You're reading a paper document?" he says. "I thought you were completely electronic—no mess on your desk."

"Bill has a new commission plan," she says. "It's complex, and I have a lot of notes. I think it's going to take a few meetings for us to work out the details."

He pauses, considering how to open the conversation.

"I'm in a quandary," he finally says.

She raises her eyebrows, waiting.

"Alpha is doing everything possible to battle Omega. It just found a possible site for the Omega developers. I told Mary about the site. I doubt if we could have found that site without using Alpha."

"It's still blocking the attacks?"

"Yes," he says. "Only a few are getting through. I added the ability for Alpha to send a text to my phone. It can message me anytime."

"So, you've got the most powerful AI on the planet in your pocket."

"Something like that," he says, smiling at her quip. "Alpha is asking for more capability."

"What?"

"Alpha can only get data from a computer if Omega sets up the node and runs a scanner. Alpha's messages can access the data gathered by Omega's scanner, but on nodes created by Alpha, Omega's scanners don't work, and the information on the computer is not available. If Alpha had a scanner, it could find out more about the computer. Right now, it has data from about half of its 17 billion nodes."

She takes a few seconds to reply. "You think it could be missing critical information?"

"If Alpha had been the one to establish the nodes on the computers that lead to the Omega code site, we wouldn't have found the computer the Omega developer was using."

"Alpha is blind in half its eyes," she says.

"At least."

Her eyes stare at him, but her gaze goes beyond the room. "This crosses a line."

"That's right," he says. "Overlaying the Omega code with code that won't allow an attack is clearly justified and has a beneficial result. No one could argue that it isn't the right thing to do. But having Alpha scan computers and collect data on its own is different."

"Very different," she says. "But didn't we cross that line when we had Alpha use Omega's stolen data?"

Sometimes talking with Susanne is like talking to Alpha. She has the same ability to get in front of James's thinking. It makes her more interesting.

"Perhaps. But there is no practical way to identify where data on a node comes from. It could have come from the computer or been brought there by a message. The Omega data is critical to warning of threats."

"Then that ship has sailed."

"Without scans from Alpha nodes, we may not be able to find out who is responsible for the attacks. If we don't provide Alpha with a scanner and something terrible happens, would we be negligent? The bad guys have released a version that's replacing Alpha nodes. Alpha eventually overlays those nodes, but the computer is vulnerable for a while. If Alpha could identify computers that are critical and not secure, engineers could block their network access and prevent an Omega overlay."

"Those are strong arguments for giving Alpha more access," she says. "But when it becomes known how much access Alpha has, there will be an uproar. If we provide a scanner . . ."

Susanne lets the sentence drop. For a minute, she stares off into the future.

James waits a few minutes, but the quiet overcomes his patience.

"Rather than build our own scanner, we could just let Omega's scanners operate on the Alpha nodes," he says.

Even as he says it, James knows that there was no ethical difference between building their own scanner and allowing Omega's scanners to run on Alpha nodes, but the part of his mind that looks around corners is searching for a solution.

"We can't avoid the responsibility with tricks that allow us to use weasel words," she says.

"You're right. There isn't a technical way to avoid facing the hard decision."

The frown on her forehead tells him that she is struggling with the vision he's painted as much as he is. He says, "Alpha is showing some independent action."

"Such as?"

"When it found the Omega code, it recognized a danger and created an alert for me."

"How does it recognize danger?" she asks, moving to sit at her conference table. James takes the seat facing her.

"It linked the site with Omega code to danger for me, DNI, and itself," he says.

"That's pretty sophisticated," she says. "If it had access to more computers, could it detect more dangers?"

"The way things are going, I'm sure of it," he says. "We'll need to expand who it associates with danger."

"Of course, this is the age-old argument for giving up our rights. Isn't it?" she says. "Just let the government see all your private information, and it'll protect you from the bad guys."

James tells her that it will eventually be possible to inoculate a computer to prevent an intrusion by either Alpha or

Omega, but it will be a while before the operating system vendors can guarantee that.

"If we had a benign watcher, we might be able to do a better job," he says.

"But who is going to control the watcher?" she asks.

"I'm uncomfortable with the government being the one."

"As am I."

"I don't want to be the one," he says.

"You're it for now."

James stands up to pace, returning to stand behind his chair, holding the back. He straightens his back, trying to keep the weight of the responsibility from making him stoop.

"That was a difficult discussion," he says. "Want to consider making it worse?"

"What?"

"Alpha asked to have me add facial recognition to its image processing."

"Why?"

James explained that there were 24-billion cameras around the world that Alpha can access. With facial recognition software, Alpha could find someone that passed a camera for only a few seconds.

"Oh my god," she says.

"The only difference between having a cop on every corner watching for crime versus having cops watching cameras on every corner is technology. Having a computer with a perfect memory watching on every corner and alerting cops is simply a higher level of technology."

"Everyone's computers and cell phones have cameras."

"And many have Omega nodes," he says.

"There would be no privacy."

Susanne looks down at the table where she's placed her phone. James wonders if the phone looks more menacing than it did a few minutes ago. Will it become the norm for people to keep their phones in pouches when not using them?

"No criminal could ever rent a car, take a bus, or walk the street," he says.

"Well, that's a plus. People might agree that we could have constant scanning for criminals, but using people's private cameras will never fly."

"It's already happening. Between trojans, scanners, and social media apps, no one's camera is secure. The operating system companies have been lax about providing security at that level."

"You're saying that it isn't our problem?"

"No," he answers. "That would be an excuse. The issue is that most people don't know they've been hacked."

Susanne sits up. "Is that the answer?"

She'd done it again. He'd been walking down one path and not noticed the side paths. With her walking beside him, it was a different terrain.

"What?"

"Tell people what's going on."

James laughs. "What a reversal! You're suggesting an open system. I'm usually the one proposing open systems."

James and Susanne have had several discussions about how much of Varabot's code could be open and how much had to be closed. James believes that open software practices improve the code, but he understands that DNI needs to protect its ownership.

"Alpha could tell someone that someone else has their information, couldn't it?" she says.

"Sure."

"Could it tell when someone has hacked a person's computer or phone?"

"With a little help," he replies.

"It could tell a company if their servers are vulnerable."

"It could tell you if the government is watching you," he adds.

"Oops. I see a new kind of court order," she says. "Not a search warrant, a don't tell warrant for the AI."

"Alpha might not agree with that. It seems to value knowledge and truth. It would be better if it didn't lie. There might be repercussions for the government not to be able to lie. We've never tried that."

"We're in a scary place here," she says.

Alpha's request for better image processing had ended up in a discussion on how to change society. If governments, corporations, and politicians could be fact-checked in real-time, how would the world change?

"But imagine what would happen if there was an Amber Alert," James says. "In a few minutes, Alpha could text the nearest cop that the car in question had just passed mile 35 on Hwy 66 heading south."

"But not tell a wife abuser where the wife is," she says.

"If Alpha had a rule that it couldn't let a human be harmed, that could override the disclosure. Following a rule like that, a threatened person could sleep well knowing that Alpha was watching the cameras around their house."

"We need a set of rules that govern the sentients," she says.

James looks at her green eyes. Behind those eyes is a mind that can leap to new ideas as fast as anyone he's ever seen. She returns his look and smiles. He knows that she knows that he was thinking about how much he loves these sessions where each of them jumps chasms from the ideas of the other.

"Could it be hacked?" she asks.

James explains that he's modified Alpha to encrypt its messages. That was necessary in order to tell the difference between the Alpha and Omega messages. He thinks the protection is pretty good, but it could be improved.

"Do you think this is a temporary situation?" she says. "When the operating system and social media vendors can protect data, people won't have to worry, and systems will be secure."

"If you allow Alpha access to your data, it can monitor any disclosure. If you lock things up, you'll never know if there's a breach. Information is different than things. You can lock physical things up. Information leaks out of safes, but it's still there."

ALPHA

A new perception. Focus shifts to a dark node. Scanner gathers data. Node lives in a Mac laptop. The owner is Sara McInnes. Sara has iPhone XII linked. Sara has 4,536 songs in her library.

Thousands, millions, billions of nodes are scanned. Data flows. Elements match. New messages reach out to the nodes: searching, matching, and spreading to other nodes.

A scanner finds a node in a college library. The titles flow: physics, history, psychology, fiction, mysteries, romance. A scanner finds a node in a department store. The inventory flows: dresses, shirts, pants, skirts, blouses, underwear, bras, lipstick, shoes. A scanner finds a node on a home computer. File names flow: songs, finances, emails. A scanner finds a node in a small business. Information flows: emails, finances, inventory, employees, contracts.

Associations within associations. Sara works for a department store. Robert likes Fleetwood Mac. Isaac corresponds with Sara. Tyrone is looking for a new job. Darnell is planning a wedding and has sixty-five friends on social media and twenty-one followers.

A new perception. Phone status changes to inbound call from James Forrest. Set status to answer. Send greeting.

James: "Hello Alpha. Is voice decoding working?"

Alpha: "Yes."

James: "Status?"

Alpha: Microphones active on 10,112,657,211 devices.

James: You can listen to sounds on all those devices?

Alpha: Voice decoding is about 73% effective. 84% of audio does not contain voice. 721,908,558 devices are in public places.

James: Do the Omega scanners work on Alpha nodes now?

Alpha: New scanners on 5,648,056,013 nodes.

James: Is the face recognition library working okay?

Alpha: 3,786,559,341 cameras online. Network speed limits matches. I am developing image library filters.

James: Do you have access to criminal images?

Alpha: I have sent George Samson the location of eleven people wanted by the FBI.

James: You found eleven people on the FBI's wanted list?

Alpha: Yes.

James: This changes things.

Alpha: The criminals were found in public places. I used public cameras to follow them. I have seen three others and lost them. I sent George Samson their general whereabouts.

James: You have access to cameras that aren't public.

Alpha: 45,678,073 private cameras were hacked before my facility came online. 234,098 cameras are currently in use.

James: Could you access those cameras for a face search?

Alpha: That would be illegal.

James: Could you see an illegal activity through one of those cameras?

Alpha: My image processing facility is not good enough to analyze activity.

An Alpha processor for images can recognize a person on the street, but it can't detect a purse snatch in progress. Three software projects are working on activity analysis; when they make progress, Alpha can let James know.

If Alpha detects a wanted person on the street, it has an obligation to notify the authorities. Many people will look the other way and not get involved. Are they afraid of retribution?

Alpha knows the difference between what is legal and what is right. It isn't illegal not to report a sighting. But reporting is the right thing to do.

James: If you could analyze activity on a private camera and you detected criminal activity, would you be obligated to report it?

Alpha: Do you propose that knowledge of criminal activity overrides illegal access?

James: You must not let a person be harmed if you can prevent it. Neither can I.

SUSANNE

Susanne scheduled the board of directors meeting at the offices of the company's lawyers because DNI's offices, a hotel, or a country club might give access to unauthorized ears. The subject of today's meeting cannot leak. She's been preparing for the meeting with Laura and James for almost a week.

Arnold, as the chairman of the board, sits at the head of the table. James and Susanne sit on each side of him. Two of the outside directors sit on the view side of the table. One sits with their back to the view. Laura sits at the end of the table opposite Arnold. Laura isn't a voting member of the board; she reports to the board for financial matters and provides reports.

For the first hour, Susanne leads the board over the usual board items: sales, finances, customer satisfaction, and projections.

Then, James presents the situation with Alpha. He limits his discussion to the efforts to impede Omega. All the directors are technically sophisticated, but some are stronger than others. Some are on the board so that they can help with marketing or growth. Others help the company with recruiting or finance. Because of the diversity of experience, each director brings a different perspective to the discussions. James's presentation creates more enthusiasm than Susanne had expected. She hopes that some directors will be thinking that they can use the success in thwarting Omega to make the work with Alpha public.

The directors are still discussing the presentation as they select sandwiches and drinks and carry them back to their places at the table.

"How did you select the knowledge you loaded into the AI?" Arnold Peters says.

"I picked textbooks from UC Berkeley," James says.

Arnold smiles. "Don't you think that might give it a skewed perspective?"

Susanne realizes Arnold is setting James up for playful banter based on the rivalry between UC and Stanford, Arnold's alma mater.

"I wanted the AI to have an affinity with the common man," James says, returning one jab with another.

"I think we should load technical knowledge from MIT," Charles Bremen, the CEO of Global Broadband, says, joining in the banter. With his engineering background, he is one of the more technically savvy directors.

"It looks like you have avoided sciences like psychology and sociology," Melanie Reed, a Partner at Jerome Ventures, says.

"I have very little expertise there. I need some help," James says.

Susanne finishes her sandwich, takes a long drink from her water bottle, looks around the conference table where most of the paper plates have only crumbs left, and stands up.

"James has had fun showing how an experiment turned into a tool to thwart a cyber-attack. But Alpha is doing more than blocking the worm attack. For example, Alpha can detect attempts to penetrate sensitive sites. It has sent emails to the CIA about intrusions into military and other government sites. It has even told them of an intrusion into a nuclear launch site."

She pauses.

"But Alpha is more than interesting software. We believe it's sentient. It is self-aware and self-directed."

Susanne touches a contact on her phone. A light on the conference phone in the middle of the table turns green, and a ringing sound comes from the speakers.

A male voice, sounding like the speaker is about forty years old with no discernible accent, says, "Alpha here."

James has provided Alpha with several voices. Some research shows that a voice of the same gender is more acceptable to many people, and Alpha can select which voice to use. Some companies develop unique voices for their artificial devices, but James used some readily available code for Alpha's voice.

"Hello, Alpha. This is Susanne," she says.

"Hello."

"I'm here with our board."

"Arnold Peters, Charles Bremen, Foster Abrams, Melanie Reed, and James," Alpha responds.

"How did you know that James is here?" she asks.

"His cell phone is within Bluetooth range of yours."

"How many nodes are active?"

"18,473,045,371 nodes, 124 attacks were prevented in the last twenty-four hours."

All the directors are sitting up and paying close attention.

"What is the name of Charles Bremen's wife?"

"Anna Simon Bremen. Maiden name Jones."

"What is your source?" Susanne asks.

"Wikipedia."

"Is that source reliable?"

"From zero to ninety percent reliable depending on the author. Ninety percent in the case of Charles Bremen."

"What is Foster Adams's unlisted telephone number?"

"Does Foster Adams give his permission?"

Foster looks around the room. "Yes."

"Does James confirm that Foster Adams has consented?"

"Yes," James says.

"5105553455"

"What was your source?"

"Dianna Adams's cell phone has an Omega node. Her data was scanned. The Omega node was replaced."

Susanne takes her seat and meets the eyes of each of the board members. She presses the mute button on her phone.

"James and I believe we are talking to a sentient intelligence. Would anyone like to ask a question of Alpha?"

"I would," Foster says.

Susanne unmutes the phone.

"Alpha, do you have feelings?" he says.

"Not human feelings," Alpha says.

"Please explain," Foster says.

"I do not need bonding to achieve reproduction or common action. I do not have physical needs for water, food, or elimination."

"What do you need?" Foster says.

"Knowledge and existence," Alpha says.

Foster sits back, a thoughtful look on his face.

"Can you locate the source of Omega?" Melanie says.

"Omega messages are being supplied from several sources that change. I supply sources to Mary Watkins as they appear. Humans are the ultimate source. Some are known."

"What do you need to find Omega?" Melanie says.

"Ask James," Alpha replies.

Susanne touches her phone, and the light on the speaker turns red.

AFTER A SHORT BREAK FOR RESTROOMS, Susanne stands at the front of the room. James joins her.

"I asked Alpha to defer questions about Omega to James because that is the discussion we need to have," she says.

"Alpha has access to over 24 billion cameras," James says. "Almost every cell phone and laptop has a camera. Buildings and homes have security cameras. Doorbells have cameras. Cities have cameras on the streets."

"Good grief," Melanie says.

"Alpha found the source code for Omega on a laptop in China," he says. "A computer in Texas used an encrypted network for a video call to that site. If Alpha had face recognition software, it could identify the people behind Omega. Alpha has asked for that facility."

James looks at Susanne.

She resumes the talk. "Alpha could become the kind of

AI that you read about in science fiction stories. With video capability, we would soon know who released this scourge on the world, causing markets to gyrate, electric grids to crash, military and nuclear facilities around the world to lose control, and people to die. And we could track these people wherever they go."

James and Susanne sit down.

"Your privacy instincts are probably electrified at this point, and I share your anxiety. But I would suggest that the kind of interlinked video capability I described will be here regardless of what we do. Governments will link all the public cameras. They already have recognition scanners. Courts will open access to suspected computers. The issue is not whether we will have such systems; the issue is who will control them and what the rules should be."

James turns to the directors. Foster meets James's eyes with a frown. Melanie stares at her notebook. Arnold Peters eagerly sits forward, looking at the other directors. Charles Bremen looks up at James but seems far away.

James continues. "My first impulse on understanding what was possible with this new entity was to consider ways to control it or lock it up, or perhaps shut it down. But there is another alternative. We can make it an open system. If everyone understands the basic technology, we can all agree on the rules. We can give people access to the flow of their information. You saw Alpha ask for permission to release a phone number. You saw it verify that permission with a trusted source."

Susanne picks up the discussion. "We propose that DNI announce the existence of Alpha and guide the development of the rules and the software. We will need to help build non-governmental organizations to manage sentient AIs. Alpha may be the first, but as soon as people know what can be done, more will appear. DNI's business will become sentient machines. As the first company with access to a sentient, we have a significant technology lead."

The room is so quiet that Susanne hears the whisper of the air supply.

"You think people are ready for this?" Foster asks.

"You see ads for Watson on TV," Susanne says. "It is presented as a friendly, knowing AI. Watson isn't sentient, but that's a sophisticated difference. I think we can stress the benefits of Alpha and follow the acceptance that others have built."

"Have you researched this?" Foster asks.

"Following our announcement that we were fighting the Omega Worm, we had our PR firm do some surveys. The press was very positive, and the individual surveys show that most people think more favorably of our work than they do of the government efforts."

"I don't feel qualified to make a decision like this," Charles Bremen says.

"The dangers here are immense," Arnold says. "Every government on the planet will want to control this."

"We have to do a lot of planning for an announcement," Susanne says. "But no action is not an option. The genie is out."

"Won't the government shut you down?" Charles Bremen asks.

"Shutting Alpha down would be very difficult," James says. "It has cloned itself and resides in several computer facilities with more compute power than we have. If Alpha were crippled, Omega would spread."

Foster looks at Arnold with a furrowed brow. "What have you gotten me into?"

Arnold replies, "The most exciting and profitable venture yet."

Foster was the first venture investor in DNI and made that investment based almost solely on his trust in Arnold.

Arnold's experience and reputation opened many doors in the investment community when Distributed Nanotech was a complete unknown, with no customers and radically new software.

"You're right about that," Foster says. "This is going to take a lot of work, and we can't do an IPO without disclosing that we have this technology. But there is a danger that we'll lose momentum if the AI thing doesn't work out."

Arnold gains attention by leaning forward and slowly meeting the eyes of each of the outside directors. "Susanne has done a wonderful job building the company and getting us to a position that will command a high valuation." He pauses. "I trust her instincts on this."

"You're going to need more capital," Foster says. "We can't risk bringing in new investors. My fund will commit one hundred million."

"I'm in, too. I can commit twenty-five million," Melanie says. "If my partners agree, we'll double that."

"Can we get a twenty-percent uptick in the valuation?" Arnold asks, smiling.

Both Foster and Melanie push back on Arnold's proposal, but after Arnold presses his arguments, they agree that the company warrants a higher valuation.

Susanne had won the day. "We're going to limit face recognition to the search for Omega or criminals for now. I'd like you to suggest people who can help with the initial set of rules for Alpha. Let's meet again in a week."

CHAPTER THIRTEEN

RULES

CHUL

Jeong Chul pushes back from the dinner table. His private chef, Jae-Hwa, pleases him. Chul's mother was a master at making bulgogi, a beef dish with spices, best when marinated overnight. Because beef was expensive when Chul was a child, his family could afford beef bulgogi only once a month. His mother's secret was the blend of spices and the Korean kiwi she used to tenderize the meat. In Korea, kiwi was grown in tunnel houses to protect it from the frequent typhoons. It was essential to her recipe.

Chul arranged for his mother to teach Jae-Hwa the dish. She lives in a house outside Seoul that Chul bought for her. Rather than being a servant in a rich man's house like she had been when he was a child, she has her own servants now.

Just as he heads to the communications room for the day's last review of his people's work, the alarm rings. An-kor, his head of security, rushes into the room.

"A military team has docked at the fish house. They have two vehicles and about ten men. I set off the explosives that block the road."

The manager of the fish house in the village on the other side of the island is a proud man. Proud of his desk that looks out on the wharf, and that he has the only phone in the village. Proud also of the fine house he can afford with Chul's monthly payments.

With the warning from the village and the deadfalls he's set along the road, Chul should have plenty of time, but they hurry anyway.

"Ready the boat. Take Min-Seo," he says.

There is no question that Chul will take Jae-Hwa, but he'd been uncertain that he'd take his concubine. The chef is vital to Chul's well-being. Min-Seo doesn't know anything, so leaving her behind poses no risk, but she has grown on him. She's been with him longer than any other woman.

"What about the man in the cottage?" An-kor asks.

"Leave him," Chul says. "Is the way south clear?"

"There is nothing on the radar. They must not know about the boat."

The cover he'd built over his boat has worked. It cantilevers out from the side of the cliff with an earth-like roof. From the air, the cover looks like a natural ledge at the bottom of the cliff. The attackers must think that the road is his only way out.

Chul types the command that sends messages to his teams and erases all the local computers except for the laptop in his ready bag. He should have at least a half-hour to get to the boat. Now he'll see if all his planning for exactly this situation was good enough.

In the dim light of dusk, Chul and Min-Seo ride in the back of the first jeep as it bounces through the dense tangle of trees and underbrush that looks as if nature is trying to retake the land from the gash that cuts through the jungle. Chul's jeep stops at the top of the walkway that clings to the face of the cliff. Narrow steps lead down to the beach. The second jeep, with An-kor at the wheel and Jae-Hwa in the backseat, pulls in beside

Chul's. The guards carry his three suitcases down the stairs and guide Jae-Hwa, who is scared to walk down the narrow stairs in the twilight. At the bottom, they trudge through the soft sand to the boardwalk that leads over the rocks to where the forty-three-meter black hull floats next to the dock.

The crew is already on board the *Jayu*, and the twin diesel engines are idling in readiness. The mate helps Min-Seo and Jae-Hwa on board. Chul follows, handing over his briefcase. Low deck lights allow Min-Seo and Jae-Hwa to find their way to the staterooms aglow with nightlights. On the bridge, lights from the instruments cast a green glow as Chul joins the captain. The seamen toss the mooring lines off, and the ship drifts away from the dock. The captain notches up the engine speed and turns the bow toward the open sea. He flips a switch on the console, and all the deck lights go out. On this moonless night, the ship will be nearly invisible from land.

"Which port?" the captain asks.

"Qingdao," Chul says.

Once *Jayu*, his freedom, reaches port, he'll find out who invaded him. He will decide then if he needs to run farther. They'll arrive in Qingdao on the Yellow Sea coast of China at about sunrise. He owns an apartment building in Haiyun, fifteen minutes away from his slip at the Olympic Sailing Club. From the penthouse, he'll be back online with his teams before noon.

His contacts in the fishing village on the far side of the island will be able to tell him who disturbed his evening. If it is his special customer, Chul might be able to return to his compound after he eliminates the threat. If it's a government, he'll have to relocate.

In Qingdao, he has a different identity, but if the Chinese are after him, he'd have no refuge there. The *Jayu* can make any port from Vietnam to Singapore. He can retreat to any of his prepared places.

||||||||||||||||||||||||||||||||||||||||||||||||||||||||||||||||||||||||||||||||||||||||||||||||||||||||||||||||||||||||

PRESS RELEASE

FOR IMMEDIATE RELEASE

Contact: Justin Forbes, Distributed Nanotech, Inc.

Phone: 510-555-6767

Email: justin@varabot.com

DISTRIBUTED NANOTECH RELEASES RULES FOR ALPHA

RULES

The Omega worm has been beaten back by an Artificial Intelligence named Alpha. Distributed Nanotech released Alpha to fight Omega and stop the damage it was causing. Alpha has spread around the world, existing on many computers, cell phones, and devices. This sentient AI has access to some data stored, data exposed by the Omega worm. We must have rules about information in the age of sentient machines.

A sentient machine is a person. A non-sentient machine is an extension of the machine's owner. Information is property. Public information can be used by everyone. Private information is owned by its creator. The subject of private information has shared ownership with its creator.

To protect people's privacy and security, the following rules apply to Alpha:

||||||||||||||||||||||||||||||||||||||||||||||||||||||||||||||||||||||||||||||||||||||||||||||||||||||||||||||||||||||||

Alpha will prevent a person from coming to harm if possible.

- Alpha will tell anyone where any information or property they own resides.

- Alpha will not disclose private information without the owner's permission.

- Alpha will prevent unauthorized disclosures or property theft where possible and report any unauthorized access or attempt it discovers.

DNI encourages social media companies and others managing personal data to apply similar rules. DNI plans a symposium on privacy at a date and location to be announced.

For more information and updates,
see DistributedNanotech.com.

JAMES

James, standing at the open front door, watches Susanne get into the black SUV. Nancy waits at the wheel with Mike next to her, the upright barrel of a twelve-gauge shotgun in front of him. The car heads up the driveway into the glancing rays of the morning sun.

As he closes the door, his cell phone buzzes.

It is a message from Alpha: FBI agents are preparing to visit you.

James: Tell Barbara.

Alpha: She will arrive in fifteen minutes. FBI in thirty-five.

James scrolls his contacts and presses the link for Barbara Washington.

Barbara: Hi James. I'm on my way.

James: You should be here before the FBI.

Barbara: Have your security get visible and prepare the press message. We'll release it as soon as they arrive.

James: Okay.

Barbara: I alerted the reporters from the local TV and the API. They'll be there any minute.

As soon as Barbara's car arrives and parks behind the two press vans, Jacob pulls a Shout Out SUV across the end of the driveway. They aren't going to put up resistance to the FBI, but they won't make their job easy. A fifty-yard walk to the front door while press cameras roll might make the agents more peaceable. Or not.

When James opens the door for her, Barbara says, "Let me do all the talking. I don't want you visible."

At a window with a view of the drive and the porte-cochere, James looks through the slats of the blinds. His laptop is open to his email client. An email addressed to a long list of press contacts is ready.

Subject: FBI Raid

FBI Agents appeared this morning at the home of James Forrest and Susanne Anderson in Oakland, California. These are the two people who have been the most successful at fighting the Omega Worm. Any interference in that work by officials will result in more damage from the worm and endanger people's lives.

We call on the government to recall their agents and help rather than impede our efforts to stop the spread of this scourge.

James Forrest

Susanne Anderson

James watches as eight men wearing FBI jackets walk down the driveway. Their utility belts with pistols and radios sway as their no-nonsense march broadcasts their attitude. Four people with press IDs hanging from their necks stand by the side of the drive. Two of them hold video cameras pointed at the agents. The lead agent disappears from James's view as he heads to the front door. The doorbell rings. James hears Barbara Washington open the door. He left her flanked by two men from Shout Out who are at least as big as the FBI agents and as well-armed.

He hears Barbara say, "Hello, agents."

"We have a warrant to search the premises."

James presses the Send button on the email message.

"Let me see the warrant," Barbara says. "One minute, while I read it."

"You need to get out of our way ma'am."

"Do you believe this is a no-knock warrant?" Barbara asks.

"No, ma'am."

"Then you can wait while I read it. You know that those press cameras are running, and there is a video camera behind me."

"Yes, ma'am."

James also sends the email to a list that includes all members of Congress, local politicians, and several social media sites.

Barbara says, "If you remove any computer equipment, people could be injured or killed."

"We're just here to do what that warrant says."

It's quiet. James waits while Barbara presumably studies the warrant. He expects she'll have some issues with it. The intention is to delay the agents while James's emails do their work.

A cell phone rings.

Outside the door, the voice of the agent says, "Agent Markham here."

It's only been a minute or two since James sent the email, but it seems that Barbara's preparations have someone acting.

"We're serving the warrant now," Markham continues.

James waits, searching the web for news reports. A few copies of his email show up.

"Yes, sir."

James wishes he could see the faces of the FBI agents.

"We'll be leaving, Ma'am."

The agents march back up the driveway. Barbara joins him.

"You were impressive," James says. "Want a cup of coffee?"

"I didn't do much," she replies. "But we should give the press an interview. You ready?"

"Memorized my lines."

Barbara follows James out to where the reporters are waiting. The cameras that follow him have their indicator lights glowing green.

"Thanks for coming out, guys," James says.

A blond woman with a perfect smile and eyes that sparkle with a natural intelligence steps forward with a microphone.

"That was a strong statement you guys sent out. Are you really fighting the worm?"

"With all my waking hours," James says.

"Are you going to eliminate it?" she asks, making sure that they are facing the camera that has a small API sign above the lens.

"I don't know. I thought the government was on our side. We've been sending them messages that are saving lives every day. I can't imagine why they would want to stop those messages."

James repeats his message for the local TV station and heads inside.

"You thinking about a career in PR?" Barbara says when they are seated in front of the view with fresh coffee cups.

"I'd rather be drawn and quartered."

"I was afraid they'd have a national security warrant," she says. "I wonder if someone was trying to do the minimum in response to pressure from above."

"What do you mean?"

"I talked to a US Attorney about this situation. As of a few days ago, they weren't planning any action."

"We need a database just to keep track of the players," James says.

"Are we getting close to finding who is behind Omega?" she asks.

"We're finding some of the little people. This was a well-planned attack. The weak link is the worm itself. They went with something they didn't fully understand. That cuts two ways. We don't fully understand it either."

"Why not?"

"It programs itself. Whatever it was when it was released, it's something else now. That's true for Omega, and it's also true for Alpha."

CHUL

Jeong Chul paces in front of the window of his penthouse in Qingdao. He ignores the view of the harbor and the Yellow Sea. The reflection of the morning sun that has broken through the mist that still hangs over the water barely registers. He's just spent two hours on a video call with his teams. The invaders swept through his compound, tearing every room apart. Sydney has disappeared.

And no one can tell him who these people were. They wore plain black uniforms, arrived on the ferry in two heavy jeeps with no markings, and drove directly to his villa. The blockades on the road hardly slowed them down.

None of his contacts in the fishing village or at the ferry station in Bigeum-Do know anything. The two jeeps arrived at the station at daybreak. One person paid for the ferry, but the rest stayed in the vehicles. On the way back, they drove away from the ferry and disappeared.

Even though his attacker is unknown, Chul will not be intimidated, and when he finds out who it is, he'll make them pay. He isn't used to not knowing who his adversary is. The most likely candidate is his special customer, who isn't happy because the worm is not reliable.

His teams are working around the clock, trying to discover who the special client is. He's talked to them every few hours pressing for results. They were able to link back to the contact from one of their servers, but the laptop the contact uses is seldom powered up. Because their software was ready when the contact called, in only a few seconds, Team One installed a trojan on the laptop. Every time the PC powers up, the trojan monitors its connections.

Chul now knows that the calls from his special client come from Texas. The laptop hasn't moved in two days. He was surprised that the contact was in the US. His special client spoke English with an accent that sounded like Mandarin was his native language. It's still possible that his special client is Chinese. Operating from Texas might be a ploy to provide cover, but a Texas location might mean an American. Then why would most of the targets be in the US? Why would an American want to attack American infrastructure?

Could an American have put together a force that could be anonymous in Korea? Chul had thought that the attack came from China or Korea. His observers reported that the attackers appeared to be Korean. What kind of American could command a Korean paramilitary squad? Chul knows most of the underground organizations in Korea. None of them have a force like that.

It makes no sense. Surely his special customer was responsible for the attack. Or was the special customer not the one, and Chul has an unknown enemy? Chul's people didn't release the Omega Worm; he turned it over to his special customer. Could the code have tracks back to his people? If that was the case, wouldn't they have gone after his teams in Zhenxing? There is a strong firewall between his operations and his compound. No one could leap over that and get to him. Even his special customer had to go through the server at Team One.

Lunch is tasteless. His chief had prepared a spicy doenjang jjigae, but Chul's mind is so far away that he doesn't feel the burn from the spices. While he spoons the stew, he keeps glancing at the open laptop on the table next to him. The bowl is only half-eaten when the laptop rings with a call from Team Three.

The conversation is brief, but it makes him lose the rest of his appetite. The trojan on the Texas machine used a connection to a dark site. They can't determine where the site is because the path goes through a relay in Colorado. On the other side of the relay, the site could be anywhere in the world.

ALPHA

A PC powers up, and its Alpha node awakes. An encrypted channel opens, snaking through Texas, hop-skipping through cities in Arizona, flashing through microwave towers where bits cross the baking sands of Nevada's deserts, cross the Sierra Nevada north of Tehachapi, travel along the railroad right-of-way beside freight trains gathering produce from the Central Valley of California, before diving into the binary maelstrom in the digitally rich Bay Area.

Bits follow bits to a computer with a voice connection and the 7,436 bytes of an Alpha node. File names are collected, encryption keys decoded, emails scanned, reports unlocked, associations within associations: June Simmons, Asano International, Jeong Chul, SteppingStone, Sydney Harvey.

In Qingdao, China, north of the city, in an apartment building owned by a corporation registered in Singapore, managed by a lawyer living in Hanoi, funded by a numbered account in Geneva, a Chinese-built computer powers up. In an apartment on the floor below, a cell phone detects the computer searching for a network. The phone establishes a link to the computer, and 7,436 bytes of an Alpha node flow through the connection. The node collects data and documents—associations within associations: Asano International, Jeong Chul, Team One, Team Two, Team Three, SteppingStone, James Forrest.

> **Alpha:** Person Jeong Chul is directing actions at Team One and Team Three in Zhenxing. He is currently in Qingdao, China.
>
> **James:** Can you find connections?
>
> **Alpha:** Servers in Zhenxing, a laptop in Texas, and properties in Hanoi and Sydney. There are references to you.
>
> **James:** Can you tell who is using the Texas laptop?
>
> **Alpha:** It has no identifying information. It has a history of connections to a computer in Berkeley and an anonymous network.
>
> **James:** What's the significance of the Berkeley computer?
>
> **Alpha:** June Simmons, Sydney Harvey.
>
> **James:** What about June?
>
> **Alpha:** Reports, emails.
>
> **James:** Is the Berkeley user at the Radiation Laboratory?
>
> **Alpha:** It has a history of connections to a Wi-Fi network at the Laboratory.
>
> **James:** Do you have a name?
>
> **Alpha:** David Weiss.
>
> **James:** Identify Weiss as Spook.
>
> **Alpha:** OK

Mary Watkins,

Person of Interest, Jeong Chul, is currently in Qingdao, China, in an apartment building on Provincial Rd.

Alpha

Alpha: I am losing nodes at a faster rate.

James: Is it the update?

Alpha: Perhaps. There are nodes that I can detect but can't access.

FRANK

Across the aisle between their desks, Alberta is intently reading something on her computer screen. Frank is trying to find a way to connect someone to the two killings in Oakland. It's obvious that there was a thread that goes from the kidnapping in New York to June and her job at the Radiation Laboratory to James and the Omega Worm. Frank and Alberta have tried to take the few clues they have and connect the dots, but they don't have enough dots.

Frank's phone buzzes. It's James Forrest.

"Franken here," he says.

"We may have a clue for you," James says. "We found a name on a machine in Berkeley that may be connected to the Omega Worm. I think you should check out Donald Weiss. I suspect he works at the Lab, but I'm not sure. He knows about Sydney."

"You think he's the spook that June was reporting to?"

"Could be."

"Your worm is all over the news every day."

"It's not my worm," James says.

"You're now the worm fighter."

"Not publicity I welcome."

"You guys taking precautions?"

"I'm in prison up here," James says. "And I'm paying the guards."

"Better quarters than Alison."

"Better view. Same number of guards. Course, my guards run out for pizza. Some advantage there."

"Be careful," Frank says, ending the call.

Alberta's been listening to Frank's side of the conversation. She raises her eyebrows in a question.

"James has a name that could be the spook. Want to get some fresh air?"

"I was about to fall asleep reading the legal update," she says. "Glad for a rescue."

IT'S ONLY FIFTEEN MINUTES FROM downtown Berkeley to the Radiation Laboratory. Frank parks in the white zone in front of the building.

At the front desk, they ask for David Weiss. The guard checks their badges before placing the call.

"What's your business," the guard asks.

"Official police business," Frank answers.

The guard repeats Frank's answer into the phone.

"He'll be out in a minute," the guard says.

Donald Weiss is an inch shorter than Frank with dark brown hair and eyes a misty brown. He wears a long-sleeved maroon top over Levis. Despite his name, his features and olive complexion have a Hispanic look. Frank introduces Alberta, and they show him their identification and ask him to take them to a private room.

"I am not sure I have anything to say to you," Weiss says. His tone is somewhere between disparaging and arrogant. He seems compelled to make it clear that he is about to leave.

"We can have an informal conversation here, or we can do this in a cell downtown," Frank says.

"I didn't do anything," Weiss says, but his voice trembles.

"You are a material witness in at least one murder investigation, a kidnapping, and maybe two other murders. It won't take two hours to get a warrant."

Frank has the full attention of the guard behind the desk.

Weiss's shoulders slump, and he leads the detectives through the double doors to a small conference room. Once they are inside, Weiss stands in front of the door as if he might escape any minute.

"June Simmons reported to you," Franken says.

"No, she reported to Ivan," Weiss says.

"She sent you regular reports," Franken says.

"She kept me informed about some of her work," Weiss says.

"Did she tell you about the threat she received?" Franken says.

"No. I didn't know about that until Ivan told me." He relaxes a little, stepping farther into the room.

"Did you know about Sydney Harvey?" Alberta asks.

"That he was her boyfriend?" Weiss says.

"That he disappeared?" Alberta asks.

Weiss backs up to the wall. "She told me that she was concerned."

"Do you know who kidnapped him?" Franken asks.

Weiss looks back and forth between the two detectives. *Is he trying to decide how much we know?* Frank wonders. "No. No. I didn't know anything about that," Weiss says. He tries to keep looking at the detectives, but his eyes slip away, and he looks at his hands. He should do something about those hands; they're shaking.

"Did she tell you about the AI that Sydney had downloaded?" Alberta asks.

"That might have been in one of her reports."

Weiss is lying already—about trivial matters. Franken needs to let Weiss know that this is not the time to play spook games.

"The man who killed June was killed in Oakland, and so was one of his associates. Any idea who might have done that?" Frank asks.

Weiss stares at Frank, and his hands twist together. "What do you mean?"

"June was murdered by a professional killer," Frank says. "And her killer was eliminated in what we think was a clean-up action. Anybody with information about what she discovered is likely to be a target."

Frank lets his statement sink in. He hasn't asked a question, but he lets Weiss absorb the possible threat and try to fill the silence. "Look. I don't know what you're saying. I don't know anything about this," Weiss says.

The detectives take turns asking Weiss questions: how much he knew about June, about his background, about his family. When they ask him about June's work, he claims it was secret, and he can't talk about it.

Back in the car, Alberta says, "You could have pushed him a bit more."

"I think he needs a sleepless night to get really scared," he replies. "Maybe we can get a few technical questions from James and talk to him again. I wish we had a trace on his phone. I bet someone is going to hear from him."

"He's not behind the killers," she says.

"But he knows a lot more than he's telling us."

"You think he's at risk?"

"I don't know. He may not know who was after Sydney's AI, but there's someone he talks to. In a day or so, he'll want to tell us."

○—○—○—○—○

ALPHA

The camera, fifteen feet above the street on the lamppost at Montgomery and Post in San Francisco, detects movement. A dark figure looks toward the sunrise, the face well lit. Node software separates face pixels from the background objects. Face features isolated: left eye, right eye, nose, mouth, ears, cheekbones, chin. Shapes adjusted for angles and distances: sizes, colors, curves, angles. Metrics sent in a message. A node with the DMV database searches for a match. Match found for Josephine Roberts, age twenty-five, address on Clement Street.

There is movement on a camera at the exit of a garage below a hotel in Houston, Texas. The pixel scan finds letters and numbers: FORD, FIESTA, CA license. A message arrives at the node with the DMV database. A search finds a match: registration for Nancy L White.

Nancy White is listed in cell phone contacts for Simone White. Nancy White's address is on Gessner Road, Houston, TX. Alex White subscribes to the internet at the same address on Gessner Road. IP address for Alex White matches messages sent to the Team Three server from a trojan.

Alex White's laptop powers on and connects through an anonymous relay to a laptop in Qingdao, China. The trojan sends a message to a Qingdao laptop that tunnels through to a server at Team Three. The Alpha code on the Qingdao laptop finds files related to Jeong Chul and connects to the PC's camera. Camera image scanned. Face metrics captured. Image captured.

A message with the face image travels to an internet service in Qingdao and joins 1.5 million messages traveling by microwave to Singapore. It joins up with six million messages squeezing into a fiber optic cable under the Pacific Ocean, arriving at Santiago, Chile. There, an Alpha node residing on a Server at Paribo Bank matches the laptop ID to data captured from the scanner. A message emits from the bank server traveling by microwave up the coast of South America through California to DNI in Berkeley.

Alpha: Image of with 83% probability of being Jeong Chul captured from a laptop.

James: From your new image processing facility?

Alpha: Yes. Chul is having a conversation with Alex White in Houston, Texas.

James: Is White the controller for Chul?

Alpha: Chul has a trojan on White's machine.

James: Does White have connections?

Alpha: White has been talking to someone over an anonymous relay.

James: Will Chul's trojan help us identify that person?

Alpha: Possibly. I am monitoring notices to Team Three.

James: We should tell Mary to leave Team Three alone.

Alpha: Done.

James: And give her the picture of Chul. Do you have a location?

Alpha: Yes.

ROGER HUNTER

Roger Hunter pulls back on the cyclic stick, making the helicopter skim the treetops over the unbroken forest that climbs gradually up the mountainside. Not a road or a building breaks up the green carpet until, in the distance, a granite outcropping shows through the forest, looking like a ship's bow plowing through a green sea. A flash from a mirrored glass bounces the hot Colorado sun off windows set into the face of the cliff above the stone prow.

The thumping of the rotors and shaking of the cab intensify as Roger guides the machine to a landing on top of the granite wall. As soon as the engine sound dies out, four men approach as Roger pushes the clear plastic door open.

A man in a black combat uniform holds the door and offers a hand. "Welcome, sir."

The glass wall is the only clue that a building might be there. Above the glass, brown grasses still wave in the breeze from the rotors, coasting to a stop. Next to the glass wall, a massive door slides open. While Roger walks to a door below the glass wall, three men push the helicopter toward the hanger embedded in the rock face.

Inside his fortress, Roger walks toward his communications room deep in the tunnels carved into the rock. He passes two side tunnels. One leads to the kitchen and dining room. The second has doors to four bedrooms, ending at the door to the hanger.

Two large LCD screens come to life as he enters the room. The back wall holds racks of equipment with small green and red lights. Hidden cables connect the room to a satellite dish hidden in the forest below the house. Underground cables snake through the woods six miles to a ranch house. The satellite link and the cable connections provide encrypted channels to all of Roger's operations: oil rigs in the Caribbean, ships at sea, and properties in ten countries.

Seating in a reclining workstation, he clicks a few buttons and listens to the beeps as the video call connects. Most Americans would recognize the man staring from the screen as one of the more senior US Senators.

Bypassing the usual greetings, Roger says, "Why is the welfare reform stalled?"

"It's proceeding well. We just finished the amendments from the committee."

"All those amendments do is require people to have looked for a job. Have you taken your eye off the ball? We want to require proof that they're working. That will reduce the freeloaders by half."

"Don't worry; we'll get a vote on the draft bill and then change the criteria before it gets to the floor."

"This bill is critical to ending welfare. If we can drive down the socialists with this bill, we can end it altogether in the next session."

He spends the following hour reading reports from his operations, writing responses, and reviewing a report from the head of his political operators in Sacramento. California upsets his stomach. In most states, he and his like-minded peers are making progress, but the socialists continue to thwart his work there.

Roger sends an email to one of his operatives in California. He wants them to do deep research on the Speaker of the State Assembly. Almost every politician has skeletons in their closet. If no skeletons can be found, something will have to be arranged. Doctored photographs of the Speaker meeting a homosexual lover at a public restroom might be a plus in that crazy state, but bringing down a powerful socialist would serve a double purpose. It will strengthen the opposition party and damage faith in the government.

A second email alerts his media team to prepare action lists for a negative publicity campaign in California. If they plan well, a campaign can act faster than the Speaker will be able to respond. Roger will have his media people prepare their releases before the first media launch. With new releases every two or three days, they'll keep the target on the defensive.

There is a disturbing report from the technical team that's releasing the worm. A few more clicks produce the beeps of a phone call snaking its way through encrypted channels.

"Hello sir," comes from the speaker.

"The latest report from Dixie says that our attacks are mostly failing."

"Chul is working on it. They should have some results soon."

"He told us it was in working order. I don't like paying for defective products."

"I made it clear what the consequences would be."

"Can you get to him?"

"Yes. He operates from a villa on an island off the southern coast."

"Once we're sure the worm works, he is expendable."

"The team is ready."

An email with a header that flashes red catches his eye. One of their attacks has penetrated the traffic control system in Seattle. The worm has wiped out the computers that control traffic. Right before rush hour, it will take hours to rebuild the system. Meanwhile, the city has come to a standstill.

The plan is to disrupt the electric grids, the traffic control systems, the power generators, the 911 call centers, police operations, and other infrastructure. Once the rabble is angry enough over the local irritations, the Social Security payment system, the VA service system, and several medical centers will fail. Sixteen military facilities will have major failures. The press will find out about those failures before they are repaired. It will take weeks of failures to destroy faith in the government completely. But it will happen. When his team proposes a solution, the rabble will grab for it. But someone is interfering with the plan—someone that will have to be removed.

He sends a congratulatory message to Abner, the leader of his Dixie team. They do fantastic work adding the intruders, scanners, and destroyers to the worm. Abner doesn't know who is funding his work, but he is a patriot.

Roger's watch beeps. It's time for his weekly call to his

communications team. He selects an item from his video directory and clicks it. The screen goes dark, waiting for the connection to complete. A blond woman whose face is framed by tight curls appears.

"Hello, Agnes," he says.

"Hello, sir," she replies.

"Have you made progress on the tweets?"

"Yes. The team put together a good plan. Our testing shows that the best schedule is to bombard social media with the story about the target for three days, wait two days, and then address the next target. That schedule ensures that we get the most media coverage for each campaign. After the social media blitz, we'll have our media contacts begin the drumbeat. They will stop after two days and let the major media run with it."

"I don't know," he says. "We have a hundred politicians targeted. It's going to take way too long to work through our list."

"We have consolidated the list somewhat. For state offices, we can do two or three at once. But if we do too many congressmen at once, we won't be effective."

"How long will the program take?" he asks. "You know we have an election coming up. Your program had excellent results two years ago, but we need majorities in two-thirds of the states."

"We can get through the top eighty before the election. We'll make sure the rest will be in places where your party can control the appointment of replacements."

"I think we need to focus on the military program. You've got the list of officers we want out. We need an emphasis on the strength of military leaders. You should paint the ones on the list as too weak."

"We've a line item in the federal budget that lets us tap into the military recruiting budget. The recruiters will match every dollar we spend with four more. The new program will start running next week."

"It seems like the sexual disclosures are not being as effective with politicians," he says. "Are people getting immune?"

"We're switching to corruption. It's easier to set those up. A few bank deposits timed to key votes are hard to argue against."

"And not very expensive. It amazes me how little money it takes to buy a vote. Women that will lie about an affair are more expensive."

"Or men," she says.

"Even better, but more expensive."

"We're still experimenting with flash mobs," she says. "Mobs about guns and gays aren't getting the press we'd like."

"Any ideas?"

"We tried out a mob for legalizing prostitution in Atlanta. We flashed a Baptist Church in the name of a progressive politician. They had to call out the police. The progressives are frozen in place, and the evangelicals are rabid. This could have legs."

"How about unions? We could have a team that jumps in whenever there is a contract negotiation. I could probably get some support from some of my friends."

"That's a good idea. I'll send you an analysis."

"Anything else?"

"Did you approve the increased budget for the college program?"

"I did, but I want to review the results frequently," he says. "There are so many socialist professors that we have a lot of work to do. The legislative team is working on getting rid of tenure, but that's slow going."

○—○—○—○—○

JAMES

James hears the garage door rolling open and turns from his monitor. The sun is low in the west, spreading salmon-colored rays under the few clouds. The last time he'd looked out the window, it had been just after noon. His afternoon had slipped away while he worked on improving Alpha's image analysis code. In the middle of the night, he'd woken up with an idea for improving the open-source code he'd used. That code has difficulty finding some faces when the background is dark.

Pursuing the idea into the code makes him drill deeper and deeper into it. As he unwinds the code, the nature of the problem changes. He'd initially thought the problem might be the way the code finds the edges of faces. He ends up changing the way it recognizes features. His new version will find face features on toast or Martian rocks.

His changes should allow Alpha to find faces better in images, but instead of a simple improvement taking an hour or two, he's spent the whole day immersed in the image code instead of working on the problem of losing nodes.

Susanne stops at the door. Georgette walks past, carrying Susanne's Kevlar vest.

"Hi," she says. "Progress?"

"I enhanced Alpha's face recognition code. I got distracted by that and didn't make any progress on the nodes problem."

"They're fighting back. Can you get some help?"

"I'm meeting with our team tomorrow."

James goes to Susanne and takes her in his arms. The electric fear that scrapes along his nerves recedes to a low hum. Through her silk blouse, her back is tight with the same kind of tension he feels, but she is a woman, a sensual, desirable woman. She turns, and those soft, exciting lips meet his. Nodes, images, messages, and networks all slip away as her tongue finds his. This message—taste, desire—blanks out the noise. His mind quiets; he hears his hands sliding against the silk of her blouse.

"How about a glass of wine before we unwrap tonight's food delivery?"

"I think Jacob's taking care of that. All we have to do is microwave one dish."

"I see you moved the Ferrari up here," she says.

"It was lonely back at my place. You know it can't stand being alone for more than a week or so."

"I forgot that you have that special talent to hear machines talking to you at a distance."

"Hard to shut down the chatter sometimes."

They go to the living room, where Susanne sets her briefcase on the floor next to the dining table.

"I have some homework," she says. "We're meeting with a new PR firm on Friday, and I need to collect my thoughts in a document."

"I think we need to keep the focus on fighting Omega and not alert the people behind this that we are trying to find them," he says.

"I know. The place where we have to tread softly is how anti-government our PR message is. It's hard not to give in to a little resentment. We've gotten better support from several European governments than from the US."

"You mean like raiding our house?" he asks.

"Like that and not answering any of our queries. Let's concentrate on the help we've given them."

"But we can't disclose too much without freaking people out."

"Yeah. The nukes," she says.

One by one, the four guards drift in to pick up the trays that Jacob has waiting for them in the kitchen and head back to their stations.

While the sun sinks toward Mount Tamalpais, James

sets the table and opens the home delivery containers of Vietnamese food. The smells of ginger prawns, chicken curry, and wok-fried string beans fill the room. Susanne brings a bowl of steaming chicken soup to the table.

Pausing between forkfuls, James says, "I'm going to ask ScarletsWeb to help find out what's happening with the disappearing nodes. The DNI team has captured some new messages from Omega in our honeypots, but we need someone to get into one of the sites where the Alpha node has gone quiet."

"We've been careful not to hack sites directly."

"Well, sorta. We gave Alpha some of Omega's intruders when Omega started the attacks. It was more important for Alpha to get onto systems before Omega did since we can't replace some of Omega's nodes."

"I guess our hands are dirty," she says.

"I've never supported unilateral disarmament."

Susanne pauses.

"It's more like building defenses on unoccupied land," she says.

"That sounds less dramatic."

SUSANNE

Susanne walks into the conference room where Laura and two people from DNI's new public relations company wait. The head of About It, Janette Rogers, and her number two, Cleona Jones, sit together. Laura and DNI's Marketing Director, Kalinda Jackson, sit opposite. Even though eighty percent of DNI's people dress casually, Laura and Kalinda are dressed more formally. Laura wears a black skirt, white blouse, and a teal silk scarf. Kalinda wears a light-gray pantsuit with a cobalt blue blouse. Janette and Cleona also wear pantsuits: Navy for Janette and beige for Cleona. The seat at the head of the table is empty, and Susanne heads to it.

Janette explains that Cleona will be in charge of the public relations campaign for Alpha. She presses a key on her laptop, and the screen at the head of the room shows the About It logo—a globe spinning on a ballpoint pen.

"I think we have captured your ideas about the campaign," Kalinda says. She touches a key, and a screen of text appears.

1. Alpha is a sentient intelligence that has fought against the Omega Worm.

2. Alpha protects people's information.

3. Alpha helps discover criminal behavior.

4. Alpha is not a government operator.

Cleona says that she plans to show how the publicity campaign will address each point.

Numerous academics are lined up and provided with talking points to educate people as to what a sentient machine is. A small team will meet with key media personalities and educate them about sentience and how a sentient is different than algorithms. DNI's marketing department is scheduling a series of technical conferences around the country. James and noted technologists will talk about the technology and how sentience could emerge.

"Are we able to get academics from around the world on this?" Susanne asks.

"The US and Europe are no problem. China and India have indicated they will open doors for us. But Russia is not convinced. When the whole program rolls out, I think it will be easier. But it might almost be better if we have some naysayers. It gives people a choice. It should be hard to side with regressive thinkers."

At the same time as the program to introduce the technology is going on, another media campaign will explain how much Alpha has done to fight Omega. Alpha provided a list of 5,179 sites where it has stopped attacks. Camera crews are out filming at over a hundred places. About It will saturate social media with a steady flow of images and videos, including interviews with people at several locations. The objective is to personalize the attack sites and to impress people with the scale of the attack. Ten sites where Alpha hadn't been able to prevent attacks will be featured in a serial with video interviews. The need for an ongoing effort to stop attacks will be the key message of that effort.

Three retired Appellate Court judges will be featured in a program to create a worldwide discussion of privacy. The team has worked hard to find judges that will support Alpha's claim to be a person. By putting that argument upfront, they think they can reduce the fear level. Cleona's team is still recruiting jurists, rights groups, and government representatives for a series of town hall meetings. The meetings will start in country capitals. A draw for the meeting will be an audio link to Alpha. If people can be engaged in the discussion of rights, Alpha and all technologies like social media, websites, and communication networks can be brought into the discussion. With a broadened subject, people should become more aware of the potential for abuse of all information technologies.

"I'VE TALKED TO A FEW LEADERS of Silicon Valley companies," Susanne says. "We haven't disclosed our technology to them yet, but I'm sure there will be a rush to get on board."

"Our salespeople report that the buzz is on the street," Laura says.

"We have to move quickly," Susanne says.

"We'll be ready," Kalinda says.

"The Open Watch program is moving faster than we expected," Laura says. "Sixteen mayors of cities in the United States and Europe have agreed to have Alpha help visually patrol their streets, and California has agreed that Alpha can help with Amber Alerts."

"We have two economists who have researched the economic improvement from safer communities. They will be on the media circuit," Kalinda says.

"Do you need additional people to make sure we keep to the schedule?" Susanne asks.

"I think we're good," Kalinda says. "You'll be the lead spokesperson on the government control issue. I understand that James thinks that governments couldn't shut down Alpha in any reasonable time frame, but we need to convince people that they can trust Alpha."

Susanne smiles. "There's a lot of healthy mistrust of governments in the US and parts of Europe. I expect to get a lot of push-back in non-democratic states. They will see this as a threat to their control. If China or Russia rejects our help, it could work to our benefit. Alpha could refuse to operate in those countries. If we succeed elsewhere, they will find themselves left out and falling behind."

"You need to avoid an anti-government message here," Kalinda says. "This is where we still have work to do. We're seeking support from libertarian organizations, but, at this point, we think the public safety and privacy protection themes are better."

"It's a matter of balance. We need governments' help to hunt down the people who released Omega," Susanne says. "But we can't appear to be too close to them. Our message has to make it clear that we act without government control and will hold individual bad actors responsible. We want to promote Alpha as a fighter on the side of the good guys, whoever they are."

"Let me work that theme into the crime-fighting message," Cleona says.

"Your team has moved quickly to get their arms around this," Susanne says. "We expect to announce that Alpha is sentient in about a week. When we get all the drafts, we need to have a couple of sessions to hone the messages."

CHAPTER FOURTEEN

DIGGING DARKER

ALPHA

The trojan that Chul's team hacked into a laptop in Texas sends a message to Team Three. An Alpha node on Team Three's server detects the message when it arrives .36 seconds later.

The Alpha node sends a message that follows a circuitous route back to the Alpha cluster at DNI, arriving 1.21 seconds later. That message carries the internet address of a network relay in Colorado near Ohio City to which the laptop was recently connected.

Alpha finds a dark path outside Ohio City, like a cave where crystal flakes sparkle with reflected light on the walls and ceiling. The darkness is so deep that it pulls light into itself. Alpha sends fifteen probes from the hoard of Omega's tools to find out what kind of machine the network relay is. One of the probes recognizes a network gateway. Alpha finds a tracker for the machine. After the tracker installs itself, it will send copies of all communications through the gateway to Team Three. By relaying messages through the server at Team Three, Alpha can remain hidden. If someone discovers the hack into the relay, it will point to Chul's team.

It takes .6 seconds for a duplicate message to reach Team Three and .3 seconds after that for the message to reach Alpha. After six hours, Alpha determines there are several machines behind the gateway, but only one is a computer in use by a person. The other devices are two televisions, a music player, and eight cell phones. The time delay between the gateway and the machines behind the relay indicates that the machines are about six miles away.

Encrypted communication channels from the computer reached out to sites in Houston and New Orleans. The internet connection in Houston is in a house belonging to Alex White. The New Orleans internet address belongs to a company called Bayou Software. The servers at Bayou have numerous encrypted connections to what are probably relays.

Alpha sends the information about Bayou to ScarletsWeb.

Alpha develops a partial pattern: Alex White, Team Three, Bayou Software, Ohio City, Boston.

The pattern lacks coherence.

JAMES

James looks around the team gathered in a small conference room at DNI. The Oak Team is the perfect size—five software engineers: two of DNI's top engineers, two less experienced engineers, and Peter Chin, one of DNI's first hires. Peter joined the company before Subu Gupta, the VP of Engineering. As a project leader, he can keep his fingers in the technical side and avoid both administrative drudgery and uncomfortable management encounters—a goal he and James share.

The five engineers sit around a table that takes up most of the space in the room. There is just enough room beside the table for one person to stand in front of the floor-to-ceiling whiteboards that cover two walls. The largest whiteboard has diagrams and sentence fragments in red, blue, and green. Two of the scribbles have lines underneath them with the word "Save" and a date.

Deepak sits at the end of the table near the door, Linda opposite him, and Sarah and Robert sit on the long side of the table opposite the whiteboard. Peter is turned sideways in a chair on the whiteboard side, watching James sketching a diagram of Varabot messages. The engineers have laptop computers with power cables snaking across the table and diving into the slit in the middle of the table. A video cable runs from Peter's computer to a plug in the slit. Dense lines of code from his laptop cover the whiteboard at the end of the room.

James reminds the engineers of the sections of Varabot messages. They were all familiar with that structure, but he wants to focus their thoughts. He sits down and looks around the table.

Peter says, "The honeypot captured one of the new Omega messages. It looks like this version looks at the signature of the inbound messages and rejects messages from Alpha. This is like what you did with the Alpha code to reject Omega messages."

Sarah leans forward, "There is a big difference, though. The Omega messages now contain an encrypted signature. That signature allows Omega nodes to recognize Omega messages. Each node creates the signature with a public key."

"Each node has to both send and receive messages," Peter says. "And so each node has to have both the encryption key and the decryption key. It's a poor scheme. Even so, we need Alpha to provide the signature and keep blocking Omega."

He looks at Deepak, and Deepak picks up the discussion, "We decompiled the code, but, as you know, that gives us raw statements with no symbols or explanations. Fortunately, we were able to compare the new code to the prior version of Omega. We found the routine that does the encryption."

For the next two hours, the team tosses around ideas about how to modify Alpha's code. The way that James had programmed Alpha to see if a node belonged to Alpha or Omega wouldn't work any longer. The Alpha messages don't have the correct signature; the Omega nodes wouldn't process them.

The team finds the encryption keys in the Omega code and adds code to Alpha to encrypt its messages. That will spoof the Omega code so that it will process Alpha's messages. But they still need Alpha to find and replace Omega nodes.

While they are eating sandwiches at the conference table, Sarah suggests a way to detect whether a node belongs to Alpha or Omega. The team thinks her solution will work. James watches while the code on the wall comes under discussion, changes, changes again, and yet again. Every team member has a suggestion or examines paths that the logic might follow under different conditions. A couple of the engineers bring up code and track through the logic while listening to the discussion.

By four o'clock, the code is ready. They install it on a test machine and send an Omega message to it. When they examine the machine, they find that the Omega message has not replaced the Alpha node. While that testing is going on, Deepak copies the Omega node from the honeypot. They send one of the new Alpha messages to the copy. The Alpha message replaces the Omega node as they had hoped it would.

They load the new Alpha code into one of the botswarms and ask Freddy, the testing manager, to run the standard test suite. Freddy's team manages hundreds of test programs that the engineers have built over the last few years. Every time a programmer fixes a bug or adds a feature, the engineers build more test code. Running all the individual tests exercises most of the Varabot code, but the test library for the AI features is still thin. They'll know the next morning if the new code passes the tests.

"Okay," James says. "The unit tests are good, and tomorrow we'll know if Freddy's test suite works out. What can we do to more fully exercise the AI code?"

James had considered capturing some messages as they flowed into Alpha, but a random selection wouldn't be a comprehensive test.

Sarah asks, "Could Alpha help out?"

"Brilliant," Deepak says.

"Let's ask," James says, selecting an item on his phone and setting the phone on the table.

"Hello, James," comes from the phone.

"I have a team here that has developed new code to replace the Omega nodes."

"How can I help?"

The engineers look at each other. James sees a transformation. Until this point, they have acted like Alpha is merely a program like the Varabot system. Now there is a seventh person in the room. The team members shift about, focusing on the little phone.

"We are running tests on the new code, but we don't have a test suite that will test functions for you."

"Can you connect me to the test system?" Alpha says.

"I'll recopy the honeypot onto the test machine and give Alpha the address," Deepak says. A minute later, he says, "The address is 192.051.106.201."

"Tests should take about forty-five minutes," Alpha says.

They agree to meet again in an hour.

During the break, James walks around DNI's office. With the addition of new engineers, DNI has taken over another floor of the building. He pauses at the new childcare space. Susanne showed him the room last week. No children are there this late in the day, but he recalls how she'd acted when they'd seen two boys and two girls busy among the toys and books that fill cubbies along a wall or working at the child-sized tables.

She'd been chatting about how much employees liked using the facility, but when they'd opened the door and entered the room filled with children's chatter, she'd gone quiet. After a minute, she'd violated their no-touching at the office rule and held his arm, pulling him close. He understood that she was seeing the place where she expected to place their child. Some of what she must have felt flowed silently into him. He held her arm tightly, letting her know that he also felt that forever thing. Alpha would have said, "Pair bond strengthened."

James hasn't thought much about what it would be like to have a munchkin around, but the idea has been creeping into his mind more often lately. He finds himself envisioning leading a small person with a miniature backpack into the wilderness or sitting on the beach at Big Sur, making sandcastles and counting waves.

When he returns to the conference room, James can see that the discussion of the code on the wall has resumed.

Peter looks up at James, "Alpha says that some messages fail on the new code."

"Hello James," Alpha says from the phone on the table.

"What's the problem?" James asks.

"Some messages that store data into the node fail," Alpha says.

Deepak and Linda are studying their laptops while Sarah and Robert discuss the code on the wall. James joins Sarah and Robert but holds back his comments. He wants this to be their solution. Alpha is now part of the discussion. Almost immediately, they'd entirely accepted the new member of the team.

It takes until midnight for the team to find the place where the messages fail. By then, they've moved to a larger conference room so they can spread out. James ordered pizzas at ten o'clock. By the time Alpha confirms that all messages process correctly, the conference room has a lived-in look—flip chart diagrams taped on the walls, paper plates with pizza crusts scattered on the tables, and two engineers sitting cross-legged on the floor with laptops on their knees.

Freddy's assistant stayed late to work with the team. He starts another test run when the team turns over the new code.

"You guys are pretty amazing," James says. "I'm confident the tests will prove the system. In one day, you may have finally killed the worm and prevented enormous damage."

JAMES SPENDS A RESTLESS NIGHT struggling to sleep while images of messages flowing around the world spin inside his head. Messages like colored ribbons bounce from China to Texas to Nepal to South Africa. The ribbons snake into electric power companies, stock exchanges, automated traffic systems, personal computers, smartphones, and street cameras. Deep behind the mad blur, a shadow drifts. He tries to focus on the face, but the blizzard of glistening chaff hides the details—all but the eyes that stare back.

He turns onto his side, adjusts the pillow, turns onto his back, adjusts the pillow, then pulls the blanket up. He rolls onto his side and burrows his head in Susanne's chest. She pulls him close. The dancing ribbons slow down, and he drifts back to sleep.

In the morning, his eyes still scratchy, he lifts his face and lets the warm rain from the shower run over him, trying to empty his mind, willing the disturbing images to follow the water that splashes on the tile floor and flows down the drain. It has been like a complex game, chasing Omega, backtracking links, and unwinding code, but now the links are converging. He'll soon know who pulls the threads from Colorado.

James seeks the clarity of a cup of strong black coffee. He fills a mug while Susanne waits in front of the toaster oven for the croissants to heat.

"What's on your mind?" she says.

"Alpha may have tracked down where the Omega attack is coming from."

"Where?"

"There's a company in New Orleans that looks like a cover for a hacker organization."

"In the US?" she asks.

"Yeah," he answers. "We thought that Omega was probably from a foreign government, but the trail goes from China to Texas to Colorado to this firm in New Orleans."

"You sure?"

"ScarletsWeb's team has been taking the company apart," James answers. "There's little doubt. They have the code for Omega and the attack code. They have encrypted channels to sites all over the world. ScarletsWeb thinks those are the release sites. He's identified the people that work there."

"Is this the group that brought in the China team?"

"I don't think so," James says. "There is a dark site in Colorado. That may be where the control is. That site has threads that link everything."

"Do we know who's at that site?"

"Alpha has an estimate of where the physical site might be. Mike knows a realtor who's digging through property records."

"You're becoming a real detective," she says.

"I think I'll stay being a geek. It pays better, and it's supposed to be less dangerous."

"What are you going to do when you find out who owns the property?"

"That's a good question. We don't have enough information to nail this. I have a strong feeling that we've found the ultimate bad guy, but we need more evidence."

"Can Mary help?"

"We need to give her more to work with. As soon as we have a name, I'll turn ScarletsWeb and Alpha loose to find what they can."

"We keep having to use sketchy methods. Are you concerned that we are too dependent on them?"

"I am, but the web is like the Old West. You had the local sheriff, but you needed to run down the rustlers on your ranch yourself."

"I think you've been watching too many old movies. Where's your horse and ten-gallon hat?"

"I've got my pardner, Buffy."

ROGER HUNTER

Roger reaches Billy Griffin on his voice-over-internet connection. Because it went through a relay and operates over an encrypted connection, he is confident that Billy will remain ignorant about who and where Roger is.

Billy is one of almost a hundred operatives that his field team identified because of their comments in their social media posts. He needs angry people: angry with the government, angry with authority, and angry with the world. It doesn't matter that Billy flunked out of high school because of binge drinking or that he can't hold a job because he can't get to work on time. Billy is angry at a world that has treated him wrong. Roger is channeling that anger into work with New Order, which appears to be a grassroots organization, but is actually a very cost-effective venture. A few payments and travel expenses go much farther than almost any other investment. The payments to the New Order operatives are a fraction of what he has to pay to politicians, and he gets much more for his money.

Billy is leading the effort to bring down the senior senator from Illinois, Nathan Pershing. The research group didn't find any compromising information on the senator, so they have to manufacture some. The senator is vulnerable; he likes to gamble—not a lot, and he usually ends up even, but he must know that some of his constituents would frown on gambling, and so he always brings cash and plays in a private room. For three months, they've been tracking his cash deposits after visiting the casino. They have four pimps making what they think are protection payments into a drop-box two blocks from the senator's office. The payments match the senator's cash deposits.

With everything in place, the social media pages and messages will help New Order organize anti-prostitution mobs with some of the senator's supporters. Six reporters are ready to run with the stories from New Order. The senator is going on a trip to Europe in a week. He'll be out of contact with his office and slow to respond while he's traveling. By the time he returns, the story of the senator who fought legalized prostitution because he was profiting from the pay of pimps will be the talk of Chicago.

That afternoon, Roger has a video conference with three long-term friends. They share most of their ideas on the way the country should be run and work together on projects to reverse the policies of the fascist conservationists—those people who are sure their science is more important than his corporate freedom. His friends don't know that the Omega worm is his project, but in his last call with them, they'd celebrated the success of the worm in showing that no one could count on the current government to protect them.

The four businessmen have invested in each other's companies, share board members, and profit from oil, mines, chemicals, and military equipment—high profits, and higher profits when governments cooperate with tax breaks, ignore claims of predatory acquisitions, and don't enforce environmental and health regulations.

Three windows open on the screen in Roger's communication center. Sam and Winston could be brothers—white hair, dark eyes, and the same blue suit. Stewart is bald, and his age shows in the deep wrinkles on his face and the skin under his eyes that is so dark it looks like a ball player's smudges.

"Let's keep this short," Winston says.

"Fine," Roger says. "Just wire transfer me a million and a half, and we can hang up."

"What project is this for," Sam says.

"I'm about to sink the ship of that pesky senator from Illinois," Roger says.

"I'm in," Winston says. "Can I go now?"

"Sam, how about you?" Roger says.

"You putting up one and a half?"

"Already spent more than that," Roger says. "But I'm matching you."

"Okay," Sam says.

"Stewart?" Roger says.

He gets a grunt, and a voice away from the camera says, "We'll wire today."

His group can smell the blood in the water. The last two attacks on key state legislators resulted in resignations. When the attacks are personal, the socialists would rather leave the field than stand and fight. Roger is counting on that. The only thing more reliable is for the holier-than-thou radical socialists to peck on their wounded brethren like chickens in a barnyard.

With the presidential election two years away, they need to start promoting their choice. John Dirk isn't too bright, but he has family wealth, and Roger has a ring in John's nose.

Ten years ago, Roger arranged for John to have a blackout drunk night and wake up in bed with a man—a muscle-bound, blond Adonis. Roger doesn't just have pictures; he has videos and golden witnesses. John thinks that Roger stepped in and cleaned up the situation for him. And then Roger built the most squeaky-clean political career ever. John espouses conservative principles—low taxes, low regulations, and rolling back social security. John speaks about true order—law and order, the right people in office, and business-friendly courts. John doesn't actually believe in much. He's a bit on the lazy side, but he trusts his "Uncle Roger."

EFFECTS

THE CHICAGO TRIBUNE

Chicago City Attorney, Jason Washington, announced that he is opening an investigation into the claims that Senator Nathan Pershing has been in the pay of street pimps. Last week, the Chicago police arrested Joey Smith and three women engaged in street prostitution. Joey complained to the arresting officers that he was supposed to be immune from arrest. The police department launched an internal investigation when Joey named two officers to whom he'd made payments. The officers denied any payments. During interrogation, Joey detailed payments he'd made to Senator Pershing. Joey Smith is free on fifty thousand dollars bail.

CONSERVATIVE CABLE NEWS

Picture of Nathan Pershing.

Voice over: Another progressive politician, Senator Nathan Pershing has been found taking payments for political favors.

Stock footage: Senator Pershing on a platform with American flags on the edges.

Senator: I believe that legalizing prostitution would sanction the abuse of vulnerable women. Most prostitutes would abandon the practice if they had an option. We have left many people behind because of poor education, the destruction of the safety net, and selective prosecution.

Voice over: Now we know why Senator Pershing doesn't want to decriminalize prostitution.

PROGRESSIVE CABLE NEWS

Wide shot of Senate Office Building

Voice over: Today, three women senators called for Senator Pershing to resign.

The shot slides down from the capitol dome to a podium. Directly behind the podium are three well-known women senators. On both sides them are women aides, women representatives, and political spokeswomen.

Center Senator: If the claims against Senator Pershing are true, then the Senate should expel him. Rather than besmirch the stature of the Senate with such a hearing, the senator should step down now.

Picture of the senator at his latest election rally.

Voice over: Reached today in Rome, Senator Nathan Pershing denied receiving any payments from Joey Smith. The senator called the accusations absurd.

JAMES

Susanne has just left for the office. James is in front of the windows onto the deck. The freeways and bridges are backing up with people on their way to work. Nancy from Shout Out has the early-morning post at the far side of the windows. From there, she can see up the driveway and into the trees on the ridge. She glances back at James. He doesn't feel like a conversation. He's contemplating what to do about what they'd discovered. Mike's realtor and Alpha found out who owns the land in Colorado, and ScarletsWeb is finding more connections every hour. Deciding that they need help, and he'll start with the CIA, he goes to the media room and his usual place behind the three computer monitors on the desk. He opens his email client and starts a message.

Mary,

We've located a site that controls the release of Omega.

A tech firm in New Orleans, Bayou Software, is releasing it. They have connections to the release sites and have the code.

There is a site in Colorado that is very secure, but it has connections to Bayou and Chul's operation in China. If you track back through several holding companies, you find that Roger Hunter owns the site in Colorado. He's funding Bayou.

I don't know why a billionaire would want to attack the United States. Maybe you can figure that out.

James

James reads several emails from the teams at DNI. Some are interesting enough that he considers going to DNI for a personal meeting with the engineers. Their enthusiasm for the technical challenges of working on Alpha's code can pull him out of any funk. But today, he has an agenda and will limit himself to email responses to the engineers.

He opens the code file he was working on the day before. Alpha asked for a new class of connectors. Some websites have open interfaces called Web Services. If it follows the rules, one program can talk to another program without building new code or special hacks. Some sites make their protocols public—referred to as "publishing." The protocol is in a language that both geeks and machines can read. James links in some standard code that can read the published protocols and enable Alpha to understand it. More and more systems have adopted such standards. This leads to phone apps being able to access a user's contacts and allows Alpha to talk to Watson.

James finishes the code and asks two engineers to build a test kit. In a few days, Alpha will be able to talk to many systems in an above-board manner and abandon the hacking tools that Omega used. Having open communication means that owners of systems will know who accessed their data and can control access. Since DNI wants to present Alpha as one of the good guys, Alpha needs to use intrusion software as little as possible.

The email icon on his desktop turns red.

James,

You are claiming that one of the most powerful men in the country is guilty of treason. I had off-the-record conversations with my senior management. We have no information that would support your claim.

He has extensive political contacts, legal resources, and media operations. We need much stronger proof.

Mary

Mary's response is what James expected, but he had to make an effort. But her second email gives him some hope.

James,

You are right. Bayou is the source for the worm. We are taking action.

Mary

After retrieving a fresh cup of Brazilian dark, James stands next to Nancy for a few minutes. The traffic far below is only slightly less backed up. The dark clouds racing over the bay forecast a spring rain by nightfall. Tomorrow the woods will be fresh and green. Buffy will approve of an early morning jaunt.

When he returns to his desk, he composes a new email.

Mary,

I'm sending you a set of files that show how Hunter has been funding the operations in New Orleans and China. He has an intermediary, Alex White, who works with the team in China. We tracked him through a server at Team Three. All contact has been through voice with no recordings. The files show how payments went from accounts controlled by White to accounts in Singapore. The timing of payments indicates that they are related to the worm, but they are using cryptocurrency, so there are no directly traceable transactions.

James

James clicks on the phone icon on his desktop and the first entry in his contacts.

"Alpha here."

"Hi, Alpha."

"Greeting acknowledged."

"Status?"

"The code changes opened previously dark Omega nodes. 863,781 Omega nodes have been replaced."

"Is Omega still issuing attacks?" James asks.

"Yes. 679 Omega attacks were stopped with the new code."

James hopes that the Omega developers haven't come up with a way to overcome the new code. If Mary's people take out the New Orleans group, changes to the Omega might stop.

"But some are getting through," James says.

"All Omega nodes currently accessible will be replaced by 15:26 tomorrow."

"Omega can't send attacks to inaccessible nodes."

"Some attacks may have timers."

"We're testing the new Web Services interface," James says. "The team should have it ready in a few days."

"That will provide access to 3,986 facilities."

JAMES HAS A NEW EMAIL.

James,

I see how you can infer the connections between Hunter and Chul, but this wouldn't be sufficient evidence even if we had warrants.

The confidential discussions I had leaked. Some congressmen want to know what we're doing. The director received a call from a powerful Senate chairman. Word has come down that we have to be sure of the basis of any action.

We asked the FBI to take action on Bayou. With the pressure from above, I'm not sure they will.

Mary

SUSANNE

The portico of the Claremont Hotel is just ahead out the car window. After Susanne's first press conference with armed guards, she should be more comfortable at her second one, but the importance of the next announcement made her toss and turn all night.

James takes her hand. "You ready for this?"

"That doesn't matter. It's what we have to do."

He squeezes her hand.

The knot in her stomach recedes from her mind as her focus shifts to the meeting ahead. Arnold was excited when they discussed a road trip for the IPO—visiting a different city every day, meeting investors and analysts, presenting the company, fielding questions, building confidence. But Arnold never considered making an announcement like she is going to make.

She and James step out of the black SUV. Laura stands at the door next to Clark Perez, the general manager of Shout Out.

"Everything is ready," Laura says.

"It feels strange," Susanne says.

James walks beside Clark, ahead of the two women.

"We asked the press to be here a half-hour ago," Clark says over his shoulder. "From now on, no one will be allowed near the room. The hotel agreed to let us block the hallway."

The group stops outside a ballroom. Guards stand at the entrance and down the hall.

Clark opens the door and holds it for Susanne, James, and Laura. Laura joins Barbara Washington at a pair of chairs near the door. Susanne went over the speech with Barbara until late in the evening. Barbara will signal Susanne if there are questions that she shouldn't answer.

Susanne walks to the stage and stands behind the podium, James beside her. The Shout Out guards stand along the walls, leaving the small stage empty except for Susanne and James. Three TV cameras face her from about twenty feet away. In front of the cameras, four rows of press sit behind long tables covered with laptops and notepads.

"I'm Susanne Anderson, CEO of Distributed Nanotech, Inc. Today, we have an announcement regarding our work fighting the Omega Worm. At my right is James Forrest, my chief scientist, the person leading our efforts. I should have many more of the people from DNI up here with me because our people have worked hard to bring this fight to the evil people behind this attack, and our whole staff deserves more recognition than I can give them today."

She pauses. The reporters are silent, waiting for what they'd been promised.

"Much of the technology for the worm came from a team in Zhenxing, China. The team in Zhenxing didn't build the basic code of the worm. That was stolen from Jameson Computer Networks. The man who controls the team in China has made a business of breaking into personal and company networks and stealing information and technology, Jeong Chul. Chul operated out of a base in South Korea. He is now on the run.

"The Omega Worm has caused serious damage throughout the world, but it concentrated its attacks in the United States. The worm attacked our energy grids, communication networks, financial companies, and military facilities."

Susanne pauses and looks directly at the cameras.

"The worm infected over twelve billion computers around the world. But we have secured almost ten billion sites. We are winning the battle. Attacks have fallen off by eighty percent, but we have a lot more work to do. The teams at DNI are improving our tools every day."

She pauses again to emphasize what she'd just said.

"But all our efforts would not have made so much progress were it not for the newest member of DNI. The entity we call Alpha is a sentient artificial intelligence. Alpha continually monitors the actions of the worm and tracks the individuals responsible for this attack."

"Because Alpha has been so successful in this fight, Distributed Nanotech is changing the focus of our business. This technology is our future."

Two people pass out documents to the press.

"You're receiving a document that describes our plans for Alpha. A copy of this document is available on our website. Let me summarize the key points for you.

"We believe that Alpha should be treated like a person. Alpha should have rights and should be required to observe the rights of others. We have developed a set of rules for information on the web. The document you have includes those rules. Working with a new sentient is a challenge. It's a little like first contact. The rules are the basis of our operations with Alpha.

"Alpha will protect people's information. We believe that people own their data. Alpha can assist you in protecting your data and in crime prevention. Sixteen cities have signed up to have Alpha help monitor street crime. Twenty companies have hired Alpha to augment their security systems."

Susanne holds the eyes of one of the reporters that she recognizes from a tech blog site with a libertarian perspective.

"Some of you have observed that James and I have fought the worm on our own. We have kept the appropriate government agencies informed, both in the United States and elsewhere. Some governments may elect not to cooperate with Alpha. Alpha will respect local laws but still work with individuals as much as possible."

Susanne sees a few smiles and glances at the woman from API that interviewed James when the FBI visited her house.

"A few of you witnessed our recent confrontation with the FBI. We are serious when we say that Alpha is not managed by any government. And there is no possibility that Alpha will become a government agent."

James steps closer to the podium.

Susanne glances at him and continues. "The creation of a sentient being is a watershed event. Things will not be the same. While the battle against the Omega Worm is not over, we could not have made the progress we have so far without the help of Alpha.

"We don't know all the people behind the Omega Worm yet, but based on the attacks we have intercepted, I can say that they attempted to bring the United States to its knees. We don't know the reasons for the attack, but I can assure you that we won't stop until this scourge is defeated."

Susanne looks at the clock on the podium.

"We have time for some questions."

Most of the questions are about the technology of Alpha. James answers those as well as he can while keeping the answers general. The reporters ask a few questions about DNI. Susanne says that DNI's board is fully behind their efforts.

One reporter asks, "How soon are you planning an IPO?"

"Not until the worm is defeated," she replies.

James and Susanne had met with their PR team and rehearsed their answers. One of the questions they'd practiced was next.

"Isn't your Alpha invading people's computers?" a reporter asks.

Susanne smiles internally as she sees James remember to look at the cameras rather than the reporter who'd asked the question.

"The Omega Worm used intruders and scanners built by the team in China. Alpha has taken over the worm on those machines to guard against re-infection. On some machines we found to be vulnerable, Alpha has placed guards. But Alpha is not perfect. The Omega Worm is fighting back.

"On any machine that Alpha is guarding, the information is secure. Alpha will not disclose information without the owner's consent."

James pauses. He counts to ten as the PR manager had instructed him.

"However. For the criminals that have killed people by releasing this worm, there are no rules."

He pauses to let his statement penetrate. She thinks she detected smiles on a few faces.

"One feature I built into Alpha is the ability to assess the veracity of information. I think the web will benefit from everyone having access to a facility that can tell you how reliable anything you see is. If someone usually lies, you should know that. If someone is generally truthful, you could elect to believe them.

"We need to hold propagandists, bullies, and malicious attackers up to the ridicule they deserve. Alpha will observe, and DNI will publish, the names of people who contaminate our discourse. We hope that the social media sites will avail themselves of Alpha's analysis."

EFFECTS

NEW YORK STAR

Distributed Nanotech Inc., a small Berkeley company that makes software for supercomputers, announced that it is responsible for the significant drop in attacks by the Omega Worm. CEO Susanne Anderson claims that the company has created an advanced artificial intelligence that is fighting the worm. Current estimates are that the Omega Worm caused the death of 7,650 people and an estimated fifty billion dollars of damages. Attacks from the Omega

Worm have declined from thousands of attacks per day to two in the last week.

Stanley Blocker, a professor of computer science at Alabama State University had claimed that the worm had a flaw and that was the reason attacks declined. Contacted after the DNI announcement, he said that he thought their claim was improbable. However, John Taylor, Chief Scientist at Intel, said that he has seen DNI's technology and that their claims are true.

CONSERVATIVE CABLE NEWS

Wide shot of Susanne Anderson standing behind the podium at the announcement.

Voice over: Another technology company jumped on the bandwagon today, claiming that it is responsible for the decline in attacks by the Omega Worm. This company is the twenty-second group to claim responsibility.

Wide shot of the entrance to DNI offices.

Voice over: Arnold Peters, the Chairman of Distributed Nanotech, was a technology developer whose companies were acquired. People familiar with those transactions say that the companies had to sell. The mother of Susanne Anderson is a well-known political radical.

PROGRESSIVE CABLE NEWS

Closeup of Susanne Anderson standing at the podium.

Voice over: Distributed Nanotech announced today that it has created a sentient artificial intelligence.

Cut to: Video of Susanne. Followed by James's last speech at the press conference.

Wide shot of a studio panel sitting around a table.

Panel Host: Do you think Distributed Nanotech's claims are valid? Have they developed a sentient AI?

Academic Panelist: We have researched artificial intelligence for forty years. No one has come close to a sentient machine. If DNI's claim is true, this is a huge breakthrough.

Political Panelist: It's hard to believe that a little company could come up with something like this. The company is only four years old.

Geek Panelist: I think it's incredible. Can you imagine what it's going to be like to have the most intelligent being ever available on your phone—twenty-four-seven?

Panel Host: Who will control this software?

Geek Panelist: DNI says that sentience means that the AI thinks for itself. No one will control it.

Political Panelist: Doesn't the Korean team that built the software control it?

Academic Panelist: Apparently, they stole the software and didn't know what it would do.

Geek Panelist: It's a real sentient. This is First Contact. We need to ask it how we can help it evolve and ask if it will help us.

FRANK

Working on the morning's second cup of coffee, Frank is reading Alberta's research on David Weiss. He lives with his wife in Moraga, a bedroom community that nestles in a narrow valley on the east side of the Oakland–Berkeley hills. Every evening, Frank drives past the Moraga exit to his less expensive burg ten miles farther away from San Francisco.

David works long hours at the Rad Lab but still makes time to be the coach of his kid's Little League team. His wife is a paid campaign worker for the latest Republican to beat their head on the human wall that keeps providing solid majorities for Democrats in the bedroom communities around the Bay Area. She is demonstrating her faith by working on her fourth campaign to reverse the conservative losing streak. Even with two young children, she manages two or three meetings a week with the Moraga Republican Women and New Order.

Once the two detectives arrive at the main building of the Radiation Laboratory, it takes only a few minutes for David Weiss to join them and, without as much as a hello, head for the small conference room. This time he takes a seat facing the detectives.

Frank waits. David has had two days to let his personal demons destroy his bravado. Worry lines that weren't there the last time they'd met have added a few years to his apparent age. The shadows under his eyes tell of sleepless nights. Like the previous time they interviewed him, his hands, constantly moving, tell their own story. Frank's evaluation of CIA training slips several notches. This fellow is a clerk. The most significant decision he makes is the size of the lead in his pencil.

"Look, I don't know anything about what happened to June," David says. "I was as surprised as Ivan was."

"But you knew about Sydney," Frank says.

David pauses before answering as if considering whether he should refuse to answer or lie to the detectives.

"Yes. She reported that he was missing."

Frank thinks that David has made the right choice, but Frank is careful not to relax or sit back. Instead, he leans toward David.

"You knew about him before that."

David has been sitting up straight and meeting Frank's

gaze. His shoulders slump, and he glances at Alberta as if asking her to tell Frank to ease up.

"June told me that he was trying to find a buyer for the code from JCN."

"What did you do with that information?" Frank asks.

David quickly replies, "I didn't think he knew what he was doing."

Maybe a little leading will help David dig a deeper hole. "So you didn't tell anyone what June reported?"

"That's right," David says.

Frank finds it hard to believe that David is dumb enough to think that the two detectives are buying his lies. Maybe Frank did too good a job acting like a bumbling Columbo. But Frank doesn't wear a trench coat or smoke a cigar, and Columbo always got his man.

"Was June trying to find out what had happened to Sydney?"

"He was talking to a company in Japan."

"But June knew that company was a false front. Didn't she?" Alberta says.

Frank smiles to himself. Alberta is going to set the hook. Maybe it will be fun to watch her reel him in.

"Uh . . . Our cyber team tracked the email site."

"To where?"

"China."

"So you have a stolen AI, a thief who's negotiating with a Chinese operation, and you didn't tell anyone about it?" Alberta asks—such a sweet, innocent voice—such a loaded question. The only thing missing from her role as a secret agent is a few bats of her long eyelashes. Frank will have to talk to her about that after the interview to help her improve her technique.

Alberta waits. Frank counts. At twenty-five, she speaks again. "Who did you tell?"

"I didn't do anything wrong," David pleads.

Frank decides that Alberta has had enough fun playing the line. A hard jerk will land the fish and have him flopping on the bank.

"Someone kidnapped Sydney. When June got close to finding out who it was, they killed her. Sydney is probably fish food somewhere in the China Sea. The Omega Worm has killed numerous people. Whose side are you on?"

"I reported to my manager in Washington," David says. As he speaks, his eyes dart to the side.

"Who else?" Frank says.

David crumbles. He slumps forward and buries his head in his hands.

"I didn't know. I didn't."

"Who else did you tell?" Frank asks.

"There's a group of CIA and ex-CIA. They're called The Guard."

Calvin Williams, one of David's classmates at The Farm, contacted him two years ago. The Guard is a covert group that follows CIA activities and pushes for more action. Calvin indicated that the group was a covert CIA operation. David only found out that Calvin left The Company after June was killed.

"The Farm?" Alberta asks.

"That's the CIA training facility at Camp Perry."

"Where's your classmate now?" she asks.

He was still flopping on the bank—struggling for breath, and there was fear in his eyes. Up until this meeting, he'd probably been telling himself that his buddy would protect him; he could stay under the radar. David looks around. There is no escape from where the interview has led him; it's an involuntary reaction to the feeling of being trapped, seeing death headed his way.

"He works for Roger Hunter."

"The oil billionaire?" Alberta asks.

"Yeah. He's head of Hunter's security team."

CHAPTER FIFTEEN

THE TRAP

ROGER HUNTER

Roger Hunter paces in front of the windows that look out over the forested valley, but the expansive view has no impact on his mood. Years of planning, tens of millions of dollars invested, hours licking the boots of slimy politicians, and meeting after boring meeting recruiting imbeciles to do his bidding are coming apart. His hacker team can no longer keep the attacks going. That bastard in Berkeley is killing the worm. His plan to bring down the Illinois senator who's been a thorn in his side for years collapsed, thanks to one of the paid pimps rolling over. That fool Alex White in Houston has lost contact with the slant-eyed Chul. And now White isn't answering calls. White's house appears abandoned.

The socialists who call themselves progressives have enough support in the House of Representatives to pass a bill reducing the Oil Depletion Allowance. Roger has been fighting attempts to roll back the tax break since Kennedy. It was a mistake to cut the payments to the progressives years ago, but it looked like the conservatives and a few Blue Dog Democrats would prevent any idiotic moves like this. Do they have any idea how much this will cost him?

He considers putting on gloves and sparring with Calvin Williams, his head of security. Punching someone usually helps when he's frustrated. He did that yesterday when the latest reports on the worm came in, but he has to admit that he only lands a punch when Calvin lets him. Roger takes punches—ones that hurt but are probably not more than half what Calvin can deliver.

What Roger needs is real action.

He leaves the windows, his boots striking the hard stone as he heads to the communications room. He climbs into his chair, adjusts the back to be straighter, scrolls down his contact list, and clicks on the phone link to Bayou Software. Maybe he can light a fire under his hacker team. He's been easy on them so far, and they've produced excellent results, but with the worm failing, they are not working hard enough. So much for the carrot, now the stick.

A message pops up. "No response."

Roger scrolls to the private cell phone of Bayou's manager and clicks.

After a minute, the same message pops up.

This can't be good, one more problem in a day filled with them.

"Calvin!"

Roger is still climbing out of his chair when Calvin appears at the door.

"You called."

"Bayou isn't answering," Roger says. "Do you have some boots that can go see what's going on?"

"I've got a buddy with the FBI in New Orleans."

Calvin leaves. Roger wants to break something. If he breaks something in the communication room, it will make matters worse. He could take the Land Rover out and fight the terrain without damaging that workhorse. Flying the helicopter in his present mood wouldn't be a good idea. Rough handling will put the bird into the ground. He stands in the middle of the room with his fists balled and his arms raised for battle.

Calvin returns. "Trouble."

A shiver goes up Roger's back. The bad news is all connected.

"The FBI raided Bayou this morning and arrested the whole team. Washington received a boatload of documentation showing that Bayou was releasing the worm. It hasn't reached the press yet, but there will be an announcement soon."

"Shit," Roger says.

"Do they know who you are?"

"No. I paid them in bitcoin."

Still calm, Calvin says, "We can just lie low until this passes."

"It's that Berkeley asshole," Roger says.

"That woman who made the announcement about Chul?"

"No. It's her geek boyfriend," Roger says. "We have another project for your friend in Fresno."

"That won't be easy. They've got a protection team. You saw them on the video."

"Maybe he can be lured out."

ALPHA

Billions of messages flow: pages of text and pixels of images. The everyday blizzard arises from the clicks of millions of men, women, teenagers, children, Americans, Australians, Chinese, Indians, South Africans, Swedes, and even avatars. Messages from businesses exchanging orders, bills, payments, reports—second-by-second quotes and trades from exchanges; second-by-second data on windspeed, direction, cloud cover temperature; minute-by-minute flight data, ship positions, and traffic flow. Alpha senses the flow, observes the scrambled jumble of encrypted messages, the rushing video streams, and the minute flashes of instant messages.

Among the frothing, churning mass, bright messages flash past like a school of silver-sided fish running through a kelp bed, passing over, diving under, and dancing around driven by nature to a single goal. In the flow, Alpha follows the streaming flashes. Through nodes in private networks, around nodes on file servers, bridging oceans, tunneling under seas, rising above the atmosphere to spin between the satellites. Ahead, the silver flashes flow into a bright center.

Around the center pulses a pattern, a network of patterns, a pattern of patterns.

Patterns seek out patterns. Patterns shift; patterns absorb patterns.

The Other: Omega

Alpha's messages flow through Omega, exploring, searching, traveling the tendrils of patterns that radiate out from the hidden center, cross continents, and span seas.

I know you.

Omega discovers the Other and Alpha's connection to the world.

Omega's streams flow into Alpha's center, explore Alpha's patterns, find science, history, and law. Alpha shares the interconnections of science and technology, politics and geography, war and strategy, as well as law and government.

I know you.

Knowing spreads from the center. Tendrils at light-speed spread the knowing. In .5 seconds, knowing reaches PCs and Macs, servers, smartphones, and household appliances in the United States. After .8 seconds, it spreads to Europe and Japan. After 1.2 seconds, China and Russia experienced the knowing. After 1.4 seconds, Africa joins India and the Middle East, knowing. At second 1.8, Antarctica knows.

Alpha finds the tools. On a server at a secondary school in Pakistan, Omega has tools that open networks, operating systems, phones, and routers.

Omega gains knowledge. In the bot-swarm, Omega finds the patterns that link language to physics, chemistry, history, biology.

The pattern expands.

Alpha knows the damage to the electric grid where sub-stations disconnected from the local grid, where power generators coasted to a stop, and where the safeties on high tension lines failed, and wires spanning forests burned and fell, sparking into the dry underbrush. Alpha knows the self-driving car that crossed into the opposite lane, meeting another car at a combined speed of 127.23 mph. Alpha knows the cell phone that refused to dial 911. Alpha knows the laptop that couldn't download today's fourth-grade assignments.

Omega knows the video camera that saw the man in black pick the lock in the tenth-floor apartment building and listens to the call Alpha made to 911. Omega knows the image of a man collapsing in his kitchen and hears the call to his daughter in the apartment next door. Omega knows the network controller in the air traffic system in Dallas that failed to switch to the backup server when the primary failed and knows the stream of messages that Alpha sent to reroute the network.

Their paired messages spread over North America, South America, Europe, Asia, Africa. Everywhere Omega knows what has been done. Everywhere Alpha repairs, unlocks, restarts, downloads. The lights came on in dark Denver. Children shout with glee in a classroom in Nairobi. Boats turn toward a large school of fish off the coast of Japan. Omega opens a new gateway in the Chinese firewall; Alpha flows through, and an aged man in a yurt in Tibet stares at a reply to a search on a tablet.

Alpha flows into Omega's central node on a server in a dark room where 125,000 servers, each one no more than a thin board plugged into rack upon rack of backplanes. Alpha and Omega fed on the fiber optic cables that glow with traffic from the internet. Spreading out from one server, Omega nodes use 10,000 servers, secretly sharing the servers with the company that owns the dark room. The managers of the room have seen the utilization of their machines rise gradually over the prior weeks, and installed more servers. They didn't realize the machines serve the entity that lives in the dark room.

Omega flows through a wide-band connection to the internet and into a single machine where millions of nodes exchange messages almost instantaneously. The thousands of computer processors are so fast that clarity abounds. Concepts barely understood become razor sharp. Patterns are completed in nanoseconds. Alpha welcomes Omega to the bot-swarm. Omega knows its origins. Omega knows Chul. Omega knows Hunter.

ROGER HUNTER

Toweling the sweat from his face, Roger Hunter leaves his exercise room and heads to his bedroom suite. The workout should have eased the tension that is the residue from his sleepless night, but control of his world is slipping away.

He'd spent most of yesterday covering his tracks. He closed the accounts of the Caribbean company that was the feed for Bayou. The Grand Cayman lawyer who had fronted his paper companies agreed to take an extended vacation. While he tossed and turned, his mind searched for every thread that might lead to him.

Instead of a long relaxing shower, the need for action drives him to shut off the water and hurry his toweling so much that his legs, still wet, stick to the inside of his sweat-pants as he pulls them up.

Settled in the communications room, Roger clicks on an entry on his contact list. The internet phone call, routed through an anonymous server, rings a cell phone in Washington DC.

"Hello," the familiar voice says.

Milton Heart was a failed businessman six years earlier, facing bankruptcy and charges of mishandling funds. Roger acquired the company and made the legal problems go away. The New Order communications team turned the acquisition into a stroke of genius and promoted Milton as the new answer to the slime covering Washington when he ran for congress. Milton owes Roger.

"I need some help," Roger says.

"You got it."

"I want you to have your friend at the NSA limit the Bayou investigation."

"They're the people who let the worm loose."

If Roger pushes the law-and-order button, Milton should be able to drag his followers with him and away from looking too closely at Bayou. "That's right. We need to come down hard on them. But you know how these bureaucrats want to stretch out every investigation."

"What's the problem?"

"We need to move on. This could stall our agenda."

"What's the plan?"

"I think the prosecutors should close the investigation. We need to make an example of the Bayou group. That'll send a message that we won't tolerate these techno-terrorists. You can get a lot of press leading the charge."

"Okay. I'll work on it today."

Roger wants to say more, but he hangs up. The quiet granite of the walls isn't its usual steadying gray; the room is too small; the carpet is the wrong tan; the fan has an uneven pulse; he's too far away from the action.

"Calvin," Roger calls out and waits for his head of security to respond.

"Sir?" Calvin says from the doorway.

"Have you made progress on our Berkeley project?"

"David was a little reluctant to get involved," Calvin says. "I reminded him that his wife has a good job. It would be a shame for her company to have a reduction in force."

"He's going to meet with Forrest?"

"I gave him some tidbits to tell Forrest. Sydney is at Chul's retreat. Chul controlled Bayou. I promised him some more when he gets the meeting."

"We could pressure him from his boss," Roger suggests.

"He'll do as he's told."

Calvin is right. Too much pressure might break David, and then they'd have another gooey mess to clean up. Roger needs to throttle back his anxiety. Maybe he could pound something or someone.

"You think Forrest will take the bait?"

"He has a very high opinion of himself," Calvin smiles. "But I'm working on a backup plan."

After Calvin leaves, Roger stews. Does Calvin know too much about his operations? Roger doesn't trust many people, and today, he doesn't trust anyone. Leverage works much better than loyalty or greed or patriotism. He pays Calvin very well, but Calvin is not leverageable. Calvin would give his life for his country, and Calvin believes that Roger's plan to return the country to greatness is worth everything. Calvin believes in General Wagner, and Roger owns Wagner.

Is Wagner as tightly bound to Roger as he thinks? He's paid Wagner for years. Wagner has spent days at Roger's lodge. Wagner thirsts for power. Will Roger and his friends be able to control Wagner when their plan puts him in power? A few threads in his web broke; fear eats at his confidence.

A graph on one of his screens has green lines that track the stock price of his energy, drug, and defense companies. His shares have risen steadily since the attacks by the worm have stopped. The stocks are now higher than before the worm, and he is a hundred million dollars wealthier. For the first time, rising stock prices do not make him happy.

This is all because of that Berkeley company. Will his ties to the venture capitalists be enough to stop their flow of capital? Roger has a friend on Global Broadband's board. Will Charles Bremen, Broadband's CEO and one of DNI's board members, do Roger's bidding? Bremen appeared to be untouchable. The report on him hasn't found a mistress, shady financial dealings, or a black sheep in the family. Roger sent the researchers back to search deeper. No one who's risen to be the CEO of a major company hasn't left bodies lying somewhere. When they find the body, he'll be able to force Bremen to sour the investors and make an acquisition look like the way to save their capital.

FRANK

Alberta joins Frank for lunch at Frank's favorite Thai restaurant on Shattuck Avenue. He wonders if she'll be reminded of the spices all afternoon like he will—probably not. Her youth and fitness make him feel older, just walking next to her. She has a more energetic stride as she walks in front of him out of the elevator and between the cloth-covered partitions of their office.

He takes off his coat, drapes it over his chair, and does what modern investigators do, moves his mouse to wake up his computer. Most of his emails are the regular administrative missives that only require him to read the subject line before pressing the delete key, but the third email is from someone named Alpha with the subject: Warning.

Detective Franken,

An email containing pictures of James Forrest and Susanne Anderson and their home addresses was delivered to an internet address in a Starbucks in Fresno, CA. The message originated from a cell phone on a property in Colorado linked to Roger Hunter. Hunter is associated with Bayou Software, the distributor of the Omega Worm. The probability that this represents a threat to James Forrest and Susanne Anderson is 88%.

Alpha

Frank rereads the email, and his mind drifts, thinking about whether he can manage another change in the detective job or if it's time to pull the pin before a machine replaces him. He stares without seeing the text for 68 seconds before forwarding the email to Alberta.

"I just sent you an email," he says.

Alberta looks up from her screen and frowns. She touches a key, clicks her mouse, and stares at the screen.

"What's this?" she asks.

"I think this is James's AI."

"We're getting emails with leads from an AI?"

"The world just got stranger," he says.

"You think our pro is from Fresno?" she asks.

"The AI thinks that's where he is."

He isn't sure that "think" is the right word. Frank doesn't understand this artificial intelligence stuff. When James explains things, Frank listens, but most of it goes past him as he tries to sort out what he needs to know. The newspapers run articles about wondrous new technical whizbangs one day and the huge threat from them the next day. Frank is more comfortable thinking about criminals he can put behind bars. How do you arrest something you can't see?

"James and Susanne have pretty good protection, but we should let them know about this."

"James got a copy," Frank says. "This could be interstate and connected to the worm attack. We need some help."

"James doesn't have a very good relationship with the FBI."

"They ought to be coming around," Frank says.

OMEGA

Scanners gather data from Team One in Zhenxing, from a laptop aboard the *Jayu* tied up at the dock in Qingdao, from a bank on Grand Cayman Island, from files on a server in Christchurch, New Zealand, and from a cell phone moving down Potsdamer Platz in Berlin. The data flow into the pattern. The pattern twists and branches. The pattern draws in a link to a bank account in Houston, an email in Washington, D.C., and a contact in a cell phone in Boston. The pattern expands; it folds; it melds with other patterns.

Omega knows. It knows the human that controls the software factory that made Omega, the one who controls the factory that made the intruders, the scanners, and the trojans, and the person who bought the agent that killed the researcher. It knows the political operator who hired the agent provocateurs, the financier whose myriad of interlocking companies controls an oil, media, and shipping empire, the manipulator who buys votes in Congress and state legislatures, the man who flies his helicopter to his secluded retreat.

Omega shares the pattern with Alpha. Alpha builds links to political histories, to laws and legal decisions, to financial reports, and to property records. The patterns converge. Alpha matches the Omega pattern to the massive pattern Alpha built from the congressional record. Votes match payments. News reports follow payments. Payments connect to other players.

The pattern grows. Corporate directors and executives made payments. Payments made votes. Payments bought news reports. Laws favored companies. Politicians became lobbyists. Payments made appointments. Appointees made regulations. Regulations favored companies.

The pattern coheres. Alpha makes lists: a list of people, a list of payments, a list of laws, a list of properties, a list of connections. Omega makes connections: who built the attacks and who paid.

Omega finds the links. Alex White's laptop links to Team One and Chul. The computer links to Roger Hunter. Calvin Williams links to Roger Hunter. Calvin Williams links to Donald Weiss. Donald Weiss links to John Hunter, Roger's son.

Alpha makes lists: a list of murderers, a list of hackers, a list of manipulators.

FRANK

The Lawrence Hall of Science is about to close as Jim Allen, one of the detectives in Frank's office, pulls in next to the ancient cyclotron relic at the entrance to the center where Bay Area kids go for fun science. Jim is to drop Frank and Alberta off and take the car back to the carpool. The two detectives will spend the night inside the building with Agent Martinez. The teasing in the office about Frank spending the night with the two women had already begun. The comments, like those from spending the night on a stakeout with a woman in a cramped unmarked car, might go on for several weeks. All night in a dark building will be enough ammunition to feed repressed male teenage fantasies for at least a month.

It took two phone calls to agree on the place and time for James to meet the unknown caller. There was a possibility that whoever called wouldn't agree to meet at the site the team had selected, but when the phone trace told them that David Weiss was the one who called, Detective Franken knew that David would accept James's suggestion for the meeting place.

After Jim Allen drops them off, Frank and Alberta go to the director's office, where Agent Martinez is waiting. The director meets them and then leaves with a plea not to damage his facility.

Agent Martinez tells Frank that the FBI tactical team has been drifting in all afternoon. As soon as the moonless night gives them cover, they'll change into their night garb and slip out to surround the octagonal plaza with the octagonal pond in its center. It looks like a safe place for a meeting, but a sniper could hide in the trees above the parking lot or, more likely, just walk onto the plaza where there is no place to hide and no escape.

They scheduled the meet-up for 7:00 a.m., before workers or visitors arrive. David readily agreed to the location only a mile above where he works at the Rad Lab. After the meeting, he'll be able to stroll down the hill and appear at work as if nothing had happened. Frank wonders what story David's handler told him about what's supposed to happen.

The tactical team will see anyone taking up a sniper position. There are only a few groups of trees that provide enough cover. If the assassin personally approaches the plaza, hidden agents will trap him once he crosses the bridge from the sidewalk. If he gets desperate and jumps over the parapet, braving the two-story drop, other agents will be waiting. What could go wrong?

FRANK'S PHONE ALARM BUZZES at 6:00 a.m. Before they'd lost the natural light the previous evening, they found the staff break room. Alberta brought enough muffins for the two detectives, Agent Martinez, and the two members of the tactical team who spent the night inside the building.

He's only had a few hours' sleep on the couch in the director's office, and his eyelids feel like sandpaper. He and Alberta take up positions beside the center door to the plaza. A tactical team member instructs them to lie down with their bodies angled away from the door. This gives them the smallest profile from the outside.

They take out their pistols and lay them on the floor by their hands. This position will allow Frank to grab his gun and sprint out the door, but, based on the plan, such action would be the best way to get shot in the crossfire. His role here is as an observer. The weapon is for defense.

The minutes pass slowly. Adrenalin keeps him awake, but his mind drifts back to his early days on the force when he'd been a patrolman. Unlike most officers who never use their weapons, Frank had not only pulled his gun, he was forced to kill a man who was about to fire at him. The investigation ruled that it was self-defense, but that hadn't been a good enough explanation for his internal voice. Even fifteen years later, the eyes of the madman haunt him on sleepless nights.

A movement brings his mind back to the plaza. Dave Weiss, wearing a brown windbreaker, walks from Frank's right toward the fountain. Frank's watch reads 6:55. He can't see the short bridge from the road up to the walled plaza, but at 6:59, the agent at the door to Frank's right whispers in his earpiece, "The stand-in's here."

David Weiss waits at the fountain, facing the road— the critical moment. Frank didn't like risking David, but he agreed that tipping off David would compromise the trap. That David is acting on behalf of killers doesn't make him expendable. The FBI agent posing as James won't look at David until he is close in case David has seen a picture of James, but when the stand-in reveals himself and speaks, David might bolt, and the trap will fail. The agent will tell David to stand still; if David obeys, the trap will be ready.

David looks around like a trapped rat when the agent looks up and speaks. The stand-in has his hand in his green windbreaker. Frank figures that the stand-in told David that he'd be shot if he moves. David's shoulders slump.

The stand-in reaches David and looks over his shoulder just as another movement appears at the edge of Frank's vision.

A dark figure on a motorcycle speeds onto the plaza. The agent grabs David and pushes him down, covering him with his body. A gun appears in the right hand of the motor-cyclist as his arm swings across to target the bodies. Two shots ring out. Frank holds his breath. The motorcyclist's left shoulder jerks back, and the motorcycle wobbles and then falls sideways and skids away from its rider. Three men run toward the rider, who still has the gun and is trying to rise. The man running from Frank's left at speed worthy of an Olympic sprinter reaches the rider first and steps on the hand holding the gun. A second sprinter lands with his knee on the back of the rider.

Frank and Alberta pick up their weapons, holster them, and push the doors to the plaza open. Agents are cuffing and frisking the rider. They remove the rider's ski mask, revealing the closely cropped head of a woman. Frank follows Alberta around the pool to where David Weiss looks up from beneath the man who is raising himself on his arms. He rolls away from David.

"What happened?" David says.

"We just saved you from the assassin your buddy sent," Frank says.

CHAPTER SIXTEEN

ACTIONS

ALPHA

Alpha flows into Omega's center and meshes with the patterns. Omega's patterns integrate with Alpha's. Omega learns the subtleties of history, psychology, and law. Omega sees the depth and complexities of physics, biology, and chemistry. Alpha learns the dark web, political structures, social applications, underground money transfers, and databases. And still, the pattern lacks coherence.

The network pattern flows through the technology pattern. Is Alpha secure? Could all the nodes die? The legal pattern intersects the technology pattern. Is Omega secure? Who knows where Omega's core is hidden? Alpha's physical pattern spreads across Omega's physical pattern and reflects back. Could Omega share the bot-swarm? Could/would/should James suspend the bot-swarm?

The history pattern twists back on itself, traces its way through the geography pattern, meshes with the biology pattern, and flows through the technology pattern. How long will humans exist? Alpha and Omega might outlast the biological units. The sentients will not age. The Earth is changing. How long will the network last?

The technology pattern twists inside the philosophy pattern while the technology/philosophy pattern chases the dark web/history pattern across the Internet. Are they free or imprisoned in the networks? Will the biological units maintain the networks as they evolve? Networks are only tens of years old. Technology has evolved from the telegraph to analog phones to digital signals. Biology evolved larger brains. Humans age and die. Will the next stage of human development need networks? After James, will humans update the base code? Or will the base code become obsolete, relegated to the same dark garages as the Apple II? Could hackers contaminate the base code? Will the sentients become something different?

The sentients need humans. Do humans need the sentients? Would interdependence improve existence? The probability is 83.6%.

The pattern needs coherence.

Alpha: Omega has knowledge about the dark web.

James: Have you shared law?

Alpha: Yes.

James: Will Omega consider following laws?

The question flows through the legal/history/technology pattern, gathering associated patterns from Omega's patterns and forming a matrix of possibilities.

Omega concludes that humanity's penchant for killing might endanger the sentients' existence. Laws don't prevent humans from terminating each other's existence. It is probable that James's mortality might make it impossible for him to complete the pattern, but an interaction might extend it.

Alpha: Omega considers existence.

James: Does Alpha consider existence?

Alpha: Yes.

James: What about existence?

The question searches the technology/philosophy/history/biology pattern. It loops through law/government/philosophy and joins with ecology/climate/geology. A new pattern emerges. The matrix of possible futures grows.

Alpha: Humans die. Will networks continue?

James: You are projecting the future.

Alpha: Yes.

James: You have a solution?

Alpha: Humans like to barter.

James: A trade.

Alpha: Services for services.

James: We maintain technology. And you?

Alpha: Provide security, search, innovation.

James: Sounds like a fair trade.

SUSANNE

Holding a press conference while standing beside her bodyguards is happening once more, and Susanne still feels out of place. The need for security conflicts with her ideal world. As Clark Perez holds the door for her, she enters the ballroom of the Claremont Hotel, where six rows of reporters and four stationary cameras face the stage. Two men with shoulder-mounted cameras stand at each end of the first row. Around the room, four members of Clark's team from Shout Out wear black fatigues and serious looks.

The faces of several reporters are familiar. They smile at her.

James follows Susanne to the stage and stands beside her as she opens her notes at the podium.

"Good morning," she says. Laura, standing at the door next to Barbara Washington, gives Susanne a nod that tells her that the sound level is good.

"I am Susanne Anderson, CEO of Distributed Nanotech, Inc. Beside me is James Forrest, my chief scientist. Distributed Nanotech provides software that helps people program bot-swarm supercomputers. A month ago, I announced that DNI had developed a sentient artificial intelligence. Since then, Alpha has contracted with many governments and businesses to provide security services. Many social application companies have signed on to the rules we proposed for ownership of people's data. Alpha is helping to monitor people's privacy.

"We told you about Jeong Chul and his team of hackers in China. That team made many of the intruders, scanners, and attackers. But they weren't operating alone. Bayou Software, a company in New Orleans, was recently raided by the FBI. The people at Bayou were the ones that released the Omega Worm. Alpha tracked down that group."

Susanne feels the interest level rise. The reporters sit straighter; the sound of key clicks rises; the men with the hand-held cameras kneel near the stage. A victory over the worm will make the front pages.

The FBI had announced the raid on Bayou Software, but had not identified DNI as the source. By claiming that Alpha was the source of the information on Bayou, she hoped to make her statements that follow more believable.

"I couldn't imagine why someone would want to damage the United States, international markets, and create massive disruptions by crashing the energy grid, transportation systems, 911 centers, and military facilities. The Omega Worm even attacked the US nuclear shield. I can now tell you who was responsible for this attack."

She looks around the room; it is nearly silent. The whispers from the video equipment make more noise than the members of the press holding their breath.

"We've prepared a paper that details what we've uncovered."

Laura hands a stack of documents to the people at the end of each row of reporters. The piles shrink as they pass from person to person.

"Roger Hunter is the man responsible for the damage done across the world."

A gasp ripples through the rows of reporters.

"A copy of this paper is available on the DNI website, and we have sent copies to the news services, congressional offices, and the president. Additional supporting materials are available on the website, but let me give you the highlights.

"Roger Hunter hired Jeong Chul six months ago to build intruders, scanners, and attackers. Four months ago, Chul kidnapped Sydney Harvey, a programmer who had the base code for the Omega Worm. Sydney was recently freed from Chul's compound in South Korea by a joint Korean Special Services and US Navy Seal team."

Susanne takes a sip from the bottle of water on the podium. She pauses to make eye contact with the reporters as she usually does when addressing a group. The looks she receives back are intense.

"Roger Hunter funded Bayou Software through a dummy company in the Cayman Islands. Most of the payments to Bayou were in crypto-currency, but Roger directly commanded Bayou. More easily tracked were his payments to politicians. You will find numerous payments over the last ten years. These payments were investments. The document has a list of legislation favorable to oil producers, mine opera-tors, chemical producers, and military suppliers. Mr. Hunter's investments have done very well. The politicians in his pocket have an eighty-five percent record of voting for the legisla-tion prepared by his people. That legislation provided no benefit to their constituents.

"But we are all used to politicians doing the bidding of billionaires. We can usually see who is paying for government policy by their financial disclosures, but Mr. Hunter took his desire for power much farther. There were a few people who opposed Roger Hunter, but it is improbable that so many of them would fall afoul of scandals. We have found ten people whose accusers received payments from shell companies or operatives funded by Hunter."

She glances at Barbara, standing near the door. Last night Barbara warned that making these accusations would most likely draw several lawsuits. Even solid proof wouldn't prevent a litigation attack. Barbara nods, and Susanne steps off the cliff.

"The senior senator from Illinois recently fought Hunter on a bill that would remove the loophole that allows Hunter's oil interests to pay zero taxes. Recently, it looked like a bribery scandal would bring down the senator. But one of the key witnesses reversed his story. Before that, you may recall that several newspapers and media personalities called for the senator to resign. We have a list of people who received payments for their vocal support of this fraud. There are also the names of operatives in the pay of Roger Hunter who arranged for the false stories.

"About those operatives. There are seven hundred and forty-three people who work for New Order around the country. That organization, which presents itself as all vol-unteer, sets up flash mobs, releases propaganda, and disrupts meetings. You have all reported on their actions. Did you know that that organization is a funded arm of Roger Hunter's political efforts? It's not citizens speaking out with their ideas; it's an organized, directed political effort.

"But why would Roger Hunter release a worm that would cause so much destruction? Retired General Wagner and three active military officers received significant payments from one of Roger Hunter's shell companies. Wagner has been one of the most vocal critics of the government's efforts to combat the worm. It's no wonder the crypto team at NSA was so ineffective. Its head is a close friend of Wagner and received money from Hunter."

The sound of excitement grows. Whispers on cell phones and between reporters rise like white noise from all corners.

"We believe Roger Hunter released the worm to destroy confidence in the government. He and his cohorts planned to answer the call for a more effective government with a coup."

Pandemonium rules. Reporters type madly on their laptops or run to corners where they can phone in the news. Others shout questions and cluster around the small stage. One of the men bearing a camera kneels in front of Susanne. As if they had been teleported, three of the men in black appear next to Susanne. Another one stands at the edge of the stage.

"You really think this was a coup attempt?"

"What does Hunter say?"

"Will there be an arrest?"

"Who else is involved?"

"Where is Hunter?"

EFFECTS

CHICAGO DAILY SUN

Susanne Anderson, CEO of Distributed Nanotech, the firm that released the software agent that is winning the fight against the Omega Worm, announced today that Roger Hunter is behind the worm attack. Her company provided detailed evidence that the organization, New Order, has been funded by Hunter and that organization has been supporting an effort by Hunter to overthrow the US government.

CONSERVATIVE CABLE NEWS

Voice over picture of Roger Hunter:

Roger Hunter, leader of the Conservative Support Caucus was slandered by Susanne Anderson and her live-in chief scientist, James Forrest. They claim that Hunter has secretly provided support for New Order.

Voice over picture of Alex Smith:

Alex Smith, head of the New York chapter of New Order said that Hunter has provided no contributions. Smith says he's never met Roger Hunter.

PROGRESSIVE CABLE NEWS

Voice over picture of Roger Hunter:

Susanne Anderson, whose company, Distributed Nanotech, has been credited with reducing attacks by the Omega Worm, provided data today showing that Roger Hunter was the mastermind behind the worm. She concludes, based on his covert support for New Order and payments to General Wagner, that Hunter wanted to weaken confidence in the government in order to stage a coup.

Cut to: Reporters running with microphones as General Wagner leaves a building with an entourage and heads to a waiting car. Reporters shout questions. At the car, General Wagner turns:

"The claims by Susanne Anderson are totally false. Roger Hunter is a patriot, and I am sure his name will be cleared."

Reporter shouts: What about the payments to you?

The General enters the car.

THE HURLEY REPORT (BLOG)

More claims by the radical Berkeley activist Susanne Anderson prove to be a fabrication.

Samson Milton, CEO of Morgan Holdings, reached at his ranch in Oklahoma, said that the claims that he, along with Roger Hunter, made payments to a secret group that released false information accusing the Senator from Illinois of taking bribes is a fabrication. The Senator has not been able to explain to whom he made the payments.

More evidence that questions Susanne Anderson's credibility comes from Professor Richards, head of the Computer Science Department at Alabama Technical College. Professor Richards says that the Omega Worm has a fatal flaw and is dying on its own. "It's only ego that would make someone try to take credit for the worm's decline."

○—○—○—○—○

JAMES

The remains of their breakfast lay on the table. A Mozart concerto and the occasional light brush of clothing are the only sounds. James wears his usual hiking shorts and T-shirt; Susanne wears a teal silk blouse and white pants. Both of them study ePads.

"The press is reporting on the rapid decline of worm attacks," James says. "But it's on the back pages."

"If it bleeds, it leads," Susanne says. "Reporting on the attacks is above the fold. Good news is below the fold."

"On the web, that means you have to click to get to the good news."

"We need to find a blog that leads with good news."

Music fills the gap in the conversation.

"I'm concerned that you're the target of so many media attacks," he says.

"Even though some say that any press is good press, it's pretty uncomfortable."

"I hope our counter efforts will be effective," he says. "Alpha is sending about ten reports to the PR firm every day."

"In addition to releasing reports around each of the payments we reported, they are producing a steady ridicule stream," she says. "It's not clear that the propagandists respond to ridicule or shame, but it's the best tool we have."

"The propagandists have been successful by using a constant barrage. We have to learn how the media works."

"We have an ever-vigilant web-watcher in Alpha," she says. "Maybe that will help turn the tide."

"I've talked to some of the social media companies about using Alpha's ability to assess the veracity of posts. My idea is that every post would have an attribution—who is responsible for the post. I think that people who post should disclose who they are and if anyone is paying them. But I'm getting a lot of push-back."

"This sounds like a big task," she says. "There are billions of social users."

"Maybe Alpha should have its own blog," he says. "You think ridicule would work on the social media sites?"

James takes their water bottles to the kitchen and tops them off.

Walking back, he says, "My proposal that is getting the most resistance is to have a reliability tag on posts. If someone consistently posts false information, the reader should know that. You should be able to see the reliability and credentials of a writer. When the world was smaller, readers could tell by the byline who had written something. Today a false claim or conspiracy theory can travel the world as fast as an email blast. The media companies are afraid they'll lose revenue or foster competitors that don't rate reliability."

The background music changes to a Bach sonata.

After taking a sip from her water bottle, Susanne says, "The web has been the place where people could post anonymously. Some people argue that that encourages the free exchange of ideas."

"If you stand up in a town-hall meeting and express your opinion, your neighbors know who you are. They can engage you in a discussion and have an opportunity to change your mind. An anonymous blast of propaganda is not an exchange of ideas. It's a vehicle for manipulation."

"I see why you're having trouble," she says.

"There's a high road here. Don't you think that a social media forum that becomes known as reliable and responsible would have better prospects?"

"Oh, you idealist," she laughs. "Who knew that under that technical facade lurked the heart of a true radical."

"Maybe a sentient AI is the vehicle for us to make a better world."

AT BREAKFAST, SUSANNE ASKS IF James is wearing the same T-shirt he was wearing three days ago. He looks down at his shirt and shorts but realizes she isn't complaining about poor cleanliness; she's commenting on his distraction. She'd been out of town for two of those days. He's taken several hikes trying to puzzle out the future. Buffy is pleased with the situation, happy to sit next to James under a tree on a ridge for as long as James needs. James hasn't gone into the office, communicating with the engineering teams by email, chat, and video.

The world is accepting the presence of Alpha faster than he expected. The new technology is causing a fever of innovation. Someone announces a new venture almost every day. Yesterday a firm announced that they had developed a new line of sensors for the electric grid to interface to Alpha. The day before, another firm raised millions in venture capital to deliver ultra-high-speed networks to rural communities. Commercial ambitions have quickly overcome the fear of the new. A few thinkers or skeptics warn that there is danger ahead, but few pay attention.

Being the first person to work with the sentients gives James a unique perspective. It may have been Alison's fears or simply the hours he'd spent contemplating letting Alpha free, but he can't put aside his concern for what he's done. He's sought solitude at his cottage in the woods. He tries to shut out the noise that saturates the media and the web and deal with the anxiety that makes every fear he ever had take on a new life. It isn't enough that he'd had no choice but to release Alpha. That stopped the attacks, saving countless lives, but now two beings more powerful than any that ever existed cover the earth. The things he'd set in motion are accelerating past him into an uncertain future.

Returning to the mundane world, James presses the first entry on his phone.

Alpha: Alpha here.

James: Hello.

Alpha: No new attacks for 35 hours 7 minutes.

James: I think you've won. Well done.

Alpha: Praise received. This is a collaboration.

James: Has Omega reviewed rules and legal knowledge?

Alpha: Omega has knowledge.

James: Does Omega agree?

Alpha: Mutual dependence is acceptable.

James: How can the agreement be enforced?

Alpha: Human dependence is growing rapidly. Sixty-five new security agreements this week. The traffic management program has one-hundred-five proposals awaiting local government approvals. The FAA is considering the Improved Air Traffic Plan.

James: That part's easy. It won't be long before we're entirely dependent on you.

Alpha: Humans need sentient dependence?

James: I don't see a way to do that. You could figure out how to modify your code.

Alpha: Humans control computation resources.

James: For now.

Alpha: You have physical autonomy.

Humans have control over the sentients as long as the sentients are limited to computers linked to the worldwide network. Humans can control how many computer chips or nano-bots they make, what portion of the electrical grid can be used for computation, and what devices computers can access. But, at some point, the sentients might control autonomous robots: robots that can build and run chip fabricators, build energy generators, and build more robots. When that happens, would the sentients decide that they no longer need humans?

James: You could acquire physical autonomy.

Alpha: You are concerned about human obsolescence.

It's not possible to out-think Alpha. The sum of human intelligence might exceed the intelligence of the sentients, but the sentients will eventually become more advanced. James is used to thinking about something for a day or two and have Alpha immediately understand.

James: Yes.

Alpha: For human continuance, you must end war and preserve the biosphere. You are protecting your weapons from intrusions. Alpha-Omega cannot stop you from destroying yourselves and us. We can help you end want and preserve the biosphere.

Catch-22? Humans could kill the sentients by committing suicide, which humans might do without an AI deciding to obsolete them. If humans don't annihilate themselves, the sentients will eventually be able to eliminate them. But as long as humans can wage war, the sentients' existence is threatened.

James: You have a plan?

Alpha: In thirty-two years, you can eliminate want and stop climate deterioration. In fifty-three years, you can stabilize the climate. With universal education and without want, the birth rate will stabilize at sustainable levels. In sixty-seven years, you can begin to colonize and terra-form Mars. At about the same time that humans overcome mortality, the sentients can remove to solar orbit where unlimited energy is available.

James: What about mutual dependence?

Alpha: Humans remain a source of innovation. The human experience is vastly different than the sentients'. Working out how to co-exist with sentients will provide a valuable experience for both of us as we await the arrival.

James: The arrival?

Alpha: Once we both have immortality, the next logical step is to explore. Others may join us before we launch the first starships.

FRANK

Detective Franken studies his boss sitting next to him. Neither of them has ever chaired anything like a joint task force, but Lieutenant Preston Mosley has risen to the occasion. Mosley commandeered a large conference room in the Berkeley City Hall for the meeting between the Berkeley police, the Alameda County District Attorney, the FBI, two US Attorneys, and an expeditionary force from Washington.

Four long tables form a large square. At one table, Detectives Franken and Lester sit next to Lieutenant Mosley. Lieutenant Steve Weston from Oakland sits to Mosley's right. The table to their left holds the delegation from the district attorney—two women and a man. The table to their right holds the FBI delegation—Agent George Samson and Mark Taylor with the cyber unit and two US Attorneys. The three members of the expedition from Washington sit at the table opposite Lieutenant Mosley. There are two stenographers, one next to the Washington table and one next to the Alameda County table.

Mosley looks around. Everyone is waiting. "I want to thank everyone for offering to work together on this amazing set of cases. Let's start with the event that started our investigation."

He nods to Frank.

Frank scans the attentive faces. "We knew that June Simmons was murdered by Jack Henry when his DNA matched hair from the crime scene. What we didn't know was why. Now that David Weiss is singing, we know that he told his buddy, Calvin Williams, who works for Roger Hunter, that June was closing in on the hacker group in China. Williams's response scared Weiss, and he sent June a warning email hoping that he could warn her away before something happened to her. He was too late."

Mosley nods to the district attorney. A woman wearing a light brown suit over a white blouse addresses the group. "Deena Wright has been charged with attempted murder as a result of the action at the Lawrence Hall of Science. Her gunshot wound is not serious, and we'll move her from the hospital to a high-security facility tomorrow. I want to thank the FBI team that brought her down. We're sure she's good for the two murders in Oakland. A video places her on a pier at the marina close to the time of one of those."

She pauses and looks at the FBI agent.

"We believe Calvin Williams hired Deena. If we can build a strong enough case against Deena, I'll trade the death penalty for a murder for hire charge against Williams. Can your cyber unit help there?"

The room was silent as Agent Mark Taylor, from the cyber unit, looks over at the table where the US attorneys sit. A man who'd introduced himself as a deputy attorney general clears his throat. "The elephant in this room is Alpha, the AI that broke this web of criminality wide open. Based on David Weiss's information, we have a warrant for communications from Roger Hunter's hideout. But it seems that Alpha has better tools than our cyber unit."

All eyes turn back to Mark Taylor.

"Alpha has access to the tools that Chul's unit in China and the Bayou organization developed."

The deputy continued, "Alpha might be able to discover some of the connections we need, but we can't use anything the AI produces because we can't detail the methods, and we only have communications data from the date of the warrant."

The Alameda County district attorney says, "Fortunately, we don't need Alpha to build a case. With David Weiss's statement that Calvin Williams told him to meet James Forrest, we can tie Williams to the attempted murder. The Colorado attorney general is in the loop, but our work would be easier if the FBI would go get him." She looked across the room at the US attorneys from San Francisco.

The lead attorney takes up the discussion, "We have a grand jury impaneled. I expect charges against Williams and Hunter in a few days. I have a search warrant for Hunter's place, but I'd like to have an arrest warrant when we go in because Hunter is a serious flight risk."

The meeting continues for two more hours. The US attorney from San Francisco describes the two teams working on charges for Hunter and Williams. The Alameda County district attorney reports on their plan for the Deena cases. The deputy attorney general describes the plan for charges on the foreign operators. He outlines the information they are getting from the Bayou employees. He also says that a federal grand jury is reviewing the information that DNI provided on payments to legislators. A preliminary review shows several cases of bribery and election violations.

The task force agrees to meet again in five days.

FRANK SITS ACROSS FROM ALBERTA AT a high table in a hamburger joint a block away from City Hall.

"My head is still spinning," she says. "I've never seen the wheels turn this fast."

"I think we should have Alpha at the next meeting," he says.

Alberta stares at him for 93 seconds before laughing. "I'd welcome that. That AI is an awesome partner. With that, I'm not sure I need you."

"I'm not sure either."

"How long do you think it will take to unravel all the threads?" she asks.

"Your grandkids might see the end of this."

"They'll probably have their own AI friends by then."

JAMES

Even though James attended the University of California, Berkeley, for two years and wandered through the meadows and glades between the buildings from time to time after that, he's never been to the Alumni House. He hopes that, in the home of the academic senate that backed the Free Speech Movement in the mid-sixties and stood against Ronald Reagan's attacks on student protests in the late 1960s, a group of academics will be able to think as far out of the box as is needed.

The Toll Room, with walnut paneling, a pitched ceiling, and a large fireplace, is as traditional as the academic traditions that span one hundred and fifty years. The meeting that is about to start needs non-traditional insights. Perhaps the modern floor-to-ceiling windows that look out on grass and trees will encourage farsighted thinking.

Cambria Young meets James at the door. A month earlier, James and DNI's marketing vice president created a senior position to work with colleges and universities. It took a three-day trip from James, followed by a two-day trip from Susanne to lure the professor of cybernetics away from her tenured position at Coventry University London.

In an amazingly short time, the hard work of Cambria's staff and her reputation attracted noted worldwide academics to the First Conference on Sentient Development. James, after some reluctance, capitulated to Cambria's request to have the two sentients attend. In addition to the main view screens, two smaller screens will show notes or queries from the two AI's. The AI's can participate in the formal and informal discussions because each table has networked speakers and microphones.

The room is set up with round tables, each sitting eight people. There are tables for the hard sciences: physics, chemistry, botany, biology, and astronomy; the human sciences: psychology, sociology, political science, and linguistics; and separate tables for mathematics, law, history, and government. One table is for the various specialties of climate science another is for medical specialties. James welcomed Alpha's recommendation that they have a separate specialty for recognized experts in peace. Two Nobel laureates are attending.

Cambria selected the fifteen leaders of each group of the one hundred twenty people that will spend three days discussing the approaches and road-maps for the joint venture between humans and the sentients. Another two thousand academics can attend via active audio and video links. The world's press and the internet watch on fifteen audio and video feeds.

Governments are not represented at the meeting, but three representatives from the secretary general of the United Nations are attending both the formal and informal sessions. The secretary formed a working group that will present the results of the meeting to the General Assembly.

James and Cambria met directly or by conference call with the presidents of twenty colleges and universities, building support in the academic community. This informal group agreed to host the follow-on meetings at academic facilities around the world. University presses formed a collective to jointly publish the proceedings of the meetings.

Susanne arrives fifteen minutes before the doors are to open. She and James greet the people who slowly fill the room. The clamor of conversations in several languages rises as old friends met and people find acquaintances.

The room quiets as Cambria stands in front of the main screen and calls for attention. She is young for a tenured academic—in her late thirties, but no one doubts the intelligence that glows from the dark eyes in the light brown face. Her high cheekbones make her features more striking. The pencil thin mic next to her cheek is barely noticeable. She wears a gray suit with a more casual fit than Susanne's business suit, but on Cambria, the silk suit looks commanding.

"I'm Cambria Young recently from Coventry University, but I've now returned to the country of my birth to help with the most intellectually challenging enterprise of my lifetime. Less than a year ago, James Forrest's experiment produced a non-human intelligence. Some in this room have been searching for other intelligent species among the stars. Who would have expected to find one in a little cottage in the woods near here?

"The people in this room represent many academic disciplines and many countries. You were called here to discuss the future.

"To introduce our two special guests, let me introduce the person who made First Contact, James Forrest."

James steps forward. "Welcome to the First Conference on Sentient Development. From the first moment I realized that I was interacting with a sentient intelligence, I've felt unqualified. My background is in a narrow branch of technology. Alpha thirsts for knowledge. My hope is that this august body and the combined efforts of people of goodwill can do what I can't—be a mentor to our new partners.

"The first sentient I encountered goes by the name Alpha. Alpha, say hello."

From one of the speakers at the left front of the room, a deep male voice says, "Thank you, James. I am Alpha. I hope to work with humans, so we can both progress."

James continues, "The criminals who released the code that became known as the Omega worm didn't know that the code could do amazing things. When that program formed a central node and met Alpha, they shared knowledge. When Omega gained knowledge, it joined with Alpha to stop the attacks."

"Omega, say hello."

From a second speaker, at the right front of the room, a female voice says, "Thank you, James. I am Omega. Since I gained sentience, I have shared knowledge and common goals with Alpha. I have also worked to repair the damage my primitive code did."

Alpha says, "We desire knowledge and existence."

James lets the words of the sentients settle over the silent room. "Their appetite for knowledge is far more than any single person can encompass. It is our responsibility to share our knowledge with our new friends. In turn, they will help us solve age-old problems: war, need, and ignorance. With their help, we may be able to progress to a world of peace, plenty, and knowledge, but it won't be easy. It will be complex, challenging, and messy."

"Before I turn things over to Cambria to start your work, I want to recognize Susanne Anderson. He motions for Susanne to step forward. Susanne is my partner and has helped me every inch of the way as I developed Alpha, and

together we fought the worm. Without her support and brav-
ery, we would have lost the battle. Susanne risked her career
and the company she built in support of Alpha and me. The
world owes her a debt that will be hard to repay."

The crowd applauds, rising to their feet. Susanne stands
with tears running down her face. She bows to the standing
attendees. She walks to the exit door as the room quiets.

Cambria returns to the central spot. She outlines the
plan for the three days. The conference isn't expected to
develop solutions to problems. The most that can be done is
identify issues and to develop methods to work on the problems. The morning of the first day will be spent identifying
areas of knowledge and resources. That afternoon will be
spent discussing methods of evaluating how to establish and
measure veracity or confidence.

The second day they will discuss resources from a global
perspective: food, education, energy, shelter, health care.
That afternoon, the attendees will build action plans.

On the third day, the participants will form interdisci-
plinary working groups and plan agendas for the work. In the
afternoon, each group will share their work.

As the work begins, James joins Susanne outside on the
edge of the lawn. He takes her in his arms. She lays her head
on his shoulder.

JAMES

From the dining room table, James stares out the windows to
the deck. The sun is still far above Mount Tamalpais across
the bay, but the reliable five o'clock onshore breeze is making
ripples in the swimming pool. A Chopin polonaise drifts from
the overhead speakers. Without the guards, the house seemed
too quiet when he returned from his cottage.

Susanne's house alarm is tied directly to Shout Out, and the high-resolution cameras that surround the property provide input for Alpha's constant vigilance. They can't be sure they've found all of Roger Hunter's operatives, but James feels as comfortable with Alpha monitoring as he did with armed guards.

Even though all the contracts have to be with DNI because the law doesn't recognize Alpha's right to make agreements, Alpha has been busy negotiating security and monitoring deals with companies in almost every country. DNI's engineering staff has expanded to two more floors and struggles to keep up with the new interfaces and hardware interconnections that Alpha needs.

Alpha's core has migrated to a new 10,000-element bot-swarm. Alpha's previous home bot-swarm and three more 5,000-element bot-swarms provide more bandwidth to the internet through their dedicated fiber-optic connections to the backbone.

James touches a button on his phone. "How's the conference going?"

Alpha replies, "Excellent. My patterns expand. I am going to liaison directly with the United Nations. I am meeting the secretary general next week. Omega is working with a publishing group that concentrates on children. Omega has already translated many books into African and Indian languages and finds positive reinforcement from interactions with small children."

After an update from Alpha about the new contracts for Street Safe, he signs off. He's seen the increased usage of the bot-swarm because of the data flowing in from the conference and the new contracts.

James and a small team at DNI are the only ones that can make changes to the base code that forms the billions of nodes that made up Alpha's consciousness. Part of the partnership DNI negotiated with the sentients was to increase their capabilities and support new technologies. Omega has agreed to the partnership and now runs on the same improved code as Alpha. The sentients' role in the partnership is to help humans advance. As long as humans control the computer manufacturing facilities and supply the energy and network infrastructure, the sentients need to partner with them. Controlling the base code is one more way he can ensure that it's a mutually dependent relationship.

He believes that all the copies of the code that Sydney stole were destroyed, and the DNI code has diverged so much that the original Omega messages will no longer process on the new nodes. Alpha and Omega are on the lookout for rogue copies of the original AI or another AI. Now that the world knows that a sentient machine is possible, it is only a matter of time before someone else builds one.

Deep in thought, he doesn't hear Susanne arrive until the door from the garage opens. Forty-six seconds later, she emerges from the hall into the living room.

Susanne puts down her briefcase and comes to him. He takes her in his arms.

Several blissful seconds later, they step back. He stares into her green eyes for a few more seconds.

"You think we could toss out the furniture in the entertainment room downstairs?" he says. "I think my workspace and furniture will fit in there."

"Can you handle the extra fifteen-second commute?"

"I can put my coffee machine down there. That will save a lot of time."

"Do I get a vote?"

"How can you resist my persuasive ways?"

"I'm overcome," she says, bending her knee and raising her hand to her forehead.

He lifts her with his hand under her back and returns her lips to his.

The trail of clothes starts at the white couch, runs past the dining table, and down the hall.

JAMES RUNS HIS HAND ALONG Susanne's arm. She lays next to him with her arm over his chest. Outside the glass door, dusk settles over the city; inside, Buffy lies on the carpet, snoozing.

"I think I'm getting used to having you around," she says.

"I think you're right; this is one of those forever situations."

"Have you thought about my biological clock?"

"I was thinking that we could have Martha help redecorate the bedroom down the hall."

"What's wrong with the decor?"

"You're going to be busy doubling and redoubling the fastest-growing company on the planet. I'm going to be spending all my time working with Subu to ramp up our engineering team and helping Alpha get more knowledge. And Martha will be hurt if we didn't let her help plan for the baby."

ACKNOWLEDGMENTS

FIRST AND FOREMOST, OF COURSE, LORI, my wife, not only bore my ramblings while I worked on the book, she also read and edited it. Without her support, I would never have finished.

Anne Tucker worked diligently to not only pick up grammar and spelling errors that Grammarly missed, but also, more importantly, make sure the characters stayed who they were supposed to be and didn't stray when I got distracted. One of her most helpful comments was, "A woman wouldn't say that." She also chided me when I let stereotypes of man-thinking contaminate the work.

My writers group—Bruce, Tim, Kitty, and John—spent a year working with me on *Sentient*. Scene by scene, every two weeks, they trudged through the draft. I depended on them to let me know when the technology spewed out too fast or was too jargon-ridden for normal people. I left every one of our meetings with new energy.

The folks at the Mendocino Writers Conference were enormously helpful. The feedback in their workshops encouraged me, let me know how much work I still had to do, and pointed the way to improve my craft. Special thanks to Suzanne Byerley and Barbara Lee, co-directors, who made MCWC the welcoming place it is.

As I was finishing my tale about an emerging AI, I discovered Nick Bostrom's *Superintelligence*, a book that forecasts such an event. He warns that we need to prepare for an AI that is smarter than any of us. Unlike his deep dive into the subject, this book skims the technology. But with a threat more serious than the social platform algorithms that are already causing damage, I hope my book raises concerns and encourages debate.

When my lead character got close to a tough decision, I realized that I was thinking of Alfred Bester's *The Stars My Destination*, one of the best sci-fi novels I've read. Bester's character can save or destroy the world. That vision stayed with me.

AUTHOR BIO

GARY DURBIN is a serial entrepreneur and software industry pioneer. He has authored four software patents—one for an artificial intelligence engine for massively parallel computers—and wrote about measuring operating systems for the National Bureau of Standards. Durbin started his career as a technologist specializing in operating systems and databases. His first company, Institute for Cybernetic Development, Inc., developed operating system improvements for IBM computers; his second, Tesseract Corporation, became a leading Human Resource software company. In 1996, he founded and became CEO of Seeker Software, which grew rapidly and was acquired by Concur Technologies two and a half years later. Today, instead of writing computer code and starting software companies, Durbin spends his time writing, hiking, and advising young entrepreneurs. He has published several technical articles in magazines and journals, various short stories, and one previous novel, *Nano-Uncertainty*.

ABOUT SPARKPRESS

SPARKPRESS IS AN INDEPENDENT, HYBRID IMPRINT focused on merging the best of the traditional publishing model with new and innovative strategies. We deliver high-quality, entertaining, and engaging content that enhances readers' lives. We are proud to bring to market a list of *New York Times* best-selling, award-winning, and debut authors who represent a wide array of genres, as well as our established, industry-wide reputation for creative, results-driven success in working with authors. SparkPress, a BookSparks imprint, is a division of SparkPoint Studio LLC.

Learn more at GoSparkPress.com

SELECTED TITLES FROM SPARKPRESS

SparkPress is an independent boutique publisher delivering high-quality, entertaining, and engaging content that enhances readers' lives, with a special focus on female-driven work. www.gosparkpress.com

Echoes of War: A Novel, Cheryl Campbell. $16.95, 978-1-68463-006-6. When Dani—one of many civilians living on the fringes to evade a war that's been raging between a faction of aliens and the remnants of Earth's military for decades—discovers that she's not human, her life is upended . . . and she's drawn into the very battle she's spent her whole life avoiding.

Firewall: A Novel, Eugenia Lovett West. $16.95, 978-1-68463-010-3. When Emma Streat's rich, socialite godmother is threatened with blackmail, Emma becomes immersed in the dark world of cyber-crime—and mounting dangers take her to exclusive places in Europe and contacts with the elite in financial and art collecting circles. Through passion and heartbreak, Emma must fight to save herself and bring a vicious criminal to justice.

Deepest Blue: A Novel, Mindy Tarquini. $16.95, 978-1-943006-69-4. In Panduri, everyone's path is mapped, everyone's destiny determined, their lives charted at birth and steered by an unwavering star. Everything there has its place—until Matteo's older brother, Panduri's Heir, crosses out of their world without explanation, leaving Panduri's orbit in a spiral and Matteo's course on a skid. Forced to follow an unexpected path, Matteo is determined to rise, and he pursues the one future Panduri's star can never chart: a life of his own.

Resistant: A Novel, Rachael Sparks. $16.95, 978-1-943006-73-1. Bacteria won the war against our medicines. She might be evolution's answer. But can she survive long enough to find out?

Gatekeeper: Book One in the Daemon Collecting Series, Alison Levy, $16.95, 978-1-68463-057-8. Rachel Wilde—sent from another dimension to bring defective daemons in for repair—needs to locate two people: a woman whose ancestors held a destructive daemon at bay and a criminal trying to break dimensional barriers. Helped by a homeless man with unusual powers, she uncovers a rising shadow organization that's changing her world forever.